Thea Harrison is the pen name for author Teddy Harrison. Thea has travelled extensively, having lived in England and explored Europe for several years. Now she resides in northern California. She wrote her first book, a romance, when she was nineteen and had sixteen romances published under the name Amanda Carpenter.

Please visit her website at
www.theaharrison.com
www.facebook.com/TheaHarrison
www.twitter.com/theaharrison

Dragon Bound

THEA HARRISON

piatkus

PIATKUS

First published in the US in 2011 by The Berkley Publishing Group,
A division of Penguin Group (USA) Inc., New York
First published in Great Britain as a paperback original in 2012 by Piatkus

A CIP catalogue record for this book
is available from the British Library.

ISBN 978-0-7499-5706-3

Printed and bound in Great Britain by Clays Ltd, St Ives plc

Papers used by Piatkus are from well-managed forests
and other responsible sources.

MIX
Paper from
responsible sources
FSC® C104740

Piatkus
An imprint of
Little, Brown Book Group
100 Victoria Embankment
London EC4Y 0DY

An Hachette UK Company
www.hachette.co.uk

www.piatkus.co.uk

ACKNOWLEDGMENTS

I have a lot to be grateful for and a lot of people to mention. I am so remarkably fortunate for everyone I have met and worked with while journeying with this book to publication.

First, I'd like to thank my fabulous agent, Amy Boggs, at the Donald Maass Literary Agency for her all-around bestitude and for being such a patient champion of my writing. I'm thrilled beyond words to thank my editor, Cindy Hwang, for her powerhouse enthusiasm and expertise, her assistant, Leis Pederson, for such friendly, prompt replies, and to the entire team at Berkley for their awesome work.

I would also like to offer special thanks to Ann Aguirre, Nalini Singh, Shannon Butcher, J. R. Ward, Christine Feehan, Angela Knight and Anya Bast. They are amazing women and accomplished writers, and I am honored to have their support.

And here's a shout-out to my superheroine beta readers. Thanks to Anne, Shawn, Fran B., Suzi, Fran H. and Amanda for coming along and joining in the fun. And I don't know what I would have done without Steven's, Pamela's and Anne's encouragement and friendship these last few years; they helped to keep me sane through some pretty insane times.

I also would like to offer heartfelt thanks to Lorene and Carol for their incredible support. They know what they've done, and it's been miraculous. And last but certainly not least, thanks to Matt for his generous work on the website, and to Erin, who loves me even though I'm weird.

Doing business with a dragon. Now that's a cutthroat experience.

—ATTRIBUTED TO DONALD TRUMP

≈ ONE ≈

Pia was blackmailed into committing a crime more suicidal than she could possibly have imagined, and she had no one to blame but herself.

Knowing that didn't make it easier. She couldn't believe she had been so lacking in good judgment, taste or sensibility.

Honestly, what had she done? She had taken one look at a pretty face and forgotten everything her mom had taught her about survival. It sucked so bad she might as well put a gun to her head and pull the trigger. Except she didn't own a gun because she didn't like them. Besides, pulling the trigger on a gun was pretty final. She had issues with commitment and she was so freaking dead anyway, so why bother.

A taxi horn blared. In New York the sound was so common everyone ignored it, but this time it made her jump. She threw a glance over one hunched shoulder.

Her life was in ruins. She would be on the run for the rest of her life, all fifteen minutes or so of it, thanks to her own foolish behavior and her *shithead* ex, who had screwed her, then screwed her over so royally she couldn't get over the knifelike sensation in the pit of her stomach.

She stumbled into a narrow trash-strewn street by a Korean restaurant. She uncapped a liter-sized water bottle and chugged half of it down, one hand splayed on the cement wall while she watched the sidewalk traffic. Steam from the restaurant kitchen enveloped her in the rich red-pepper and soy scents of *gochujang* and *ganjang* sauces, overlaying the garbage rot of a nearby Dumpster and the acrid exhaust from the traffic.

The people in the street looked much as they always did, driven by internal forces as they charged along the sidewalk and shouted on cell phones. A few mumbled to themselves as they dug through trash cans and looked at the world with lost, wary eyes. Everything looked normal. So far, so good?

After a long nightmarish week, she had just committed the crime. She had stolen from one of the most dangerous creatures on Earth, a creature so frightening that just imagining him was more scariness than she ever wanted to meet in real life. Now she was almost done. A couple more stops to make, one more meeting with the shithead, and then she could scream for oh, say, a couple of days or so while she figured out where she would run to hide.

Holding on to that thought, she strode down the street until she came to the Magic District. Located east of the Garment District and north of Koreatown, the New York Magic District was sometimes called the Cauldron. It comprised several city blocks that seethed with light and dark energies.

The Cauldron flaunted caveat emptor like a prizefighter's satin cloak. The area was stacked several stories high with kiosks and shops offering Tarot readings, psychic consultations, fetishes and spells, retail and wholesale sellers, imports, those who dealt with fake merchandise and those who sold magic items that were deadly real. Even from the distance of a city block, the area assaulted her senses.

She came to a shop located at the border of the district. The storefront was painted sage green on the outside, with the molding at the plate-glass windows and door painted pale yellow. She took a backward step to look up. DIVINUS was spelled in plain brushed-metal lettering over the front window. Years ago her mother had on occasion bought spells from the witch who owned this shop. Pia's boss, Quentin, had also mentioned the witch had one of the strongest magical talents he had ever met in a human.

She looked in the storefront. Her blurred reflection looked

back at her, a tired young woman, built rather long and colt-ish, with tense features and a pale blonde tangled ponytail. She looked past herself into the shadowed interior.

In contrast to the noisy none-too-clean surroundings of the city street, the inside of the shop appeared cool and serene. The building seemed to glow with warmth. She recognized protection spells in place. In a display case near the door, harmonic energies sparked from an alluring arrangement of crystals, amethyst, peridot, rose quartz, blue topaz and celestite. The crystals took the slanting sunshine and threw brilliant rainbow shards of light onto the ceiling. Her gaze found the single occupant inside, a tall queenlike woman, perhaps Hispanic, with a gaze that connected to hers with a snap of Power.

That was when the shouting started.

'You don't have to go in there!' a man yelled. Then a woman shrieked, 'Stop before it's too late!'

Pia started and looked behind her. A group of twenty people stood across the street. They held various signs. One poster said, MAGIC = HIGHWAY TO HELL. Another said, GOD WILL SAVE US. A third declared, ELDER RACES – AN ELITIST HOAX.

Her sense of unreality deepened, brought on by stress, lack of sleep and a constant sense of fear. They were yelling at her.

Some of humankind persisted in a belligerent disbelief of the Elder Races, despite the fact that many generations ago folktales had given way to proof as the scientific method had been developed. The Elder Races and humankind had lived together openly since the Elizabethan Age. These humans with their revisionist history made about as much sense as those who declared the Jews hadn't been persecuted in World War II.

Besides being out of touch with reality, they were picketing a human witch to protest the Elder Races? She shook her head.

A cool tinkle brought her attention back to the shop. The woman with Power in her gaze held the door open. 'City ordinances can work both ways,' she told Pia, her voice filled with scorn. 'Magic shops may have to stay within a certain district, but protesters have to stay fifty feet away from the shops. They can't come across the street, they can't enter the Magic District and they can't do anything but yell at potential customers and try to scare them off from a distance. Would you like to come in?' One immaculate eyebrow raised in imperious challenge, as if suggesting that to step into the woman's shop took a real act of bravery.

Pia blinked at her, expression blank. After everything she had been through, the other woman's challenge was beyond insignificant – it was meaningless. She walked in without a twitch.

The door tinkled into place behind her. The woman paused for a heartbeat, as if Pia had surprised her. Then she stepped in front of Pia with a smooth smile.

'I'm Adela, the owner of Divinus. What can I do for you, my dear?' The shopkeeper's face turned puzzled and searching as she looked Pia over. She murmured, almost to herself, 'What is it? . . . There's something about you. ... .'

Crap, she hadn't thought of that. This witch might remember her mom.

'Yeah, I look like Greta Garbo,' Pia interrupted, her expression stony. 'Moving on now.'

The other woman's gaze snapped up to hers. Pia's face and body language transmitted a CLOSED sign, and the witch's demeanor changed back into the professional saleswoman. 'My apologies,' she said in her chocolate milk voice. She gestured. 'I have herbal cosmetics, beauty remedies, tinctures over in that corner, crystals charged with healing spells—'

Pia looked around without taking it all in, although she noticed a spicy smell. It smelled so wonderful she breathed it in deeply without thinking. Despite herself, the tense muscles in her neck and shoulders eased. The scent contained a low-level spell, clearly intended to relax nervous customers.

While the spell caused no actual harm and did nothing to dull her senses, its manipulative nature repelled her. How many people relaxed and spent more money because of it? Her hands clenched as she shoved the magic away. The spell clung to her skin a moment before it dissipated. The sensation reminded her of cobwebs trailing across her skin. She fought the urge to brush off her arms and legs.

Annoyed, she turned and met the shopkeeper's eyes. 'You come recommended by reputable sources,' she said in a clipped tone. 'I need to buy a binding spell.'

Adela's bland demeanor fell away. 'I see,' she said, matching

Pia's crispness. Her eyebrows raised in another faint challenge. 'If you've heard of me, then you know I'm not cheap.'

'You're not cheap because you're supposed to be one of the best witches in the city,' said Pia as she strode to a nearby glass counter. She shrugged the backpack off her aching shoulder and rested it on the counter, pulling the tangle of her ponytail out from under one strap. She stuffed her water bottle inside and zipped it back up.

'*Gracias,*' said the witch, her voice bland.

Pia glanced down at the crystals in the case. They were so bright and lovely, filled with magic and light and color. What would it be like to hold one, to feel the cool, heavy weight of it sitting in her palm as it sang to her of starlight and deep mountain spaces? How would it feel to own one?

The connection snapped as she turned. She looked her own challenge at the other woman. 'I can also feel the spells you have both on and in the shop, including the attraction spells on these crystals as well as the one that's supposed to make your customers relax. I can tell your work is competent enough. I need an oath-binding spell, and I need to walk out of the shop with it today.'

'That is not as easy as it might sound,' said the witch. Long eyelids dropped, shuttering her expression. 'This is not a fast-food drive-through.'

'The binding doesn't have to be fancy,' said Pia. 'Look, we both know you're going to charge more because I need it right away. I still have a lot to do, so can we just please skip this next part where we dance around each other and negotiate? Because, no offense, it's been a long bad day. I'm tired and not in the mood.'

The witch's mouth curled. 'Certainly,' she said. 'Although with a binding, there's only so much I can do on the spot, and there are some things I won't do at all. If you need something tailored for a specific purpose, it will take some time. If you're looking for a dark binding, you're in the wrong place. I don't do dark magic.'

Pia shook her head, relieved at the woman's businesslike attitude. 'Nothing too dark, I think,' she said in a rusty voice. 'Something with serious consequences, though. It's got to mean business.'

The witch's dark eyes shone with a sardonic sparkle. 'You

5

mean a kind of "I swear I will do such-and-such or my ass will catch fire until the end of time" type of thing?'

Pia nodded, her mouth twisting. 'Yeah. That kind of thing.'

'If someone swears an oath of his own free will, the binding falls into the realm of contractual obligation and justice. I can do that. And have, as a matter of fact,' the other woman said. She moved toward the back of her shop. 'Follow me.'

Pia's abused conscience twitched. Unlike the polarized white and black magics, gray magic was supposed to be neutral, but the witch's kind of ethical parsing never did sit well with her. Like the relaxation spell in the shop, it felt manipulative, devoid of any real moral substance. A great deal of harm could be done under the guise of neutrality.

Which was pretty damn self-righteous of her, wasn't it, coming fresh as she did from the scene of her crime and desperate to get her hands on that binding spell. The urge to run pumped adrenaline into her veins. Self-preservation kept her anchored in place. Disgusted with herself, she shook her head and followed the witch. Here goes nothing.

She really hoped that wasn't true.

They concluded business in under an hour. At the witch's invitation she slipped out the back to avoid more heckling from the protesters. Her backpack had been lightened by a considerable amount of cash, but Pia figured in a life-or-death situation it was money well spent.

'Just one thing,' said the witch. She leaned her curvaceous body in a languid pose against the back doorpost of her shop.

Pia paused and looked back at the other woman.

The witch held her gaze. 'If you're personally involved with the man that is intended for, I'm here to tell you, honey, he isn't worth it.'

A harsh laugh escaped her. She hefted the backpack higher onto one shoulder. 'If only my problems were that simple.'

Something moved under the surface of the other woman's lovely dark eyes. The shift of thought looked calculating, but that could have been a trick of the late-afternoon light. In the next moment her beautiful face wore an indifferent mask, as if she had already mentally moved on to other things.

'Luck, then, *chica*,' the witch said. 'You need to buy something else, come back anytime.'

Pia swallowed and said past a dry throat, 'Thanks.'

The witch shut her door and Pia loped to the end of the block, then moved into the sidewalk traffic.

Pia hadn't shared her name. After the first rebuff, the witch knew not to ask and she hadn't offered. She wondered if she had TROUBLE tattooed on her forehead. Or maybe it was in her sweat. Desperation had a certain smell to it.

Her fingers brushed the front pocket of her jeans where she'd slipped the oath binding, wrapped in a plain white handkerchief. A strong magical glow emanated through the distressed denim and made her hand tingle. Maybe after she met with the shithead and concluded their transaction, she could take her first deep breath in days. She supposed she should be grateful the witch hadn't been more of a shark.

Then Pia heard the most terrible sound of her life. It started low like a vibration, but one so deep in power it shook her bones. She slowed to a stop along with the other pedestrians. People shaded their eyes and looked around as the vibration grew into a roar that swept through the streets and rattled the buildings.

The roar was a hundred freight trains, tornadoes, Mount Olympus exploding in a rain of fire and flood.

Pia fell to her knees and threw her arms over her head. Others screamed and did the same. Still others looked around wild-eyed, trying to spot the disaster. Some ran panicked down the street. The nearby intersections were dotted with car accidents as frightened drivers lost control and slammed into one another.

Then the roar died away. Buildings settled. The cloudless sky was serene, but New York City most certainly was not.

Alrighty.

She pushed upright on unsteady legs and mopped her sweat-dampened face, oblivious to the chaos churning around her.

She knew what – *who* – had made that unholy sound and why. The knowledge made her guts go watery.

If she were in a race for her life, that roar was the starter pistol. If God were the referee, He had just shouted Go.

He had been born along with the solar system. Give or take. He remembered a transcendent light and an immense wind. Modern science called it a solar wind. He recalled a sensation of endless flight, an eternal basking in light and magic so piercing and young and pure it rang like the trumpeting of thousands of angels.

His massive bones and flesh must have been formed along with the planets. He became bound to Earth. He knew hunger and learned to hunt and eat. Hunger taught him concepts such as before and after, and danger and pain and pleasure.

He began to have opinions. He liked the gush of blood as he gorged on flesh. He liked drowsing on a baked rock in the sun. He adored launching into the air, taking wing and riding thermals high above the ground, so like that first endless-seeming ecstasy of flight.

After hunger, he discovered curiosity. New species burgeoned. There were the Wyrkind, Elves, both Light and Dark Fae, tall bright-eyed beings and squat mushroom-colored creatures, winged nightmares and shy things that puttered in foliage and hid whenever he appeared. What came to be known as the Elder Races tended to cluster in or around magic-filled dimensional pockets of Other land, where time and space had buckled when the earth was formed and the sun shone with a different light.

Magic had a flavor like blood, only it was golden and warm like sunlight. It was good to gulp down with red flesh.

He learned language by listening in secret to the Elder Races. He practiced on his own when he took flight, mulling over each word and its meaning. The Elder Races had several words for him.

Wyrm, they called him. Monster. Evil. The Great Beast.

Dragua.

Thus he was named.

He didn't notice at first when the first modern *Homo sapiens* began to proliferate in Africa. Of all species, he wouldn't have guessed they would flourish. They were weak, had short life spans, no natural armor, and were easy to kill.

He kept an eye on them and learned their languages. Just as other Wyrkind did, he developed the skill of shapeshifting so he could walk among them. They dug up the things of Earth he liked, gold and silver, sparkling crystals and precious gems, which they shaped into creations of beauty. Acquisitive by nature, he collected what caught his eye.

This new species spread across the world, so he created secret lairs in underground caverns where he gathered his possessions.

His hoard included works of the Elves, the Fae and the Wyr, as well as human creations such as gold and silver and copper plates, goblets, religious artifacts and coinage of all sorts. Money, now, there was a concept that intrigued him, attached as it was to so many other interesting concepts like trade, politics, war and greed. There were also cascades of loose crystals and precious gems and crafted jewelry of all sorts. His hoard grew to include writings from all Elder Races and from humankind, as books were an invention he (only sometimes) thought was more precious than any other treasure.

Along with his interest in history, mathematics, philosophy, astronomy, alchemy and magic, he became intrigued with modern science. He traveled to England to have a conversation on the origin of species with a famous scientist in the nineteenth century. They had gotten drunk together – the Englishman with rather more desperation than he – and had talked through the witching hours until the night mist had been burned to vapor by the sun.

He remembered telling the clever drunken scientist that he and humankind civilization had a lot in common. The difference was his experience was couched in a single entity, one set of memories. In a way, that meant he embodied all stages of evolution at once – beast and predator, magician and aristocrat, violence and intellectualism. He was not so sure he had acquired humanlike emotions. He had certainly not acquired their morality. Perhaps his greatest achievement was law.

Humans in different cultures also had many words for him. Ryu, they called him. Wyvern. Naga. To the Aztecs he was the winged serpent Quetzalcoatl whom they called God.

Dragos.

When he discovered the theft, Dragos Cuelebre exploded into the sky with long thrusts from a wingspan approaching that of an eight-seater Cessna jet.

Modern life had gotten complicated. His usual habit was to focus Power on averting aircraft when he flew or, simpler yet, just file a flight plan with the local air traffic control. With his outrageous wealth and position as one of the eldest and most powerful of the Wyr, life scrambled to arrange itself to his liking.

He wasn't so polite this time. This was more a get-the-fuck-out-of-my-way kind of flight. He was blinded with rage, violent with incredulity. Lava flowed through ancient veins and his lungs worked like bellows. As he approached the zenith of his climb, his long head snapped back and forth, and he roared again. The sound ripped the air as his razor claws mauled an imaginary foe.

All of his claws except for those on one front foot held a tiny scrap of something fragile and, to be frank, inconceivable. This tiny scrap was as ludicrous and as nonsensical to him as a hot fudge sundae topping an ostrich's head. The cherry on the hot fudge sundae was the elusive whiff of scent that clung to the scrap. It teased his senses into a frenzy as it reminded him of something so long ago that he couldn't quite remember what it was –

His mind went white-hot and slipped from its mooring in time. Existing in his wrath he flew until he came to himself and began to think again.

Then Rune said in his head, *My lord? Are you well?*

Dragos cocked his head, for the first time coming aware that his First flew behind him at a discreet distance. It was a measure of his rage that he hadn't noticed. Any other time Dragos was aware of everything that happened within his vicinity.

Dragos noted that Rune's telepathic voice was as calm and neutral as the other male's physical voice would have been had he spoken the words aloud.

There were many reasons why Dragos had made Rune his First in his Court. Those reasons were why Rune had thrived in his service for so long. The other male was seasoned, mature and dominant enough to hold authority in a sometimes unruly Wyr society. He was intelligent with a capacity for cunning and violence that came close to Dragos's own.

Most of all, Rune had a gift for diplomacy that Dragos had never achieved. That talent made the younger male useful when treating with the other Elder Courts. It also helped him to navigate rocky weather when Dragos was in a rage.

Dragos's jaw clenched and he ground massive teeth shaped for maximum carnage. After a moment, he answered, *I am well. How may I be of service?* his First asked.

His mind threatened to seize again in sheer incredulity of what he had found. He snarled, *There has been a theft.*

A pause. Rune asked, *My lord?*

For once his First's legendary coolness had been shaken. It gave him a grim sense of satisfaction. *A THIEF, Rune.* He bit at each word. *A THIEF has broken into my hoard and taken something of mine.*

Rune took several moments to absorb his words. Dragos let him have the time.

The crime was impossible. It had never happened, not in all the millennia of his existence. Yet it had happened now. First someone had somehow found his hoard, which was an incredible feat in itself. An elaborate fake setup complete with state-of-the-art security was located below the basement levels of Cuelebre Tower, but no one knew the location of Dragos's actual hoard except himself.

His actual hoard was protected by powerful cloaking and aversion spells older than the pharaoh tombs of Egypt and as subtle as tasteless poison on the tongue. But after locating his secret lair, the thief had managed to slip past all of Dragos's physical and magical locks, like a knife slicing through butter. Even worse, the thief managed to slip out again the same way.

The only warning Dragos had received was a nagging unease that had plagued him all afternoon. His unease had increased to the point where he couldn't settle down until he went to check on his property.

He had known his lair had been infiltrated as soon as he had set foot near the hidden entrance to the underground cavern. Still, he couldn't believe it, even after he had torn inside to discover the indisputable evidence of the theft, along with something else that trumped all other inconceivability.

He looked down at his clenched right foot. He wheeled in an abrupt motion to set a return path to the city. Rune followed and settled smoothly into place behind him, his rear right wingman.

You are to locate this thief. Do everything possible, Dragos said. *Everything, you understand. Use all magical and nonmagical means. Nothing else exists for you. No other tasks, no other diversions. Pass all of your current duties on to Aryal or Grym.*

I understand, my lord, Rune said, keeping his mental voice quiet.

Dragos sensed other conversations in the air, although no one dared direct contact with him. He suspected his First had begun giving orders to transfer duties to the others.

He said, *Be very clear about something, Rune. I do not want this thief harmed or killed by anyone but myself. You are not to allow it. You should be sure of the people you use on this hunt.*

I will.

It will be on your head if something goes wrong, Dragos told him. He couldn't have articulated even to himself why he pressed the matter with this creature who for centuries had been as steady and reliable as a metronome. His claws clenched on his implausible scrap of evidence. *Understood?*

Understood, my lord, Rune replied, calm as ever.

Good enough, he growled.

Dragos noticed they had returned over the city. The sky around them was clear of all air traffic. He soared in a wide circle to settle on the spacious landing pad atop Cuelebre Tower. As soon as he settled he shifted into his human shape, a massive six-foot-eight dark-haired male with dark bronze skin and gold raptor's eyes.

Dragos turned to watch Rune land. The gryphon's majestic wings shone in the fading afternoon sun until the other male also shifted into his human form, a tawny-haired male almost as massive as Dragos himself.

Rune lowered his head to Dragos in a brief bow of respect before loping to the roof doors. After the other male had left, Dragos unclenched his right fist in which he held a crumbled scrap of paper.

Why had he not told Rune about it? Why was he not even now calling the gryphon back to tell him? He didn't know. He just obeyed the impulse to secrecy.

Dragos held the paper to his nose and inhaled. A scent still clung to the paper, which had absorbed oil from the thief's hand. It was a feminine scent that smelled like wild sunshine and it was familiar in a way that pulled at all of Dragos's deepest instincts.

He stood immobile, eyes closed as he concentrated on inhaling that wild feminine sunshine in deep breaths. There was something about it, something from a long time ago. If only he could remember. He had lived for so long, his memory was a vast and convoluted tangle. It could take him weeks to locate the memory.

He strained harder for that elusive time with a younger sun, a deep green forest and a celestial scent that drove him crashing through the underbrush –

The fragile memory thread broke. A low growl of frustration rumbled through his chest. He opened his eyes and willed himself not to shred the paper he held with such tense care.

It occurred to Dragos that Rune had forgotten to ask what the thief had stolen.

His underground lair was enormous by necessity, with cavern upon cavern filled with a hoard the likes of which the world had never seen. The treasure of empires filled the caves.

Astonishing works of beauty graced rough cavern walls. Items of magic, miniature portraits, tinkling crystal earrings that threw rainbows in the lamplight. Art masterpieces packed to protect them from the environment. Rubies and emeralds and diamonds the size of goose eggs, and loops upon loops of pearls. Egyptian scarabs, cartouches and pendants. Greek gold, Syrian statues, Persian gems, Chinese jade, Spanish treasure from sunken ships. He even kept a modern coin collection he had started several years ago and added to in a haphazard way whenever he remembered.

On the ostrich's head was a hot fudge sundae. . . .

His obsessive attention to detail, an immaculate memory of each and every piece in that gigantic treasure, a trail of scent like wild sunshine, and instinct had all led Dragos to the right place. He discovered the thief had taken a U.S.-minted 1962 copper penny from a jar of coins he had not yet bothered to put into a coin collecting book.

. . . and on the hot fudge sundae atop that ostrich's head perched a cherry. . . .

The thief had left something for him in place of what she had taken. She had perched it with care on top of the coin jar. It was a message written on a scrap of paper in a spidery, unsteady hand. The message was wrapped around an offering.

I'm sorry, the message said.

The theft was a violation of privacy. It was an unbelievable act of impudence and disrespect. Not only that, it was – baffling. He was murderous, *incandescent* with fury. He was older than sin and could not remember when he had last been in such a rage.

He looked at the paper again.

I'm sorry I had to take your penny. Here's another to replace it.

Yep, that's what it said.

One corner of his mouth twitched. He gave himself a deep shock when he burst into an explosive guffaw.

⇒ TWO ⇐

Pia spent the next hour trekking across town. She witnessed how the city transformed after that unholy sound, as if it were a painting some artist smeared with sinister streaks of dark colors. Stress carved itself into the expressions of the people she passed on the street. Anger erupted in shouted confrontations, and clumps of uniformed policemen appeared. Pedestrians moved with greater urgency. Smaller shops and kiosks put out CLOSED signs and locked their doors.

In normal circumstances she would have taken the subway, but as ugly as the mood had turned on the streets, she wasn't about to risk getting trapped underground. At last she stood in front of the shithead's door.

The tenement where he lived was in miserable condition. She breathed through her mouth and tried to ignore the used condom on the floor of the stairwell and the baby squalling two apartments down. After she did this one last thing and she stopped by work to say good-bye to Quentin, she was so out of here.

The door yanked open. Her fist was moving before she had fully laid eyes on him. He doubled over as she punched him in the stomach.

He wheezed and coughed. 'Fuck, bitch!'

'Ow!' She shook open her fist. Thumb outside, not inside, dummy.

He straightened and glared at her as he rubbed his abdomen. Then he started to smile. 'You did it, didn't you? You actually, really did it.'

'Like you gave me a choice,' she snapped. She shoved at his shoulder. It knocked him back enough so she could stalk inside and slam the door shut.

His smile turned into a gleeful laugh. He fist-pumped the air. 'Yes!'

Pia regarded him, her gaze bitter. Shithead, aka Keith Hollins, had amiable good looks with shaggy dishwater blond hair and a surfer's body. His cocky grin had women flocking to him like flies to honey.

She had been one of those flies once. Then disillusionment had set in. She had thought him kind when he was charming. She had taken his caressing manner for real affection and called him boyish when the truth was he was selfish to the bone. He was Captain Fantastic in his own mind. He created the fiction that he was a risk taker when in reality he was a gambling addict.

She had broken up with him a few months back. Then just last week his betrayal had punched her in the teeth, but it felt like much longer.

Pia had been so lonely since her mother died six years ago. There was not another single creature who knew her for who and what she was. Only her mother had known. Her mother had loved her so much she had devoted her life to safeguarding Pia's welfare and safety. She had raised her daughter with a fanatical attention to secrecy and with every protection spell she could muster or buy.

Then Pia had thrown away almost everything her mom had taught her for a sweet smile and the promise of some affection. I'm so sorry, Mom, she said in her head. I swear I'll do better now. She stared at Keith doing a touchdown shimmy. He pretended to slam a football on the ground and grinned at her.

'I know I had that punch comin' to me. I owed you one. No hard feelings, sugar.'

'Speak for yourself.' Pia's words were coated in frost. 'I've all kinds of hard feelings going on over here.'

She dropped her backpack to the floor and glanced around even though she was pretty sure they were alone. Fast-food wrappers littered the thrift store coffee table. A dirty T-shirt draped the back of the couch. Some things never changed.

'Aw, come on, P., there's no need to be like that. Hey, listen, I know you're still pissed, but you gotta understand somethin', sugar. I did this for us.' He reached for her shoulder, but she jerked back before his fingers could touch her. His smile dimmed, but he didn't lose his easy, caressing manner. 'P., you don't seem to get it. We're gonna be rich now. Really fucking rich. Why, you can have anything you want. Won't you like that, darlin'?'

Keith was the one who didn't get it. The dimwit didn't realize he was collateral damage. He had constructed this fantasy world in which he was a player while his gambling debts grew worse, and he fell more and more under the control of his business associates.

Those 'associates' were shadowy connections a couple times removed from Keith's bookie. She imagined them as a cackle of hyenas gathering around their prey with languid purpose. Keith was lunch, but they had decided to play with their food before the kill.

She didn't know who his contacts were and she didn't want to. It was awful enough that she knew there was real Power somewhere up that food chain. Human or Elven, Wyr or Fae, it didn't matter. Something nasty had turned its attention this way. It had enough magic and muscle to take on one of the premiere Powers of the world.

And here was Captain Fantastic, a mere human with not a single spark of Power in him and not a lick of sense, either. The fact that she had ever hooked up with him, even for a few months, would keep her humble forever.

She told him, 'You sound like the dialogue from a bad movie.'

Keith's flirtatious manner fell away and he glared at her. 'Yeah? Well, fuck you too.'

'And it goes on,' she sighed. A headache had begun to pulse in her sinuses. 'Look, let's get this over with. Your handlers wanted me to steal something from Cuelebre—'

'I *bet* my *associates* that I could get them anything from anywhere,' Keith sneered. 'And they *suggested* something from Cuelebre.'

Today had been a long bad day on top of a long bad week. It

had started the moment Keith had put an object of Power in her hand and told her she was going to find Cuelebre's lair with it. The shock still clung as she remembered the pulse of serious magic that had seared her hand.

The feeling was compounded by a rush of terror for whoever, or whatever, had the kind of mojo to create that artifact and hand it to Keith.

That was sure a special moment, when she discovered Keith had betrayed her. When she realized that, between Cuelebre and the cackle of hyenas, she was screwed. If she stole from Cuelebre, she was dead. If she didn't, she had no doubt Keith would tell his hyenas, and she was still dead. Rock, shake hands with hard place.

Having the charm sit in her hand was like holding on to a cluster bomb. The design had been deceptively simple. It had felt like a finding charm with a onetime activation, but it had had the Power to slice through all of Cuelebre's protections.

Her breath shook as she remembered the terrible walk she had taken earlier that day, through an innocent sunlit city park where coffee-drinking adults watched over shrieking children as they threw sand and pelted from the merry-go-round to the jungle gym.

The sounds of traffic and barking dogs had punctuated the blistering pain in her hand, as the charm's activated Power flared and drew her along a flower-lined path to an anonymous, utterly forgettable rusted metal maintenance door set into a park viaduct. The charm drew a thin shimmering path that led through an invisible mist of cloaking and aversion spells, which had her convinced with increasing urgency that she was lost, mistaken, cursed, trapped in her worst nightmare, in mortal danger, *damned for all eternity* –

Pia's fragile control snapped. She slapped Keith's chest with both flattened hands, driving him backward a few feet. 'You blackmailed me into stealing from a dragon, you asshole!' she shouted. She pushed him again and he staggered back. 'I trusted you with my secrets.' Although not all of them, thank the gracious Powers, not all. She'd somehow retained a few last scraps of self-preservation. 'I thought we loved each other. God, what a wretched joke. I could crawl under a rock and die from embarrassment, except you. Are. Not. Worth it.'

Her last shove knocked Keith into a wall. The look on his face would have been comical if she'd had a sense of humor left.

His astonishment turned ugly. His hands shot out faster than she expected. He shoved her back so hard she tripped and almost fell. 'Well, I must have done a good goddamn job of faking it,' he snarled. 'Because you've got to be the most miserable fuck I've ever had.'

Pia never knew until that moment that she was capable of killing someone. Her hands curled into claws. 'I am an excellent fuck,' she hissed. 'I am the best thing that ever happened to your sorry, deluded, preejaculating ass. You just didn't have the good taste to recognize it. And you know what? Now I don't even know why I put up with you. I had a better sex life with five minutes and my hand in a hot shower.'

Captain Fantastic's face turned puce. She stared. She'd never seen that color on a person before. He cocked back his arm as if to hit her.

'You do that and you never get what you want. Plus you lose a hand.' The frost in her voice turned to an ice pick. He froze. The ruthless stranger that had taken over her body brought her up nose to nose with him. 'Go ahead,' she said, settling into a soft and even tone. 'Amputation might be a little therapeutic right now.'

She stared him down until he dropped his hand and took a half step back. The move wasn't much, but it meant a lot to her battered pride. In a contest of wills she'd pinned him to the mat.

'Let's get this over with,' he snapped.

'About time.' She dug into her jeans and gave him a folded piece of paper. 'You get what I stole when you read that out loud.'

'What?' He gave her a blank look. It was clear things had taken a turn beyond his comprehension. As a nonmagical human he couldn't feel how the paper glowed with Power from the binding spell.

He unfolded it and scanned the contents, and his face contorted again with rage. He dropped the paper like it was on fire. 'Oh no, bitch. This isn't gonna fuckin' happen. You're gonna give me what you took and give it to me *now*!' He lunged for her backpack. She took several quick steps back, letting him rifle through the contents. Wallet, tennis shoes, the half-empty bottle of water and her iPod spilled onto the floor.

He made an incoherent strangled noise and rounded on her. She danced back another step and kept on her toes, both empty hands held up as she gave him a mocking smile.

'Where is it!' Spittle flew. 'What did you take? Where did you hide it? *FUCK!*'

'*You* said it didn't matter,' she said. As Keith advanced on her, she kept moving in counterpart, keeping a few feet between them. '*You* said your keepers—'

'Associates!' he roared, fisting his hands.

'—didn't care what I took as long as it was from Cuelebre, since they had the means to verify the take. I suppose that means they can spell it somehow to prove it really is from him.' The back of her shin came in contact with the coffee table. She gathered herself and sprang backward as Keith made a lunge for her. She put a lot of push into her jump and landed in a crouch on the couch as Keith stumbled into the table. 'And you know what?' she said. 'I don't give a damn, except for one thing.'

Pia paused and straightened. She bounced a little as Keith scrambled back to his feet. His good surfer looks had twisted into an expression of hate.

She wondered if it would occur to him that her backward jump had been too far and high for a normal human woman to make, but she supposed none of that mattered anymore.

'The thing about blackmail is it never stops at just one payment. All the TV shows say so, anyway,' she said. She didn't know she had any more disappointment left until her stomach sank at the cunning expression that flashed in Keith's eyes. 'Did you think I wouldn't guess you meant to keep using me? After all, why would you stop at just one theft? It was always going to be like, "Hey, Pia, I'll keep quiet about you if you'll do just one more little thing for me." Wasn't it?'

His top lip curled. 'We could have been a real partnership.'

He had the gall to sound bitter. Unbelievable. She dropped her flippant tone and became serious. 'Either you would keep blackmailing me, or sooner or later – if you haven't already – you would tell your owners about me. Or' – she held up a finger – 'how about this scenario? You're going to give them what I stole, which will prove to them you were doing more than just idle boasting. It's going to make them take you seriously.'

His mouth tightened. 'They already take me seriously, bitch.'

'Riiight.' She continued, 'They probably promised to wipe out all your gambling debts if you could pull off the theft. Maybe they said they'd give you a good chunk of cash as well. You're hoping this will save your miserable hide. Then they'll finally sit up and give you the kind of attention you deserve. They'll have to take you as a real player and not some chump up to his ears in bad debt. But don't you see – if that happens, they're also going to get seriously interested in how you pulled it off. They're going to want to ask you a lot of questions.'

The anger faded from Keith's face as what she said sank in. 'It wasn't going to be like that,' he said. 'I didn't tell them hardly anything about you.'

Hallelujah, it looked like he was turning thoughtful. Or what passed for thoughtfulness, for him. She relaxed enough to step off the couch and sit down. 'You know, I think I believe you on that,' she said. 'At least I think you believe it. But what you "hardly didn't tell" was already too much.'

She could see how his thought process would have gone. He was going to retain all the power. He would keep her strung along in a pseudo-partnership where he held all the strings and got her to do whatever he wanted. His 'associates' were going to be admiring and respectful. He probably thought he would end up being a real broker for them too and get them whatever they wanted for exorbitant fees. Then Keith was going to get to live the good life.

'Okay,' she said, scraping at the dregs of her flagging energy to adopt a brisk attitude. She braced her hands on her thighs. 'We have to step outside of Keith's fantasy land now. Here's how it's going to be. You swore you would keep what I said in confidence. This is all about keeping a dishonest man honest. You blackmailed me, so now I'm blackmailing you, because however you look at the scenarios I just painted, I'd be screwed.'

He shook his head and said, 'No, you wouldn't, P. All you gotta do is work with me. Why can't you just fuckin' see that?'

'Because I'm not like you, Keith,' she snapped. 'And damage control is the only way I have a remote chance of getting out of this nightmare.'

'I can't believe you would just walk away.' He looked as petulant as a little boy.

'I walked away a couple of months ago,' she reminded him. 'You just wouldn't stay gone. Now pick up that piece of paper and swear the binding oath, or I'm leaving and you're never going to get what I stole. That would mean you'll have to rene-gotiate a different payment plan with those "associates" of yours on the money you owe them. Wouldn't it?'

She didn't have to say how those different payment options would go. She could tell he knew his life was on the line. Keith regarded her, his mouth turning down at the corners. 'You know, it could have been good.'

She shook her head. 'Only in your dreams, cowboy.'

He walked over to the spell and picked it up, reluctance in every step. She held her silence as he paused one last time. She could tell he was trying to think of a way to get out of reading it. But there was nothing he could do, and they both knew it.

He read it in a fast, ill-tempered tone. 'I, Keith Hollins, hereby swear never to talk about Pia or her secrets in any way, either directly or by inference or silence, or I will lose my ability to speak and suffer unremitting physical pain for the rest of my life.'

He gave a shout as the magic activated. The paper burst into flame. Pia sighed as a weight lifted, just a little, from her shoul-ders. She went to stuff her things into her backpack.

Keith said, 'Okay, I did what you wanted. Now we go to pick up what you stole. What is it – a gem, a piece of jewelry? It had to be something you could carry.' Avarice crept back into his eyes. 'Where did you hide it?'

She shrugged. 'I didn't hide it anywhere.'

'What?' Realization dawned. He bared his teeth like a feral dog. 'You had it on you the whole time.'

She drew a folded linen handkerchief from her jeans pocket and handed it to him. He tore it open as she shouldered her backpack. She walked out the door as the swearing began.

'Oh, fuck me. You stole a goddamn PENNY!'

'Bye, baby,' she said. She walked away. The hall misted in front of her. She gritted her teeth until pain shot through her jaw. She would not spill one more tear for that loser.

He shouted after her, 'What is a dragon doing with a penny in his hoard? How do I know this goddamn penny is even his?'

Well, there was a question.

She thought about reminding him his 'associates' could verify a real theft. She thought about telling him she knew a fake would have gotten him killed, but the poor dumb schmuck was doomed anyway.

Either Cuelebre would find and kill him, or sooner or later he would piss off one of his 'associates.' They would want to know how he got hold of Cuelebre's property. And now Keith wasn't going to be able to tell them. How awkward was that.

Then she thought of telling him about her own stupidity since it hadn't occurred to her to try to pass on a fake to him. Despite a few unusual abilities, Pia didn't have a larcenous bone in her body. She couldn't think with the cunning of a criminal.

Besides, she hadn't dared to do anything but the job once she had realized real Power moved in the shadows behind him. Something was brewing. It was bigger and worse than anything Keith could imagine or she would want to. It smelled dark like assassination or war. She wanted to run as far and as fast as she could away from it.

Never in a million years would she have imagined finding a jar of pennies amid all that blinding treasure in Cuelebre's lair, or that 'take a penny, leave a penny' would come to mind. Everybody did it at gas stations. Why the hell not.

She thought of a whole conversation she could have had with him. Instead she shook her head. It was past time to leave.

'You'll be sorry!' he shouted at her. 'You'll never find anyone else that will put up with all your bullshit!'

She gave him her middle finger and kept walking.

A low-level panic continued to urge Pia to run. After several lip-chewing minutes, she decided not to return to her apartment. The difficulty of the decision surprised her. She didn't own many things that mattered. Her furniture was just furniture, but she did have a few mementos from her mother and she was fond of some of her clothes. Aside from possessions, the real wrench was breaking from the continuity of what home she did have.

Don't let yourself get too attached to people, places or

23

things, her mother had said. *You have to be able to leave every-thing behind.*

Be prepared to run on a moment's notice.

The definition of their lives had hinged on this. Pia's mother had kept stashes of cash and different identities for them in a half-dozen places throughout the city. Pia had memorized pub-lic transportation routes, lock combinations and safety deposit numbers for all the locations by the time she was six years old. They'd had regular escape-from-New-York drills where she would go through the routes and get access to the documents and cash while her mother followed and observed. The picture IDs got updated as Pia had grown older.

Still, while Pia had nodded and said she understood, the events of last week showed just how much she hadn't really understood or internalized things. Her mother had died when Pia was nineteen. Now, at twenty-five, she was beginning to realize how sloppy her behavior had become.

It wasn't just her monumental foolishness at trusting Keith. She had kept up with the regular self-defense and martial arts classes, but she had fallen out of the habit of taking them seri-ously. Instead she treated them like they were for exercise and entertainment. Now her mother's early lessons were com-ing back to haunt her. She only hoped she would survive long enough to appreciate what it meant to be sadder and wiser.

Earlier Pia had wiped out one cache to pay the witch for the binding spell. Now she took a circuitous path to Elfie's bar in south Chelsea. She managed to hit one safety deposit box before banks closed and a second, less conventional cache hid-den at her old elementary school playground. She had three new identities and a hundred thousand dollars in unmarked non-sequential bills stuffed in her backpack, along with a renewed paranoia weighing her down.

When she pushed through the front door to Elfie's bar, she had begun to feel like she was wearing half the dirt in the city. She felt grubby and hollowed out, emotionally drained and physically hungry. Stress had clogged her throat for days and she hadn't been able to choke down much food.

Elfie's was open for lunch during the day. Lunch, served from eleven to three, was a supplemental part of the busi-ness, as Elfie's came alive at night. Quentin, the owner, could have turned it into one of New York's premiere clubs if he had wanted to. He had the charisma and style for it.

Instead Quentin kept a lid on the business getting too big. Elfie's was known as a good neighborhood club with a steady, loyal clientele of mixed breeds from all three races. They were the city's very own Island of Misfit Toys, the flotsam and jetsam of societies, not being fully Wyr, Fae, Elven or human and thus not fully belonging anywhere. Some were open about their mixed-breed nature and argued the benefits of living out of the closet. Many, like Pia, hid what they were and pretended to fit in somewhere.

She had worked at Elfie's since she was twenty-one, when she had pushed through those same front doors and asked Quentin for a job. It was the only place she had found after her mom had died that came close to feeling like home.

She pushed her way to the servers' end of the bar and sagged against it. The current bartender on duty, Rupert, paused in slinging drinks and looked at her in surprise. He lifted his chin, silently asking if she wanted him to get her a drink.

She shook her head and mouthed at him, 'Where's Quentin?' The bartender shrugged. She nodded, waved at him, and he went back to work.

Air-conditioning licked her overheated skin. Her eyes threatened to water again as she looked around familiar surroundings. She liked bartending at Elfie's. She liked working for Quentin. She hoped Captain Fantastic and his hyenas rotted in hell.

The after-work crowd cluttered the large trendy space and lined up three deep for drinks. Low-level magic items and Power sparkled through the constant buzz of conversation. Sports channels played on huge HDTVs on the other side of the bar. Most people watched the wide-screen mounted high in one corner of the bar. She looked up to a CNN newscast.

'. . . and in local news, reports continue to roll in on the extent of the damage from this afternoon's mysterious event. Meanwhile, speculation continues to run rampant as to the cause.' A blonde lacquered woman, one of CNN's regulars, gave the camera a professional smile. The reporter stood in front of a sidewalk where crews of workmen were sweeping up mountains of broken glass.

The barfly next to Pia said in a voice that sounded like tumbling rocks, 'Hey, gorgeous. Weren't you taking a week of vacation? What are you doing here on your time off?'

She glanced at the hulking, squat half troll perched on a custom-made steel stool. On his feet, he slouched at eight feet tall with pale gray skin and a thatch of black hair that refused to lie down. 'Hey, Preston,' she said. 'Yeah, I'm still off. I just need to talk to Quentin for a minute.'

Preston was one of Elfie's regulars. He declared he lived life on his own terms. A freelance computer programmer, he worked from home during the day and warmed the bar stool at Elfie's at nights. He drank like a fish and occasionally acted as volunteer bouncer when things got dicey. 'You know it's a bad sign when you can't leave work at work, honey,' he grunted as he slurped down a tall Coke glass filled with scotch.

'It's a curse,' she agreed. Pulled by an invisible string, her gaze drifted back up to the overhead screen. She watched in equal parts fascination and horror.

'Quentin went somewhere about twenty minutes ago,' the half-breed troll told her. 'Said he'd be right back.'

She nodded as the CNN reporter continued. '. . . Meanwhile public officials confirm that the origin of the event occurred some distance from Cuelebre Tower on Fifth Avenue, in a local park near Penn Station. Cuelebre Enterprises has released a press statement claiming responsibility for the unfortunate "research and development accident." We now go to Thistle Periwinkle, PR director for Cuelebre Enterprises and one of the more famous spokespersons from the Elder Races.' The scene cut to a small figure surrounded by reporters in front of Cuelebre Tower's polished chrome and marble veneer.

The crowd at the bar broke into two-fingered whistles, scattered stamping and applause. '*Woot!*' 'Faerie Barbie – yes!' 'My GIRL!'

The petite figure wore a pale pink business suit that accentuated an hourglass figure with a tiny waist. Standing close to five foot ten, Pia always felt like a galumphing horse when she saw the faerie on television. Cuelebre's famous public mouthpiece wore her fluffy lavender hair in a chic flipped-up bob. She wrinkled her tilted nose with a sympathetic smile as a dozen microphones were thrust in her face.

'God, she's hot.' Preston heaved a sigh. 'What I wouldn't give for a chance at that.'

Pia gave the huge craggy male a quick glance and scratched at the back of her head. The fact that the cutesy faerie was Cuelebre Enterprises' PR spokesperson always seemed manipulative to her. Look at how nice and friendly and safe we are, oh my.

The faerie held up a delicate hand. As soon as the shouting quieted, she began to speak. 'This will be just a brief statement today. We'll follow up later with more details as we better understand the situation. Cuelebre Enterprises regrets any inconvenience this incident has caused the good people of New York and promises a prompt resolution to any and all property damage claims.' The faerie's gamine smile died. She looked dead-on into the lens of the camera, her normally merry expression grim. 'Rest assured that Cuelebre is using every resource available to conduct a full investigation. He gives you his personal guarantee that what caused today's incident will be taken care of swiftly and decisively. There will never be another occurrence.'

So much for cutesy. The crowd of reporters around the faerie stilled. In the bar the constant burr of noise died. Even Rupert stopped serving drinks.

Someone nearby said, 'Damn. Did that twee little chick just pull off scary?'

On the wide-screen the scene erupted into chaos again before it cut back to the main newsroom at CNN where the blonde reporter said in an urgent tone, 'And there you have it, Cuelebre's public statement, and didn't it sound like a loaded one, folks.'

The news show went on to do a brief biographical sketch on Cuelebre. There wasn't much documented about the reclusive multibillionaire. He was universally acknowledged as one of the oldest Powers in the Elder Races and recognized as the iron-fisted ruler of the New York Wyrkind demesne. He was also a major, if shadowy, power player in the Washington political scene.

Close photographs and film segments of him always blurred. The most detail cameras had been able to capture of him was from pictures taken at a distance. The network showed a couple of snapshots of a group of tough-looking, powerful males. In

27

the midst of them towered a massive, dominant figure caught in aggressive midmotion, dark head turned away.

Cuelebre had never made a public acknowledgment of what he was, but news shows loved to speculate. They avoided claiming anything but made much of how his first name, Dragos, really meant 'dragon' and Cuelebre was a mythological giant winged serpent.

Even the most marginalized half-breed that crept around the edges of the Elder Races' politics and society knew what and who Cuelebre was. Every one of them would have felt in their bones the dragon's roar that had shaken the city to its foundations.

Pia groped for Preston's scotch. The troll handed the glass to her and she gulped at it. The liquid slid down her parched throat and exploded into a burning fireball in the pit of her stomach. She gasped and handed it back to him.

'I feel you,' said the troll. 'They've been playing stuff like that all afternoon. Apparently the "incident"' – he made finger quotes in the air – 'broke windows in buildings as far as a mile away and cracked one brownstone down the middle. I heard it myself, and I'm man enough to admit the sound made my stones shrink.'

Panic pulsed through her again. She dropped her hands below the bar to hide how they shook. She cleared her throat. 'Yeah, I heard it too.'

'Whoever made him that mad?' Preston shook his head. 'I can't imagine, but it's gonna make Judgment Day look like a picnic.'

A deep voice said by her ear, 'You look like shit.'

Pia almost leaped out of her skin. Then she pressed the heel of her hands against her eyelids until she saw stars before turning to face Quentin.

'That's my boss,' she said over her shoulder to Preston. 'A compliment a minute.'

The troll snorted.

Quentin leaned against the wall by the swinging doors that led to the back. He regarded her with a frown. He was six feet two inches of lean tensile strength and spare graceful features, one of those scary-gorgeous guys that could make the cover of *GQ* if he had been a model. His dark blond hair, when loose, would fall past broad shoulders, but he normally kept it pulled back in a queue. The severe style emphasized the long bones of his face and piercing blue eyes.

Pia's emotions took another wild swing. Her lips tightened and she looked down to tug at a backpack strap. 'I need to talk to you,' she told him.

'Figured as much.' He straightened from the wall and turned to push open one swinging door.

Pia wiggled her fingers at Preston and walked to the back, Quentin behind her. The door swung into place, muting the bar noise.

She continued through the stockroom and stepped into his spacious office. She stopped in the middle of the room, dropped her backpack and just stood there, her tired mind a blank.

A beautifully proportioned hand came over her shoulder and hooked under her chin. She allowed him to turn her around, though she could only meet his intent gaze for a moment before her own drifted to an area somewhere over his right shoulder. Her chest hurt. She could feel his scrutiny travel down her body.

'I'm leaving town,' she told the area over his shoulder. Her voice sounded choked. 'I came to say good-bye.'

Silence stretched and grew thin. Then Quentin put a hand on her forehead and wrapped the other around the back of her neck. Her gaze flew to him, and the concern she saw in his expression almost did her in. He said, 'You have a headache.'

Golden warmth began to flow from his hands, infusing her head and spreading through her body, easing pain away. 'Oh God, I had no idea you could do that,' she said with a sigh. 'That feels so good.'

When her knees sagged, he pulled her into his arms and held her close. 'I'm afraid I can't do anything about the heartache.'

Pia's mouth trembled. He must have read misery on her face like a road map. She rested her head on his shoulder. 'Aren't you supposed to yell at me for not giving you two weeks' notice?'

'How about I don't and we'll just say I did.' He rubbed her back. 'Deal?'

She sniffed and nodded, wrapped her arms around his waist.

Quentin's age was indeterminate. He could have been any-where from 35 to 135. There was something stern and age-less about him in repose and his aura carried a hint of violent

29

secrets, so Pia had always put her money on older. She'd had a flaming crush on him for years. Usually she enjoyed it. It was a comfortable indulgence, made all the more so because she knew she would never act on it.

There had been a frisson of awareness the moment they laid eyes on each other. Quentin bore a low-level hum of Power that pulled at her bones. She recognized what it was. He carried a glamour that helped him pass for human, which was very similar to hers and the other half-breeds who camouflaged themselves. She wasn't sure what he was but she guessed part Elven.

She knew he had no idea what she was either, and because he didn't pry she had tolerated the speculative glances he had given her at the beginning of their acquaintance. One of the things she appreciated most about her relationship with Quentin was that they didn't ask each other questions that were too personal.

After the first couple of months of wariness, they had relaxed in each other's company, having come to a tacit understanding. They both knew they had things that were better left hidden in the shadows. They were both content to leave them there.

He began to untangle her ponytail, combing through the strands with long fingers. 'Did Keith have anything to do with this? You haven't seen him since you broke up with him, have you?'

She was shocked at how good it felt to have Quentin stroke her hair. Going boneless, she turned her face into his shirt. He smelled like warm, virile male and green growing places. It felt so good to be held by a strong, steady man. For a few moments she allowed it to banish her chill as she pretended she belonged in his arms and that she was safe. What a dangerous, stupid pretense.

She stiffened and pulled out of his arms. 'Yes, I have seen him, and no, it wasn't romantic. Keith has contributed to this,' she admitted, not willing to lie, not only because she cared for Quentin but also because she had never been able to figure how much truthsense he had. 'But it's complicated.'

Quentin strolled to close his office door. He leaned against it and folded his arms. 'Okay, so I'll get it uncomplicated. Just tell me where he lives.'

Alarm flared. 'No! You've got to swear to leave him alone.'

Quentin cocked his head, regarding her with far too much acuity for her comfort. 'Why? You don't still care for him, do you?'

'God, no!' She scratched at her head with both hands and then rubbed her face. 'That isn't it at all. Look, you don't understand because you don't know anything, I get that. And I can't explain it to you. I shouldn't have even come to say good-bye. This was a big mistake.'

She gestured at him to move from the door. He didn't budge. Only then did she realize his position at the door had been deliberate. She huffed, angrier at herself than she was at him. She had to start getting smarter real fast, or she was going to be barbeque.

Quentin caught and held her gaze, his eyes going stormy. 'Just tell me what kind of trouble you're in,' he said slowly and deliberately. 'And I will take care of it. I won't ask questions you either can't or don't want to answer. All you've got to do is tell me what's wrong.'

Just like that her panic was back, only this time it was for him. She leaped forward and grabbed him by the shoulders. 'You listen to me.' She tried to shake him but he was too big. The stubbornness in his face made her snarl. 'I mean it. You have got to take me seriously. Shit's happened, and I'm not telling you about it. I'm leaving and that's that.'

Still watching her, he took her hands from his shoulders, wrapped them together and held them against his lean chest. 'Pia, we've known each other for four years, and we've respected each other's privacy very well up until now. Whatever else you are, I know you're a smart cookie—'

'You say that to me with a straight face after I fell for Keith. What a joke,' she said. She tried to jerk her hands away, but he wouldn't let go.

'You made a stupid mistake. That doesn't make you stupid,' he said, crushing her hands against his chest until she felt them throb. 'I've seen you watching how things work around here. Do you think I don't have contacts or influence? Let me help you.'

She stopped struggling since she wasn't able to get loose anyway. 'I know you have influence. There's got to be lots of reasons why Elfie's has such a large loyal clientele of half-breeds and why you talk with so many of them back here in your office. And I'm sure there's got to be a lot of interesting conversations during your Monday night poker games. Judging from other visits and back door deliveries, I'm also quite sure you have contacts from the Elven demesne, and God only knows who else.'

'Then you should know I can help you,' he said. He seemed to realize he was hurting her and loosened his hold. 'All you have to do is let me.'

She rolled her eyes. She knew he was stubborn, but this was ridiculous. 'You are still not listening to me. You. Can't. Help. Me.' She turned her hands over and clasped his. 'We're *still not going to talk about it*, but just think for a minute, will you? Dragon?' She curled her hands into claws. 'Rowr? Me leaving town?'

He whitened as he stared at her. 'What did you do?'

She shook her head. At least he was taking her seriously now. 'All you need to know is my kind of trouble has got you outclassed and outgunned. Do nothing. Even better – don't even think of doing anything. And God, Quentin, whatever you do, don't go after Keith. There's something really bad and scary out there that thinks it can mess with Cuelebre and get away with it.' Leaning forward, she let her forehead chunk on his chest. 'After telling you just that much, now *I'm* going to have to kill you. Please, listen to me. You've come to mean a lot to me and I don't want to hear you've been hurt or killed. Especially when there's nothing you can do, anyway.'

His arms came around her again and he squeezed her so hard she lost her breath. Then he put his lips next to her ear. 'I am not,' he said, 'going to let you go on the run without helping you. Deal with it.'

She groaned and pushed against him but he wouldn't let her go. 'What is the matter with you, moron? Do you have a death wish?'

'Oh, shut up. Of course I don't. I just look after my own,' Quentin said. He let her go and strode to his desk. Surprised, she staggered and pivoted to track him. His mouth thinned into stern lines. She saw again the shadow of something scary darken his face. He flashed her an ironic glance. 'Even if she does incomprehensible stupid things and squeals like a girl.'

'Fuck you. You're not the boss of me. Anymore, anyway,' she muttered. She watched him open his wall safe with swift efficiency.

'He pulled out an envelope and handed it to her. 'You're going to go here,' he told her. 'To a little place I own.'

His autocratic attitude caused a brief impulse of anger to sputter like an engine ticking over, but she was losing the energy to fight with him. She opened the envelope, pulled out two house keys on a plain metal ring and just looked at him.

'Ask me where it is. Say, "Quentin, where is it?"' he said. 'Go on.'

'Quentin, where is it?' she parroted without expression as she started to throw the keys onto his desk.

'Why, thank you for asking, Pia. How uncharacteristically polite of you.' He strode back and told her, 'It's just outside of Charleston.'

She froze in midtoss. 'South Carolina, Charleston? The seat of the Elven Court Charleston, smack in the middle of their demesne?'

Quentin smiled. 'That's the one. The one Cuelebre can't enter without the Elven High Lord's permission, or he breaks all kinds of treaties and things get really fucked-up for him.' His smile faded and he searched her gaze. 'I don't know what happens after you get there or what your next step is. This may do nothing more than leverage some Elder politics to buy you some breathing room. But it's a first step.'

'Yes, it is,' she breathed, staring at the keys. She stuffed them into her pocket and threw her arms around Quentin.

Maybe, just maybe, there was hope for her after all.

Quentin pushed another set of keys on her and walked her out the back to the small parking lot adjacent to the back of the bar. He stopped by an unassuming blue 2003 Honda Civic. 'Take it,' he said.

'This is too generous,' she said, her throat clogged. 'And you're too involved as it is.'

He refused to take the keys back. 'Look, the car can't be traced to you, or back to me. I keep half a dozen of these. It's no big deal. Shut up and get in.'

'I'm going to miss you,' she said.

He gave her a fierce hug. 'This isn't good-bye.'

'Sure it isn't.' She wrapped her arms around his long waist and held him tight.

'I mean it, Pia. Find a way to keep in touch to let me know you're okay, or I will come after you.'

She could only hope that something would happen to keep him from making good on that promise. He had to stay out of this mess. She couldn't bear to think she might have gotten her boss and friend killed because she couldn't leave without saying good-bye.

He pressed his lips to her forehead and stepped back. 'Go on, get out of here.'

She pushed the unlock button on the key ring, threw her backpack in the passenger's seat and climbed in the car. When she pulled to a stop at the end of the block, she looked in the rearview mirror.

Quentin stood at the edge of the parking lot watching her, his hands on his hips. He waved at her.

There was a break in the traffic. She pulled onto the street and he was gone.

Quentin had said the drive took more or less twelve hours, depending on traffic, from New York to Charleston, most of it on I-95. She wanted to get as much distance between herself and the New York Wyr demesne as she could. After forty minutes, she stopped at a Starbucks and bought a tofu salad sandwich and a large coffee so strong it could have scoured her bathtub clean. Then she drove until she couldn't see straight.

The demesnes of the Elder Races lay superimposed over the human geographical map. There were seven Elder demesnes in the United States, including the Wyr demesne seated in New York, and the Elven Court that was seated in Charleston.

Each demesne had its own lord or lady who enforced its laws. Some Elder rulers preferred to live at a distance from humankind. They kept their Courts in Other spaces where only those with magical aptitude could discern and cross dimensional boundaries. Others, like Dragos, lived in the human realm.

She wasn't clear where the Wyr-Elven border was so she drove until she was sure she had crossed over. Sensible or not, she felt a little of the fear peel away. Finally around 3:00 A.M., the exhaustion she had been fighting wouldn't take no for an answer. She pulled into a motel and got a room with one of her fake IDs. She put the door chain on, dropped her backpack onto a chair and sank onto the bed. The room spun as she toed off first one shoe, then the other.

I could sleep for a month, she thought as she got sucked down a whirling drain into black.

She wasn't that lucky.

Dragos stood at the edge of his penthouse balcony atop Cuelebre Tower. He looked out over his city as the sun approached the horizon. This late in the day the deepening sunlight was a heavy golden weight with the richness and complexity of a rare, aged white-burgundy wine. His feet were planted wide apart, hands clasped behind his back.

The balcony was one of his favorite places to meditate. There was no railing. It was a large ledge that ran the circumference of the building, which took up a city block. The balcony was a handy, more private place to launch or land when he didn't feel like going to the roof, which was used by his sentinels and certain other privileged members of his Court. He could enter or exit the penthouse from any number of large French-style doors.

Cuelebre Enterprises was the umbrella for any number of businesses, and it consistently ranked in the top ten of the world's largest corporations. Casinos, hotels and resorts, stock trading, shipping, international risk assessment (private army for hire), banking. He employed thousands of Fae, Elves, Wyr and humans worldwide, although the majority of Wyrkind preferred to live in New York State so that they could live within the law and protection of his demesne.

Those Wyr who clustered in Dragos's Court and occupied key positions in his companies tended to be predators of some sort, the type of shapeshifter that thrived in a competitive, volatile, sometimes violent environment, although there were a few tough-minded exceptions like Cuelebre Enterprises PR faerie Thistle Periwinkle, known to her friends as Tricks.

Like Rune, his First, all seven of his sentinels were immortal creatures strong in Power. They were also raptors of some sort. There were the four gryphons, Rune, Constantine, Graydon and Bayne, each responsible for keeping the peace in one of the four sectors of his demesne. The gargoyle Grym was in charge of corporate security for Cuelebre Enterprises. Tiago, one of the three known thunderbirds in existence, headed Dragos's private army.

Last but not least was the harpy Aryal, who was in charge of investigations. She had not taken well to giving over the investigative reins on this theft to Rune. She was not known for having a serene temperament. There was a reason she had risen to such preeminence in his Court. Dragos's smile was grim. The harpy was one hell-spawned bitch when she lost her temper.

He reached into his shirt pocket and withdrew the scrap of paper left by his thief. The message was scribbled on the back of a 7-Eleven receipt. The thin paper was already getting dog-eared from his handling. He opened it and read what the thief had bought yesterday. A pack of Twizzlers and a large cherry Coke Slurpee.

Rune, he said telepathically.

His First's response was immediate. *My lord.*

You will go to – he squinted at the faded lettering on the receipt – *the Forty-second Street 7-Eleven store and retrieve all of their security footage for the last twenty-four hours. There* is *a good chance our thief may be caught on it.*

Re-eally, drawled Rune, his hunter instincts engaged. *Leaving now. Back within the hour.*

Oh, and Rune?

Bring back Twizzlers and a cherry Coke Slurpee. He wanted to know what these things were.

Sure. You got it, said his First, clearly taken aback. *Dragos?*

What. He squinted and stretched, basking in the last of the sunlight.

Any idea what size Slurpee you want? His First's mental voice sounded odd.

They had known each other and worked together for several hundred years now. Dragos said, *You know my tastes well enough. Will I like it?*

Now that Dragos was back in control of his temper, Rune fell into their normal friendly informality. *Uh, I don't think so, buddy. I've never known you to do junk food before.*

Make it a small, then. Dragos held the receipt up, sniffed and frowned. Even to his sensitive nose the receipt was starting to lose that delicate feminine scent and smell like him.

He strode inside. The penthouse took the Tower's top floor. Just below that were his offices, meeting rooms, an executive dining hall, training area and other public areas. The third floor down housed his sentinels and other top Court and corporate officials. If it had been a stand-alone building, it would have been a mansion. All the rooms and halls were built on a massive scale.

Dragos located the kitchen in the penthouse. It was a foreign place filled with chrome machines and countertops. No one was there. He went in search of the communal kitchen responsible for serving the dining hall and all the sentinels, Court and corporate executives' needs. He located it on the next flight down.

He strode through the double doors. A half-dozen kitchen staff froze. In the corner a brownie gave a squeak of dismay and faded into invisibility.

The head chef hurried forward, wringing her hands. She was a dire wolf in her Wyr form, but she kept her human shape, that of a tall gray-haired middle-aged woman, during work hours. 'This is an unexpected honor, my lord,' she gushed. 'What can we do for you?'

'There are plastic bags with zippers on them. I've seen them in commercials,' Dragos said to her. He snapped his fingers, trying to remember the name. 'You put food in them.'

'Ziploc bags?' she asked in a cautious voice.

He pointed at her. 'Yes. I want one.'

She turned and snarled at her staff. A faerie leaped to a cupboard and then bounded to them. She bowed low to Dragos, head ducked and eyes to the floor while holding a cardboard box up. He pulled out a baggie, placed the 7-Eleven receipt inside and zipped it closed.

'Perfect,' he said, placing the small bag in his shirt pocket. He walked out, ignoring the babble that rose behind him.

While he waited for Rune to show up, he went to his offices to confront the most urgent of issues waiting for his attention. His four assistants, all Wyr handpicked for their quick intelligence and sturdy dispositions, occupied the outer rooms that were adorned with works of abstract expressionism by such artists as Jackson Pollock and Arshile Gorky and sculpture by Herbert Ferber.

Located in a corner of the building, his office was decorated in natural tones with wood and stone. As with the penthouse, the outer walls of the office were plate glass set with wrought-iron French doors that opened to a private balcony ledge. The interior walls were adorned by two mixed-media canvases he had commissioned from the late artist Jane Frank. They were from the artist's Aerial Series, which depicted landscapes as if seen in midflight. One canvas was a landscape by day, the other by night.

As he sat at his desk, his first assistant, Kristoff, poked his dark shaggy head in the door. Dragos clenched his teeth on a surge of irritation. Head bent to the contracts laid on his desk, he said, 'Approach with caution.'

The Wyr's ursine nature and shambling demeanor masked a Harvard-trained MBA with a quick-witted, canny mind. Clever bear that he was, Kristoff said the two words guaranteed to grab his attention. 'Urien Lorelle.'

His head lifted. Urien Lorelle, the Dark Fae King, was one of the seven rulers of the Elder Races; his demesne was seated in the greater Chicago area, and he was the guy Dragos most loved to hate. He sat back and flexed his hands. 'Bring it.'

Arms overflowing, Kristoff lunged forward and spilled documents onto his desk. 'I've got it – the link we were looking for between Lorelle and weapons development. Here are hard copies of everything. Transcontinental Power and Light's 10-K filing with the SEC, last year's proxy statement and annual report and its quarterly corporate-earnings conference calls. I've marked the relevant pages and typed up a report.'

Formed in the latter part of the nineteenth century, Transcontinental Power and Light, Inc., was one of the nation's largest investor-owned utility companies. The Dark Fae King was the largest individual shareholder.

Dragos picked up the 10-K filing and began to flip through it. The U.S. Securities and Exchange Commission document was thick, some 450 pages in length and dense with statistics, tables and graphs.

Urien Lorelle and he shared so many differences of opinion. Lorelle's utility company was partial to mountaintop-removal

mining. Dragos preferred mountaintops to stay where he could
see them. Urien's fleet of aging coal-burning power plants
emitted over one hundred million tons of carbon dioxide annu-
ally. Dragos preferred to breathe clean air when he flew. Urien
wanted to see him dead. Dragos preferred to see Urien not just
dead but utterly destroyed.

'It's because you prefer to live in an Other land. You don't
care how much you pollute this side of things, you anachro-
nistic bastard,' he muttered. He said to Kristoff, 'Summarize.'

His assistant said, 'Transcontinental has set up a partnership
called RYVN, the acronym – well, it doesn't matter. RYVN
has applied for a Department of Energy grant to clean up an
old Energy Department site in the Midwest that produced
nuclear fuel and defense applications back in the fifties. RYVN
says they want to explore building a new electricity-generated
nuclear plant on the site, along with new contracts with the
Defense Department.'

His eyes flashed lava hot. He hissed, 'Defense applications.'

Kristoff nodded, dark eyes bright. 'Weaponry.'

The financial documents he held smelled like printer ink
and paper, but Dragos scented the blood of an imminent kill.

'Get a hold of our DOE contact,' Dragos said. 'Make sure
he knows to reject RYVN's grant application and why. After
you've done that, I want you to destroy the RYVN partnership.
When that's gone, go after the individual partners and disman-
tle them one by one. Head the project yourself.'

'Right,' said Kristoff.

'No mercy, Kris. When we're done, no one will dare partner
with Urien on something like this again.'

Kristoff asked, 'Project budget?'

'Unlimited.' The Wyr-bear turned to go, and he added, 'And
Kris? Make sure they know who shut them down. Especially
Urien.'

'You got it.' Kristoff gave him a grin.

So many differences of opinion between him and the Dark
Fae King. So much hate, so little time.

Just then Rune appeared in the doorway wearing torn jeans,
combat boots and a Grateful Dead T-shirt. The gryphon's tawny
hair was windblown. He carried two drinks in a cardboard box
drink holder, a plastic bag and a bulging manila folder under

one arm. He dumped out the contents of the bag. Packets of Twizzlers tumbled across the desk.

Dragos tore open one packet. Rune shoved straws into the drinks, gave him one and kept the other.

'I've got the footage,' said Rune, gesturing to the folder under his arm. 'Do you know what we're looking for?'

'Make prints of anyone who buys Twizzlers and cherry Coke Slurpees and bring them to me. Just those two things, nothing else. It will be a female, although she may be in disguise.' Dragos bit into a red rope of candy. He stared in disgust at the remaining half in his hand and threw it in the trash can. Then he picked up the drink and sucked on the straw with caution.

Rune burst into laughter at his expression. 'I said you wouldn't like it.'

'So you did.' He slam-dunked the Slurpee. 'Apparently you will be watching the tapes for someone with no taste.'

'This shouldn't take long. Thank the Powers for fast-forward,' Rune said. He swiped up a few of the Twizzlers packets, winking at Dragos. 'Since you don't like them,' he said, and left.

Dragos went back to work, but his concentration had splintered for other matters. He kept three wide-screens on the opposite wall on different news channels. His other three assistants came and went. The ticker tape headlines of one channel caught his attention and he turned the volume up. The preliminary cost estimate for the property damage he caused that afternoon was already in the tens of millions.

The news crew conducted interviews of pedestrians. One woman said tearfully, 'Forget about property damage. I heard that sound earlier today and I'm going to be in therapy for the rest of my life. I want to know if Cuelebre is going to pay for that!'

He pushed the mute button. It was turning out to be one expensive damn penny.

Outside the wall-sized windows, early evening fell into full night. Then Rune came loping back into his office, paper in his hands.

'I've got it, got *her*,' his First exclaimed. 'Lots of people bought lots of crap, but only one woman bought only Twizzlers and a Slurpee. What are the odds?'

Dragos leaned back in his chair. He felt a pulse of dark anticipation as Rune handed him the paper. He shuffled through all of the photos. They were of a fixed scene of the 7-Eleven's registers and the glass front doors. Rune threw his large frame into a chair and watched as, with an impatient shove, Dragos wiped clear the large expanse of his desk and began to lay the photos out one by one.

Rune had printed several sequential eight-by-elevens. As Dragos laid out the grainy black-and-whites he could almost imagine the woman in the photos moving. He couldn't wait to see the footage and watch her move for real.

There she was, opening the door. She moved to the left and disappeared from the camera. There she was again, reappearing, holding a packet of Twizzlers and a Slurpee drink in slender hands. She paid, gave the cashier a smile. The last photo was of her pushing out the front door.

He went over them again with more care.

The angle of the shots made it difficult to say for sure, but she seemed a normal height for a tallish human woman. She was whippet graceful with long bones and delicate curves. The camera caught the dip and hollow of her collarbones. She wore her thick hair in a ponytail that was somewhat disheveled, and it was either white or some other light color. He was betting on some shade of blonde. Her triangular face was far too young for it to be gray.

The slash of Dragos's dark brows lowered over his blade-straight nose. The woman looked tired, preoccupied. No, she looked more than tired – she looked haunted. The smile she gave the cashier was courteous, even kind, but sad. She wasn't what he expected, but he knew in his old wicked bones that this was his thief.

He traced a finger down the silhouette of her figure as she walked out the 7-Eleven door. It was the only one of her walking away. He didn't like this picture. He slammed his flattened hand down on it and crumpled it in his fist.

'I've got you,' he said.

'I have just one question for you,' Rune said. The gryphon's long legs were spread out, his eyes curious. 'How did you know to send me there and what to look for?'

Dragos looked up with a flash of secretive jealousy. 'Never

41

mind how. We've found her and your part in this is done. You can go back to your regular duties.'

Rune nodded at the photos. 'What about her?'

'I'll take care of her.' Dragos bared his teeth. 'I'm hunting this one. Alone.'

He sent Rune away, climbed to his penthouse bedroom and opened the French doors. The late-spring air licked into the room. He stood in the doorway looking at the gleaming city lights.

Where are you, thief? I know you're running somewhere, he said to the night. He lifted his head to the breeze, which carried the city's complex mélange of scents.

Power, magical or otherwise, has its own set of habits. He realized he had fallen into a bored complacency. Either life conformed to what he desired or he bent it to his will. He didn't ask, he took. If a business interest threatened him, he had them destroyed. No mercy. He had settled into the unsophisticated laziness of brute force.

Dragos summoned his Power and began whispering beguilement into the night. He held the image of his thief firm in his mind. The magical threads flexed like long-unused muscles and began curling outward on the breeze. It was only a matter of time before they found their target.

I've got you now.

≡ THREE ≡

Pia dreamed of a dark, whispering voice. She tossed and turned, fighting to ignore it. Exhaustion was a concrete shackle. All she wanted to do was sleep. But the voice insinuated into her head and sank velvet claws deep.

She opened her eyes to find that she was standing at the edge of a spacious balcony that hung high over New York.

The night scene was dazzling. Lights of all colors were spray-painted on massive skyscrapers against a purple-black background. She looked down. She was barefoot and stood on flagstones, not concrete.

There wasn't a railing.

She shrieked and fell on her ass as she stumbled back. She scrambled backward until she put several feet between herself and the precipice. Then she noticed her long bare legs pouring out from a simple white negligee. The negligee accentuated her runner's light, strong build, slender muscles both racy and muscular.

Negligee? She fingered the satiny material. She didn't own a negligee. Did she? She could have sworn she hadn't gone to bed in it. By the way, where had she gone to bed again?

A gentle pearly luminescence lit the flagstones around her. The blood rushed through her body on a surge of adrenaline.

Oh shit, she was glowing.

This was so not good. She pushed the hair out of her face. The glow made her feel more naked than she would have if she'd been nude. She hadn't lost control over the dampening spell since she was a child.

She fumbled for the spell that would shield the luminescence and make her skin appear human. It was dangerous for her to be so exposed, but she seemed to have forgotten how to cast the spell.

'There you are,' a deep, quiet voice said. 'I've been waiting for you.'

That voice. Whiskey and silk, ageless and male. It poured over her and set her body on fire. She was bereft of air. Her lips parted on a soundless gasp.

She turned toward elegant open French doors wrought of black iron. White, gauzy, floor-length curtains billowed in the breeze. They obscured as much as they revealed.

'You want to come inside now.' That incomparable beautiful voice created a deep yearning that shook through her. She scrambled to her feet.

A small part of her mind rebelled. Um hello, that part of her mind said to her. Not into yearning much. Remember what happened the last time you gave in to yearning. You fell for a shithead who blackmailed you? You lost everything and had to go on the run?

The scene around her flickered and started to fade. The dark whispering surged in strength until it was all she could hear or think about. She was so lonely her chest ached. It actually, physically ached. She pressed a hand between her breasts and looked around in confusion.

The hypnotic voice ordered, 'You will come inside now.'

All of a sudden that was the only thing she wanted to do. She went to the curtains and gathered them up in one hand as she looked inside into a huge shadowed bedroom. She caught an impression of a fireplace and large sturdy furniture sprinkled throughout the room.

A male reclined on pale covers on an enormous dark-framed bed. He had a massive physique, thick muscles bulging over long limbs, the bare skin of his torso dark against pale linen. The fall of hair onto his strong forehead was darker still. A sensual mouth quirked in a cynical smile. Only his eyes gleamed against the darkness with a faint, calculating, witchy glow.

Unease skittered on light mice feet down her back. There was something important she had to remember about his eyes. If only she could think of it.

Power like champagne filled the room until she felt like she was swimming in it. She had never been in the presence of so much magic before. It pressed against her skin, exhilarating and terrifying, addicting. It turned the fire the voice had ignited in her into liquid desire. An animal sound came out of her.

The man uncurled a long muscular arm and extended a hand to her. Resistance melted. She went to him in a rush. She had barely reached the bed when he exploded into action. He took hold of her arms, dragged her across his body and slammed her into the mattress as he rolled on top of her. Pinning her down with his heavy body, he locked his hands around her glowing wrists and yanked them over her head. The corded strength in his fingers make the flesh and bone they shackled feel slender and fragile.

Magic and desire choked her. Her breathing turned erratic at his controlled violence and the dominance of his body pressing her down. Sexual heat pooled low in her body as the juncture between her thighs grew slick.

A rumble started low in his throat. The bed shuddered with the feral sound. His harsh, shadowed face was hewn out of the same indomitable mountain that had formed his body. There was something familiar about his spiked black hair.

'Look at me,' he said, thrusting his face down until they were nose to nose. *'Look at me.'*

In the pearly glow of her body, his gaze flashed gold like a falcon's eyes. Predator's eyes. Sorcerer's eyes.

Something shouted a warning in a distant part of her mind but it was too late. She had already flung back her head and looked into his eyes. Just like that she was snared like a spider in a web. He could do anything he wanted to her now, anything at all.

She found it impossible to care. She found she wanted to be snared. She rubbed against his taut, sexy body. It felt so good to be pinned by him, a renegade pleasure that went against everything she'd been taught or thought she understood about herself.

'Oh, what's the matter with you,' she groaned. She arched her neck and tried to angle her hips just right. That area between her thighs was beginning to throb with a deep, insistent, empty ache. 'What are you waiting for?'

He stilled as if she had surprised him. Then something changed between them. She didn't know what it was, but she could feel when it happened. The air grew even more electric, a live wire jumping ungrounded, building force as it bounced back and forth between them. Then he shifted with slow deliberation, settling full on her. His growl deepened, the rumble vibrating in that immense, muscled chest. His eyes were wild, ravenous. His head came down on her with the force of a raptor's plummet.

Hard open lips captured hers. The gentle seductiveness that had been in his voice earlier was gone. He shoved into her mouth, penetrating her with a hot, hungry tongue while he ground her into the bed with his hips. Something lay stiff and heavy along her flat stomach. With a thrill of shock she realized it was an enormous erection.

Her lips shook beneath his as she whimpered, 'That's so good.' She worked her back muscles, trying to rub her hips on his cock.

He sucked in a breath and muttered a shaken curse. He made his body into an enormous cage constructed of bone and muscle and starvation as he bowed around her, pinning her with arms and legs and weight. She arched up with all her strength, exhilarating in the cage, which gave her a paradoxical feeling of release. She moaned as they ate at each other's mouths, frantic to consume each other. His hands moved on her wrists, a restless shackle. His tongue thrust an aggressive rhythm as he fucked her mouth.

The ancient primitive rhythm only made her need flash hotter. She needed him to penetrate her in other ways. She writhed and he moved so that thick muscled thighs were on either side of hers, which brought his hips in full alignment with her aching pelvis.

It also brought the length of his erection against her clitoris. He ground against her, flexing like a great hunting cat, rubbing the hot, hard length of flesh along the graceful ridge of her pelvic bone. Pleasure raked frenzied claws through her. She cried out into his mouth and pushed her hips against his.

Vaguely she knew something was wrong. She was acting out of character even for a sexual dream. It had something to do with a lifetime of loneliness, with the electric sensuality this male exuded, with him calling her to him with sorcery and with her looking into his eyes and becoming snared, with his seductive, cunning patience. She tried to hold on to those thoughts but they ran like water flowing through her fingers. Her sexual frenzy – his sexual frenzy pouring over and through her – overrode all of it.

He dragged his mouth from hers, turned his head to one side and gasped something. The words were foreign, the language harsh and burning with Power. They sounded like curses. His hands slid away from her wrists. One dove to the small of her back to yank her hips tighter against him. The other came up to palm her small breast while he lay hard against her. His marauding lips plunged down the side of her face to her throat.

He bit her, a savage and archaic gesture that sent an earthquake through her body. She shrieked and raked her nails down the immense musculature of his back while she wrapped her legs around those taut pumping hips and pulled him even closer.

They were almost there, almost there. He rolled with her until she lay sprawled on top of him. She adjusted to the new position with an eager wiggle, mouth turned to him, seeking his. Hard hands sank into her hair and held her head imprisoned against his hairy chest. She needed him to push inside her like she'd never needed anything before. She plunged one hand between them to grip the velvety, broad head of his penis. It was damp at the tip.

Then, his lungs working hard, he pulled her head back until their lips were just touching. Still pushing his hips against her pelvis in that slow, hard sexual rhythm, rubbing his thick cock against her palm, he whispered into her open mouth, 'Tell me what your Name is.'

Okay, wait. She had to remember something about that. She struggled to think past the burning need for him.

'Tell me,' he whispered, the words winding around her, snaring her tighter.

47

Wait a minute. Her breath shook. Names have Power. Power, like that in his voice.

She cast around in her desire-fuddled mind for a good lie but heard herself say, 'P-Pia Giovanni.'

She panted in real pain and rubbed herself along the length of his body, trying to rediscover the rhythm he had begun. She needed to come so bad she could have screamed.

'Pia.' He didn't so much say the name as breathe it. His hot breath coiled around her like tendrils of smoke from an infernal fire. 'Pretty.'

God, it felt unbelievable, as he stroked her all over with nothing but the Power in his voice. He licked her hot skin and murmured, again with that caressing, dark, seductive voice, 'But that's your human name, isn't it, darling? You're some kind of Wyr. I need to know your real Name.'

Then as if he couldn't help himself, he cupped the back of her ass and pushed up against her so hard his hips left the bed.

But just wait.

Giving him her real Name would give him Power over her.

'May all the gods have mercy, *tell me.*' The agonized groan came up from his core and blasted her swollen, moistened lips.

The ghost of her mother's voice touched her desire-crazed thoughts with cool lucidity.

Don't ever tell your real Name to anyone, my love, she had said to Pia. Over and over her mother had repeated this lesson. She spoke it with Power of her own in her voice, so that the lesson would be fixed in Pia's mind because she had been a bit of a flighty child at times. *If you tell someone your real Name, you have forever given that person Power over you. It is your most precious, private treasure. Keep it safe as you guard your life, for your Name is the key to your soul.*

The dream spell shattered. 'No,' she whispered.

Was she denying him or her mother? She tried to clamp down with her legs on his torso to hold on to him, clutching at that black spiky hair with greedy fingers.

He roared. He sounded like he was in as much pain as she was. He wrapped hard arms tight around her, but she was already growing insubstantial. The raw silk of his hair melted through her grip.

She threw out her hands, reaching for him. For a moment she felt his questing fingers brush along hers. Then he was gone.

She hurtled to wakefulness and plunged upright in her bed with a soundless shout. Her heart hammered like she had just raced a marathon. Her dirty clothes were soaked in sweat, the motel bedspread tangled underneath her. The air conditioner rattled, blowing stale, deodorized air through the room. The remnant of magic lay flat in the air like soured champagne.

Her hungry body wept. With a moan, she plunged one hand between her legs and pressed. It only made her ache more.

She had never felt such a wretched, unconsummated lust. She curled into a miserable ball, starving for that dream lover and terrified of him at the same time. Something deep inside her started to whisper his name. Then panic shut it down. She couldn't think it, couldn't let what happened become too real because that would be beyond disastrous.

Then she jerked as she realized that she was still glowing. The low-level glamour that hid her skin's pearl-like sheen was fed from her own life force. It was supposed to remain active at all times, even when she slept. Her mother had helped her put the spell in place. She hadn't lost control over it in years.

She renewed the spell and dampened herself to look human again.

She was so screwed.

Grimacing, she curled into a tighter ball.

Dragos exploded out of his bed, face contorted, one hand holding his painful erection. His balls ached so badly he stumbled forward to grip at the edges of a nearby mahogany dresser. He bowed over it, shuddering.

What the hell?

The beguilement he sent was supposed to seduce his thief with her deepest fantasy, her most heartfelt desire. He had expected anything but this, a dream of riches or power, success or even fame, but sex? The ultimate opportunist, he had laughed to himself and had been quick to oblige, as he beguiled her deeper into his dream trap.

Then she stepped into his bedroom and his world stopped.

She was lovelier than he could have imagined, her body glowing with its own internal moonlight. His mind seized. What was she? His knowledge of the Elder Races was near encyclopedic, compiled as it had been over the long ages. He cast back, searching for any memory of this type of creature, and slammed into a blank wall. All that came to mind was that distant tantalizing memory of the time he had caught the hint of a scent on the breeze that had driven him wild.

He remembered now. Centuries ago he had plunged into the forest in North Umbria and chased after an elusive wild scent very like his thief's, catching and losing it again in fitful spurts, sure that he heard the sharp rustle of foliage as some mysterious creature bounded away from him. The forest had teemed with the Power of green growing things, back when both he and the world were so much younger.

In the dream he concentrated everything he had on this woman, greedy to understand and categorize what was happening, to find its appropriate place in his vast memory. Yet he met with absolute failure. The magic that was an inherent part of her was delicate and filigreed, layered with feminine complexity and beauty. It felt wild and mysterious, cool like her moonlit glow. His whole body had tightened with shock as he watched her walk toward him with a graceful roll of slim hips, generous lips parted and her gaze radiant with sensual yearning.

Yearning for him, the Great Beast. Cuelebre. Wyrm.

He did not recognize himself then, or the volcano that erupted inside him. The beast pounced and took her with violent, voracious force.

And she had loved it.

Blind lust took him over then, scorching him in a way he had never experienced before. He fell prey to it and to her, body and old wicked soul. The beguiler became the beguiled. The sensual undulation of that graceful female form underneath his felt like some kind of epiphany. Eating at her plump, eager mouth made him ravenous. All he could think about was plunging his cock inside her in an ecstasy of ravishment.

He had managed to hang on to the reason for the spell he had cast, as he recognized in one corner of his mind that however intense and pleasurable this dreamscape felt, it was designed to feed a hunger, not assuage it. It worked to use his prey's weaknesses and desires against it so that he could pull it into his control. Neither of them would gain fulfillment from the dream, only increased appetite.

But when he tightened the spell and pressed her for the ultimate surrender, she denied him.

His thief *said no to him*.

He snarled and tore the mahogany dresser apart. He picked up the bed and hurled it across the room, then whirled and drove his fists into the wall. He must have hit a girder because something inside the wall groaned and buckled.

The door to his bedroom slammed open. He whipped around, almost faster than sight, teeth bared. Rune and Aryal entered like twin cyclones, half-dressed bodies aimed like weapons. His First was armed with a sword while Aryal carried a semiautomatic. Rune went left and the six-foot harpy dove right before they both realized he was not under attack. They slowed to a stop.

To give his sentinels credit, they didn't run when faced with the nude figure of their enraged lord. In fact, Dragos had to admit it was brave of them to enter his bedroom in the first place. That thought was the thread that helped him to gain enough control so that he didn't tear their heads from their shoulders.

'Bad dream?' Rune said, keen gaze steady as he straightened from a fighting crouch and let the tip of his sword fall to the floor.

'I've got her human name,' he said. They all knew who he meant. 'Pia Giovanni. Find out what you can about her, quickly, and get me the witch. I need a tracking spell.'

The harpy Aryal's sleek brows lifted as she glanced from his ruined room to the predawn sky. For a moment her life trembled by the merest thread. If she had spoken a single word just then, she would have died in flames.

'DAMN YOU, MOVE!'

The floor of the penthouse shuddered at his roar. They raced out the door. So they were smart as well as brave.

The lingering traces of the beguilement clawed at him. He yanked clothes on and stalked outside to pace the balcony. The penthouse was a prison. Even the vast, spread-out, noisy panorama of the city felt like a cage. He wanted to lunge into the air. He felt the impulse to slaughter something but he was trapped and flightless until the witch arrived.

The dragon stood at the edge of the ledge, fists clenched, and with narrowed eyes he watched the small quick-moving humans in the street eighty floors below.

A short time later, Rune said telepathically, *My lord, the witch is here.*

My office, he said. He moved along the penthouse balcony until he stood one floor above his office. Then he leaped to the ledge below.

Rune and the witch had already entered the room. The gryphon was unaffected by his sudden appearance but the witch stared as he straightened to his full height. A human Hispanic woman with a tall imperious beauty, she was quick to lower her gaze when he opened the French door and strode inside.

Cuelebre Enterprises had for some years contracted with the best witch in the city. Dragos had never bothered to learn her name but he recognized her. She was afraid of him, which he ignored. All humans were afraid of him. They should be.

He growled, 'I need a tracking spell put on a woman.'

The witch inclined her head. She said, 'Certainly, my lord. Of course, no doubt you already know that the more information I can be given on a target, the better I can craft a tracking spell for it.'

'Her name is Pia Giovanni,' Dragos said. He handed her the stack of photos from the 7-Eleven security footage. 'This is what she looks like.'

The witch went still, her eyes on the top photo. Her expression was a perfect blank, but something, some minuscule change in her posture or breathing, roused the predator in him. A smooth, fluid shift of his body brought him closer to her. He could sense her body heat and the pulse at her neck and wrists, which beat more rapid at his proximity. He scanned her with truthsense as he asked, 'Do you know this woman?'

The witch's dark gaze lifted to his. She said, 'I have seen her in the Magic District. I didn't know her name.'

Her face remained that perfect blank, revealing nothing. It was not, he thought, the blithe calm of innocence but one of educated discipline. Still, she did speak the truth. The predator in him eased back. He nodded at the photos. 'Is her name and a photo enough for you?'

The witch said, 'I could cast a spell with these things. But it would be more durable, and it would last longer, if you had something of hers that I could use as an anchor. A good tracking spell is more complicated than a finding. It must shift and move as the object changes direction.'

Unsurprised, he reached into his shirt pocket and pulled out a Ziploc bag that held a battered receipt. 'It just so happens I do have something we can use.'

≡ FOUR ≡

Shaken by such a rude awakening, Pia rolled off the bed and lurched into the bathroom to take a shower. She hadn't carried any toiletries in her backpack beyond hand lotion and Chap-Stick so she had to make do with the motel's paper-wrapped sliver of plain soap. It took forever to work some through her long hair and lather a washcloth, but at least the water was hot and plentiful. The skin at the side of her neck felt tender as she scrubbed herself.

She paused and rubbed at the tender area. What was that?

After a quick final rinse, she wrapped her tangled hair in a towel, grabbed another towel to dry off and then wiped the fogged sink mirror to peer at her neck.

Bite. It was a bite mark. She fingered the area at the juncture of her neck and shoulder. The skin wasn't broken but there was an impression of teeth, and a suck-bruise was already forming.

She whispered, 'The bastard gave me a hickey?' In a dream?

Goose bumps rose on her skin. She rubbed her arms and avoided looking at her white face with the dark-circled eyes.

Somehow that horrible dream had been real. His magic had found her. He knew what she looked like. She told him her name.

Get out now.

Good thing she had three other names, with picture IDs that said so, because she had to hit delete on the one she'd lived with her whole life. Pia Alessandra Giovanni had to go. She felt another pang, another loss. Her mother had given her that name from long-held fondness for the time she had spent in medieval Florence. How much more did Pia have to lose? Apparently everything.

It was too much for her tired mind. She yanked a brush through her hair, miserable at how it had snarled without conditioner, and then she dressed in her dirty clothes.

When she started the Honda, the dashboard clock said 6:30 A.M. She had slept just under two hours.

She went through another drive-through and bought juice, more coffee and apple slices, although she could only choke down a few bites. She drove south as the sky grew pastel and brightened into full day. The temperature warmed the farther she went until she rolled down the windows and opened the Honda's moon roof.

If she'd been making the trip for any other reason, she would have enjoyed herself. The sky was cloudless. The scenery in South Carolina was different from what she was used to. The foliage was a couple weeks farther along in bloom than in New York, and the land felt strange to her senses. She began to pass properties vivid with greenery and profuse with camellias, roses, azaleas, and magnolia trees blanketed in pink blossoms. Silvery Spanish moss draped along the branches of old oak trees like fashion stoles adorning beautiful women. Charleston and the surrounding area had a grace and beauty that was quite different from the brisk urban setting she had just left.

She had given an ironic chuckle when Quentin had handed her directions to a beach house in a place called Folly Beach. Folly. Ha. It was about twenty minutes south of Charleston. Most of the houses, he told her, were vacation rentals. He had owned his for over thirty years and kept it furnished and stocked with linens and kitchenware.

When she got close to her destination, she stopped at a superstore to buy clothing essentials and toiletries, aspirin, a prepaid cell phone and food supplies. When she reached the checkout lane by the liquor aisle, she caved and bought a bottle of scotch as well. A girl's got to have priorities. If she didn't deserve a drink after the nightmare week she had just suffered, she didn't know who did.

She threw her purchases in the Honda's trunk. Soon after, she drove at a slow pace down a small coastal road on Folly Beach. She stared at the glimpses of the Atlantic Ocean she could see between cottages. The smell of the ocean gusted into the car.

The sunlight was different here, clearer and thinner, and she got the sense of a nearby place drenched in magic. There was a dimensional passageway somewhere near to Other lands. She wasn't surprised, given that the seat of the Elven Court was located either in or near Charleston.

Quentin's house was at the end of the road, on the beach side. It was larger than many of the cottages she had passed, with its own short off-street driveway and garage. After parking, she shouldered her packages and entered the house, which had an empty feel to it, although thanks to a monthly cleaning service, it was at least fresh and clean.

There were three bedrooms to choose from. She put away the food and then picked the largest bedroom with an en suite bathroom. She threw the toiletries on the bathroom counter and piled her new clothes and underwear on top of a dresser. She found towels and bed linens and made the bed, moving slowly and methodically. As soon as the bed was made, she took off her jeans, climbed under the covers and curled up as she hugged a pillow.

Soon she would start thinking about her next steps and try to make a plan. Even if Cuelebre couldn't come this deep into the Elven demesne, he had more money than God and probably more employees too. She didn't dare stay too long.

She would close her eyes for just a little while.

She woke with a start several hours later. For several bleary moments she couldn't remember where she was or why. Then memory flooded in, and she sagged back against the pillows.

Okay. Life sucked. But at least she didn't have another freaky sex dream where she got *bitten*.

The room felt sticky and overwarm. Though the curtains were drawn, it seemed from the diffuse light that the sun was at a much lower angle than when she had first lain down. She pushed out of bed and dressed in some of her new clothes, low-hipped capris, sandals and a red tank with spaghetti straps. Her breasts were high, rather small and firm, so she didn't bother with a bra.

She peered outside. It was early evening, maybe around five o'clock. She went to the bathroom to splash her face with cold water. After dragging a brush again through her recalcitrant hair, she pulled it back in another ponytail. Then she went to the kitchen/dining room area, which was separated by a counter and bar stools. The dining area had sliding glass doors that opened to a large deck with a few simple pieces of patio furniture. Stairs led to the beach.

She went down the stairs. She stood on the sun-warmed sand and breathed deep for several minutes as she gazed at a limitless horizon and listened to the murmurous dance of a calm ocean as it played against the shore. Kicking off her sandals, she walked close to the water's edge and let sea foam surge across her toes. It was very cold. The tension that had taken up residence between her shoulder blades eased. She watched a seagull hover over the water and let herself exist in the moment. Then she walked along the water's edge.

With the onset of early evening, there were few people on the beach. A woman with two children wandered along the water's edge about fifty yards away, picking up shells and rocks, until someone shouted from a cottage and they went inside.

She sighed and tried to think through the obstacle course in her head. She bounced from idea to idea like a pinball in an arcade machine. At least the sleep had helped to clear her mind.

She wondered if Keith were still alive. She was surprised to find she felt sadness at the thought. She wondered at the shadowy Power that had given her an artifact strong enough to get past Cuelebre's aversion wards. She shied away. Don't think about that.

Then she thought about Quentin's fierce protectiveness, his stubborn insistence on helping her and the bone-cracking hug he had given her. Her eyes watered. Okay. Don't think about that either. Keith was gone. Quentin was gone. Her life was gone.

She scowled and scrubbed at her eyes. So what did she know? Cuelebre knew her name. Got that problem covered. He knew what she looked like. He might even know what she smelled like, so she could change her appearance, maybe dye her hair and cut it short, but she would have to be extra smart to obscure her scent trail.

I can't stay here, and I need to ditch the Honda. I need to get new wheels and make it an arbitrary switch, difficult to trace, maybe change rides a couple of times fast. It might slow him down. I need to move in a random way and disconnect completely from Quentin and my past. And I need to find a way to block that bastard from my dreams.

To do that, she would need more magical expertise than she could muster. Her mother could have kept herself obscured, in both a psychic and physical sense, but her blood didn't run as strong in Pia. While she had a highly educated sense for magic, she couldn't do half the things her mother could have done.

The last gift Quentin had given her the night before had been an 800 number that he had made her memorize. *I know people in Charleston*, he'd said. *If you need help, call them.*

Did she dare? Who were these people? She turned north and started walking back to the beach house. And did she dare stay here another night?

She glanced at the sky and paused. In the distance over the water, a patch of the sky rippled. It looked like the watery shimmer of heat waves off an asphalt highway on a hot summer day. But the May evening was cooling down, the sky just starting to darken in the east and there was no asphalt anywhere near that ripple.

She shaded her eyes. What was it? It was big and seemed to be getting bigger fast. She watched the patch grow, her stomach clenching. She'd never seen anything like it before, but she knew it was wrong.

Wait a minute. That shimmering patch of air wasn't growing bigger. It was getting *closer*.

Oh shit.

Pia's thinking splintered into raw instinct. She whirled and sprinted. She may not have inherited many of her mother's abilities, but if there was one thing she could do with an extravagance of talent, it was run. Her bare toes dug into the sand and she nearly flew down the beach.

But nearly flying isn't the same as really flying. Even as she pushed with all the speed she had in her, she knew she wasn't going to be able to outrun what hurtled toward her.

A shadow engulfed her from behind. She caught just a glimpse on the sand in front of her of an enormous winged shape with a serpentine neck and a long wicked head. Then the shadow collapsed in on itself and a split second later, a mountain slammed into her back.

She crashed into the sand so hard it knocked the breath out of her. The mountain resolved itself into the hard, heavy body of a male. Muscle-corded arms came down on either side of her. Huge hands latched onto her slim wrists while a long thigh crossed over the backs of her legs.

She wheezed, struggling to get her bruised rib cage to expand so her lungs could function, her palms and knees abraded from the impact. She stared at those imprisoning hands. Like the arms, they were powerful, colored a dark bronze that looked very dramatic against her pale skin.

Her mind wailed. She was so dead.

The male put his nose in her hair and took a deep breath. A convulsive shiver racked her body in response. He was *sniffing* her. She felt his nose at the back of her neck. He rubbed his face in her hair. A whimper was born and died at the back of her throat.

'Good chase,' he growled, his voice a dark rumble at her back.

She coughed and sand puffed up in front of her. 'Not long enough.'

The weight lifted from her back, and he flipped her with mind-numbing swiftness. She slammed back into the sand, arms spread-eagled as he held her by the wrists again.

He bared his teeth at her in a machete smile. 'We could always do it again.'

She thought of him letting her go and pouncing again, playing with her like a great cat, and shuddered.

'You're not supposed to be here,' she whispered. Her eyes had gone watery from the force of the impact that knocked her down. She tried to focus on the dark, fierce face bent over her. Then her vision came clear.

Cuelebre was breathtaking. Energy and Power boiled from him; he radiated it like a dark sun. He had a handsome brutality, facial features cut into bold lines and angles as if a sculptor had hewn him from granite. His skin was a dark brown with a bronze hue, and those brilliant dragon's eyes were hot gold. In his human form he was almost seven feet tall, three hundred pounds of dominant Wyr male sprawled like an avalanche across her body. In comparison she felt delicate, very breakable.

His hair was inky black. Just like in the dream. It had slipped through her fingers like silk.

The shock of his assault had not begun to pass, but through it she noticed one astonishing thing. He had thrown his thigh over hers again. He stared at her neck. Realization pulsed. He was looking at the bite he had given her. A hard length was growing against her hip.

'So, is that your long, scaly, reptilian tail, or are you just happy to see me?'

No, she did not just say that.

Did she? She cringed in mortification, screwed her eyes shut and waited to be splattered all over the beach.

Nothing happened, good or bad. Yet. Maybe if she kept her eyes closed it wouldn't.

She whispered through shaking lips, 'I didn't mean to say that. Um, pay no attention to the lunatic inhabiting this body.'

As silence continued she opened one cautious eye. He studied her, lava gaze alert with interest. 'Are you possessed?' he asked.

She had to clear her throat twice before she could answer. 'You would think so, wouldn't you, with all the dumbass moves I've made over the last couple of months. I've been acting out a lot with all the stress. This stranger seems to have taken over my mouth. She doesn't seem to come installed with a brake. No offense.' The corners of her lips lifted in a tremulous smile. 'I bet you want your penny back, huh?'

He shifted with sinuous grace, letting go of her hands to kneel over her. His predator's stare narrowed further. 'What do you think?'

Her hands fluttered up and, unable to help herself, she straightened his shirt collar with shaky fingers. Her fingers looked like delicate white twigs against the thick column of his neck.

Dragos stared down at her hands. She let them fall to her chest and clasped her hands together. 'I think,' she said in a low voice, 'that you would do anything to get your property back. No matter what was taken, no matter what it took, no matter where you would have to go to find it.'

'No one takes what is mine.' His growl reverberated through the ground. He bared his teeth and bent down until he was nose to nose with her. *'No one.'*

Holy mother, he was terrifying and magnificent. He disappeared in a blur as her eyes watered again. She nodded and whispered, 'I know. I – I don't suppose this matters much to you, and I don't expect it to change anything, but I am sorry.'

Dragos cocked his head, his attention sharpening. 'So your note said.'

Voices grew closer. She craned her neck and saw a couple walking hand in hand toward them. Dragos put a hand over her mouth to keep her silent. As they both watched the oblivious couple pass not five feet away from them, she realized he had to be shielding them from curious eyes. Only thing to do. Otherwise someone might call the cops if they saw a man assaulting a woman on the beach. Then there might be a wholly avoidable massacre.

After the couple walked away, Dragos shifted his weight onto one hand and traced a finger down her cheek, followed her jaw down the side of her neck. He watched the path his finger took as it traced the delicate curve of her collarbone down to the edge of her shirt.

His finger felt hot and abrasive against the softness of her skin. She shivered harder and bit back a moan. Wow, she'd had no idea her sexuality was so messed up. Here was this predator of all predators exuding menace as he crouched over her. He was the only known real dragon in existence. It was like he was a natural monument or something.

Oh my God, not only is he older than the Grand Canyon, but he's like the pope and the Fae King and the president of the United States all rolled up into one. To some ancient cultures he had been a god.

He was going to hurt her so bad before he killed her so dead, and all she could think of was how hot his kiss had been in the dream and how delicate the touch of his finger was as it traced down her body. Her mind stuttered. She looked down at his hand. Her breathing roughened as her heart raced.

Dragos picked up a lock of her hair and fingered it. Then he held it up to the evening sunlight. He turned it this way and that, staring at the strands. He did nothing at all to keep her pinned in place. The possibility of her escaping from him was that inconceivable. The force of his regard was such that her whole body trembled. A flush of sensual heat torched any coherent thought she might have had left. Her sex moistened in a liquid rush.

She couldn't have been more humbled, more mortified, or felt more naked. With a Wyr's ultrasensitive nose, of course he could smell every minuscule body change. He had to be aware of her growing arousal. He could no doubt read every passing emotion in the pheromones she exuded, whereas she couldn't tell anything about him. His gaze was so shuttered, his expression so severe, she knew nothing at all about what he was thinking – except –

Pia looked down the length of that tremendous male body as he held himself poised over her, down the long torso that tapered from those wide shoulders to the hips that looked so lean and tight. He was dressed for function not fashion, in jeans and a plain white Armani button-down silk shirt, rolled at the arms and tucked at the waist.

She sucked at her bottom lip, staring at the indisputable evidence bulging underneath the zipper of his jeans. The bulge, like the rest of his human form, made her eyes widen. Alrighty. As far as size went the details in the dream hadn't been wish fulfillment in the slightest.

She wondered if he could still be aroused while he ripped her head from her shoulders. He was a dragon, a Wyrkind beast, by general knowledge one of the most ancient of the Elder Races and by reputation wicked and cunning and ruthless. Normal humanlike thought patterns just didn't apply.

'Well, this is socially inexplicable,' she muttered.

'Hush,' Dragos said.

She hushed, blanked her mind and waited, while she watched him study strands of her hair.

Her hair had always seemed somewhat coarse to her, so thick and such a pale blonde it was almost white. The ends sparked with gold highlights in the sun. When she wore it loose instead of in the usual ponytail, it hung halfway between her shoulders and waist.

Dragos fisted his hand in the long bright strands and held it to his nose, inhaling. There it was. There was the mystery he didn't know how to solve. He'd thought of it as wild sunshine, but that was when he'd had the merest scrap of scent on a piece of paper.

The actual reality floored him. Somehow her delicate feminine fragrance did more than capture the essence of the sunlit air. Somehow it took him back almost further than he could go, back to the morning of everything when he basked in transcendent light and magic. That ancient time, so piercing, young and pure.

He found his unhurried way back to the present and studied her hair again as he fingered it. It felt like Chinese silk, and the highlights were the same color of some alluvial gold deposits he had known. He had a thirteenth-century Peruvian statuette that was the same color. He dropped the handful of hair and proceeded to study everything else about this mysterious, unpredictable female.

'I didn't think you would be so young,' he said. He felt the same wild surge of excitement he had in that other long-ago time, when he had lost control and crashed through the undergrowth in chase of – something. He looked at her supine body lying so still and submissive underneath him and exercised a ruthless clampdown on his self-control. 'There is Wyr blood in you. Also human.'

He watched her long graceful neck muscles as she swallowed. 'I'm twenty-five,' she said, her voice turning husky.

The predator in him noted she made no mention of the Wyr blood. But she gleamed with subdued Power, and he remembered in the dream she had been as luminescent as the moon. Had that luminescence been symbolic or literal? What Wyrkind or Fae would gleam like that? The Elves carried a light within them but not like what he had seen in the dream.

'Look at you,' he murmured, almost to himself. 'You're a baby, nothing but a moment, a heartbeat.'

She took a quivering breath. 'I'm more than that.'

He quirked an eyebrow but otherwise ignored the faint protest.

For all her paleness she was rather jewel-toned. There were the gold highlights in her hair. The cream in her light skin was like pearls. Those large eyes that watched him with such frightened, perplexed arousal were a violet blue as deep as the midnight sky. Like sapphires. He could almost fancy he saw distant stars in those eyes.

He sat back on his heels and stood while he yanked her to her feet. 'We'll go now to wherever you are staying.'

She staggered a bit as she regained her footing, watching him with the wariness of a wild creature ready to bolt again. 'Why?' she asked, dark blue eyes flashing. 'You're just going to kill me. Why don't we get this over with already?'

'You have no idea what I am going to do,' he told her. That had to be true, because he didn't know himself. He was awash in strange emotions and impulses. His lids dropped as he watched her face. He said, 'I have a lot of questions. Just tell me what I want to know, and I'll let you go.'

'You mean that?' She searched his face.

He laughed, a husky, wicked chuckle. 'No.'

Fury flashed across her face and was dampened. 'Fair enough,' she said, voice flat. She turned and strode toward the beach house.

Dragos followed, frowning. Just like he didn't like the photo of her walking away from the camera, he didn't like her voice dull and flat or her expression shuttered. It muted those jeweled tones. The fear and stress in her scent jangled, depressing the intoxication of her arousal, the addicting young wildness of her normal fragrance.

That flash of fury had been much more interesting. Fury also had a scent, like the crackle of a bonfire.

She scooped up a pair of sandals. He watched her trim ass and long slender legs as she climbed wooden stairs to a balcony and entered a beach house by sliding doors. She dropped the sandals again just inside. As he entered, he closed and locked the door behind him.

She went to the kitchen sink and focused on scrubbing the sand from the abrasions on her palms. The house was growing chilled, the kitchen floor tiles cold under her sandy feet. Her ponytail felt like a rat's nest attached to the back of her head.

Still in that flat, dull voice, she asked, 'Are you hungry?'

He paused, surprised again by her. He leaned against a wall. There was no telling what the lunatic in her body would say next. 'What if I am?' he said.

She glanced at him, face tight. 'If you are, I'll need to order delivery. I'm a vegetarian and you're rather famously not. Assuming I'm not on the menu for your dinner, I don't have anything to feed you that you'll like.'

She meant to feed him supper?

He had serious questions for this female, his property to locate and an outrage and fury he had set aside, not banished. He had justice to mete out and vengeance to claim, but first he had to map out this unfamiliar territory he traveled in.

He realized something. For the first time in a long time, perhaps even centuries, he wasn't bored. From the moment he picked up that scrap of paper in his lair, his little thief had continued to surprise him.

Dragos rubbed his jaw and prepared to be entertained. 'Get something,' he said.

She began thumbing through a telephone directory on the kitchen counter. She flipped past the yellow pages, and the red pages for business, to the green pages for Elder businesses. Her head was ducked as she muttered under her breath.

Dragos leaned forward, barely catching what she said. 'What?'

She paused and looked at him, eyes wide. 'What – what?' she asked.

'You whispered, "Get something, please,"' he told her. 'What is it you want me to get?'

Despite the grimness of her situation, she was surprised to find amusement bubbling up. She kept a stern grip on it.

'It's normal,' she told the dragon, 'for people to say please when they make a request. You said, "Get something." Most people would say, "Get something, please."'

'Ah.' Dragos folded his arms. 'But I did not ask for anything. I ordered it.'

She pinched the bridge of her nose. 'That you did.'

Her finger traveled down the green page and stopped at the number for an Elder restaurant. Hands shaking, she punched in a number.

A youthful, musical voice answered the phone. Elven.

All too aware of the keen gold gaze focused with relentless patience on her, Pia said, 'I'm calling from a beach house on Folly Beach.' She rattled off the address. 'Will you service this area?'

'Of course we will,' said the voice. 'We know the address well.'

'We would like a dozen porterhouse steaks,' she said. She looked at her captor. 'Dragos, do you want them raw or cooked?'

'Just seared,' he said.

The person on the other end of the connection drew in a swift breath. 'We will be with you soon as we can,' he said. 'It may take a little while. Delivery in about an hour.'

'Soon as you can will be fine,' she said.

She deleted the number from the cell phone's memory, clicked the off button and placed it on the counter. She didn't think Dragos had looked away once since they had entered the beach house. It was just one more thing to add to a growing list of things that felt unreal.

Then she stood, staring at her hands. An hour, she thought. God, it felt like forever. Her shoulders sagged. She didn't think she had any more adrenaline left to pump into her system. 'They'll be here soon. Now what?'

He pushed himself away from the wall. 'Now,' Dragos said, 'you tell me why you stole from me. And how. Most especially we will discuss how.'

≡ FIVE ≡

Pia kept her gaze down. She touched one abraded palm with a finger. 'My ex-boyfriend blackmailed me into doing it.'

'Keith Hollins,' he said.

Startled, her head jerked up. 'You know who he is?'

His black eyebrows rose. 'I know a lot of things.'

His sentinels had worked fast that morning before he left New York. While the witch had cast the tracking spell for him, Aryal and several others had run a background check on Pia Giovanni. They winnowed through other possibilities until they found the right one. A team had been dispatched to search her apartment and follow any leads they found. Soon after the spell was in place and he had collected preliminary information, Dragos had taken flight, arrowing south for his prey.

'Your boyfriend is dead,' he told her.

Just like that, she had had too much. Her vision grayed and the world tilted.

Dragos leaped forward, hard arms snaking around her before she could collapse. He eased her onto a bar stool and pushed her head down. Her ponytail was a mess, he noted with disapproval as it spilled toward the floor. He kept one hand at the back of her neck. With the other, he worked the puffy elastic thing out of her hair until it fell free, if still somewhat tangled. He slipped the puffy thing into his pocket.

She asked, muffled, 'Did you kill him?'

'No. Nor did my people.' The skin at the back of her neck was chilled. He felt the shiver ripple through her. 'They found him earlier today. Bad death.'

'Damn that poor idiot. I tried to warn him.' She covered her face with her hands.

Jealousy spiked. His lip lifted in a silent snarl. She was his thief, nobody else's. 'You loved him.'

'No,' she said, wretchedness in her voice. 'Yes. I don't know. I thought I did once, but he wasn't who I thought he was. After I broke things off with him, the bastard blackmailed me. I knew he was going to get himself killed. I even tried to warn him but he wouldn't listen to me. He got what he deserved, but it's still hard to hear about someone I used to care about.' She clenched her fists. 'Let me up. I'm not going to faint.'

He released the pressure he had been putting on her neck. She sat upright in the bar stool. She looked composed but her skin was ashen. There were goose bumps along her bare arms and shoulders.

'You are too cold,' he said. 'That means shock, I think. We will change that.' He noted the bottle of scotch on the counter by the sink. He retrieved the bottle along with a coffee mug from the cupboard. He poured a drink and shoved it into her hands. 'Drink that while I find a blanket.'

She looked at him askance as her fingers curled around the mug.

'Yes, I know,' he said, impatient. 'I am going to rend you from limb to limb. Someday. When I feel like it. In the meantime, you will not faint, you will get warm and you will stop being distressed.' His nostrils pinched. 'I don't like how it smells.'

Her pretty mouth fell open. 'You don't . . . like . . .' A hysterical giggle bubbled out and turned to outright laughter. She listed on the bar stool, the coffee mug tilting.

He covered her hands with one of his own, steadying the mug, and pressed a finger against her lips. 'Stop that.'

'Sure.' She hooted. 'Whatever you say.'

He wasn't by any stretch of imagination an expert on emotions, let alone female emotions. Scowling, he tapped her lips.

'I'll just, I don't know, be happy until you decide to start rending.' She hiccupped. 'How will that do, Your Majesty?'

'I was being sarcastic,' he said.

'Which is very reassuring, coming from a pissed-off dragon,' she told him. 'Kinda like the whole "tell me what I want to know and I'll let you go" joke. Definitely has its own charm. I bet all your other prisoners love it.'

Her slender body continued to shake. She was out of control. He would get no sense out of her as long as she was this overwrought. Dragos cupped her chin. He stared into her eyes, intending to beguile her into a sense of calm. Instead he came up against a mental barrier. Intrigued, he inspected it, feeling along the borders.

The barrier seemed to be both natural and intentional. There was the echo of another feminine Power interwoven in it, a subtle presence very like her own and yet separate. It was an altogether beautiful construction, an elegant citadel that protected the female's core.

This was why she was able to break the beguilement in the dream. He could batter that wall down if he wanted to, but that would be like taking a sledgehammer to an opal. There would be nothing coherent left to salvage of her afterward.

'Stop it,' she whispered. Her body had stiffened, straining away from his touch. 'Get out of my head.'

He held fast and used his voice instead of his mind. 'Quiet, female,' he murmured. 'Be quiet now.'

His deep voice murmured. Tendrils of the sound curled into the air and wrapped around her. It soothed and reassured. Her breath shuddered and she grew still.

She stared in Dragos's gold eyes. Impossible depths existed in those brilliant pools. She could fall into his gaze and never come out. 'Valium's got nothing on you,' she murmured. 'Bottle that, and you could make another fortune.'

'You are calmer now,' he said. His severe dark face was inscrutable.

'Yes.' She wrenched her gaze away and stared into her coffee mug. She forced herself to say, 'Thank you.'

He let go of her chin and hands and stepped back. 'Drink.'

She looked up as he disappeared into the hall. Then she raised the mug to her lips and drank it all down. Scotch napalmed her veins, hitting her all the harder since she hadn't eaten well the last week.

She put the mug on the counter and inspected her hands, felt along her jaw. She had taken a battering when he slammed her into the ground, but his handling of her since then had been quite careful. How remarkable. What did it mean?

He strode back into the kitchen, the light blue hoodie she had bought earlier bunched in one hand. He nodded at the empty mug and dropped the hoodie in her lap. She shrugged it on as he crossed his arms. Perched on the bar stool as she was, he towered over her even more than he would if she were standing upright. She had thought the house was quite spacious until he had walked into it.

'We will begin again,' he said.

She kept her gaze focused on his crossed forearms that looked very dark against the white silk shirt. The distance across his pectorals was extraordinary. On another man it would be too much. On him, those heavy muscles armored a body long enough to carry them with power and grace.

'Keith blackmailed me into stealing something from you,' she said. 'It didn't matter what it was. He owed some people a lot of money.'

'Gambling debts,' he said.

She lifted her head. He had settled into a hunter's patience. 'You got that far already?'

'We found his bookie. Also dead.'

Icy fingers slid down her spine. She pulled the hoodie closer around her torso. 'I dated Keith for a few months. For a little while I thought – it doesn't matter what I thought.'

He tilted his head. 'You thought what?'

'You're not interested in all that.' Color tinged her cheeks.

'Don't make assumptions about what I am interested in or what I will think or what I will do. You have no idea what interests me,' he told her. He settled back against the edge of the dining room table and crossed one ankle over the other. 'We clear?'

She nodded, her color deepening. She went on, 'We've already established I was an idiot. Keith came along when I was feeling low, and I fell for his charm. I was . . . indiscreet. I should have known better, and I screwed up.' Her throat closed.

'You said you had broken things off,' he prompted when she fell silent.

She nodded. 'I had, a while ago. Then last week he showed

70

up. He was full of this scheme that was going to pay off all his debts and make him rich. Of course by then my rose-colored glasses were gone. I didn't want to have anything to do with it, or him. Then he . . . made me.'

'Blackmail, you said. Over your indiscretions.'

He spoke in a neutral tone. He had throttled the aggression down. She was very aware that he was 'managing' her, but he still sounded pitiless. She covered her throat with one hand as he dissected her expression.

'Can we please not talk about that?' She tried to steady her voice. 'Please?'

His lids dropped down, hooding his gaze. 'Go on with your story.'

'There's what I know.' She stressed the last word. 'There's what I think, and then there's what I've guessed. Keith was all about his "associates." People he met through his bookie that he was going to do business with. He was somehow a bigger man in all his stories than he was in real life, know what I mean?'

He nodded, keeping silent.

'Well, I think he was half desperate, half boasting and all-the-way manipulated. He started promising those contacts of his anything he could. His loans had come due. He said he told them he could get them anything they wanted.' She swallowed hard. 'And they said, how about something from Cuelebre, then. They gave him a charm that would locate your lair, and Keith came to me.'

'Did they, now.' He hadn't moved, but he had tensed all over. What radiated off him had her heart pounding.

She licked lips that had gone dry and whispered, 'I think Keith told them something about me but not much. He would have wanted to keep me a secret because he wanted to be the big player, and he thought he could control me. He was hoping to set up a repeat business. But I think someone very nasty and Powerful was manipulating him, and now, thanks to me, they've got something of yours.'

'They do indeed.' He bared his teeth in that machete smile. 'I'll have to thank you later for that one.'

She whispered, 'That charm scared the shit out of me. If I didn't do what he wanted, I knew Keith would sing like a canary. Would he give me up? In a heartbeat, if it would save his own ass. Then they would come after me. So I was in that damned if you do, damned if you don't place.'

'Where's the charm now?' His eyes had gone pure gold, all dragon.

'It disintegrated when I used it.'

His eyes narrowed. 'I would have felt my spells fail if it had nullified them, but they were all still in place when I went to investigate.'

She cupped her ear with one hand and rubbed her neck, a stressed, defensive gesture as she remembered the pain from using the charm. He moved closer as that pitiless dragon gaze dissected her face. She whispered, 'The charm didn't nullify anything. Between it and your spells, I felt like I was being ripped apart.'

'Yet you still got through them.'

She didn't bother to reply. Instead she searched his face. His expression was savage, catapulting her thoughts forward to consequences that were more far-reaching than just her own future. Her lips felt numb. 'A charm that Powerful could find anything hidden, couldn't it?'

'Depending upon the strength of the user, yes.'

Anything hidden. There were things in the world that should never be found, dangerous things, or fragile, and precious creatures whose lives depended on secrecy. A finding charm as strong as the one Pia had used could slice like a knife through someone's every defense. She shivered and huddled into herself. Despite her fears and preoccupation for her own safety, this had never been about her.

Dragos frowned as he considered the minefield she had maneuvered in order to get to his hoard, the unknown charm acting in opposition to his spells. The conflict of opposing magics might have killed another person. That elegant citadel inside her mind was probably what had saved her life. Despite her obvious upset, he didn't think she realized how much danger she had been in.

He wondered if it was her conscience that made her so upset. He was fascinated by the concept of a conscience. He dropped a heavy hand onto her shoulder, gripping the slender bone and sinew. Her body shifted in subtle ways as she leaned into his bracing hold.

He shifted the conversation back to an earlier point. 'Hollins might have given you up anyway, before they killed him.'

'No,' she sighed. 'He didn't, which may actually be why they killed him.'

'How can you be so sure?'

'After he blackmailed me, I blackmailed him,' she told him. She squinted at him with one eye. Was that approval gleaming in his gaze? 'I wouldn't give him what I stole unless he read the binding spell I bought yesterday. He would have lost the ability to speak if he tried to talk about me.'

Her stomach twisted as she imagined what must have been done to Keith. It had been a bad death, Dragos said, and Dragos wasn't exactly known for being squeamish. Was Keith's death on her conscience if he had been the one to start the whole damn thing? Or did she start the whole damn thing by opening up her big mouth? The morality of it all was getting too convoluted for her to figure out.

'How did you get past my locks and the wards?'

She closed her eyes and put her hands over her face. What did it matter anymore? 'I'm a half-breed. I don't have much Wyr blood or many abilities. I can't change into a Wyr form, and I don't have a lot of Power. I don't have anything interesting about me.' She pulled her hands away and looked at him. He was staring at her. 'What, have I grown two heads?'

'You believe you don't have anything interesting about you,' he said. 'Or that you don't have much Power.'

She gave him a blank look and a shrug. 'Except, I guess, for one stupid parlor trick I was too fucking stupid to keep to myself,' she said. 'I showed Keith when we were both drunk and goofing around.'

'What was it?'

'It's easier to show than tell.' She walked over to the sliding glass door, unlocked it, stepped onto the deck and shut the door again. Outside, the evening had darkened to dusk. Still staring at her, he stalked over and put a fist against the glass as if to break through it. She told him, 'Go ahead and lock it again.'

His dark brows lowered in a scowl.

She just looked at him. 'Oh, go on. You know you could catch me again if I tried to run.' His gold dragon's gaze holding hers, he did as she told him.

She opened up the door and stepped back inside. 'See?'

He looked at the door and back at her again. 'Do it again.' She stepped outside. She walked back in after he locked the door. He said, 'I didn't feel you cast a spell.'

'That's because I didn't. It's just a part of me.' Locks, wards – you name it, and she could walk through it. Nothing could cage her. Nothing, that is, unless it plummeted out of a clear blue sky and sat on her. She dug the heel of her hand into one temple where a headache was starting to throb and sighed. 'That's all I know. That, and again, I'm sorry. I suppose you'll want to do the rending now.'

He hadn't moved back when she stepped inside. She was so close she could feel his body heat on her skin. He had a kind of strength and vitality that was a constant shock to the system. She felt small and cold and pale by comparison. Despite the colossal danger this creature represented, she had quite an irrational desire to curl up in his warmth.

He cupped her head. The broad palms and long fingers cradled her skull. Oddly, she didn't feel afraid and she didn't resist when he tilted her face up.

The predator bent over her. 'You committed a crime,' he said. 'And you owe me. Say it.'

What was this? She could gain no hint by searching his face. Her shoulders sagged and her mouth drooped. 'What if I don't want to say it?'

'You will make recompense,' said the Lord of the Wyr. 'You will serve me until I deem the debt is paid. Is that clear?'

'No rending?' she asked. Her gaze clung to his. Could she believe him this time, or was this another cruel joke?

He shook his head and smoothed back her hair. 'No rending. You told me the truth,' he said. 'I could sense it as you talked. You committed a crime, but you were also a victim. This is justice.' He bent his head until his nose just touched the top of hers, inhaling. His voice was much softer as he continued, 'But when I go after who orchestrated this? That will be vengeance.'

She shuddered, going limp with relief. Her hands smoothed over the heavy muscles in his chest. She felt encompassed by him, and against all good sense or sanity, she felt safe. Her spine lost its starch. She leaned against him. Just a little. She did it sneakily so he wouldn't notice. 'I don't like that word "serve." What would you want me to do?'

'I'll make use of you somehow,' he said.

'What if I don't want to do it?' Her head started to lower, a drooping flower on a stalk. His hands guided her to rest on his chest. 'I'm not stealing again,' she warned. 'So if that's what you want, we might as well get back to the rending right now.'

Listen to her. Big tough girl.

'There is nothing you could steal that I couldn't get in any number of other ways. I will not put you in harm's way.' He kept her head cradled in one hand and put an arm around her. He murmured, 'I do not endanger my treasures.'

What did he mean by that? She was mesmerized by his hold in a way that had nothing to do with beguilement. She tried to focus. 'I'm not agreeing, mind you,' she grumbled. 'I'll have to think about it.'

But it didn't sound so bad. It was much better than rending. And she *did* steal from him, along with telling him too much about herself. She bit her lip. What if he decided to blackmail her too?

'I wasn't aware that I gave you a choice,' he said. Was that amusement in his voice? 'Crime and judgment, remember, not negotiation. You lived in my demesne, you lived by my law. But you go ahead and think about it all the way back to New York.'

A car horn sounded from the street side of the house. She jumped and yanked herself away. He looked at her with his eyebrows raised.

'Oh God,' she said, 'that's the . . . that's the delivery. I'll go get it. Be right back.'

She charged for the door to be brought up short by his hand circling her wrist. 'I'll get it,' he said.

'Don't be silly,' she told him. A wild horse galloped in her chest. 'I said I would buy you supper, and I will. It's the least I can do.'

'No.' He brushed past her, long legs eating up the distance to the front door.

Oh damn. She caught him by the arm just before he opened it and tried one last time. 'Please, Dragos. Let me do it.'

He put his hands to her shoulders and nudged her back into

the living room. 'Something is not right. I can feel it. You are not going out there,' he said. He had turned into a stone-cold killer. His Power revved like fighter plane powering up. 'It's not safe.'

How did this get so messed up? She wrung her hands. He not so much walked outside as flowed, that great magnificent body of his turning into a weapon.

A sound sliced the air. Dragos spun backward, his legs buckling. It all happened too fast. She caught up a heartbeat later. She stared at Dragos, who had collapsed on the walk. A dozen tall Elves stepped out of various hiding places, from behind her Honda, the nondescript Ford idling at the curb and nearby shrubbery. They held weapons trained on the sprawled figure. Six-foot longbows.

She launched toward Dragos, who was lying on his back. Darkness appeared on one white-clad shoulder. It began to spread. She fell to her knees beside him.

'You shot him!' she shouted. She stared at the stern-eyed Elves encircling them. 'Do you know who he is?'

One of them stepped forward. He was a silver-haired male, beautiful in the way that all Elves are, with a gracious light that somehow made all other creatures leaden by comparison. Despite his slender build, he not only looked powerful, he carried more Power than anybody else in the clearing except for Dragos.

'We know who he is,' said the Elf. He stared down at Dragos, his beautiful face cold. 'Wyrm.'

She turned back to Dragos. Even though he lay wounded, he looked utterly without fear, his raptor's stare turning from the Elves to focus on her. She tore open his shirt to stare at the bleeding hole over his left breast. Her uneven breathing sounded loud in her ears.

'I don't get it. None of you are carrying guns. Where's the arrow?' she asked. She tore off her hoodie and pressed it to the wound.

'Elven magic,' Dragos responded through gritted teeth.

'No simple arrow could mark him,' said the Elf. 'But this one has already melted into his body. It will continue to release poison into his bloodstream for a number of days.'

'What did you do!' she shouted. Her face contorted. She

clenched her fists and started to her feet. Dragos grabbed her wrist.

'Pia,' he said when she fought against his hold. 'It would take a lot more than this to kill me.'

'We have disabled him,' the Elf told her.

'You don't understand,' she told Dragos. 'I called them. It's my fault.' She tried to pry his fingers open. It was like trying to pry open a steel shackle. She looked up at the Elf.

He had shifted his attention to Dragos. 'You entered our lands without permission. Treaties have been broken. There will be consequences. For now, the poison will keep you from changing into the Great Beast. Since we have clipped your wings, we will give you twelve hours to get beyond our borders. If you are not gone by then, there will be more than twelve of us who will come for you.'

'I broke his law,' Pia said. 'He was just coming after me.'

'His law is not our law,' said the Elf. 'And he broke ours. Wyrm, release your hold on the female.'

'She is mine.' Dragos bared his teeth, gold eyes flaring to lava. His growl shivered through the ground at her knees, and long fingers clenched on her wrist. He tensed and began to rise.

The other Elves sighted down their longbows at him. 'You will release her now or forfeit the twelve hours' grace,' their leader said.

Pia flung her free hand out at the Elves, fingers spread and palm out. 'Stop!' She leaned over Dragos. Bending close to that feral face was one of the braver things she had done in her life. Some instinct she could not have verbalized had her gentling her voice. 'Dragos,' she murmured. Calm and quiet, like she would speak to a wounded animal. 'Can you look at me, please? You know how normal people say "please." Pay attention to me, not them.'

That lava gaze turned to her, burning and alien. He may not be able to change, but he was immersed in the dragon.

'Thank you,' she breathed. She dropped her free arm and stroked at his black hair. Dragos tracked the movement and then looked at her face. 'I know you're very angry, but I promise you, this is not worth fighting over,' she whispered. She tugged just a little at the inky ends. Inspiration struck. 'And you promised me you wouldn't put me in harm's way. Just a few minutes ago. Remember?'

His dangerous face clenched. 'You're mine,' he told her.

For a blistering instant, she had no idea what to say to that. Then hey, another lightbulb moment came along and she was on a roll. 'Letting go of my wrist doesn't change a thing,' she murmured. She mimicked what he had done to her earlier and stroked a finger down the side of his face, then laid her hand against his cheek. 'Please.'

His fingers loosened and he let her pull away.

She got to her unsteady feet, somehow managed to stay upright and turned to face the Elven leader, who gave her a slight bow. He stared at her. 'Do I know you from somewhere?'

Interior alarm bells started to ring, but all the lightbulbs had left her high and dry. She shook her head and said, 'We've never met.'

'I'm sure I've seen you before. You look—' The Elf's sea-colored gaze widened. 'You look exactly like—'

Dragos curled a hand around her ankle.

'Yeah, I look like Greta Garbo,' she interrupted in a loud voice. A pulse of dread dampened her skin. Shut up, Elf. 'I get that a lot.'

'My lady, I am so honored to meet you,' the Elven leader breathed. He bowed low to her, his previous generic respect turned to reverence. When he straightened, his face was alight with joy. 'You have no idea how we hoped and prayed that something of your mother still remained in this world.'

All the other Elves stared at them, their faces alight with curiosity. She scowled at the Elven leader. 'I have no idea what you are talking about,' she told him.

He seemed to start and come to himself. His joy became muted but she could still feel it beating in him. He smiled at her and said, 'Of course, forgive me. I am mistaken.'

Then his telepathic voice sounded in her head like deep bell chimes in the wind. *My name is Ferion. I knew a woman once who looked much like you. Meeting her was one of the greatest gifts of my life.*

I am honored that you would share that with me, she said. *But it is dangerous for me that we talk of this, and I am not that woman. In fact, I am very much less than that woman.*

Not to my eyes, he said. *Please allow us to offer you sanctuary. I know our Lord and Lady would greet you with joy every bit as deep as my own. We would treasure your presence among us.*

She hesitated and for a moment, oh, she was tempted. The thought of such a welcome wrung at her lonely heart. But Ferion's reverence brought her up short. She didn't think she could bear to live with such regard. Not when she was so much less than what he thought she was, nothing very special at all, just a glow-in-the-dark night-light and a stupid parlor trick and a big mouth that got her into too much trouble. Living with the Elves, where she would feel like a fraud while she aged and died and they remained forever the same, would just be a different kind of loneliness.

The jealous hand on her ankle tightened. She looked down at Dragos, who was watching her with a narrowed gaze.

I thank you for the offer of sanctuary. Perhaps one day I may take you up on it, she said to Ferion. While she couldn't accept, she couldn't bear to say no, either, to what might be the only home ever offered to her. *In the meantime, I have a debt to pay.*

Ferion said aloud, 'Lady, I beg of you, come away with us. Do not stay with the Beast.'

She squatted by Dragos and dared to peek under the hoodie covering his wound. It had stopped bleeding. She mopped the blood streaks from his shoulder as gently as she could, wiped her hands on the material and folded the bloodied part into the rest of the hoodie.

'This train wreck all is my fault,' she said. 'I have to do what I can to make it right.'

Dragos's grip on her leg eased. His fingers slid along her calf in a subtle movement.

It annoyed her so much, she snapped at him. 'But no matter what ridiculous thing you say, I am not yours. You wouldn't be here except for me so I will see you to the Elven border. I know you lost your head, and you got all scary and obsessive and territorial, and you want to get back your property and all that, but come on. All I took was a freaking penny. Besides, I already gave you another one.'

One corner of his long, sexy, cruel mouth lifted in a smile.

The Elves refused to touch Dragos, so she had to help him as much as she could. By the time he had pushed himself off the ground and she had gotten herself insinuated under his good arm, the Elves had disappeared. She knew better than to believe they were gone.

'You took a 1962 penny,' Dragos said. His teeth were gritted. 'You left a 1975 penny. It's no replacement.'

She stared at him. 'Oh my God, it's scary you noticed that.'

'I know everything in my hoard and exactly where it is,' he told her. 'Down to the smallest piece.'

'You could go to a doctor, get checked out for OCD,' she panted. 'There might be medication for that.'

His chest moved in a silent laugh.

She focused on putting one foot in front of the other. He leaned on her as little as possible – otherwise they both would have crashed to the ground again. He still felt like a Volkswagen had been hung around her neck.

They got inside. He collapsed on the couch. He draped an arm over his eyes and stretched out one leg until his boot hung over the end. He left the other foot planted on the floor. Between the blood and the buttons she'd popped when she ripped it open, his Armani shirt was ruined. She eyed his chest that went both wide and far, narrowing to an eight-pack that rippled into his jeans.

For God's sake. The male was injured and here she was ogling him like a pervert in a porn store. 'I'm just not right in the head,' she muttered.

He said from under his arm, 'I'll pursue that comment later.'

She turned to the kitchen. 'I'll get you some water.'

'Scotch.'

'Okay. And water.'

She brought the bottle of scotch along with a jug of water and a cloth. He swiped the scotch bottle from her, uncapped it and drank half without pausing. She waited until he came up for air. Then she sat on the wood-framed coffee table and used the washcloth to wipe the blood off his chest. The entry wound was already nothing more than a white scar.

'Does it still hurt?' she asked, anxiety gnawing at her.

'Yes.'

'I'm sorry.'

'Your voice is too loud. Shut up,' he told her. She bit both her

80

lips as she finished washing him. He sighed and shifted. While he had lost none of that lethal animal grace, it was obvious he was in pain. 'Keep doing that with the cloth. It feels good.' He paused. 'Please.'

After freezing for a moment, she said, 'I'll get a clean one.'

She dropped the bloodied cloth in the sink, grabbed another and hurried back. He hadn't moved. She began to smooth the dampened cloth over his chest and shoulders. If he had felt hot before, now he was an inferno. She took the arm draped across his washboard stomach, pushed up the sleeve and bathed it. Then she put it down and reached for the arm he had covering his eyes. He let her, eyes glittering under half-closed lids.

'It was the phone call,' she said. 'For the steaks. I didn't call a number from the phone book. I had memorized a help line number somebody gave me.'

'I got that.' His reply was very dry.

She nodded, dipped the warm washcloth in the water from the jug to cool it down and started over again. The words kept pouring out of her. She said, 'I was scared when I called them. I thought you were going to kill me.'

'Got that too.'

'I'm sorry,' she burst out. She grabbed the scotch bottle from him and took a deep swig.

As she lowered the bottle, she caught him smiling. 'Good,' he said. 'You should be very sorry. In the last two days, you have cost me an untold amount of manpower, tens of millions of dollars in property damage—'

'Hey. Let's keep the record straight. I wasn't the one who threw a hissy and hollered fit to wake the dead.' Her spine straightened and she glared at him.

His smile broadened, a slash of white in the room's gathering darkness. 'You've caused me all kinds of broken treaties with the Elven community, and now I'm sick as a dog.'

She pointed at him. 'You broke those treaties. You weren't supposed to come here. How crazy is that.' A pause. She looked at him with sad eyes. 'Are you really sick as a dog?'

'Pretty much.' He gestured for the bottle and she handed it over. 'My body's fighting off the poison. It's better than it was. In a little bit I'll be able to move around on my own.'

She turned and sat with a small grunt on the floor. She

leaned back against the couch facing away from him. She drew up her legs, put her elbows on her knees and pushed the heels of her hands against her eyes. Her headache had grown. 'I'm not sure where the Elven demesne ends, but it won't take long to drive it. Couple hours. We've got some time.'

He dug his fingers into her hair and lifted up the strands. 'I want some of your hair.'

She lifted her head. 'What?'

'I said I want some of your hair. Give me a lock and I'll forgive you for breaking and entering.'

'Oh-kay. Sure.' She squinted at him. 'So I give you a lock of my hair, take you to the Elven border and drop you off?'

He laughed. 'I never said I was letting you go. I just said I'll forgive you.'

'I knew that had to be too easy,' she muttered. 'You're just not a straight road, are you? Okay, so why will you forgive me but not let me go?' Her shoulders sagged. 'Never mind. I'm too tired for this conversation.'

He kept running his fingers through her hair. 'Did you ever give your boyfriend any?'

Her eyes tried to close. The gentle tugging on her scalp was making it all but impossible to keep her head upright. 'Ex,' she mumbled.

'Ex,' he amended.

'No.' She fought against the drugging pleasure, to wake up. She gave his hand a halfhearted push. 'Stop it. I can't keep my eyes open when you do that.'

'So don't.' He smoothed his palm over her head. He liked how her voice got soft with drowsiness. He liked that she didn't smell of fear any longer, that her scent was tinged with a lingering faint arousal. 'Go to sleep,' he murmured.

'Gotta meet that deadline. Set an alarm.' She tried to struggle to her feet.

As she was rising off her knees, he hooked an arm around her waist and pulled her down on top of him. It wasn't hard. She was off balance to begin with and wobbly with fatigue. She oophed and tried to push off him, but he wrapped his arms around her and trapped her in place.

'Lie down,' he ordered. 'I'll make sure we leave on time. Go to sleep.'

She collapsed on him like a house of cards. He pulled her head into a comfortable spot on his uninjured shoulder. 'Quit giving me orders,' she yawned. Under the guise of shifting to get comfortable, she rubbed her cheek against his chest, wallowing in the sensation of warm, powerful male. It seeped into the cold cracks that ran deep inside her. 'You're not the boss of me.'

'Sleep,' he told her.

Just like that, from one moment to the next, she was asleep.

No one was around to witness when he experimented with pressing his lips against her forehead.

He decided he liked that too.

≡ SIX ≡

The bed shifted underneath her. Pia yawned and rubbed her nose. Why was the mattress so uneven and warm? Her eyes popped open. The room was full dark. All she could see were shadows.

She was sprawled on Dragos, their legs entangled. She stiffened and tried to push herself upright, but the heavy arms encircling her refused to let her go. And her head was pinned. She gave a tug. He had wrapped her hair around one thick wrist.

Gravel seemed to be lodged in her throat. She croaked, 'You think I would try to run away again while you slept? I wouldn't leave you when you were hurt.'

He unwound her hair and let go of the ends, smoothing it back. 'I didn't sleep.'

This time when she pushed onto her elbows, he let her, allowing one arm to loop across her waist. Not going to think about that nap. Not going to think about sleeping in his arms or how shocking it was that it felt so good. Whoops. She just thought about it.

'How could you not sleep?' she asked. 'Did you feel too sick?'

'It's not my usual habit, but I can go days at a time without eating or sleeping if I need to.' He kept his voice at a sedate pitch. The sound rumbled through her. 'I have no intention of sleeping in the Elven demesne. Besides, all I needed to do was rest.'

'How do you feel now?' Too groggy to keep her head up, she sank down again and rested her cheek on his pectoral. Mmm. Satin skin over iron.

'Better. My shoulder feels like ice, but the pain has eased. I'll be able to get up and move around, but I don't think I'll be able to shift until well after their deadline expires. The magic of their poison was well constructed.'

She ran light fingers over his injured shoulder. The area felt feverishly hot, much warmer than the rest of his body, not icy. 'That doesn't hurt?'

'No.' He captured her hand and brought it up to his mouth. She stiffened as he slipped her forefinger into his mouth and sucked.

Just like that the intense lust from the dream came roaring back. His hold on her waist shifted her until he brought them into better alignment, pelvis to pelvis. The evidence of his arousal jutted long and thick under his jeans. She groaned and tried to wriggle away. All she managed to do was rub their bodies together.

She choked, 'Stop it.'

He took his time sucking his way to the tip of her finger. His dark voice brushed her like a lazy tiger rubbing against her skin. 'Why? You wanted me in the dream. I wanted you. I have smelled your arousal since. Only a few hours have passed. We have time before we need to leave.' He licked her palm, a sensation that shot all the way down her body to throb between her legs.

She gasped. 'What happened was in a dream!'

'So? We both still want it.' His lips moved to the delicate skin of her wrist.

The pulse at her wrist beat a frantic tattoo against his mouth. His tongue traced the vein. She was not just shocked but bewildered. He was such a sledgehammer kind of male, but this sensuality had a knowledgeable gentleness she didn't know how to handle. She had to work to find her outrage again. When she did, it was whimpering in delight.

'The dream was a spell! It wasn't real.'

'It was the truth,' he said. Long fingers began to tease their way under the hem of her shirt to trace along the skin at her lower back. 'The beguilement brought you what you wanted most.'

Her skin prickled and she felt suffocated. She struggled hard to get free and meant it this time. For a moment his arms tightened on her as if he would refuse to let her go. Then his hold loosened.

She scrambled to her feet, collided with the coffee table and knocked something over. Wetness soaked the carpeting at her bare foot. She had kicked over the jug of water she'd used to sponge him clean.

She held out her arms as she went forward until she came to the wall. Her fingers slid along the smooth plaster until she found a switch. She flipped the switch and then stood with both hands braced on the wall, eyes squeezed shut against the sudden light.

Her face felt like it was on fire. Keith and the horrible mistakes she made. Ignoring her mother's advice, opening up and sharing, all because she wanted to be in love and to be loved, she wanted to be trusted and to trust. All because she wanted a lover and a mate, a real home, a safe house, a place she didn't have to run from, and dare she think it, maybe someday even children.

The muscles in her arms were too tight. She rubbed her damp cheek on her shoulder.

The couch springs protested. She felt rather than heard him come up behind her. An inferno of energy boiled along her hypersensitive nerves.

Dragos pressed his body to her back. He pressed his hands over hers, so much bigger and darker than the slender feminine ones that trembled underneath. Her distress bruised the air. He lowered his cheek to the top of her head.

His Court was at times a tumultuous place. Some were mated. Many were single. All the Wyrkind lived with a frank sensuality, and all too easily hot emotions ran to violence.

He took a female on occasion, but his couplings were always simple. It was straightforward sex with no complications. But he had been a witness to many other couplings that were much more complex. Hurt feelings, misunderstandings, jealousies, broken hearts, infidelities, passions – it all played out in a backdrop to Court life.

This was a complex female, no simple sex for hire. He considered what to do, examples of things he had seen, discarding one thing after another. Then he said in a quiet voice, 'I don't understand. Will you please explain to me?'

Damn him. Now he knew that saying 'please' got to her, he was starting to say it. She shook her head.

He sighed. 'I am old and I am often cruel and calculating, and it is not safe to be around me when I am in a rage. I do not apologize for what I am. I am a predator, and I rule other strong-minded predators. But I did not mean to distress you.'

She calmed as she listened to him. The horrible sense of exposure faded. He surrounded her with his body, and his energy engulfed her.

He didn't understand. He thought the dream was just about sex. If it were only that simple. She leaned her head back and he moved so that she rested in the hollow where his neck met his shoulder.

She said, 'The dream was manipulative. It was outside of reality. You might choose to do things in dreams that you might not choose to do when you're awake.'

'But it was true?' His breath puffed the delicate hairs at her temple.

How strange that he was uncertain. He wore arrogance with much more ease. That shouldn't be as charming as she thought it was. She really wasn't right in the head.

'There was a truth in the dream,' she admitted. 'It is not as obvious as just sex.'

'There is more to it than I thought.' She could hear the smile in his voice. He sounded . . . pleased.

'You're glad about that?' she asked, unable to keep from smiling too.

'You're complicated. I am not bored.'

She pulled one hand out from under his and covered her mouth. 'I'm so happy I could entertain you, Your Majesty.'

He wrapped his arms around her. 'So, what is this reality that is not as obvious as the sex in the dream? How does it connect to the arousal I have sensed from you?'

She reveled in the strength of those arms and decided to let herself enjoy being held. No analysis, second-guessing motives, no looking forward, no expectations. 'Is that how I really feel?

How much might be left over from the dream spell? You're complicated too, and I've been pretty damn scared of you off and on today. And for me, attraction is one thing, but making l—' She drew in a sharp breath. 'But sex,' she amended, 'is quite another. I have to have a certain level of trust in someone before I can choose to be that vulnerable.'

'You trusted Keith,' he said.

She couldn't keep from flinching. 'Yes, I did. And he betrayed me. And that still hurts.'

'The beguilement from the dream has worn off,' he told her. 'Whatever you feel is real, and what you choose to do about it is all your own.'

He pulled her hair to one side and put his lips to the bite mark at her neck. Her pulse fluttered like a butterfly and her breathing hitched. His arms tightened and then he let her go and stepped back. She turned around, disheveled and bewildered. Graceful bare feet gleamed pale against the neutral beige of the carpet, her toes painted a glossy red. She looked delicate and delicious and his groin tightened.

He ignored it. 'We should go.'

She nodded, trying to tuck flyaway strands of hair behind her ears. 'Yes, of course we should. How long did we rest?'

'Couple hours.' He turned away, fighting to control his reaction to her.

'There's time to clean up, then. If you don't mind, I'm going to take a shower and change. I won't be long.' She hurried down the hall.

Dragos angled his head and watched her leave. He still didn't like that image of her walking away.

Someday you will trust me. Then you will tell me what more there was to the dream and why you were so shaken. You will not be afraid of me and you will tell me all your secrets. And then you will be mine.

He smiled. She didn't realize he was still on the hunt. Good. It was better that way.

In the bedroom, Pia grabbed the second new outfit she had bought along with underwear, a pair of blue jean capris and a lemon yellow stretch T-shirt with capped short sleeves and a scalloped neck. Only one more new outfit to go. At the rate she was dirtying things, she was going to have to do laundry or buy more clothes.

She closed the bathroom door, feeling silly as she locked it. Like that and the U.S. Army would keep him out if he chose to get in. She shook her head, started the shower, stripped and stepped in.

The warm water gushed over her head and body, soothing achy, tired places. She hissed when it hit her abraded knees. Working fast, she washed her hair with proper shampoo, sighing with relief as she worked conditioner through it and the ropy length became softer and more manageable. Then she soaped the rest of her body, rinsed, dried and dressed. She brushed her hair and pulled it back with a yellow scrunchie, threw the toiletries back into the shopping bag and stepped out of the bathroom.

Dragos had stretched out on the rumpled covers. He made the queen-sized bed look small and cramped. She ran into an invisible wall when she saw him. He lay on his back, eyes closed, one hand behind his head, the other resting on that long washboard stomach.

He had removed the bloodstained shirt and wore only his jeans and boots. The shoulder wound still shone white against the bronze skin. His ribs rippled under heavy pectorals and dark nipples puckered against the cool air. He had washed too, the inky sprinkle of hair still damp on that truly inhuman chest. His head was damp too. She caught the scent of clean male.

As with every room he entered, he owned the bedroom just by being there. She shivered and rummaged for her last clean shirt, a long-sleeved button-down. After she tore off the tags, she put it on and wore it like a jacket, since the hoodie had had such a short life span.

His presence was too overwhelming. She could not bring herself to sit near him on the edge of the bed. Instead she crouched to slip on anklet socks and her tennis shoes. Her gaze darted from Dragos to her various belongings scattered around the room. She looked at her backpack with the documentation for three new identities and almost a hundred thousand dollars. Then she looked back at the supine male.

'Are you ready?' she asked. She sounded as winded as if she

had run a marathon. She went around the room and collected her belongings, stuffing them into another shopping bag.

'Yes,' he said. He took a deep breath and sighed. It was an awe-inspiring sight. She licked her lips and tried to think of other things. 'You don't need those other identities,' he told her. 'I like the name Pia Alessandra Giovanni. It suits you.'

Shit. Three very expensive well-constructed identities down the toilet. And the others were back in New York. 'I can't believe you!' she exploded. 'That was my stuff! You had no right to look at it.'

'Of course I did,' he said.

How did he manage to come up with that? She threw one of the shopping bags at him. He must have been watching her with his eyelids slit. In a movement that looked lazy yet was very fast, he caught the bag with one hand. 'I bet you counted the money too!' she snapped.

'Of course I did,' he said again. He grinned, a white slash of a smile. 'Women really do take a lot longer in the bathroom. I also looked in the refrigerator, used your cell phone to call New York and pocketed your car keys. There can't be a scrap of predator Wyr in you because you aren't just a vegetarian, you're a vegan. No wonder you're so scrawny.'

'Scrawny!' Only he could think of calling a five foot ten, 140-pound woman scrawny. She threw the other shopping bag at him. He caught that too but couldn't stop the bottles of shampoo, conditioner and lotion spilling over him. 'I am not! And anyway, I'm not quite a vegan either. I'll eat honey if it's harvested in a responsible manner. But forget about all that – you give me back my car keys!'

'Not happening,' he told her.

She launched at him and smacked him in the chest. 'You bastard! You did *not* have any right to go through my things or – or steal my car!'

He started laughing, a deep, full-out belly laugh. Then in a move that mimicked the one in the dream, he grabbed her arms, rolled her over his body and slammed her into the mattress. She squeaked. He rose over her, eclipsing the light. Those golden raptor's eyes were alight. 'There is not another entity in the world who would dare to act that way with me.'

She froze and the blood drained from her face.

His expression changed. He held a stiffened finger under her nose and said, 'No! I did not mean that as a threat.'

Her lips trembled. 'What did you mean then?'

He laid a hand on her cheek. It was so long it almost covered the length of her head. 'You're mine,' he said. 'You can deny it, argue, throw fits, try to run away. But. You're. Still. Mine.'

'That's insane,' she whispered. 'I have no idea what that means. I don't belong to you or anyone else.'

'Yes, you do,' he told her. His thumb stroked her lips. 'You are mine and I will keep you. I will not hurt you and I will protect you. And you're beginning to trust me. All of that is a good thing.'

'I am not a piece of property, damn it!'

'But you are in my possession.'

She enunciated, 'I think you are a lunatic.'

'Since you are too, that works well enough.' His mouth curled into a smile. He lowered his head slowly, watching her. When she tensed, he whispered, 'You're safe. I just want to taste you. No more.'

He waited inches above her lips.

This was so wrong on so many levels. She looked from his patient eyes to his mouth. The tension melted from her traitorous body.

He felt her resistance go. His mouth covered hers. Her eyes fluttered closed. His lips, warm and firm, moved featherlight against hers, discovering their shape and texture. It was nothing like the dream when they were both hard and rough with each other. This kiss was slow, confident, unhurried and sensuous.

Pleasure spiraled down through her body and grew liquid. She murmured and touched his jaw.

He licked and nibbled at her lips, his breathing deepening. As her fingers traveled up from his jaw and threaded through his hair, he opened his mouth and drove into her with his tongue. The pleasure spiked higher, sharper.

He angled her head so he had better access and could dig deeper into her mouth, his body hardening. He drove his thigh between her legs and pushed up against the area that had grown wet in response to him. She made another muffled noise as she kissed him back with escalating excitement. He growled and pushed harder with his thigh, deeper with his tongue.

He hit just the right spot. She gasped and arched her pelvis. Both her arms were now wound around his neck. He cupped her ass and pulled her up more tightly against him. He wound his other arm underneath her neck, holding her pressed along the length of his body. He found a wicked rhythm with mouth and thigh that stole all thought from her until she was so torched, she was eating at him with the same lack of control as she had in the dream.

He devoured her with starved greed. She ran her hands over his bare shoulders. His nude torso was all over her, his thick hard erection pressing against her hip. She wanted his clothes off. She wanted him inside of her, holding her down as he pounded into her.

Oh my God, she wanted to pull way the hell back now. She yanked her mouth away and said, gasping, 'Stop. It's too much.'

He reared back his head and hissed. He crushed her to him and didn't move, his body strung tight.

His gaze had turned to lava again, golden eyes burning. She turned and buried her face against his hard, bunched biceps. She whispered, 'I'm just not ready.'

'The boyfriend,' he snarled.

'*Ex-boyfriend.* And I'm so over him.'

She peeked at him. He was looking down at her, the planes and angles of his dark face cut sharp. 'You said you were still hurt.'

She laid her fingers against that taut mouth and traced it, obsessed with the shape and texture of him. 'I am hurt because I chose to trust someone and was betrayed. I am no longer hurt *by him*, nor would I want anything to do with him if he were still alive. The most I would be tempted to do is beat the crap out of him again.'

The tension in his body started to ease. She felt his mouth pull into a smile under her fingers. 'You beat the crap out of him?'

She smiled back, eyes crinkling at him. 'Well, no,' she admitted. 'But I did get a lot of satisfaction out of pushing him until I smacked him into a wall.'

He studied her. The ivory of her skin was flushed a delicate pink, lips swollen and dusky red from being kissed. Those night-dark violet eyes sparkled at him. However she claimed she felt, her body was lax and trusting as it curved to fit his. The scent of her intense arousal was delectable. All her jeweled tones had been polished bright.

'You are utterly gorgeous,' he said. He pressed his lips against her forehead.

Her eyes widened in shock. Then she looked away, her flush deepening. She couldn't think of anything to say. On impulse she hugged him tight. It seemed to surprise him because he held still and then hugged her back, crushing her to him before letting go.

He rolled away from her and onto his feet in one smooth, lithe motion. 'Now we really must go.'

She wobbled to her feet, not as graceful as he had been. He helped her pick up the things that had spilled from the shopping bags and insisted on carrying them and her backpack. Feeling she had lost vital control of her life somehow, she trailed after him.

Before they left she went to the kitchen to collect her cell phone and to grab what she could eat on the run. She ignored the salad ingredients and dressing. She threw into another shopping bag a package of almonds, soy yogurt and a spoon she swiped from the utensil drawer, along with the bottled water she had bought.

The dryer was running in the small utility room off the kitchen. Dragos stopped it and pulled out his torn Armani shirt. He had rinsed out the blood as best he could, but the pristine white was gone. He shrugged it on but didn't bother to fasten what few buttons were left. She found herself grateful for even that indifferent coverage. Although it didn't help much. He was still distracting and sexy, with glimpses of that long brown torso showing at the open shirt. The sight of his bare chest had stolen every digit of her IQ.

They stepped outside. As Dragos closed the front door, she made a mental note to call Quentin to warn him they hadn't left the house in quite as good a shape as she would have liked.

Dragos escorted her to the passenger's side of the car as he looked around. The stone-cold killer was back. He opened the door for her and closed it after she was seated, then put the packages in the back and climbed into the driver's seat.

'Are you expecting trouble?' she asked, looking around at

the tranquil night scene. Altogether with her nap and everything else, they had used about six of Dragos's twelve-hour time limit, and it was around 3:00 A.M. Someone several beach houses down was having a party with all lights blazing, but they kept it quiet.

'Not if the Elves keep to their word,' he said. He located the lever and pushed the seat back as far as it could go.

'Why wouldn't they?' she asked, her eyes wide. 'I've never heard anything bad about their integrity.'

'You're quite a bit younger than I am too,' he reminded her. 'Every race has had its less than stellar moments now and then. Oh, for fuck's sake. This car is going to kill me.'

'What? Why?'

'Still waiting for it to pick up speed,' he told her. 'Any day now. What is it, a POS?'

'What's a POS?'

'Piece-of-shit car.'

She started to laugh. 'It's a Honda Civic, and it's a fine car. Very fuel efficient.'

'Well, we know why, don't we?' Despite his words, he kept to a modest speed until they had left the beach area and came to a main highway. When he accelerated, he held the car's speed steady at the speed limit.

'What kind of car do you have?' She opened her yogurt. She was starving.

'My favorite is the Bugatti.'

She might have known he would have a car worth over a million dollars. No doubt it did something extravagant like hit the sound barrier in sixty seconds. She started to eat. 'How many other cars do you have?'

'Maybe thirty in the whole fleet. I don't keep track of them all. The ones I drive are the Bugatti or the Hummer. Sometimes the Rolls. My people drive the others.'

'Of course they do,' she said. His people. She shook her head. Such extravagant wealth was unimaginable.

He glanced at her sideways, his lip curled. 'What the hell are you eating?'

She wiped the corner of her mouth with a thumb. 'Soy yogurt.'

'Is that food? I tried what you bought the other day, the

Twizzlers and the cherry Coke Slurpee. I couldn't get either one out of my mouth fast enough.'

She burst out laughing. 'Come on, it couldn't have been that bad.'

'It was,' he told her in a serious voice. 'It was very much that bad.'

'How did you know . . .' Realization dawned. 'Oh, the note I left you. I wrote it on the back of a receipt.' She smacked her forehead. 'That's how you tracked me.'

'We got the security footage from the date of the receipt. Between that and your human name you told me in the dream, we had you.'

She sighed, finished her yogurt and opened the package of almonds. 'So much for my life of crime.' She offered him the opened package and he shook his head. Headlights came up behind them and stayed a steady distance away. She noticed him looking in the rearview mirror and twisted in her seat. 'What is it?'

'We have an escort to the Elven border.' His profile looked hard in the dim reflected light. 'How polite of them. What do you want to bet they would offer roadside assistance if we got a flat?'

'Well, you can hardly blame them,' she pointed out. 'You did trespass.'

'Yes, and you stole from me,' he said. 'And look at how well we're getting along.'

She was taken aback. She thought back on the overloaded day. They were getting along extraordinarily well. She suspected she ought to be freaked-out by it. Come to think of it, some part of her was.

'Now that you mention it,' she murmured, 'you do seem to be running against type a bit. Aren't you?'

'Of course,' he told her in a silken voice. 'Do you think I go from possibly rending to kissing in a day with just anyone who's stolen from me?'

'I . . . I haven't had much time to think about it.' She hadn't had time to think of much of anything.

He held up a finger. 'First, you're the only one who's ever successfully stolen from me.' He held up another finger. 'Second, I am not a forgiving creature. In fact, you're the only one

I've ever forgiven before.' He put up a third finger. 'And third, I like vengeance. I'm looking forward to ripping apart the person who gave you that charm and who ended up with my penny.'

'Put like that, I should still be running away screaming,' she said. She swallowed and looked out her window at the dark night scenes passing by. 'Why is this so different?'

'Remember when I said I wasn't bored?'

She nodded as she folded the corner of her long-sleeved shirt between her fingers.

'Looking back, I think I've been bored for centuries now. That's a pretty big rut. People rush to give me anything I could want. And if for some reason that doesn't happen, I can always buy what I want.'

'I can't imagine,' she murmured.

'Well, I live that way every day. But you're different. You have been a series of surprises from the first,' said Dragos. 'I have never been so angry. Then your note made me laugh out loud. The dream? Big surprise. The ridiculous things you say, the way you smell, the color of your hair in the sunlight, in the moonlight.' He shot her a sidelong glance with that blade-sharp smile of his. 'I am very much not bored. I find that's worth a lot to me, including figuring out how to do new things.'

She turned to look out her window again. Oh great, so she could relax as long as he was entertained? What happened when he got bored with her? Would he forget how he 'forgave' her? She bit her lip.

Good thing there were still three caches in New York, with three new identities and more money. Guess she was going back to the city with him after all. She would just have to play along until she found some way to get away.

His hand landed on her knee. She jumped and turned her attention back to him. 'Pia,' he said. The smile was gone from his voice. 'I want you to listen to me. I'm serious. Do not try to run away when we get back to the city.'

Her eyes went wide. 'What are you talking about?'

'Oh come on, it's not a big leap,' he retorted. His hand tightened, as hard on her as an iron manacle. 'Remember I said I called New York? I talked to my First sentinel, a gryphon named Rune. We think we know who might have been responsible for orchestrating what happened, manipulating and killing

Keith and his bookie, making sure the charm got to you and who ended up with the penny.'

'Oh,' she said, her voice very small. 'I have a feeling I don't want to hear this.' The almond she had just swallowed seemed to stick in her throat. She folded the package, put the remaining nuts in the shopping bag at her feet and drank part of a bottle of water before capping it and throwing it back in the bag.

'I have a feeling you're right. But you have to hear it. If Keith said anything about you, anything at all, you're not safe. Can you guarantee he didn't before you made him take the binding oath?'

She squirmed, leaden with the return of fear. 'He said he had mentioned me but hadn't said much. It makes sense if he hadn't. He would have wanted to try to control how things went down.'

'But try this thought out,' said Dragos. 'He also would have had to be pretty damn convincing to someone in order to get that charm. Do you know how many people could make something like that, something with the strength to hold against my strongest spells?'

'I'm guessing by how this conversation is going, not very many,' she muttered.

'Again, you'd be right. Offhand, I can think of three.' The manacle on her leg loosened. He rubbed her thigh. 'See what I'm getting at?'

Following instinct, she grasped his hand between hers. He allowed her to hold it in her lap. 'Who are they?'

'A very old witch in Russia. The Vampyre Queen in San Francisco is a sorceress. And the Dark Fae King.'

'Shit.' Shit, shit, shit.

'I have people doing research right now to see if there might be someone else who could pull off a charm strong enough to find my hoard. Right now, it looks like there isn't. The witch is pretty indifferent to things that happen outside of her neighborhood. I don't see her as likely. And the Vampyre Queen is a friend of sorts, or at least an ally, but the Dark Fae King?' Dragos shook his head with a grim smile. 'Urien hates me beyond anything else. It just so happens that for the last two hundred years I've had something he desperately wants, and I'm not letting him get his hands on it. He wouldn't hesitate to level the continent if he thought it would take me down too. You'd be nothing but a small bump in his road.'

From what little she knew of the Fae, there were two Courts, one Dark and one Light, and more often than not they were fighting each other over something. The Light Fae were ruled by a queen. Urien ruled the Dark Fae. He could be the nasty Power that had manipulated Keith behind the scenes.

She focused on the hand she held in her lap. It was such a big, strong hand. His arm was a tree trunk. She realized she was petting him, stroking his long fingers with her own.

'My people are very good. I don't think you would be able to get far anyway, but you've proved to be surprisingly resourceful,' he said. He could be many things – seductive, coaxing, quiet – but this capacity for gentleness surprised her. 'And on the off chance you did manage to get away, I would find you again. But you would be in danger until I did, so how about that promise?'

'Okay,' she said.

'Good girl.' His hand tightened on hers and then he pulled away.

They fell into silence. Sometime later, when the sky had lightened to predawn, the headlights behind them flashed, and the car that had been following pulled away. She supposed that meant they had crossed out of the Elven demesne.

After a while her eyelids drooped again. She didn't think she could fall sleep, but two two-hour stretches and an afternoon nap wasn't enough rest, since she hadn't slept a full night through for a while.

She rubbed her temples and said, 'One of these days, I'm going to get a real meal and a real night's sleep.'

Dragos said, 'I told Rune to find someone who could cook the kind of food you eat.'

Despite herself, she had to smile. He made vegetarianism sound so foreign, like cooking dog food. 'That was very thoughtful of you, thank you.' She had a brief struggle between pride and desire, and desire won. She put her head against his arm.

It was wrong. It was foolish. She shouldn't take such comfort from the hard, muscled warmth she leaned against. And the last thing she should do is start to rely on it.

He cupped her head and then focused again on driving. She dozed.

Some indefinable time later, she came alert to a vague sense of anxiety. It strengthened as she straightened and looked around. The morning light was stronger, although the sun had not yet appeared at the horizon. The passing scenery was whipping by. She glanced at the speedometer. They were traveling close to 110 miles an hour.

She looked at Dragos. His body was relaxed and he drove with complete competence, but his dark face was fierce. 'What's wrong?'

'Something's found us. We're being tracked. I don't know if we can outrun it, but we're giving it a shot.'

Even knowing it was useless, she couldn't help but look around. She also opened her senses wide, straining to understand what she was picking up. Comprehension eluded her. She had never before experienced what she was sensing.

'What is it?' he asked.

'I don't understand what I'm feeling,' she said.

His eyebrows rose. 'Try to describe it.'

'That's just it; I don't know.' She shrugged, feeling inadequate. 'It – it doesn't feel good. It's like a feeling of dread, knowing something bad is near. Don't you feel it?'

'No,' he said. 'You're describing something different than the spell that has locked on to us. The feeling may be connected to your Wyr blood.'

'Where are we?'

'The next big city is Fayetteville. If we get there, we're going to change course.'

If we get there? He sounded so calm. She gripped her seat belt.

What came next happened so fast. At a blind curve, a large vehicle roared down on them. Dragos swerved hard, holding the car in tight control. But just then another vehicle came from ahead on the right.

The passenger's side. Light blinded her.

Dragos gave one last vicious yank at the wheel. The tires screamed as the car went into a spin. Everything whirled. Then the oncoming vehicle was about to impact the driver's side. He threw his torso over hers, jamming her head into the hollow of his neck.

A horrendous noise as everything –

≈ SEVEN ≈

Pain woke her up. Her body was twisted at an uncomfortable angle. She was surrounded by jagged metal and trapped under a heavy weight.

She groaned.

'Shh,' Dragos whispered. 'It's all right. You're going to be all right.'

She tried to take a deep breath and couldn't.

'I can't breathe,' she whimpered. 'I can't move my legs.'

'We've been in a wreck, Pia. You're pinned in, but I'm going to get you out. For now you must listen to me. Don't move. Can you do that for me? Just for a little while?'

His voice wove into her and brushed aside her panic. He was beguiling her into calming down. Someday she was going to have words with him about messing with her head. Right now didn't seem like the time. She tried shallow breaths and mouthed, 'Okay.'

'There's a brave girl,' he soothed.

The heavy weight on her chest lifted briefly. Metal groaned. It was a terrible sound. Pain seared her legs and back. She cried out, and the world grayed over.

Dragos cursed a steady stream of vitriol as Pia lost consciousness again. The impact had been so violent the car was an unrecognizable heap of twisted metal. Most creatures could not have survived the crash. If he had been less than he was, if he hadn't recovered enough from the Elven poison, if he had not thrown himself over Pia and *pushed* out with his Power to cover them both, she would have been crushed in an instant.

They were surrounded by shadows. He ripped the collapsed air bag to shreds and threw the pieces out the little twist of space that had been the front passenger's window. Then he snapped her seat belt. He glared around as the shadows crept closer. He bared his teeth and growled a warning, and the shadows paused. Over the burnt rubber and gasoline smells, the stink of Goblin made his nostrils flare. Soon the Goblins began to creep closer again, their coarse features coming visible in the predawn.

They thought they had him pinned. They were right.

His own body had taken damage, various contusions and cuts, but he ignored it. For him, the injuries were minor. If he had been alone, he would have ripped his way out of the wreck and done a WWF SmackDown on their ugly asses. But if he did that he could do incalculable damage to Pia, maybe kill her. He would have to be very careful in working to free her from the wreckage. That would take time. She was so much more fragile than he.

The Goblins grew bolder. They were misshapen creatures, gray-skinned and brutish with inhuman strength. They were one of the few Elder Races that could not maintain some kind of glamour to make them more palatable for coexisting with humans. For that reason they spent most of their time in Other lands, where magic was stronger, humankind was the rarity and certain technologies such as electrical appliances and modern weaponry wouldn't work with any degree of safety or reliability.

He expanded his senses and found a passageway nearby that led to a pocket of Other land. Big surprise.

He turned his attention back to Pia. The wreckage had wrapped them together like a ghoulish present. He was twisted at the waist, his torso covering hers. Her seat had broken. She was lying partially in what had been the backseat, while the front of the car had collapsed on her legs.

He wiggled his left arm free and reached behind him to grasp the steering column, which was pressing against his left lower kidney. Bracing himself with his right arm, he pushed.

Careful. Metal groaned and the column eased away a few inches. He stopped before he wanted to, so he could check if shifting the column would make something else pinch down on Pia. He didn't sense any further collapse. Good enough. He tried the same with the roof crumpled over his back and gained a little more room for them.

Goblins called to one another in their guttural language. One came too close. Grinning, it poked a serrated sword at him through the crunched window hole.

Dragos grabbed the sword. He punched his other arm out the hole. He locked his hand around the Goblin's throat and crushed it while the creature choked and kicked. He let go. The Goblin crumpled to the ground, claws digging at its ruined neck as it died. The other Goblins watched as their comrade kicked out his life but made no move to try to help him.

How fucking charming. Ignoring his bleeding fingers, he pulled the sword into the car. The other Goblins snarled but kept well out of his reach.

He wedged the sword near his hand and turned his attention back to Pia, ignoring when the ruined car lurched. The Goblins lifted the wreckage onto a flatbed with them still inside.

At least she was breathing easier. Contusions, cuts and bruises mottled her face. The shirt she wore like a jacket was cut and damp with blood in places. Always pale, to his grim gaze she looked too white in the dirty morning light. A delicate tracery of blue veins was visible under the fine skin at her temple.

The flatbed truck lurched into motion, turned off the highway road and cut across country. Armed and armored Goblins jogged alongside and behind, keeping them surrounded. They traveled toward the passageway that would lead them to the Other land.

Dragos scanned down her body with Power, paying close attention to her spine and legs. He breathed a sigh of relief when he found them intact. He'd managed to throw enough cover over her to prevent major structural damage. Next he checked for bleeding. He found jagged metal cutting into her right calf. No wonder she had passed out when he tried to shift things. He lowered his head and used his shoulders as he pushed up against the crumpled roof, gaining them several more needed inches.

He studied how her legs were pinned until he was satisfied he had found a way to widen the area without hurting her further. He gripped the two places he had chosen and pulled them apart. The metal protested but gave way until her legs were free. Blood gushed as the jagged metal left her leg. He slapped his palm over it. Despite the urgent need to stop the bleeding, he paused and sucked in a breath as he felt her Power welling underneath his hand.

Liquid sunlight, magic eternal, young, wild and *free.* He discarded each word as it came to him. They were all inadequate. What he now knew for sure was what he had suspected before. He was in the presence of something unique. In the series of surprises he had encountered since coming aware of her, he came to another first in his long bad life as he discovered reverence.

He sent a very gentle pulse of Power to seal the wound and stop the bleeding. He sent the pulse over her body, sealing other, smaller cuts. She would hurt and be unhappy when she woke up, but she would live. That's all that mattered.

That's everything that mattered.

He straightened as much as he could and cupped her chin. 'Pia,' he said, reaching soft and calm into her unconscious mind. 'Time to wake up. I want you to open your eyes now.'

She pushed at the fingers gripping her chin. She was tired, damn it. She muttered, 'Would you stop talking so loud?'

'Pia, look at me.'

'I want to sleep,' she said, her tone petulant. Why did that voice have to be so damn beautiful?

It crooned, 'I know, but you can't. Suck it up, baby.'

'God, you're so annoying.' She sighed but opened her eyes.

She looked up at Dragos, who smiled at her, his dark expression lit with an unfamiliar expression. On someone else she would call it relief. He propped his weight on one elbow by her head as he leaned over her. One side of his face was a dark purple bruise.

Her gaze left that puzzle and went on to others, traveling over an unfamiliar misshapen metal while they lurched in a constant, uneven motion. She lifted her head to peer out and she wished she hadn't bothered. Monsters ran alongside them. The sense of dread from before hit her full force. The surrounding land shimmered with magic that was growing in strength. It was too much to take in all at once.

'We're being kidnapped,' he told her in a calm voice. 'Car wreck. Remember? I'm pretty sure they're hauling us into an Other land.' He stroked her hair. 'You're all right. You were hurt but it isn't bad.'

She looked down at her battered and blood-smeared body. A switch flipped in her head. 'Oh God, I'm bleeding,' she stammered. She brushed at her arms, scrubbed at the wetness streaking her face.

'Whoa,' he said. He grabbed her hands. 'Stop panicking. I said you're all right.'

'Make it stop. I can't bleed.' She struggled and started to hyperventilate.

'Keep your voice down. One of them might understand English.' He put a hand over her mouth, holding her down. 'Damn it, I just closed your wounds. You're going to cut yourself again if you're not careful.'

'Dragos, I can't bleed,' she said, muffled against his palm. 'Do you understand? *I can't bleed!*' She looked at him with wild eyes. 'Can you burn it?'

He stared at her, his gold gaze arrested. 'Pia,' he said, 'you were cut all over.'

'It doesn't matter,' she panted. 'We've got to get rid of the blood.'

After a quick murderous glance at what was happening outside their private cage, he said from between gritted teeth, 'Shit. All right, hold still.'

She froze, pushing out the panic. Moving fast, he tore her capris above the knees and stripped the bloody cloth off her. He used it to wipe her legs and the edge of metal that had cut her, and wadded it up. She fought to wriggle out of her overshirt, hampered by their close space. He helped by shredding it and then he used it to wipe the cuts on her arms and her face as best he could. He added it to the wad of material he clenched in one fist.

Magic surged. The truck coughed and stalled. Goblins ran to unhitch the flatbed, calling to one another as they ran chains underneath. A dozen Goblins grabbed the chains and began to haul them forward.

'We've crossed over,' he said.

She had never been to an Other land before. Her mother refused to take her, insisting their best chance at avoiding discovery was to hide among humankind. Despite everything else going on, the feeling of the land was intoxicating.

She peered out the ruined window. Majestic old-growth trees draped with vines towered around them. There was a symmetry to the land that fed her tired spirit. Her gaze followed the thick twist of a tree trunk up until the branches spread out high overhead with the graciousness of a vaulted cathedral ceiling. Steeped with age, drenched with magic, everything looked richer, greener, and the early-morning sunlight shone more golden and bright.

Pain forced her to lie back. She whispered, 'It's beautiful.'

'I'm pretty sure it won't be where they're taking us,' he said.

They both looked down at the short-sleeved lemon yellow T-shirt she had worn underneath. The right shoulder was soaked red, along with an area at her waist where she had bled through the overshirt.

'Tear it off,' she said. She pushed away a panicked sense of exposure. She hoped her bra was clean.

His eyes went lava hot as he glared at the Goblins surrounding them. 'Fuck if I will,' he snapped.

He shoved the wad of material into her lap and then ripped the shirt at shoulder and waist until he got all the bloodied cloth. What was left of the T-shirt was a ragged mess that left her stomach and shoulder bare but the collar was intact. She peered underneath it and sighed in relief. Her bra was unbloodied.

Last of all, he tore off his own shirt, which was dotted with red spots. He tied the bundle up in the pieces of his shirt.

Then he held it up in one hand close to the crumpled window opening. His eyes narrowed. The lava in them flared just as his Power did. The bundle burst into flame.

'Thank you,' she breathed.

He said, 'We are so going to talk about this when we get home.'

She shrank against his chest, away from the flare of fire, staring as he held the ball in his fist. It burned with too much intensity, fueled by his magic. She felt the heat lick along her skin but he was unburned.

He sent a sideways glance outside, a quick evil look, then flung the flaming cloth with enough force that it slapped a nearby Goblin in the face.

'Two birds, one stone.' He shrugged when Pia stared at him. He watched with interest as the screaming started.

The Goblin ran in erratic circles, slapping at his flaming face and howling. The fire refused to die. Instead, fueled by his Power, the magic of the land and whatever was in her blood, it spread to the leather armor. Pia turned away from the gruesome sight. She covered her ears and buried her face in his chest. He cupped the back of her head and watched as the Goblin fell down and died.

Payback was a beautiful bitch. She was also a good friend of his, and they were just getting started.

There were twenty Goblins left after the two Dragos had killed. Before long they were joined by another dozen. The newcomers switched places with the ones that had been hauling the flatbed. The pace picked up.

After Dragos pushed the distorted car out in a few more carefully chosen places, they could move around a little more inside and make themselves more or less comfortable. Then he focused his attention on what was going on outside.

She had watched with wide eyes as he had bent the jagged ends of metal around her legs so she didn't cut herself again when she moved. That was some kind of scary strength he had. She fished around in the cramped, alien area at her feet and managed to find a battered bottle of water that hadn't been punctured. They shared half of it in sips; then she capped the rest for later.

She had no doubt that Dragos had saved her life in more ways than one. She was grateful he had been able to stop her bleeding by sealing her cuts. He told her it was a form of cauterization except he was able to keep her from feeling the pain. It was too bad that was the extent of his healing skills, because her body ached all over.

She peeked out now and then, staring around in awe at the landscape that was so like and yet unlike the part of Earth she knew. The fluid roll of hills, burgeoning blue-green foliage, shards of sunlight sparking off crystal veins in granite boulders, the scenes they passed veiled some invisible truth that was so essential, so palpable, she could swear she could almost scoop it out of the air with both hands. Some long-denied, starved part of her soul unfurled and wailed with the need to drink from it.

Was it the magic of the Other land that called to her? Was it the ancient canny wildness of forest that had seen no woodsman's axe, no farmer's plow, that reminded her of her deepest self, the wild creature that lived trapped within the inadequate cage of her weak, half-breed flesh?

She wanted to cut at herself to let the poor creature out. The upsurge of desperate emotion was so violent, so uncontained, the part of her that was civilized with language and culture shrank away from it. An impulse ghosted through her to try to tell Dragos about the frenzy teeming inside, but civilization and language failed her in the end. She did not understand what she felt and so she remained silent.

As powerfully as the land called to her, the Goblins freaked her out, so she didn't look outside too often. She chose instead to lie back in her broken seat and stare in thought at the mangled roof as she tried to explore the mysterious landscape she found inside herself. She became convinced the Goblins were the source of the dread that clung to her. The feeling crawled along her skin like baby spiders.

There were other layers to the mélange of contradicting, complicated emotions. Shock from the crash lingered. Fear clung, along with anxiety about what would happen next. Excitement welled that she was actually in an Other place.

Dragos existed at the center of all of it. He was her one point of stable reference, her compass point, true north.

His dark bronze skin seemed more intense, his inky hair more glossy, the gold of his eyes more burnished than it had been before. She wondered if it was an effect of the magic-saturated land, or if it was a side effect of the Elven poison working its way out of his system. Perhaps both.

She studied his dangerous face as he reclined on one shoulder and watched what happened outside. His gold eyes were calculating, and he kept the Goblin sword he had captured ready against his side.

She weighed the odds. On one hand, thirty or forty armed

Goblins, give or take. On the other hand, one seriously pissed-off dragon. She thought of the enormous strength in those hands as he reshaped the metal near her legs. Maybe she was biased, but those Goblins were toast.

The trick would be how and when he was going to toast them.

'The problem is me,' she said, pitching her voice low like he'd told her to.

'What are you talking about,' he said in a soft voice, only half paying attention to her.

'Just like it was when the Elves had you surrounded. You wouldn't fight them because I was in the way.' That got his full attention. She felt calm and clear. 'I bet you could have gotten yourself out of the wreck probably well before we crossed over.'

'Speculation like that is useless,' he told her, frowning.

'Maybe you could have gotten free of the wreck before the Goblins even got the car onto the flatbed, right?' she persisted. 'You didn't, though, because of me. I'm holding you back.'

'Let's be clear on something,' he said. 'I don't know what the hell you are. We're adding that to a growing list of things for that conversation we're going have when we get out of here. But one thing you're not is a problem. Let's say you are a tactical consideration.'

'Tactical consideration,' she huffed. 'What does that mean?'

'It means you factor into the decisions I make. Stop fretting.' He flicked her nose with a forefinger. 'Looks like we're coming to our destination.'

She propped herself up on her elbows and looked out. They had been traveling for a long time. She wasn't sure how long, because she had heard time moved at a different pace in Other lands. The sun had lowered until it looked like late afternoon or early evening, but if she went with what her body clock was telling her, it felt like they had been trapped into that awful wreck for an entire day.

The land had gotten rockier and wilder since she'd last peered out. Ahead against the bottom of a bluff was a grim-looking stone . . . fortress? Wow, she'd never seen a fortress before. A couple Goblins broke off and jogged ahead of the main group. Anxiety got the upper hand of all the other emotions in her mélange. Her stomach clenched.

Dragos's hand settled on her shoulder in a firm, steady grip.

'You listen to me,' he whispered. 'You are going to do as I say. Do you understand? Now is not the time to argue or disobey me. I am the expert here. Got it?'

She nodded. She focused on regulating her breathing as her gaze clung to his.

'Here's what you're not going to do,' he whispered, looking deep into her eyes. 'Do not draw any attention to yourself whatsoever. Do not give them a reason to believe you're anything but incidental. Do not look them in the eyes. To a Goblin, that's a sign of aggression. Do not speak to them. Do not struggle. Do you understand?'

'I think so,' she whispered back. That galloping horse was back in her chest. The way things had gone this last week, she'd lost ten years off her life from stress.

'Here's what I think is going to happen. They're going to separate us. They might hurt you.' His grip tightened to the point of pain. 'They won't kill you. They'll have seen I was tending to you in some way, so they'll want to use you as leverage to control me. Goblins have no interest in human women. They won't rape you.'

A spasm of trembling hit her, and then it was gone again and she was calm. 'It's all right,' she told him. 'I'm all right. I'm glad you're telling me this.'

'That's my good brave girl.' He let go of her shoulder and brushed his knuckles against her cheek.

'That's pretty patronizing,' she said, refusing to acknowledge how her idiotic heart had swelled at his words. It seemed pretty clear by now she had no sense or good taste.

He gave her an impatient shrug. 'So?'

Just like that she cracked up. His raptor's gaze narrowed. She clapped both hands over her mouth to muffle the noise and sobered fast. 'This is still about that penny, isn't it?' she said into her palms.

'This is about the fucking penny,' he agreed. 'I think it was used to put a tracking spell on me, much like the one we used on you. I don't sense any real Power here yet, but I bet our orchestrator of events is on his way. It's all the more reason you *must not draw attention* to yourself.'

'I won't.'

He looked out. 'Almost there now. If they're thinking what

I hope they are, they don't know I could have gotten out. From their point of view, it must have looked like I've been trying to get free. I'm hoping they have underestimated me.'

Another wave of adrenaline hit. Her system was so overloaded it was starting to make her feel high. She thought back over what had happened and nodded.

'That's it. You keep your head down, keep quiet and survive.' His gaze was fierce. 'I will come after you.'

They started to slow. She couldn't bring herself to look out. 'How close do you think you are to throwing off the last of the poison?' She forced the question out of throat muscles that had locked up.

'It might take a day, maybe two. It helps we crossed over and the land magic is so abundant here.'

A day or two. In some ways not long at all. In other ways, a lifetime.

All of this was about her. She stole the penny, she was the one he came after, and she was the one who got him shot by the Elves. He held himself back from escaping from the wreckage to help her. He still wasn't going to fight when they stopped, because she was around.

He has to wait until I'm out of the way. It's so I don't get killed. Maybe now we've come so far he's got to wait until he's healed. It's going to be a race, between how fast he can get free and how fast the Power that arranged his capture can get here.

The emotion that welled at that was indescribable.

'I think you're my hero,' she said. Only half kidding.

He stared at her, the picture of incredulity. 'Most people,' he said, 'think I am a very bad man.'

She studied his eyes to try to find out if that bothered him. He didn't seem bothered by it. He seemed discomfited by her. 'Well,' she said at last, 'maybe you're a very good dragon.'

The flatbed stopped. Showtime.

She kept crouched down as she peered out the wreckage. A Goblin had stepped out of a black metal gate. She had seen pictures of Goblins before but the drawings and sketches hadn't managed to capture their robust vigor. The real ones were not only hideous but powerfully built. The language they spoke to one another was choppy, guttural and harsh. As a few came closer, she realized how bad they stank.

Still, there was something different about this Goblin, an air of authority. He held ropes of black chains with manacles. He strode closer to them but stopped a prudent distance away. He stank too.

They were altogether repulsive, and somehow she was supposed to let them put their hands on her. Another convulsive shiver hit. In a move unseen by the Goblins, below their line of sight, Dragos put a hand on her knee. She covered it with hers.

'Buck up,' she whispered to him. 'Don't be such a wuss.'

His hand clenched and his shoulders shuddered. She hoped she made him laugh again.

The Goblin that had approached said something to them. Chop chop chop. Dragos answered him in the same awful language. Chop chop.

They went back and forth a few more times. Then the Goblin stepped closer and threw the shackles. Dragos reached outside and caught them. He pulled them into the wreck. They made a lot more sense to him than they did to her because he sorted them deftly.

The dread had become so strong it was nauseating. Some of it was coming from the chains. They reeked of some kind of horrible magic.

Dragos bent and locked a manacle to one of his ankles. She hissed, 'Stop! What are you doing? Don't put those on!'

'Shut up,' he snapped. He locked a second manacle to his other ankle.

She grabbed his arm. 'Dragos, there's some kind of bad magic in those!'

He whipped around and snarled at her, eyes blazing.

She flinched and cowered from him. Her thoughts flatlined.

He finished putting the other two manacles on his thick wrists and held them up so that the Goblin could see. The Goblin nodded and shouted to the others who swarmed forward.

When they started prying the ruined doors off the car, she curled into a fetal position and closed her eyes.

⸻ EIGHT ⸻

What followed next was ugly. She couldn't say she hadn't been warned.

They dragged her out of the wreckage first. She kept her gaze trained on the ground as one punched her in the stomach. When she lay curled on the ground trying to breathe, they kicked her. Over and over again hard-toed boots slammed into her, interspersed with harsh Goblin laughter as they taunted Dragos, until she no longer kept silent because it was the smart thing to do. She was silent because she couldn't get in a deep enough breath to scream.

She caught one blurred glimpse of Dragos standing in the grip of two Goblins every bit as huge as he was. His aggressive, dangerous face was blank, gold eyes as reflective and emotionless as two Greek coins.

A lifetime later, several Goblins with drawn swords walked Dragos through the squat stone fortress. One Goblin grabbed her by the hair and followed behind them. Another brought up the rear, still kicking at her now and then, although without much interest.

The group of Goblins guarding Dragos marched him into a cell. Her Goblins passed it by, down to an intersection in the corridor and to the right. Once they were out of Dragos's line of sight, their manner became businesslike and uninterested.

They took her by the arms and dragged her into another cell. They threw her onto a pile of rancid straw.

One Goblin said something. Chop chop. The other laughed. They left and the grate of a key sounded in the cell door lock. Sounds faded from the corridor.

She lay on the horrid straw for a while. Then she crawled a few feet, then collapsed and lay on chill, dirty flagstones. She may have blacked out. She wasn't sure. The next thing she became aware of was a blue-black beetle walking across the floor.

She tracked its progress. It fell headlong into a crack and got stuck. She dragged herself over and watched it some more. It managed to get turned around so its little head poked out of the crack. Feelers waved and its front legs worked, but it couldn't get enough purchase to crawl out.

Her fingers crept across the floor until they found some straw. She took a shallow handful. She wiggled the ends deep into the crack and lifted up. The beetle popped out and waddled on its way.

When it disappeared, she sighed, rolled over onto her back and levered herself into a sitting position. Her thinking came back online.

Do one thing at a time. Take one step.

She crawled to the wall. Step.

She got first one foot underneath her, then the other. Step.

She straightened her shoulders. When she was pretty sure she had her balance back, she opened the locked cell door and walked out.

The dragon lay spread-eagled where they had bound him. He was chained twice, first with the magical black shackles. The second set was attached in four points to the floor. He stared at the ceiling, thoughts weaving in a serpentine path. Every few minutes he would pull at the floor chains. He ignored his bleeding ankles and wrists. He could feel a weakness growing in the chain on his left arm and concentrated on that.

His cell door opened. He turned his head, the serpentine path turning lethal.

A battered, filthy Pia backed into the room, and Dragos became sane.

He began to shake. He watched her listening at the cracked door for a few moments before she pulled the door shut. She turned around. When she caught sight of him, her shoulders sagged.

'Oh, for crying out loud.' She rolled her eyes. '*Two* sets of manacles? Now I suppose we need two sets of keys. This day keeps getting better and better.'

'Come here,' he said. He gave the chain anchoring his left arm an enormous wrench. The chain groaned but didn't break. 'Come here. Come here.'

She cocked her head, her weary gaze becoming very sober. She limped across the cell and collapsed to her knees beside him. 'They beat you too,' she said. She touched his ribs with a light gentle hand.

His shaking increased. Talking to her before the Goblins took her had been easy. He had explained to her with his usual calm ruthlessness how he thought things might go. Overall she had seemed to take it well. He approached the confrontation as he always did, ready and focused to meet any upcoming challenge.

Then that first Goblin had driven his fist into her stomach, and he had gone bat-shit crazy. Every kick, every blow she suffered was like corrosive acid in his veins. He wanted to howl and rage. The dragon strained to rip their hearts from their chests while they watched.

He had clung to his self-control by the merest thread, by the realization of how much worse it could get for her if they got the reaction out of him they were searching for.

They hurt her. They hurt her, and that hurt him inside somewhere, in a place he had never been hurt before. He had sustained physical injury and pain many times before. It meant little to him. But this new hurt – he was in shock. He had never realized just how invincible he had been until it was ripped away from him.

He studied her with a hungry gaze as she knelt beside him. The brightness of her hair was dulled with dirt. Her tattered T-shirt was now gray, and the shortened capri jeans were no longer blue. Her pallid skin was mottled all over with swollen bruises so deep they were a purple black.

And underneath everything, all of it, was remembering how

just before it happened, he had made her cower from him. He had never before hated himself, but he thought he did at that moment.

'Come here, come here,' he whispered. Her beautiful eyes went from sobered to worried. She leaned over and put her cheek against his. He turned his face into her and her hair fell over him in a light canopy.

She was murmuring in his ear as her hand stroked his cheek. He focused on it. 'I'm sorry. It's all my fault. I can't tell you how sorry I am.'

'What?' he said. 'What are you saying? Stop talking that way. Shut up.' He brushed his lips along her skin, breathed in her presence. Underneath the dungeon filth and the stink of Goblin, he found her delicate, indomitable fragrance. Something cramped and injured in his soul expanded again. 'I snarled at you. I didn't mean it.'

'Don't be ridiculous; of course you did.' She stroked his hair and pressed a kiss to his cheek.

'You cringed from me. Don't ever cringe from me again.'

'Dragos,' she said in a sensible voice. 'If you turn on me and snarl like a wild animal when I'm not expecting it, I think I might cringe again. Call me a girly girl if you want, but that's just how it is.'

'I won't do it again,' he whispered. He was so quiet she almost didn't hear him. He concentrated all his attention on the featherlight trip her fingers made across his face until she touched his lips.

She sighed and let more of her weight rest on him. 'Locked things can't hold me caged, but that doesn't mean I can pull these blasted manacles open. How the hell am I going to get two sets of keys with Goblins running all over the place?'

The frayed self-control in her voice sent him a little bit back into crazy. 'You're not,' he said.

She lifted her head and scowled at him. He was relieved to see she hadn't broken down. 'What else are we going to do?' she asked. 'We can't just wait around until the Dark Fae King, or the Joker or Riddler, or whoever the hell it is, shows up.'

His mind clicked into gear again and became crystal clear. 'This is what's happening,' he told her. 'I have very good hearing. Most of the Goblins have gone to have their evening meal.

115

There are a few guards left in strategic places. I can hear where they are.'

'That's handy to know,' she said with relief.

'And this is what we're going to do,' he told her. 'You know how the corridor tees and they took you to the right?'

She nodded.

'If you go straight instead of right, there's some kind of room they use down that way. I think it's a guardroom. I could hear them in there talking about going to supper. There was the sound of metal clanking, which I hope was weapons, and the scrape of chairs, so it's a place where they gather. There's no one there now. I want you to go look for keys that might fit these floor chains or something straight and thin to use as a lock pick. Failing those two, try to grab an axe. Be quick.'

'Dragos,' she said, eyeing him in doubt. 'I don't know how to pick a lock. I've never had to learn, duh.'

'You won't have to. I know how to pick a lock,' he said. He had learned to pick locks as soon as locks were invented. People liked to lock up all kinds of pretty things that he wanted. He rattled the manacle on his left wrist. 'There's a weakness in one of these links. I'm going to break it.'

She looked at his arm and her forehead wrinkled. She said with concern, 'Your wrist is a mess.'

'Don't be such a girly girl,' he told her. Her gaze met his and lit with reluctant laughter. 'It's nothing. You'd better hurry. We don't know how much time we've got while they eat supper.'

'Right,' she said.

An echo of the pain and rage came back as he watched her struggle to her feet without any of her usual grace and he could do nothing to help her. He had paid special attention to the ones who had beaten her. There were going to be a lot of dead Goblins before he was through with this place.

But for now he turned all his considerable attention on to the weakened chain and yanked.

Pia crept down the corridor again, this time comforted by Dragos's reassurance that she wasn't in imminent danger of running into a Goblin. She found the guardroom he was talking about since the door was open. She looked inside and recoiled.

'Ugh,' she muttered. 'Filthy creatures.'

She jumped, then put a hand to her sore ribs when Dragos whispered in her ear, 'Are you all right?'

'Oh, of course you can hear me,' she said. 'Yes, I'm fine. It's just there's moldy food scraps on the table, and it stinks in here. They're disgusting.'

'They taste bad too,' he said.

'You've eaten Goblin!' she exclaimed.

'No,' he said, 'I've *bitten* Goblin.'

He sounded a little strained. She bit her lip. She hoped he wasn't damaging his arm too much.

Relevance, Pia. She shook herself and hurried through the room as fast as she could. The place was positively medieval and not in a sanitized-Hollywood-movie kind of way. Was that urine in the corner? Ugh! She tried as much as possible to avoid touching things.

She was disappointed she found no keys. But she did find a switchblade that fit into her pocket and a stiletto knife. The manacles weren't precision made. The stiletto looked like it might be thin enough to fit into the locks if he could bend the tip a bit.

She grabbed the end of a battle-axe from the rack of weaponry. It was too heavy for her to lift, so she had to drag it back to the cell. The sound of the axe scraping along the corridor floor made her uneasy, so she hurried rather faster than her abused body wanted. She was sweating and in pain by the time she propped open the cell door with one hip. She bit back a groan as she heaved the axe inside.

Dragos looked from the axe to her as she leaned back against the doorpost, panting. He held up his left arm where part of the broken floor chain dangled. She held up the stiletto.

He smiled. Game on.

After she gave him the thin blade, she leaned against the wall nearby and slid down until she was sitting. It was comforting to watch him work and let her mind drift, to know there was nothing at that point in time that she could or should be doing.

He did bend the tip of the knife by sliding it between two flagstones and pulling on the handle. He had to twist at the waist, strain to reach the floor chain manacle on his right wrist and hold steady as he worked at the lock.

She admired the strength and grace of his long body as he worked. To hold his twisted position he had to tighten those striking abdominal muscles. They rippled and flexed as he took in controlled, steady breaths. The line from his broad shoulder slid around into that clenched waist. His jeans were as filthy as hers, but the buttock and long masculine leg they sheathed were mouthwatering.

Come to think of it he looked pretty damn sexy chained to that floor. Especially if this were her castle. She would send her servants in to wash him (all male heterosexual servants, and they would of course clean up this disgusting cell, scatter candles around, put a mattress under him with silk sheets, oh, and maybe leave a bottle of wine and a couple of glasses), and afterward she would come down and tease him to madness by mounting him and rubbing her scantily clad body all over that sizzling hot torso.

Except there was no castle. She had no servants. His wrists were bleeding, which looked painful and was no fun at all, and everywhere she went it stank like Goblin. Oh yeah, and their lives were in danger.

'Still not right in the head,' she muttered.

He sent her a gleam of that machete smile over his shoulder. 'You are going to explain what you mean by that very soon now.'

She felt a blush warm her cheeks. 'Not likely.'

He removed the manacle, sat up and stretched, then slid forward and started working on his ankles. He was matter-of-fact about it, but she had to cover her mouth to muffle her squeal. She sat up straight and clapped excitedly. His smile deepened. Soon he had his ankles freed, and he took a moment to pick the lock on the manacle on his left wrist and fling it into a corner.

Then they both looked at the other black metal manacles and chains with the repulsive magic. They were two simple shackles, one hobbling his arms together, the other at his ankles, which kept him from being able to walk in his normal long stride.

'Somehow I don't think this is going to be as easy,' he said. He was right. No matter how he worked he wasn't able to pick any of the four locks. 'I think these won't come off without the matching key. I bet that's part of their magic.'

Her excitement plummeted. 'What do you think they do besides feel slimy?'

'Well, the Goblins didn't know I got shot by the Elves, did they?' he said. 'Or if they did know, they wouldn't have wanted to trust it since it is going to wear off at some point. These feel like they do the same thing the Elven poison does – limit my strength and prevent me from changing. Otherwise there would have been no hope of those' – he jerked his chin at the other set of chains – 'keeping me prisoner.'

'So now what do we do?' She threw up her hands. She could feel somewhere inside there was a crack that was getting wider. It was just a matter of time before she fell into it, like the beetle, only she wasn't so sure she would be able to crawl her way back out again.

'You're going back into your cell.' He crouched over her and put a hand over her mouth when she started to protest. He snapped, 'Did you or did you not promise no arguing?'

'Fuck you. You're not the boss of me,' she mumbled against his palm. She wrapped both hands around his wrist, careful of the bruised torn skin. 'You keep forgetting that.'

'Let me see if I've got this straight,' he said, gold eyes glinting. 'You promised not to argue when you don't want to argue. Is that it?'

Was he amused? Mad? She couldn't tell. She said, 'Of course.'

He barked out a laugh, put his hands under her arms and lifted her to her feet. He held on to her until she steadied. 'Okay, girly girl. You're going in the cell, I'm locking the door behind you and all the fuck-yous in the world aren't going to change that. It's the safest place for you. If for some reason they get back before I do, they'll never think you got out. They'll think that I did all this.' He gestured around the cell.

'I don't want to separate.'

'Tough,' he said. 'I'm going hunting and you don't want to be there.'

He hefted the battle-axe in one hand like it was made of Styrofoam and placed the other at her back. Despite his callous tone, he was careful as he led her down the corridor. Between her injuries and his shackles, they went at a slow pace.

She stepped inside and turned back. She couldn't look up at

him. She focused instead on the floor as her lips trembled. 'But what if they come back?'

A heavy silence lay between them.

Long fingers slid under her chin and coaxed her face up. She bit her lips as she looked up at his sober expression. 'I won't leave you alone for long. I'll be quick as I can.' A fat tear splashed onto his hand and he looked as if it had seared him. He swore under his breath. Then he bent his head and brushed her mouth with his. 'I swear to you, Pia, they will not hurt you again. You have to trust me.'

She nodded and jerked her head away, swiping at her face with the back of her hand. 'Go.'

He stood there looking at her. For a moment he seemed like he was about to speak, but she turned her back on him. She thought she felt his fingers brush the back of her neck, and then he was gone.

All the vitality that had been surrounding and sustaining her drained away in his absence. She looked around the dingy, horrible cell and felt so lonesome she could have lain down and died.

She sat in the middle of the floor and made herself into a small package, with upraised knees and forehead resting on her forearms. How did she do that trick before, when she went blank as soon as the Goblins took her? She hadn't meant to. It had to have been some kind of defense response to too much horror when those monstrous hands had touched her.

Now the minutes trickled by with agonizing slowness and she had no insulation from it. She wanted to check out, to disassociate and go somewhere else in her head, but she couldn't figure out how to do it again. It took everything she had not to give in to panic and walk out that cell door.

She remembered every turn they took. She knew she could get to that outside door again. Which was no doubt guarded by a couple of those skanky bat-faced freaks. She muffled a groan and squeezed herself into a tighter package.

How did I get here again? It's like I had a grocery list of all the things I shouldn't do, and I went right on down it, checking off things as I got to them. I've been very thorough about it. *Live very quietly,* her mom had said. *Leave everything behind on a moment's notice. Don't get too attached to people. And don't tell anyone anything about your real self.* Simple, simple stuff.

I've got to give myself one thing. Mom never did tell me not to steal from a dragon. No doubt she thought it was too flaming obvious to mention. It should have been added to that Jim Croce song. You don't spit into the wind. You don't pull the mask off of the ole Lone Ranger, and you don't steal from Cuelebre.

Think I might have destroyed any hope of living anonymously? Numskull.

A small sound sent her into a panic.

A key scraped in the lock.

Her body shrieked in protest as she pushed to her feet and backed against a wall. She pulled the switchblade out of her pocket and pressed the spring. The blade snicked open. She hid it along the length of her thigh, staring with a dry mouth as the door opened.

Dragos slipped in, his massive fighter's body moving with liquid grace on quiet cat's feet. He carried a leather pack on one shoulder. The black metal shackles were gone. Leather harness straps crossed his chest. The hilt of the battle-axe and what looked like a sword were strapped to his back. Knives in sheaths were laced on his forearms, and the sheath of another short sword was buckled at his waist and tied at his thigh. His chiseled features were calm. Holy cow, he made Conan the Barbarian look like a wimp.

Relief almost brought her to her knees. Black stars danced in front of her. In an instant he was in front of her, hands on her shoulders, bracing her back against the wall.

'Damn it, you look like you're going to pass out,' he said.

'Well, I didn't know it was going to be you, did I?' She showed him the switchblade she was holding against her thigh.

His severe face lit with a smile. 'Surprise number one hundred thirty-four and counting.'

'You made that number up,' she accused. She pushed the blade against her leg. It closed with a snick and she slid it back into her jeans.

'Are you sure?' he said, sounding amused. 'You know how to use that thing?'

'Well enough. I'm not really a fighter, though.' It was sad but true.

'No, your nature's too gentle for that, isn't it?' He stroked her hair and pulled her with care into his arms.

She leaned against him, her world settling back into place. On a deep level she didn't have time to examine, it was a very disturbing experience. His body warmth drove the chill away. She put her arms around his waist and hugged him tight.

'I've had a lifetime of classes, but I haven't had to use any of it in real life. Yet.' She forced herself to breathe deep until the lingering dizziness passed. 'Just give me a chance to stick one of those two-legged cockroaches though, and I'm there.'

'They'll have to get through me first.' He gave her a gentle squeeze and stepped back.

'You were faster than I was afraid you might be.' She looked at his new acquisitions. 'It looks like you found a lot.'

'I located the key to the shackles, but I didn't find the Goblin captain. I found his rooms instead. He's a greedy son of a bitch. He had all kinds of loot. Half of it looked untouched.' He moved back to the door, listened for a moment and opened it. 'We need to hurry now. There are more Goblins moving about. It sounds like their evening meal is finished.'

He led the way and this time he moved much faster. She struggled to keep up but fell several paces behind. He slowed as he reached the final turn that led to the outside door. He stalked to the corner, completely silent as he reached for the battle-axe and unsheathed the short sword in a simultaneous motion.

She caught her breath at the sight. He was an über-warrior, magnificent and terrifying. Hey, when he could shift into a dragon he was his own tank and aerial force all at the same time. Add to that his magical capability and he was virtually a one-creature army. She had known he was one of the premiere Powers in the world, but as she saw him in motion, she began to get a glimmer of real understanding what that meant.

She eased closer but was careful to leave plenty of space between them. He glanced at her, leaning back against the wall. He nodded to her in approval. He pointed the sword at her and mouthed, 'Stay put.'

She nodded back. She wanted to obey that one.

He stepped into the corridor and twisted on one foot, bringing his big body around as he flung the battle-axe like a Frisbee. Continuing in the same smooth turn, he hurled the short sword in an overhand throw with as much ease as tossing a dagger. Without pausing, he drew the long sword and one of the knives and lunged forward out of sight.

She crossed her arms and gripped her elbows, tapping her toes and flinching at the sounds of battle.

Not that it was much of a battle. It was over in seconds. A moment later, Dragos stepped around the corner and beckoned her forward. 'None of these grunts have keys. Now it's your turn to do your stuff. It's ugly,' he warned her.

'I expect so,' she said, looking at him round-eyed. She rounded the corner.

At first she couldn't make sense of what she saw. When she did, she wished she hadn't. There were four dead Goblins strewn about the end of the corridor. Or at least she counted four heads, not all of which were still attached to their bodies. And not all the bodies had all their limbs. Black blood had sprayed the stone walls and great pools of it dotted the floor.

She gagged, her empty stomach twisting. Dragos strode forward.

'If you're going to vomit, make it quick,' he told her in a matter-of-fact voice.

He yanked the battle-axe out of the Goblin it had almost split in two and wiped the blade on the Goblin's leggings. Moving fast, he collected the rest of his weapons, cleaning the blades on the corpses and sheathing them again when he was done.

She focused on the great metal door, not the carnage, and gained control of her gag reflex. She stepped around the pools of blood. She paused at one spot and tried to figure out how to get across a large patch of Goblin blood. It looked like a greasy oil spill had spread between two sprawled bodies. If she weren't injured she would have leaped over it without a second thought. Her dilemma was solved as Dragos grabbed her by the elbows and gently swung her over to the other side.

The door had been barred, but he had already moved the thick wood plank. She grasped a thick lever with both hands and pulled down. The heavy door was hung well. It swung open on silent hinges.

They stepped outside into deepening dusk. The air seemed incredibly sweet outside the Goblin stronghold. The flatbed with the Honda was still where the Goblins had stopped. She shook her head when she saw the mangled wreck. It was a wonder she had survived.

'Now we have to haul ass,' said Dragos.

She looked around at the alien, wild landscape, and just like that, she fell into the crack. 'That's it,' she croaked. 'I'm done.'

His head whipped around, eyes narrowing. He said, *'What?'*

'I said I'm done.' Lead filled her hollow limbs. She swayed and blinked, but he kept blurring out of focus. 'I . . . I haven't eaten well or slept well in over a week. Then there was the wreck and then the Goblins. I'm spent. I don't have anything else. You'll have to go without me.'

'You are a stupid woman,' he said. He sounded furious. Why was he so mad at her? The world tilted as he swept her into his arms. *'I'm* not done.'

Holding her tight, he started to run.

She tucked her head under his chin and fell into a half-waking state. Afterward, she never did remember much of that run. She remembered it went on for hours. Dragos never faltered, never slowed. He broke into a light sweat, but his breathing remained deep and even. His steady grip cushioned her from any shocks.

She did note one thing and murmured a question when she realized he was not taking them back the way they had been brought.

'Hush,' he told her. 'I'll explain later. You just have to keep trusting me.'

That seemed to matter a lot to him. He kept bringing it up. She turned her face into his neck. 'Okay.' It wasn't like she had any choice at the moment.

'Good,' he said gruffly. His arms tightened.

That was the last they spoke for a long time.

At last he began to slow. She roused from her doze and struggled to lift her head and look around. They had left the barren, rocky landscape and Goblin fortress far behind and stood in a small clearing. He had run the rest of the day away.

The moon shone brighter than she had ever seen before. It hung huge and low and witchy over murmuring trees. The silver-limned and intensely shadowed edges of the clearing shifted with a fitful breeze, the rippling contours so lifelike, hidden faces seemed to peer out at them, whispering news of their arrival.

Running water trickled nearby. Dragos knelt and placed her on the ground near the water. It was a small brook. He put a hand at her shoulder blades and supported her as she struggled to sit up.

'The water's safe,' he told her. 'Drink as much as you think you can. You've got to be seriously dehydrated.'

He moved to the water's edge a few feet downstream from her, laid on his stomach and ducked his head all the way in.

Pia fell forward, desperate to provide relief for her parched mouth and throat. She scooped up cold handfuls and sucked them down. When the need to drink eased she splashed water over her face and arms, desperate to get the stink of the Goblin dungeon off of her. She scooped up more to drink and sighed.

Dragos came up for air at last, flinging back his head in a wet spray that sparkled in the moonlight.

'That's got to be one of the best things I've ever tasted,' she said.

It wasn't just thirst talking. The water was crisp and alive somehow, more nourishing and satisfying than anything else she could remember drinking. She could feel her wilted resources soaking it up greedily. It soothed the cramped, starved part of her soul into something resembling peace. Already she felt steadier than she had in a while, the sick sense of crisis brought on by exhaustion, injury and stress easing.

He grinned. 'It's being here, in the Other land. The heightened land magic makes everything more intense. If you like that, just wait until you see what else I have for you.'

She pushed back on her knees and sat up. 'What is it?'

'I found some food you can eat. I got you other things too, but nourishment comes first.' He opened the leather pack and pulled out a flat leaf-wrapped package and handed it to her.

She took it with obvious reluctance. 'Dragos, I don't think I could stomach anything you found in that hellhole.'

'Don't jump so fast to conclusions.' He nodded. 'Go ahead, open it.'

She pulled the leaves apart and the most mouthwatering aroma escaped. He broke off an end of the wafer she held and coaxed it between her lips. When the piece hit her tongue, it began to melt. She chewed and swallowed with a moan. It was indescribably delicious.

'Elven wayfarer bread,' she breathed. Vegetarian, nourishing in a way that fed the soul as well as the body and imbued with healing properties. 'I've heard about it, of course; who hasn't? It's legendary. But I've never had the chance to taste any before.'

He broke off another piece and fed it to her, watching as she closed her eyes and moaned again with delight. 'Eat every bite of that. It'll do you good,' he told her. 'I found a dozen wafers. We have plenty.'

She stared at him. A dozen wafers would fetch a fortune on the black market. Most people couldn't beg, borrow or steal the wayfarer bread. Oh. She looked down at what she held and her enjoyment dimmed. 'You found it in the Goblin captain's rooms?'

'Among other things. Remember I said half the loot was untouched?' He frowned. 'Why aren't you eating?'

'Oh, I will,' she assured him. She broke off another piece. 'It's too precious to waste, and I need it. It's just hard to enjoy someone else's misfortune.'

He smiled a little and touched the corner of her mouth. 'For all you know, some Elf suffered a minor annoyance when his or her pack got stolen, and they've forgotten all about it by now. You go ahead and relish every bite.'

'That's true.' The unknown Elf hadn't necessarily been hurt or killed. She took a deep breath. 'Aren't you going to eat any?'

'Not my kind of food,' he told her. 'I'll go hunting if I feel the need.'

Right. Carnivore. She went back to her meal.

He reclined on his side, propped his head in his hand and watched her enjoy the wayfarer bread. He waited until she had put the last piece in her mouth. Then he started to pull other things out of the pack and lay them in her lap. A light woolen Elven blanket, a tunic and leggings, a packet of soap – soap! – and a hairbrush. She stared at the treasures.

'I know how much you hated it in there,' he said.

'Oh. My. God.' She looked at him, teary. 'I think this is one of the nicest things anyone's ever done for me. Aside from the fact you saved my life I don't know how many times.'

'You saved me too, you know,' he said. He sounded thoughtful.

The need to wash became a crisis. 'I've got to get clean.'

'Pia, you're weaving where you sit. Why don't you wait until you've slept a little? We're going to rest here while I keep watch.'

Her hands started to shake. 'You don't get it. I can't stand another minute stinking like them. It makes my skin crawl.'

'Okay,' he said, frowning. 'If you need to get clean, you need to get clean. It's going to be cold. I'll gather some wood while you wash, and we'll have a fire.'

She paused. 'We're not going to worry about the firelight being visible?'

He shook his head and uncoiled from the ground. 'I'll hear anyone long before they get near enough to be a problem.'

She turned her back to him and knelt at the stream, already consumed with the thought of scouring the Goblin stink off her body. Self-consciousness tried to take over as she stripped off her ruined T-shirt and filthy bra, but she squashed it. At least it wasn't broad daylight. He had no doubt seen thousands of naked women before. (Thousands? No, definitely not the time to go there.) Nothing mattered more than getting that stink off of her.

The soap was Elven made too and heaven sent. It softened fast, lathered well in the cold stream, was gentle on her healing cuts and had a delicate fragrance that had her sighing with pleasure.

She washed and rinsed her torso and pulled on the clean tunic. She stripped out of her capris, anklet socks and sneakers. The anklet socks were especially awful. She had bled into one of her shoes, and one anklet was crusted with dried blood. They joined the pile of clothing that was going into the fire as soon as Dragos lit it.

She pulled the blanket over her shoulders and let it drape behind her in an attempt to preserve a little privacy and finished washing the rest of her body. Her body was racked with violent shivering by the time she yanked the leggings on, but nothing was going to stop her from dunking her head in the water and lathering and rinsing her grimy hair at least once.

She dunked her head underwater, gasping at the sharp chill. She was bent over the stream, struggling with shaking hands to work the soap through her wet hair, when Dragos's hands came over hers. 'Let me,' he said.

She leaned on her hands and gave herself over to his minis-trations. His long hard fingers massaged her scalp and worked the soap with patience through the long wet rope of hair that trailed in the stream. Her teeth were chattering by the time he finished scooping enough water to rinse through the length.

He wrung out her hair and slipped an arm underneath her waist to lift her to her feet. She scooped up the dirty clothes. 'Over here,' he said. He had laid campfire kindling, which was waiting to be lit. As soon as she threw the clothes on top of the woodpile, he flicked a few fingers at the woodpile and it blazed alight.

'Cool trick.' Her teeth clicked together.

'Comes in handy.'

He wrapped the blanket around her. He had her sit with her back to him. Then he brushed out her hair.

With the fire in front, wrapped by the blanket and Dragos's heat enveloping her from behind, she was toasty warm in no time.

'I'm crashing and burning fast,' she told him.

'I'm surprised you held up as long as you did,' he replied, setting the brush aside.

He pulled her onto his lap, wrapped his arms around her and coaxed her head onto his shoulder.

Her eyelids felt cased in cement. She couldn't hold them open. A great big pile of questions, doubts, thoughts and issues had piled up, but they were being held at bay by the oncoming coma that came toward her like a black train.

She made a huge effort and opened her eyes one last time to stare up at Dragos. His dark face was always going to be hard, always have an edge of the blade to it, but as he watched the fire, he looked as peaceful as she had ever seen him.

He was wicked bad, by far the scariest creature she had ever met, yet as she rested in the circle of his arms, she felt safer than she ever had in her life. His body was as strong and stable as the earth. Her eyelids drifted closed.

'You're right, I am a stupid woman,' she mumbled. 'I don't understand you.'

'Maybe you will someday,' he said, even though he could sense she had already plunged into sleep. He traced the elegant curve of her brow with a finger, followed the delicate arch of her ear. Her still-damp hair fell over his arm, an extravagant waterfall of moonlit gold.

Maybe you will someday, just as soon as I understand myself.

The dragon held her sleeping figure closer. He lowered his cheek to her head and looked around the clearing in bafflement, as if the quiet, peaceful scene could tell him who he was.

═ NINE ═

Pia was running for the sheer joy of it.

The wind played in her hair. The moon looked down from its throne in the royal purple sky and smiled at her. The night was brighter than she'd ever seen before, a velvet carpet strewn with stars that winked diamond bright and sang faint ice-cold snatches of song, of distant journeys and enchantments in other realms. The magic in the land nourished parts of her that had been crippled and half dead. She felt stronger, freer and wilder than she ever had before. She leaped high and reached up to tickle the edge of the moon, who laughed in delight.

She was in a field miles wide, with all the room in the world to stretch her legs. Distant trees shadowed the edges. A tall dark man with raven hair and gold raptor's eyes stood in the trees and watched her.

She didn't care. He couldn't catch her. Nothing could, not even the wind, unless she let it.

Pia.

She knew that voice. She loved that voice. She turned and saw her mother running toward her. In her true shape, her mother had an incomparable loveliness and shone brighter than the moon who bowed down before her.

Mom? She slowed and turned. She felt like a little girl again. *Mommy?*

They came together. She threw eager arms around her mother, who nuzzled her. *My sweet baby girl.*

I miss you so much, Pia told her. *Please come home.*

Her mother drew back and looked at her with great, liquid eyes. *I cannot. I have faded from your world. I no longer belong there.*

Then let me come with you, she pleaded. *Take me to wherever you are.*

A roar of denial shook the trees. It ran through the earth, which trembled at their feet. Pia looked back at the male, although her mother remained untouched by the disturbance and seemed unaware of the figure in the trees.

You cannot join me, darling. Your place is among the living. Exquisite eyes smiled at Pia. *Giving birth to you was the single most selfish thing I have ever done. Forgive me for leaving. I did not mean to abandon you.*

Tears clogged her throat. *I know you couldn't help it.*

I have come to warn you, said her mother. *Pia, you must not be in this place. There is too much magic here. It is why I never dared to take you to an Other land.*

She looked around. *But I like it here. It feels so good.*

You will be exposed here, and hunted. Go back. Starlight began to shine through her mother's figure. *Go back; blend in with humankind.*

No, don't go yet. Pia tried to reach for her.

But her mother had already faded, leaving a final message on the wind. *Be safe. Know that you are loved.*

She reached after her mother, almost grasping an answer to something important. She could almost make out where her mother had gone, could almost follow her, except the whispering wind curled around her and held her to the earth.

The whispering circled around her, stroked along delicate nerve endings, coaxing her, *Pia, stay.* That was not her true Name, but the Power behind the whispering was enough to make her hesitate. The wind became a dragon twining around her, brushing against her skin like a cat. *Stay. Live.*

She brushed her fingers along the hot skin of the beautiful, feral creature. It turned its head. Great molten, hypnotic eyes stared into hers and she was caught.

She woke up.

She was lying on the ground, wrapped in the Elven blanket, beside the glowing red coals of the dying campfire. Dragos crouched over her, hands cupping her head. He was whispering in a language she didn't recognize, but it tugged at her bones.

'What is it?' she asked in a sleepy voice. She glanced down at herself. She was gleaming with a faint, pearl-like luminescence. She jolted full awake. 'Goddammit, I lost hold of the dampening spell in that dream we had too. I've never lost control like that before. I can't keep doing this!'

He took a deep breath. His body was clenched. A fine tremor ran through his heavy muscles. He was paler than she had ever seen him, eyes dilated and stark.

'What's the matter?' she asked again. She laid a bright ivory hand against his cheek. 'What happened?'

'I put you down,' he said. His blade-honed face was drawn. 'I went to go wash at the stream. I wasn't gone long . . . I was just twenty feet away.'

'It's okay,' she said. 'Whatever happened, it's okay now.'

He was so upset, unlike anything she had seen from him. To date he had been calm, arrogant, infuriating, amused, angry, cautious, downright imperious. But this was like how he had been when she found him chained in the cell, only worse. It was hard to see such an indomitable male so shaken. She stroked his face.

He sank his fists into her hair as if to trap her more completely. 'I turned around,' he gritted, 'and I could see the fire through your body. You were transparent, Pia, and you were fading.'

'That's impossible,' she said.

Or was it? Her mind raced back to her dream. If she had started to fade – could her mother have visited her in truth? Her lips pulled into a bittersweet smile.

'No smiling. This isn't something to fucking smile about,' he snarled at her, his fists tightening. 'You were almost gone. My hands passed right through you. If I hadn't started calling you back, you would have disappeared for good.'

'Maybe, I guess, but I don't think so,' she said in an absent tone, letting her fingers slide through his hair. She loved the inky black strands of silk. There wasn't a kink or hint of curl in it. 'I don't think I could have gone where I tried to go. She said it wasn't my place.'

'What are you talking about?' His eyes narrowed, but the tension in his body dialed down a notch.

'I dreamed about my mother.' Her gaze went unfocused and she said, 'And I think it actually was her. When she left I tried to follow her.'

'You are never to do that again,' he said between his teeth. 'Do you understand?'

'Dragos,' she said, speaking with care because he was still so upset. 'You've got to stop giving me orders.'

No matter how gently she said it, it was still like a spark to dry tinder.

'Fuck you,' he snapped. He thrust his face down to hers, eyes flaring to lava and features hardening. 'You're *mine*. And you. Can't. Leave.'

'Whoa, there. I don't know what to say to you. You're like some stalker guy on steroids.' She threw back her hands and rolled her eyes. 'You are aware, aren't you, that you can't have slaves any longer. You know, abolition. Big war. Happened a hundred and forty, forty-five years ago.'

'Human history, human terms,' he snarled. 'They mean nothing to me.'

She had already known she shouldn't attribute human motives or emotions to him. Here was the reminder. The dragon was very close to the surface. The big body crouching over her was taut with menace. Every legend she had ever heard of a dragon's possessive, territorial nature came to mind.

Damn, it was enough to make her swallow hard but not, she realized, in fear. Muscle by muscle she relaxed. 'Okay then, big guy,' she said, soft and easy. 'You tell me what you mean.'

'I don't know.' That fierce, proud face was puzzled. 'All I know is you're mine to keep and protect. You can't fade away, and you can't die. I won't let you.'

She thought it was not the time to point out that she was going to die at some point. She had too much human in her.

'So, I'm yours for how long?' she asked, curious now that she decided to explore this path. 'Until you get tired of me, or you get bored again?'

'I don't know,' he said again. 'I haven't figured this out yet.'

A sudden rush of affection surprised her. He wasn't faking his perplexity. He wasn't putting on an act. 'That makes two of us,' she said. She thought of the Elven wayfarer bread, the hairbrush and the soap, and his thoughtfulness surprised her all over again. She reached up to run a finger down his throat. 'So, for the sake of argument, if I'm yours as you said, to keep and protect, that seems to me like you would want me to – be all right. To thrive?'

'Of course,' he said. He looked down at her hand as she drew circles on his chest, and the menace he exuded turned darker, smokier.

'Dragos,' she murmured, 'I don't thrive when someone barks orders at me all the time.'

She peeked at him to see how he reacted to her logic. He was frowning. 'It's how I talk to people,' he said.

'It's how you talk to your employees and servants, you mean?' she replied.

His frown deepened. She bit her lips to keep back a smile. How could she be so damn charmed by such a primitive thug? She had to establish a different footing with him or be mowed under by the sheer force of his personality.

'See, here's the thing.' She kept her voice gentle while she started to rub his chest in soothing circles. 'Someone barking orders at me makes me feel trapped and stifled. I understand you've gotten into a habit, but maybe,' she suggested, 'you could try not ordering me around sometimes. You know, just until you get bored and let me go.'

He had grown heavy-lidded as she stroked him, but at that his narrowed gaze snapped up to her face. She smiled at him, nonthreatening and relaxed. 'What if I don't get bored?' he said. 'What if I don't let you go?'

She was jolted by a sense of longing that swept over her. She lost her smile and looked away. 'We don't even know what we're talking about, anyway,' she said.

He loosened his grip on her hair, shifted his weight onto one elbow and took her luminescent hand. He tilted her arm and looked at it. 'You're remarkable. No, don't!' he said, as she remembered and began to dampen the glow. 'Let me see you as you really are, for a while at least. Look at how fast you're healing.'

She looked. The ugly black bruises that had mottled her

skin had almost faded. 'I feel good,' she confessed. 'Different, somehow. Better. More. Hey, am I the Bionic Woman?'

He smiled. 'It sometimes happens with halflings when they come to an Other land,' he told her. 'The heightened magic can help them access abilities and traits that might otherwise have remained latent.'

She tried to keep a tight grip on the hope that surged at his words but questions still leaked into her thoughts. Was this the explanation for everything she felt since they had crossed over? If what he said was true about her, might she be able to shift? What if she could end this sense of living a half life, the feeling of being caught between two incomplete identities, human and Wyr?

'I had no idea,' she said. 'My mother always refused to bring me over to an Other place. I've never had enough Power to cross over by myself. I barely have enough for telepathy.'

In the dream, her mother had said it was dangerous for her to be here. She glanced around the dim coal-lit clearing. That meant they should leave soon. The thought lacked urgency.

'Ah yes, your mother,' he replied, sounding distracted as he inspected her slender fingers, the graceful tilt of her wrist. 'Very soon we're going to have a talk about your mother, who she was and why that dumbass Elf loved her so much. We're also going to talk about why you're not right in the head and if you have any more IDs or stashes of cash hidden anywhere.'

She snatched her hand back and smacked him on the arm. 'None of that is any of your business! And just because he liked me but he didn't like *you* doesn't mean he's a dumbass Elf!'

He gave her a lazy, predatory smile as he moved his torso over hers. 'You're not afraid of me at all anymore, are you?'

She sobered. Call her crazy, but she thought he would rather cut off his hands than hurt her. 'So what if I'm not?' she muttered.

His beautiful, cruel mouth pulled into a smile. 'I think if you're not, it's a very good thing,' he said. He moved, and before she realized what he intended, he had her hands pinned over her head. 'It gives me all kinds of license to do bad things to you. With you. On you. In you.'

She jumped and her heart hammered. He looked at her

splayed and helpless underneath him and insinuated one heavy thigh between hers. He pushed up with his leg as he bit her neck in the exact same place where he had in their dream. He drank in her gasp and held her with ease as she tried to tug her hands free. Not that she tried all that hard.

Excitement took the express shuttle through her body. She stretched for the sheer enjoyment of feeling herself slide against his naked torso, and his brilliant gaze tracked every movement she made. She was feeling less human by the minute.

She licked her lips. 'Dragos, I don't think . . .'

'You don't think what?' His burning gaze swallowed her up.

'I don't think I'm as good as I thought I was,' she whispered. Her eyelids dropped down and she smiled.

'That's my girl,' he whispered.

He pushed her legs wider apart, settled between them and began a sensual assault on her, nibbling and licking. He pulled her lower lip between his teeth and suckled at the plump flesh, then thrust his tongue deep into her mouth.

They both groaned. He dug deeper into her, thrusting harder and harder. She tilted her head to open more to him. He shifted her wrists to one hand so that he could push the other under her tunic, running calloused fingers up to the soft swell of her breast. He grasped the plush mound with greedy care, found her nipple and began rolling it between his thumb and forefinger. He tugged at the sensitive flesh and gave it a light pinch.

Pleasure jolted through her as he played with her breast. Her breathing became choppy. She tugged harder, but he refused to let go of her wrists, his body hardening. She raised her legs to cradle his long body, shifting underneath him until his heavy, long erection lay nestled against her pelvis.

He hissed, face darkened with lust, and he reared up to grab hold of her tunic.

'No!' she cried, stiffening.

He froze. God love him, that dragon didn't even breathe.

'I don't have anything else to wear,' she explained. She gave him a shaky smile when his eyes flashed to hers.

The stricken look left his face. He let go of her wrists and sat back on his heels as she sat and yanked the tunic over her head. She tossed it to the ground. He put his hands to her rib cage and ran them up to cup her breasts.

'Goddamn,' he said. His normal deep voice had gone hoarse. 'Will you look at that.'

She looked down at them. The lines and curvature of her torso and breasts looked ultrafeminine against the brawn of his big hands and muscular arms. Her radiance and the dusky hue of his skin seemed to feed on each other. The paleness of her skin was creamier, the blush of her nipples pinker. The sinews of his hands and wrists shifted under skin that was a richer, deeper bronze.

She put her hands on his torso and watched as she ran them up his chest. Muscles rippled underneath her palms as he took in a shaking breath. She raked at his nipples with gentle fingernails. Part of her was ecstatic with shock. I am touching him. He is touching me.

He hissed and grabbed her fingers, coming over her as he bore her back down. He put his hands at her waist and, understanding what he wanted, she lifted her hips for him to pull the leggings off. He shifted to tear off his jeans and fling them aside. Then he slid back over her, heavy and hard and naked, and they were lying skin to skin.

If he had seemed hot before, he had since turned volcanic. She could feel his heart hammering against her breast. She lost herself in the enjoyment of rubbing herself against him, running her hands up the considerable musculature of his powerful back.

He slid down her body, running his open, shaking mouth along the length of her neck, down her collarbone, until he could feast on her breasts. He sucked and bit at the succulent flesh, gripping her nipples between his teeth and flicking at them with his tongue, one after the other until she arched and cried out, incoherent with sharp delight.

Then he slid down farther, licking and biting his way along the curve of her waist. He gripped the inside of her slender knees and held her splayed as he sucked the tender flesh of her inner thighs. She writhed in his hold, crying out again as she lifted her hips up to him.

He paused to look his fill of her. Elegant bone structure, radiant cream and dusky pink, she lay on an extravagant pillow of tangled pale gold hair. He could track his journey across her body in the luscious suck-bruises that were blooming at the undersides of her breasts, the insides of her thighs. Her violet dark eyes were huge and shimmering with desire, just like they had in the dream.

Just as he had craved ever since. Desire for him, the monster, the Great Beast.

But this was no dream, and he was so hard and full from wanting her he was in superb pain. He looked at the plump, fluted pink of her labia topped with a tangle of white-gold curls. She was slick with moisture, drenched with it, and his heavy cock leaped at the generous evidence of her arousal. He whispered, 'I'm going to eat you until you scream.'

Her slender feet curled and a deep groan burst out of her. He lowered his head and continued his assault, licking and biting and sucking with shaking greed. He drew her stiff little bud into his mouth and suckled as she bucked and shook with the force of the pleasure spiraling through her.

She lifted up on her elbows, panting, and stared at what he was doing to her. That dark head and those broad shoulders between her shivering thighs, his blade-cut face drenched with arousal as he worked her, was a sight so erotic it hurtled her into a climax. She hung her head back and squealed as she came with an intensity she had never known before.

He never stopped. He kept licking and suckling, his mouth absorbing the ripples that cascaded through her. He put a flattened hand on her lower abdomen as she clenched, feeling the rhythm of her climax. He wrung her out and still he continued to suck.

The sensitivity became too much. She sank trembling fingers into his hair, tried to pull his head back. 'Stop, I can't . . . I can't . . .'

He made a throaty sound, his hot gold gaze flashing as he focused on her sweaty dazed face and suckled harder. He plunged two fingers deep inside her, and just like that, he pushed her into another climax, this one longer and more intense than the first. He gobbled that climax down and without stopping shoved her into a third.

Her torso arched off the ground and the tendons in her neck distended as a thin, breathless scream broke out of her. She was completely taken over by what he was doing to her. The brilliant star-studded night sky disappeared as her eyes filled and spilled over.

At last he pulled away and crawled up her, breathing harsh, intent carving every flex and shift of his body. She had no words as she stared up at him. He was such a splendid aggressive male, the broad muscles in his chest and upper arms quivering, his large erect penis hanging long and heavy between rock-hard thighs. She looked into his eyes as she curved a hand around the broad mushroom head and stroked.

With that he went bat-shit crazy for the third time in three days. He lunged down at her, his lungs working to take in great gulps of air. He scooped an arm under her hips to yank her up for his entry. She guided him and he slammed all the way inside.

She shrieked at the invasion and dug her nails into his back. He was no delicate, diffident lover. He was like nothing she had ever experienced, a tsunami crashing over her head and destroying her old identity, reshaping her life.

He wrapped his other arm around her, clutching her by neck and hips as he began to plunge into her in heavy, powerful strokes. He was groaning in her ear with every thrust as they mated like the animals they were. The increasing pressure, the sound of their flesh coming together, her total lack of control, had her digging her nails into his back. She stretched and whimpered, lost in the inexorable rhythm of her body, and came again.

He threw back his head, face contorted in savagery, astonishment. With a last convulsive thrust he made a muffled sound and joined her in climax. She felt him pulse deep inside and she clenched everything she had around the delicious length of him, holding on to the sensation, on to him. He rocked into her, panting, eyes closed as he gushed into her. She put a hand at the back of his head, an arm around his waist, holding him as he held her, murmuring in her ear, yes, there you are, yes.

He turned his face, found her mouth and kissed her as he held them so tight together at pelvis and hip, for a while it felt as if they had fused together and become one creature, light and dark, yin and yang.

It was then her shattered consciousness caught up with what he had growled in her ear as he fucked her. Mine, he had said. You're mine. You're mine.

She drifted, looking at the silhouette of the back of his

head against the sky as she rubbed her cheek against his, as his weight bore her down. Something in her was sputtering and trying to shift into overdrive in reaction to what just happened. It was too much. She couldn't think.

He started to move his hips again, pulling out, pushing in, his breathing deepening. Oh God, he was still huge and hard. Not human. She made an amazed noise at the back of her throat, clutching at him as he worked inside her. It was too gorgeous. She thrust up with her hips, matching his pace.

This time a moan tore through his chest and he shook all over as he started to pulse. She worked inner muscles and rocked him through the climax, murmuring in his ear. He turned his face into her neck.

He pulled out, face drawn. She woofed in surprise as he flipped her onto her stomach and yanked her hips up so that she was on her knees. Her tangled hair settled in a cloud over her face. 'Not deep enough,' he groaned. 'Got to get deeper.'

More than willing, she spread her knees and arched her pelvis back. She reached between her legs to help guide him as he pushed into her from behind. The slick, hot, velvet length of his cock felt even bigger this way. She murmured a throaty encouragement as he buried himself to the hilt. She was taken over not just by his overwhelming sexuality but by this strange creature who lived inside her body and who felt more sensuous, more female, and more desired than she ever had before.

He covered her, one arm low around her waist to hold her for his frenzied thrusts, the other hand planted on the ground beside hers so that he bore most of his weight. This time the pistoning of his hips was relentless. He drove hard and steady as he buried his face in the back of her neck, his breath shuddering against her skin. The pressure built again, but this time she wasn't sure she could take it. She sobbed and clutched at the ground for purchase. Grass tore under her fingernails.

He sank his teeth into the back of her neck as his Power curled around her. *Come with me.* He shifted to put his hand between her legs, to rub long fingers along the place where he entered her and to pinch her clitoris. He shoved in hard one last time and held taut. His Power rippled over her, through her, with his climax.

Her mind went incandescent. She flew apart.

Dragos poured everything he had into her. It came roaring up from the base of his spine as he locked himself in the tight glove of her sheath. This wasn't sex. He'd had sex countless times. Sex was a simple coupling and release. More often than not, half an hour later he would have already forgotten the female's name.

This was something he'd never done before. This was something far more elemental and necessary than sex. Feasting on her didn't ease his hunger but fed his need. Working inside her wasn't enough. Climaxing didn't assuage the lust. It built the frenzy. She absorbed everything he did to her and amplified it back, and bloomed even more lustrous and intoxicating. He had to drive into her so deep he never came back out.

He came back to awareness. He still covered her from behind, was still inside her, his hand spanning the graceful arc of her pelvis. Tremors quaked through her body. The slender muscles in her thighs quivered against his. She gasped for breath in quiet sobs.

What had he done? He pressed his lips to her neck and drew them along the sleek angle of her shoulder. He withdrew his hand from her pelvis to brush the tangled cloud of her hair out of the way as he tried to see her face. 'Ssh,' he murmured. 'Easy.'

She was too weak to stay on her hands and knees without his hold supporting her. His softening penis slipped out of her as she sank to the ground. She rested her head on her arms. He shifted to lie on his side, one thigh draped over the back of hers. He smoothed her hair, rubbed her shivering back.

Her face seemed wet. Was she crying? Had he hurt her? The questions knifed him. He could have sworn she was with him the entire way.

He stopped breathing. He eased fingers under her chin to coax her head up and turn her toward him. Her face and those brilliant eyes were devastated and wide-open. She looked as beautiful and fragile as cut crystal. His gut clenched.

'I lost control,' he whispered.

That, along with the worry darkening his eyes, anchored her back in her body. Was he trying to apologize?

'So did I,' she whispered back.

'I've never done that before.' He touched the delicate skin

at the corner of her eye, rubbed the ball of his thumb along her lower lip.

'Neither have I,' she confessed. A smile broke over her face.

His fingers dropped to trace the curve of her lips. 'Are you – all right?'

She was a mess. She was euphoric, an emotional train wreck. She needed to go into a quiet, dark room somewhere and try to make sense of everything that had happened – and that he had done – to her.

But first she had to wipe that uncertainty off his face.

Her smile widened, and she told him the truth. 'No,' she said. She leaned over and pressed a kiss to those incredible seductive lips. 'You demolished me. I had no idea anybody could do the things you did. And I want to know how soon we can do it again.'

The worry vanished and an answering smile lit his eyes. He looked at her mouth. 'I want a lot of things.'

'What you do with your tongue is a sin,' she teased.

That vulnerability he saw in her still lurked around the edges, but he chose to go with her attempt to lighten things up. He told her, 'There are many advantages to being a bad man.'

'Such as?'

He sat up and pulled her onto his lap, turning her so that she faced him, torso to torso, groin to groin, her slender legs stretched out on either side of him. It was an intimate position made even more so by their nudity, a position perfect for making love. He wrapped his arms around her and she curled hers around his neck.

Even sitting on his lap as she was, his body was so much bigger and longer than hers, he had to tilt his head down to go nose to nose with her.

'A comfortable lack of conscience,' he said. 'The enjoyment of unbroken sleep. An uncomplicated desire to discover every possible carnal pleasure with the beautiful woman in his arms.'

Her eyes brightened at the compliment and crinkled at him. He smiled back and kissed her, a long, leisurely exploration that curled her toes.

'Well, I think you keep a very well-hidden secret,' she told him when she could breathe again.

He cocked an eyebrow.

She tapped a finger against his chest. 'There is a pretty charming creature buried deep inside there. You should let him out more often.' He laughed out loud, but then the look on his face turned calculating. She laughed too as she realized she found even that charming. God, she was a goner. She warned, 'Don't make me regret telling you that.'

'I'll try not to take too much advantage,' he said.

'Oh, thank you very much.' She rolled her eyes. That probably meant he was going to wring everything he could out of it. Her stomach rumbled. 'I'm starving again.'

They sat in reach of the pack. He gave her a leaf-wrapped wafer, which she unwrapped. She ate while he tried to run his fingers through her tangles. 'We did a number on your hair,' he said. He sent a gentle pulse of Power through his hands and her hair smoothed out.

She swallowed a bite of the delicious wayfarer bread. 'You ever get tired of being a multibillionaire businessman, you could make another fortune as a hairdresser.'

'I'll be sure to keep it in mind,' he said. He didn't tell her he had no interest in anyone else's hair but hers. He looked around the clearing. 'We've lingered too long here. We should leave as soon as you finish.'

'Right,' she said, looking around also. 'And why did we come this way, instead of going back the way they brought us?'

'You've never been to an Other land before, right?' She nodded, and he continued, 'This isn't the best analogy, but it will work for now. Time and space buckled when the earth was formed, and the buckling created dimensional pockets where magic pooled. Picture them like lakes or large bodies of water. There are lakes of varying sizes. Some are quite small, more like ponds, and some stand by themselves. Others are almost as big as oceans and are linked together, with streams or rivers. I can sense that this' – he gestured around them – 'is a very large area connected to other large land areas.'

'How do you do that?' she asked.

He frowned, not, she could see, from irritation at her question but more in an effort to figure out how to explain what he experienced. It must be something he had known how to do for so long it came automatically to him, like breathing.

'I put my hand down on the land and send out my awareness. It doesn't take a heavy pulse of Power. It's more like a knowing that comes to me.'

She tried to imagine what that must feel like. Maybe it was the same kind of knowing she got when she sensed magic was around, or a spell had been cast, just more focused on the land. She wanted to try it out for herself sometime. 'So there are different ways in and out of this place.'

'Correct. We had a better chance of getting away by taking off in an unpredictable direction than going back the way they had crossed over. We may even be able to go so far north that we can connect to New York or get at least close to it.'

'Since we're talking, why doesn't technology work in Other lands?'

'That's a bit of a misnomer. Some technologies work if they're of a passive design, if they utilize natural forces that are already present like water flow, and if they don't involve combustion more complicated than a wood-burning stove or a boiler. Modern crossbow designs aren't exactly passive, but they're fine to use because they don't ignite. You can also bring over things like factory-made glass windows, artwork, various convenience appliances like Melitta or French-press coffee-makers and even composting toilets, as long as what you bring over is not dependent upon electricity and you can transport it safely through a dimensional passage.'

She chuckled. 'You sound so domestic.'

He smiled. 'I have quite a comfortable house in an Other land connected to upstate New York where we've done a lot of experimenting to see what works and what doesn't. It is designed to take maximum advantage of the sun, which heats water for an underfloor hypocaust system that keeps the house warm. Very Roman. As far as why certain technologies don't work?' He shrugged as he ran his fingers through her hair. 'There are a couple of theories bandied about, but the short answer is nobody knows for sure.'

She tilted her head back, reveling in the petting. 'A single-action revolver isn't a very complicated device, nor is a flintlock rifle, but I've heard that even simple guns are too dangerous to use.'

'You're right. Simple guns are just the application of

gunpowder, fire and lead, with a barrel. Interestingly the more primitive the gun is, the longer you could use it in an Other land. Automatic weapons seize or misfire as soon as they're brought over. You might get a few more shots fired out of a simpler, more historic model. You might possibly get as many as a half-dozen rounds fired off, but the amount is never predictable and in the end the gun will always misfire.'

She frowned. 'Good way to lose your eyesight or your hand.'

'Or your life,' he said. 'One possible explanation is the Living Earth Theory. What if the world was a gigantic entity? When you use a living creature as a conceptual model, then the earth would have discrete parts, organs, limbs, veins, muscles, a skeletal structure and arteries and so on. What if the Other lands are more essential to this organism's overall system than other places are, more like the artery than the outlying vein, or a vital organ as opposed to one you can survive without? What if the magic that is so strong over here and that dampens, even sabotages, certain technologies is Earth's defense mechanism?'

'Kind of like white blood cells?' she said. 'If you use that analogy, maybe you could shoot simpler guns a few more times because it would take the immune system longer to recognize them.'

'Exactly. The theory is more poetry than science, but I like it. There's also a modified Living Earth Theory that knocks out the concept of a world entity. It focuses instead on individual pockets of Other land as collective "minds" that are created from the magic-drenched land and regional wildlife, although these minds aren't necessarily conscious as we currently understand consciousness. In this theory, the concept of magic acting as a defense mechanism and hampering technology is still the same.'

She smiled, intrigued and delighted by this new glimpse into him and his active, curious mind. 'You're quite the scientific thinker, aren't you?' she said.

His eyebrows rose and he nodded. 'I like to look for underlying patterns and meaning to the world. I do a lot of reading in scientific journals.'

She finished her meal and licked her fingers for any lingering sweetness. His gaze dropped to her mouth, and she felt him harden against her inner thigh. Her breathing hitched.

But he moved her from him, rose to his feet and offered her a hand to pull her upright. She was too sore to be disappointed. She told herself that a couple of different times as she scooped up the crumpled tunic and leggings and the blanket. She went to the stream to rinse away the evidence of their . . . whatever.

What was the word for what they had done? Lovemaking was too pretty. Sex seemed too simple and basic. Mating sounded like it could be too permanent. She bit her lip as anxiety threatened to knock her sideways.

It's too much to think about. It's too big. He really did demolish me. I don't know who that hellcat slut was that tore up grass and screwed her brains out. I don't know who I am anymore.

She shut down those thoughts before she careened too far out of control. She reasserted the dampening spell. She sighed with resignation as she turned her hands over and looked at them. Predawn was lightening the clearing to gray, and they were just normal dim, human-looking hands.

A real hot meal, a bed, a stable schedule. Going to bed in the evening. Getting up in the morning. The things you take for granted until you don't have them anymore.

She dragged the tunic and leggings on and sat on the ground to pull on her tennis shoes. She bit back a grimace at their dingy state and added it to her list of grievances. A hundred thousand dollars down the toilet. Three IDs gone. No car. No socks. No underwear.

And what did she do? She went and had *sex* with the cause of all of her problems. Sure, it wasn't the yawn-and-make-up-a-grocery-list-until-he's-finished kind of sex. It was a kind she had never even imagined was possible, a what-the-hell-is-my-name-again kind of sex, but sex was all they'd had. She was worse than a fool if she tried to make it into anything else – she was a Wyr-dingbat, and wasn't that a god-awful sorry concept for a creature.

She yanked her shoelaces tied as she bitched to herself; then she glared at the object of her obsession.

He had rinsed at the stream too and pulled on his jeans and boots. He was on one knee by the dying fire. He laid his hand on the red coals and with one last pulse they went black. She sucked in a breath. So, okay, maybe he was a what-the-hell-is-my-name-again kind of guy.

His head came up and his body stiffened. He twisted to stare in the direction of a light breeze that blew through the nearby trees.

What is it? She drew in a deep breath, scenting the breeze. She caught a hint of stench.

He leaped upright. 'Run.'

≡ TEN ≡

She jumped to her feet and grabbed the blanket and hairbrush with shaking hands. She started to stuff them into the bag.

No more Goblins. Please God. I'll be good and eat all my peas.

'Forget all that. Drop it.' He lunged for his weapons. *'Go.'*

If there was one thing she could do well. She dropped everything, whirled and ran.

Everything inside went on red alert, all systems flashing. Adrenaline kicked her ass. Her vision sharpened, her sense of smell heightened and her hearing became more acute. She plotted out the best path ahead of her at the same time as she strained to hear any hint of pursuit.

There was nothing, no sound. There was just the wind waltzing through the trees, the sound of her own breathing gone ragged from fright and Dragos racing behind her. But she caught another whiff of Goblin stink. Her heart lurched.

Dragos said in a calm voice behind her, 'Fast as you can, Pia.'

Right. She tucked her chin in, sought and found her stride, then kicked it out.

Dragos raced after her as the sky became brilliant with sunrise. Pia seemed to have gone weightless. Damn, she ran like a cheetah. Maybe faster. Hell of a thing to watch. She sailed over obstacles like fallen tree trunks and rocks, making the leaps look effortless, as if she simply chose to pick up her feet and fly. He found room in himself for one more surprise as he discovered he was falling behind.

Good girl. If she had endurance as well as speed, they might be okay.

Pia let her mind go blank and lived in the moment. Nothing existed beyond the deep rhythm of her breathing, the athletic flex of muscle and bone, the sound of Dragos running behind her. They had plunged deep into the forest so that the infinite bowl of the sky became obscured with heavy boughs of green, but the morning light brightened and the day grew warmer until her skin was coated in sweat.

The forest was silent around them, ancient tree trunks twisted with secrets and imprisoned by creeping vines. She realized that since the Goblins had brought them over the day before, she hadn't heard another single creature nearby, not a rustle, peep or tweet. Maybe it was because she was in the presence of the most apex predator of them all. Or maybe it was because Goblins swarmed through the forest like a terminal disease. Or both.

I don't blame any of you, she thought. I wouldn't rustle, peep or tweet either if I were you.

Then like a chill mist rising from the ground, a sense of cold Power crept over her. It licked along her overheated skin and tightened over her body, squeezing like a boa constrictor wrapping around its prey.

Panicked revulsion closed her throat muscles, or perhaps the constriction of Power did. She stumbled to a halt, instinct driving her to claw at her neck.

Dragos whirled to face back the way they had come. As Pia looked over her shoulder, he roared. Tendons stood out in his neck, and the massive muscles of his chest and arms clenched with the force of his fury. The memory of what had happened in New York faded to triviality next to this apocalyptic noise. Standing as she was so close to him, even in his human form the Power in his roar ripped through the fabric of the world.

The hair at the back of her neck rose. Terror bolted through her from an atavistic place deeper than conscious choice.

The sound shredded the constriction around her throat. The

chill constriction of Power receded. Suddenly she could breathe again. She gulped air.

Dragos turned, the savage bones of his dark face transformed with rage and hate. The hot gold of his eyes were twin suns, and his pupils had changed to slits. 'Now we know for sure,' he growled. 'Urien is here and trying to slow us down. Run.'

She fell back a few steps, still staring at him. He narrowed that lambent alien gaze on her and tilted his head, the very picture of male exasperation. Alrighty. She threw up her hands in an I'm-going-already gesture, spun on one heel and ran for her life.

Not long afterward, she broke out of the edge of the forest and faltered as she looked ahead at a wide, flat plain. There was no cover for creatures of their size. She glanced back, uneasy, as he caught up with her.

He had the battle-axe and sword strapped to his back again. The rage in his hawkish face had eased but his eyes were still lava hot.

'Can you change?' she asked him.

'Not quite. I tried back in the forest.' He nodded at the plain. 'It's not like they don't know we're here.'

She bounded forward, and he got the chance to admire just how fast she could run unfettered by trees and underbrush.

To avoid wasting breath, she asked him telepathically, *I still can't hear them; can you?*

No, I think Urien has been cloaking them, he told her. *Otherwise I would have heard them a lot sooner. They would never have gotten so close.*

That, and he'd allowed himself to be distracted by her sensuality. Damn it, he had known they had lingered too long, but he had done it anyway. This was all his fault. She was in danger again because of him. She messed with his head and his old, well-honed instincts short-circuited. He was never going to get so impatient with his men again when they fell for a beautiful face.

They're chasing us while believing you can shift into a dragon? Even telepathically her mental tone indicated how suicidal she thought that was.

Unless they know otherwise, he said. *Could be why they're so aggressive. Maybe they do know about the Elven poison and that it should be wearing off soon.*

She tripped and almost went down. He leaped forward to grab her arm. She turned a horror-filled gaze toward him. *But that would mean the Elves – Ferion – knew we would be attacked.*

Or it means at the very least that one of the Elves passed some helpful information on to an interested party, he agreed. He urged her back into a run. *And to be fair, for all Ferion knew, you did what you said you would and drove me over the Elven border and left me.*

Screw fair, she snapped. *I see that Elf again, I'm gonna rip him a new one.*

He couldn't help but grin. *I want to be there when you do.*

She dropped back to keep pace at his side. When he frowned a question at her, she said, *Don't worry about me, big guy. I can beat any pace you set.*

He laughed out loud. *I just bet you can, lover.*

She tossed her head. *I'm just bored with rubbing your nose in it.*

Despite their banter, they both knew their situation was growing more desperate. He kept watch behind them and soon he saw a horde of Goblins running out of the forest. Along with them appeared a score of armed riders on horseback.

Pia glanced behind as well. *Goblins don't ride,* she said. *Even I've heard that. Horses won't tolerate them.*

That'll be their allies, the Dark Fae, he told her. He realized his raptor's eyesight was much better than hers. He could see the Fae riders perfectly.

For the first time during their flight, her face showed strain. *They have crossbows.*

Buck up, girly girl. He gave her his machete smile. *Things are just getting interesting.*

He picked up speed, and true to her boast, she kept pace, her mane of blonde hair flying behind and long gazelle legs flashing. Damn, he was proud of her.

The land broke up ahead of them, a rocky bluff rising along the horizon. They had run perhaps a half mile more when a dozen Dark Fae riders appeared along the top of the bluff.

The riders on the bluff weren't riding horses.

They were astride Fae creatures that looked like giant dragonflies. Huge, black-veined, transparent wings glimmered with rainbow hues.

Pia slowed and came to a stop when she saw them. Beside her, Dragos did the same. She pressed a hand to her side and turned in a circle. They were trapped.

She sat down on the ground and put her head in her hands. He knelt beside her and put an arm around her shoulders. He didn't say anything, and neither did she. There wasn't anything to say.

Once they had stopped running, their pursuers slowed and approached with more caution. The Goblins spread out in a half-circle formation, the Dark Fae riders interspersed among them. The Dark Fae atop the bluff remained where they were, sitting astride the giant dragonfly creatures while they watched the scene unfold below.

Pia shaded her eyes as she stared at them. The third one from the left radiated a chill Power unlike any of the others. She swallowed, trying to relieve her dry throat. 'Over there,' she said. 'The Fae King is on the bluff, isn't he?'

Dragos sat behind her and pulled her against his chest. 'Yes. He's waiting to see if he's needed.'

'Still no shift,' she said. It wasn't a question.

He shook his head. 'I need a little more time.'

He needed time they didn't have. She turned her face into his sun-warmed skin. His breathing was slow and easy. She marveled at his calm.

She wasn't calm. She was running around inside her head like a crazy person, her heart still doing the jackrabbit dance. She thought of the beating the Goblins had given her. She thought of Keith and his bookie, both dead. She thought of the switchblade in the pocket of her leggings.

Dragos released her, rose up on his knees and removed the weapons harness. He laid the battle-axe and sword aside. Then he removed the short sword he had buckled at his waist and put it on the ground with the other weapons. He stared at the approaching host, eyes narrowed, as he told her, 'Maybe if I don't fight, I can negotiate with them to let you go.'

'You can't just surrender,' she said. 'They're going to kill you!'

'Probably not right away.' His expression was all brutality and harsh angles. 'If I surrender, it may buy some time. If I can get you away, you could try to get back to my people in New York and tell them what happened. They would keep you safe.'

He meant they might not kill him right away because they would torture him. She felt her bile rise.

She studied the Dark Fae King on the bluff. She had never hated anyone so much, especially someone she hadn't met before.

He was another of the world's premiere Powers, one of the oldest of the Elder Races. His knowledge and memory of Earth's lore and history would be extensive. As Dragos had pointed out, there was no telling what Keith might have blabbed before she stopped him up with the binding spell. And Urien had Elven connections, if not Ferion, then perhaps one of the other Elves who had witnessed her discussion with Ferion and had heard enough to speculate.

'It won't work anyway,' she said in a flat voice. 'They're not going to let me go.'

He glanced down at her, not bothering to argue. 'Then we fight.'

'I won't be captured,' she told him. She dug into her pocket and withdrew the switchblade. She pressed the lever and the blade snicked open.

Quicker than sight, he grabbed her wrist. His eyes blazed. 'The fuck are you doing?' he snapped. 'You won't be captured? Then we *fight*. We don't give up.'

She glanced at Goblins and Dark Fae. There were so many of them, they were a small army. They were almost in bow-shot range.

She put a hand over his. 'Dragos, this time will you trust me? Will you let me try one more thing and not ask me any questions about it?'

His hand and face were like stone, his body clenched.

She fought a sense of rising panic and kept her voice soft. 'Please,' she said. 'There isn't much time.'

His fingers loosened. He let her go. She rose to her knees and faced him. He held still and watched her face as she put the tip of the blade against the white scar at his shoulder. She concentrated on the dark bronze of his bare skin. She bit her lip and tried to make her hand move, but all she did was start to shake. Her grip on the switchblade turned white-knuckled.

'Damn it,' she gritted. 'I can't cut you.'

His hand came over hers again. This time he gave a quick jerk and the blade bit into his skin, right over the scar. Hot, brilliant blood began to flow from the cut. She took a choppy breath and nodded to him. He let go of her again.

The second bit was a lot easier. She drew the blade across her palm. It was a good deep cut. Pain blossomed and her own blood began to drip down her wrist.

The advancing army had crossed into bow-shot range, close enough she could hear the Goblins laugh and call to one another.

Talk about a last-ditch effort. Wish I knew if this would work. Guess we'll find out soon enough.

'Here goes nothing, big guy,' she muttered. She met his falcon-sharp eyes and slapped her open cut against his.

For a few seconds it seemed nothing happened. Then something flared and flowed out of her, passed through her palm and entered him. His head fell back. He gasped as he swayed on his knees. His Power roared in response.

She swayed, dizzy from the transference. Then Dragos shimmered and expanded so fast she fell on her back.

She struggled to prop herself up on her elbows, staring up openmouthed at the appearance of the enormous dragon who stood over her.

Oh. My. God. She had imagined what he must look like. She had caught that one glimpse of his shadow flowing over the beach. Nothing could have prepared her for the impact of the real thing. He had to be the size of a private jet.

He was varying shades of bronze that had an iridescent glint in the sunshine. His wide, heavy-muscled chest was right overhead. Her head bobbled back and forth as she took in the long legs planted on either side of her. The bronze color darkened to black at the ends of his legs. His feet had curved talons that had to be the length of her forearm. His body narrowed to powerful haunches and long tail.

She stared for a frozen moment at the slit in the sheath of thick bronze hide between his hind legs, covering the region of his genitals. There didn't appear to be any part of him that was vulnerable.

Massive shadows unfurled across the ground. He had opened his wings and mantled like an eagle.

Her body rediscovered how to move. She scrambled backward on hands and feet, scuttling like a crab.

He arched his long serpentine neck. He tilted down a horned triangular head that was the length of her body so that he could look at her with eyes that were great pools of molten lava. With a sound that sliced the air, he whipped his tail back and forth.

'*That's* my long, scaly, reptilian tail. And it's bigger than anyone else's,' Dragos said in a voice that was deeper, larger, yet still recognizable as his. One huge eyelid dropped in an unmistakable wink.

She collapsed in hysterical laughter.

'Stay down,' the dragon told her. He lowered his head as he turned to the bluff, a sleek, sinuous behemoth. He bared his teeth in a vicious challenge. '*BRING IT ON, YOU SON OF A BITCH.*'

One by one the Dark Fae riders rose into the air on their dragonfly steeds. They turned and flew away.

It was impossible to see, but she sensed the predator in him vibrating with the instinct to give chase. He held himself back, though, and she knew why. He wouldn't leave her unprotected with the Goblin/Fae army so near.

She pushed up on one elbow to stare in the direction of their pursuers. The Goblins and Fae riders had turned away. They were in full retreat.

The sound of ripping soil had her looking back at the dragon. He was digging his talons into the ground as he snarled at their retreat.

'Dragos,' she said. He looked at her. She jerked her head toward the retreating army. 'Go.'

He needed no further encouragement. He crouched and sprang into the air. A roar split the sky like a thunderclap. The Goblins began to scream as the killing began. She was ferociously, vindictively glad.

It was not so much a battle as it was extermination. After Dragos's first spectacular dive and roll when he winged low over their heads and spouted fire, she couldn't watch anymore. She turned onto her stomach, put her arms over her head and waited for it to be over.

The stink of Goblin was overcome with the smell of oily

smoke. It was not long before silence fell over the plain. There was no one left to do a body count. None of their enemies made it off the plain alive.

She nestled her nose deeper in the tall, sweet-smelling grass. The sun was high in the sky. It was warm on her back and shoulders. A quiet rustling in the grass grew closer. A shadow fell over her. Something very light tickled her forearms that covered the back of her head. It whuffled in her hair.

She scratched an arm. 'Did you kill the Fae horses?'

The whuffling stopped. Dragos said in a cautious voice, 'Was I not supposed to?'

She shrugged. 'It just wasn't their fault.'

'If it helps any, I was hungry and ate one.' Another whuffle.

She couldn't help but chuckle. 'I guess that does help some.'

She rolled over. He had stretched out alongside her, his great body between her and the remains of the Goblin/Fae army. His wings, a dramatic sweep of bronze darkening to black at the tips, were folded back. His hide glinted in the sun. She lifted her head and looked in the direction of a few plumes of smoke. His triangular head came down in front of her, golden eyes keen. 'You don't need to look over there,' he said in a gentle voice.

She sat up and leaned against his snout. She laid her cheek against him. Close up, she could see a faint pattern like scales in his hide. She stroked the wide curve of one nostril. It seemed somewhat softer than the rest of him. He held very still, breathing light and shallow.

'What does that feel like?' she asked him.

'It feels good.' He sighed, a great gust of wind, and he seemed to relax. 'Thank you for saving my life again, Pia Alessandra Giovanni.' He made the syllables of her human name sound musical.

'Back atcha, big guy,' she whispered.

After a few more moments he withdrew, giving her plenty of time to straighten. She looked up, way up at his long triangular head silhouetted against the afternoon sun. 'You have,' he said, 'two choices.'

'Choices are good.' She pushed to her feet, all of a sudden feeling tired and achy again. 'Choices are better than orders.'

'You can ride,' he told her. 'Or I can carry you.'

'Ride? Hot damn.' She shaded her eyes and eyed his enormous bulk. 'That might be more excitement than I can deal with right now. I'm not seeing any seat belts up there.'

'You got it.' Giving her plenty of time to adjust, he wrapped the long claws of one foot around her with such precision he didn't cause so much as a scratch or pinch. When he tilted his foot, she found she had quite a comfortable hollow in which to sit. He lifted her up so that he could look at her. 'All right?'

'I'm feeling a little Fay Wray here, but otherwise it's great,' she told him. 'You know, if you weren't a multibillionaire, you could make a good living as an elevator.'

He snorted a laugh. Then the world fell away as he leaped into the air. Anything else she might have said was lost in the beat of his huge wings, in her earsplitting shriek.

I take it all back, she shouted at him telepathically. She had no breath left from shrieking to try to speak out loud. *Forget about producing Valium, or elevator and hairdresser careers. You could be the world's only living roller coaster. Hey, I bet Six Flags would pay you a fortune.*

I see the lunatic inhabiting your body is alive and well, he replied.

He banked and shifted direction as he sensed a passageway back to the human realm. She managed to suck in more breath to shriek again. *I'm being serious now – I don't think I can deal with this!*

Tough, he told her. *I'm not taking the chance of anything else going wrong. This is a nonstop flight to New York. Thank you for flying Cuelebre Airlines.*

'You're not funny!' she screamed out loud. Dragon laughter filled her head.

She huddled in his unbreakable grip, hands over her eyes. She discovered it wasn't a smooth, seamless flight but one that had a rhythm from the beat of his wings. She also thought she would be freezing. She was in for another surprise as he kept a velvet blanket of Power wrapped around her. It protected her from the cold altitude and the wind.

She could sense the upswell of magic that marked a passageway back to the human dimension as they approached. She peeked through her fingers. Following a directional sense she didn't share, he stretched his wings and they glided until they skimmed along just a hundred feet above a small canyon.

Are you able to open your eyes yet? he asked.

She told him, *I'm looking.*

A lot of passageways to Other lands are like this one. They're couched in some kind of break in the physical landscape, he told her. *If we flew just ten or fifteen feet higher, we wouldn't be in the passageway.*

Then we would stay in the Other land? she asked, as she became interested in spite of herself.

Correct. From the air, it's like following a specific airstream. The passageway the Goblin brought us through was somewhat unusual, he explained. *There was a break in the land but it was an old one worn down by time. It was barely visible even to my eyes.*

Somewhere along the way the sun changed and became paler. The canyon shrank until it was a mere ravine tangled with underbrush. The quality of air changed as well. They had crossed over.

Can you tell where we are? she asked. She had forgotten her fear in the fascination of watching the land scroll by underneath.

North of where we were before. I'm more familiar with the landscape along the coast. I'll know more when we hit the Atlantic. He gave the equivalent of a mental shrug. *I'm more interested in finding out when we are and how much time has passed while we were in the Other land.*

She had forgotten about that. She watched the landscape change as Dragos winged east. After about a half an hour or so, the blue line of the ocean appeared ahead of them. He wheeled to fly north alongside the land's edge, climbing in altitude until the air felt thin to her. The cities and towns they flew over looked like a child's toys.

There, he said. She looked up to see him nod to their left. *That's Virginia Beach. We've got a good couple hours' flight ahead of us.*

Oh, right. She drooped at the thought. *And here I am without my magazines or paperback novel, and no money for an in-flight movie.*

They fell silent. After a while, watching the coastline pass by between her dangling feet became so commonplace it was boring. She inspected the cut on her palm, which had sealed sometime during Dragos's healing.

The scab already looked a week old. She picked at it without much interest, then turned her attention to the long, curved, black talons that surrounded her. She rubbed one, then tapped at it with a fingernail. It gleamed like obsidian and was no doubt harder than diamonds.

After that there was nothing left to do but kick her feet and obsess over the debacle that her life had become.

After everything, now she was headed back to New York in the grasp of the very creature she had been running away from. With whom, by the way, she had also had fantastic, mind-blowing sex.

That was a head bender all on its own, without considering all the many other disasters that had occurred. She peered up at Dragos and looked away again fast.

The memories of what they had done together were so intense she lost her breath every time she thought of them. Yet they seemed surreal at the same time, almost like they had happened to someone else. And she couldn't quite connect the man who had been her lover with this splendid exotic creature who carried her with such care as he flew.

She propped her elbows on a talon and buried her face in her hands. Images from the last few days flashed across her inner eye. The confrontation with the Elves. Dragos getting shot. The car crash. The Goblin stronghold, the beating. The beautiful dream of her mother. The standoff on the plain.

She didn't know what to make of all of it. She wanted that dark room to hide in until she figured everything out. Like in maybe ten years or so.

And it was really not good that she had come to the Fae King's attention for sure this time. Front and center. He couldn't know everything that had happened between her and Dragos. But they had escaped together. Now the Fae King had to have some questions about whether she had anything significant to do with Dragos's transformation, questions he would want to have answered along with all the questions he might have had from before.

Way to stay under the radar and avoid scrutiny, dingbat.

159

If he *might* have known something and been interested in her before, he sure as hell did now. She had no doubt she'd just shot right up to the Fae King's Ten Most Wanted list. For all she knew they would be posting pictures of her in post offices and police stations and faxing them to the FBI.

She could always have plastic surgery and run away to live off the grid in a remote Mexican village. If she could collect the stuff from her three remaining caches and get out of town again. That wouldn't stop magical detection, though. Dragos had already warned her he would find her if she tried to run.

What did that make her? She didn't know. Was she his prisoner when they got back to New York? Was he serious about considering her his property now or had that been a joke? He had a strange sense of humor sometimes, so it was hard to tell.

Just tell me what I want to know and I'll let you go. Ha. She rolled her eyes. She couldn't believe she fell for that one.

She did believe he had forgiven her for the theft. She supposed that was a miracle all on its own, since not that long ago she had been convinced he was going to tear her to pieces. And she had promised him she wouldn't try to escape. She had meant it at the time.

She wondered if she was going to keep that promise. Life had turned so unpredictable she wasn't willing to bet on anyone or anything at this point, least of all herself.

All she knew for sure was that she still faced a dangerous and uncertain future.

And that she was . . . lonely again. Worse than ever before.

≈ ELEVEN ≈

She fell into a cramped, fitful doze, propping her head on one arm as she leaned against a curved claw. Come to think of it, it was quite a bit like trying to nap in an airplane seat. The change in their altitude woke her up. She straightened with a wince and looked around. New York lay spread out all around her. The panoramic splash of lights in the deepening dusk stabbed at her eyes. She winced and rubbed her face in an attempt to wake up.

Dragos banked and wheeled in a great circle. They were headed for one of the tallest skyscrapers. She groaned as her stomach lurched. Then they dropped onto the launchpad on the roof of Cuelebre Tower.

She looked around, dazed, and tried to stand without staggering when Dragos set her on her feet. The roof was a huge expanse of space, more than adequate for handling someone of Dragos's size with room for the takeoffs and landings of other creatures at the same time.

A group of people stood waiting by a set of double doors. In front of them a tawny-haired man stood with feet planted apart and arms crossed. A feral-looking beautiful woman stood beside him, hands on her hips. A Native American–looking man stood a little apart from the others in a black sleeveless leather vest and black jeans, with black hair cut short with shaved whirls of pattern throughout it and tattooed, muscular arms.

Every last one of them bristled with weapons. They all stood six feet tall or over. None of them looked like someone she would be comfortable running into in a back alley.

The air behind her shimmered with Power. She looked over her shoulder as Dragos changed, every ounce of the dragon's force and energy compacted into the tall, muscular shape of the man. By some trick of the magic in the change, he still wore his battered grimy jeans and boots and nothing else. She looked from his bare chest up into that blade-cut face and raptor's eyes and lost her breath all over again.

He took her by the arm and strode with her to the group waiting by the doors. Her face heated as curious, unfriendly eyes assessed her.

''Bout time you showed up,' said the tawny-haired man. He jerked his chin toward the Native American. 'I sent to South America for Tiago and some of the cavalry. You all right?'

'I'm fine,' said Dragos. Two of the men held the doors open. Dragos ignored the open elevator doors and took the stairs. She had no choice but to trot along by his side. The others followed. 'Conference in ten minutes. Is the room ready?'

What room? Her room? Pia looked at him sidelong as they hit the landing for the penthouse floor.

'All set,' said the tawny man just behind her. Most of the rest had broken away from them to go to the conference room.

They swept down a large hallway, turned and went down another. The halls had luxurious marbled floors. Original works of art hung placed on recession-lit walls. She craned her neck. Wait – was that a painting by Chagall?

Dragos stopped in front of a blond wood door. He pushed it open and walked her inside. The tawny male and two others stayed in the hall by the door.

Pia looked around. She got a blurred impression of a room that was larger than a small house. Her filthy sneakers sank into plush white carpet. A freestanding fireplace and sunken living area with pale leather couches and armchairs was at one end. A black wrought-iron framed bed the size of a boat was at the other end, piled with pillows and quilts. An immense plasma flat-screen hung on one wall, and a wet bar was tucked

162

into an alcove. Another wall was nothing but floor-to-ceiling plate-glass windows with French doors. Open doors led off to walk-in closets and a bathroom.

He turned her around to face him and tilted up her chin. She looked up at him, round-eyed and wary. 'I know how tired you are,' he said in a quiet voice. 'I want you to stay here, take a hot bath and rest. Everything you should need is here, clothes, drinks, and I'm going to have a hot meal sent up for you. All right?'

In some ways this present landscape was more alien than the Other land had been. The tangled mess inside of her got even more snarled. She was half afraid of him again, but at the same time she didn't want him to leave. She bit her lips, clenched her fists to keep from reaching out to him or appearing too high-maintenance. She gave him a jerky nod.

He put a hand at the back of her neck, a heavy, warm weight, his face tightening. He said, as if she had argued, 'I've been talking with Rune as we approached the city. We've been gone a week. I've got to brief them on what happened.'

'There must be a million things you've got to do,' she said. She pulled out of his hold, crossed her arms around her middle and stepped away from him. 'I can't imagine.'

He stood with his hand suspended in midair, frowning at her. She caught a glimpse of the hallway where the tawny male who must be Rune stood, along with two other great hulking males. All three were staring at Dragos as if they didn't recognize him.

He turned on his heel and strode out. He said, 'Bayne, Con, stay here. Get her anything she wants.'

'Right,' said one of the men. He exchanged a glance with the other man. 'Anything she wants.'

Dragos disappeared with Rune, leaving her alone in the great gorgeous barn of a room with two men at the door.

Armed guards. Guess she had one question answered. She was a prisoner.

One of them took hold of the door handle and nodded to her, his weather-beaten face expressionless. 'We'll knock when your meal comes,' he told her. 'Do you need anything right now?'

'No, thank you,' she said from a dry throat. 'I'm fine.'

Her guard shut the door and left her alone.

She turned in a circle, taking everything in. The empty room was draped in shadows that deepened with the onset of dusk. The strange penthouse luxury seemed colder and hollower without the vitality of Dragos's presence. She rubbed her arms and shivered.

She slipped off her disgusting sneakers and put them on the tiled floor just inside a bathroom that was bigger than the whole of her apartment. Then she padded over to the alcove that hid the wet bar.

Though small, it was stocked with a wide assortment of liquor, all top of the line, of course. She paused, distracted by the collection. She had always wanted to try a glass of Johnnie Walker Blue. There was a coffee machine on the counter and a sink. Underneath the counter was a half-sized refrigerator. She checked the contents. Bottles of Evian water and Perrier, beer and lager, various juices, white wine and champagne.

She took out two bottles of water. She gulped down the Evian. Then with her thirst somewhat assuaged, she opened the Perrier and drank that more slowly.

The fireplace was a real one, not gas. It was immaculate and laid with a neat stack of wood, ready to start. A box of long matches sat by a TV remote on the coffee table in front of two of the couches. She gave in to temptation and lit the fire. The yellow flicker of the flames helped to dispel some of the room's chill emptiness.

Next she crept into a walk-in closet and dressing room. One side was filled with male clothes. The other side was filled with her clothes.

From her apartment.

She pushed through the hangers and opened up the dresser drawers. Her underwear, socks, T-shirts and shorts, all immaculate, all pressed and folded.

She held up a small neat bundle that was a pair of white panties. Some stranger had washed her underwear – and ironed it?

The same was true for the clothes on the hangers. Her shoes were no longer in a pile but polished and stored in order. Her small cedar jewelry chest was on one of the dressers. She opened it and grew teary at the sight of her mother's antique necklace. She stroked the necklace, then shut the chest with care and leaned against the dresser.

This was both creepy and . . . thoughtful. Finding familiar things was comforting at the same time as it scared her half to death.

When had he given the order to collect her things? Had it been at the beach house when he called Rune? He had said he had told Rune to get a vegetarian cook. When had he decided to move her things into his room?

She grabbed a T-shirt, sports bra and panties and a pair of flannel boxer shorts. She went into the bathroom. She could spend a week having a vacation just in the bathroom alone. There was a bathtub the size of a small pool with steps and bench seats, and there were unopened bottles of Chanel-scented bubble bath. Her toiletries and makeup were laid out on the marble counter by the sink. New bottles of the shampoo and conditioner brand she liked were in the shower stall.

Someone had apparently thought of everything, every last freaking thing, except for asking her opinion about any of it. What a gilded cage.

Even though Dragos had urged her to take a hot bath, she felt too vulnerable and unsettled to relax. Just as she had at the beach house, she locked the bathroom door before she stripped.

The shower was several feet in size with a bench seat and multiple heads. After she figured out how to turn it on, she stood under the multiple streams of water with her eyes closed until the warmth soaked away all the strength in her legs. She sat on the bench as she lathered and conditioned her hair and scrubbed at her body until it felt like she had taken a layer of skin off. After rinsing, she wrapped her hair in a towel and dried and dressed. Rational or not she felt better as soon as she had clean clothes on.

When she walked out of the bathroom, she found that a serving cart/portable dining table and a chair had been set near the windows. There was a heavy white linen tablecloth and simple but elegant tableware and dishes with silver covers. A small bottle of white wine chilled in an ice bucket. Consumed with hunger, she uncovered all the dishes.

She found a delicate lemon asparagus risotto sprinkled with slivered almonds, a salad with mixed greens, sliced pears and dried cranberries, fresh baked bread with individual packets of soy margarine and blueberry crumble for dessert. She fell on the food and devoured every last delicious bite.

After getting clean, comfortable and filling her stomach, she had no room for alarm or offense. She couldn't even keep her eyes open. She managed to brush her teeth before she crawled between the sheets of the massive bed. As prisons went, this one would be mighty hard to beat. She yawned, gave up trying to think and fell asleep.

On the next floor down, Dragos strode into the conference room, followed by Rune. Located a short, convenient distance down the hall from his offices, it was a large executive board-room, with black leather seats, an expansive polished oak table and state-of-the-art teleconferencing equipment.

All his sentinels were present with the exception of the two gryphons Bayne and Constantine, who stood guard at Pia's door. Rune took a seat by the fourth gryphon, Graydon, and tilted his chair back. Tiago leaned against the far wall, a dark brooding presence. Aryal sprawled and tapped her fingers on the table. She never quite managed a motionless state unless she was hunting prey. The gargoyle Grym angled his chair so he could watch Aryal.

Tricks, the faerie known as Thistle Periwinkle, Cuelebre's head of PR, sat with her arms and legs crossed at the other end of the table. Her lavender cloud of hair, sporting a four-hundred-dollar haircut, was disheveled. She jiggled one tiny foot and chain-smoked.

Dragos, like Tiago, didn't take a seat. Instead he went to lean back against the oak counter at the head of the room. He kicked one foot over the other and folded his arms, tucked his chin in and brooded at the floor.

He didn't like how he felt. He didn't like it one fucking bit. He felt jittery and restless at leaving Pia alone. The feeling increased with every step he took away from her and with every minute that trickled by. She had looked very lost and alone standing in the middle of that big empty room.

He didn't like how she had looked at him either, like he was an unpredictable puzzle she couldn't decipher. Or a bomb that might go off in her face. She had looked at him with uncertainty, distrust. With something very close to fear again.

She had pulled away from him.

It was unacceptable. But before he could go and take care of whatever was brewing in her head, he had to do this first.

He lifted his gaze and looked around the occupants in the room. They were all watching him and waiting.

'Hey, Tricks,' he said to the chain-smoking faerie. 'Your uncle Urien says hi.'

Tricks started swearing, her urchinlike features contorted. She stabbed a half-smoked cigarette out in the ashtray. 'What did the bastard do this time?'

Rune said, 'Everybody knows what happened up to the point when you called from South Carolina. We've been dealing with the Elven fallout. They've invoked a trade and business embargo with anything to do with Cuelebre Enterprises, along with all other known Wyr businesses. They also swore they escorted you and the woman to the Elven border. They're insisting on knowing what happened to her.'

'You mean, aside from housing the criminal in a penthouse suite and hiring a private chef for her? Yeah, we're talking cruel and unusual punishment,' Aryal whispered to Grym, but Dragos's sharp hearing caught it anyway. He chose to ignore it for now.

'They did escort us to the border. That's true as far as it goes,' he said. He told them the rest, omitting what happened in private between him and Pia, and glossing over anything to do with her secrets. Pia was his mystery. No one else's. He intended to solve her all by himself.

The mood in the room turned ugly as he described the confrontation on the Other land plain.

When he finished, Tiago stirred. In his thunderbird form, he was as big as any of the gryphons. 'So, it's war. About damn time,' he said. Dark satisfaction gleamed from obsidian eyes.

Dragos nodded. 'It's war. We don't stop now until Urien is dead.' He looked at Tricks. 'That means you get to be the Dark Fae Queen at last.'

'Oh God no,' the faerie groaned. 'I fucking hate the Dark Fae Court.'

'Well, suck it up, Tricks. You've run from this long enough. And this time Urien's pushed me too far.'

Over two hundred years ago, humankind time, Urien had

taken the Dark Fae crown in a bloody coup. Urien had slaughtered his brother, the King, the King's wife and anyone else who had any direct claim to the throne, except he managed to miss one small person, their eldest daughter, Tricks.

At just seventeen years old, Tricks had been considered little more than a baby at the time when she had managed to escape. She had run straight to Dragos, the one entity she felt sure could stand up to her uncle without any fear, and had asked for sanctuary. She had been with him ever since.

'It's been a fun game of Fuck You, hasn't it? We managed to keep it going for quite a while, but you know it had to end sometime,' he said to her. She gave him a miserable nod.

'Okay, here's what we're going to do,' he said. 'Tiago, send some of the troops you brought back with you to scour that Goblin stronghold. They know what to do to anyone stupid enough to still be there.'

Tiago smiled. 'You got it.'

'Aryal,' he continued, 'investigate the Elven connection. I want to know who might have leaked information to Urien.' The harpy gave him a nod. He turned his attention to the gargoyle. 'Grym, I want you to work with Tricks to plot the layout of the Dark Fae palace and grounds for possible plans of attack. I've got a few ideas, but I also want to know what you come up with. Tricks, I know you're going to get really busy, but I would appreciate it if you managed to hire a replacement for yourself before you go, or at least come up with a short list of suggestions. We're going to need a new PR person.'

'Of course I will,' Tricks said. 'It's the least of what I owe you.'

'It's never gonna be the same,' Graydon said in a mournful voice. 'Watching her cute little face when she came on television and knowing how Urien must have gnashed his teeth every time he saw her.' Everyone laughed. Even Tricks managed to smile.

Rune and Graydon were looking at him. He told them, 'Until further notice, you two, and Bayne and Con, are on special detail. Get lieutenants to step in with your regular duties. You four are going to guard Pia whenever I'm not with her. Two on, two off, twenty-four/seven. She is never to be left on her own. Understood?'

Rune's chair came down on all four legs. The handsome male looked very alert. Graydon's expression was the picture of incredulity. It was more or less echoed around the room. Tricks's eyebrows rose and her lips pursed.

'You're putting four of your most powerful warriors on babysitting detail for a thief?' said Aryal. 'At a time like this?'

Dragos looked at her from under lowered brows. Grym put a hand on her arm. The gargoyle said to him, 'Unless there'll be anything else, we'll get right to work, my lord. I think we all have got a lot to do.'

He considered the harpy for a few more moments, the dragon roused and moving deep in his thoughts. Aryal dropped her gaze and bowed her head in a submissive posture.

'Go,' he said.

The others scattered. Rune and Graydon followed him as he went back upstairs. He stalked down the hall, still brooding, while they shadowed him on either side. He came to Pia's door where Bayne and Constantine lounged against the wall, talking. The two men straightened at their approach.

'Fill them in,' he told Rune, who nodded. The dragon still roused, he regarded them all. The gryphons watched him with attentive, quiet faces. He said, 'Let me make this perfectly clear. Just so there's no mistake. We've worked well together for almost a thousand years. You have all come to mean a lot to me. I treasure your service and I prize your loyalty above all others.' He looked at Rune. 'I count you as my best friend.'

They all stood taller as he talked. He pointed at the door. 'Thief or not, she is mine and I'm keeping her. If a single hair on that young woman's head is harmed, you four bastards better be slaughtered and in pieces when I find you.'

Rune's steady gaze met his. 'You needn't worry, my lord,' the gryphon said. 'We'll guard her with our lives. I swear it.'

Tired as she was and in spite of the comfort of the bed, Pia tossed and turned, unable to settle into a deep sleep. She dreamed of being chased. The scenes kept changing. First she was crawling through the secret ways of a huge house, trying to find someplace to hide. Next she was weaving in and out of a crowded, unfamiliar city street while someone menacing followed behind her. She could never quite see her pursuer's face, but he terrified the hell out of her.

Then someone lifted the bedcovers. A large, damp, naked male slid into the bed beside her. She startled, coming awake with a violent jerk.

'Shh, it's me,' Dragos whispered. 'I didn't mean to wake you.'

'S'okay,' she murmured. 'Didn't like that dream anyway.'

There was a reason why it wasn't such a good idea for him to be in her bed. Or was she in his? She wasn't awake enough to grasp any of it. She was just awake enough to feel a rush of pleasure and relief.

His arms came around her. She made a noise and burrowed into his side. His warmth and energy enveloped her. She put her cheek to his shoulder, against the damp, clean-smelling skin that covered hard, bulky muscle like silk, and rested a hand on his chest.

'Did you like your supper?' he asked.

'Lovely.'

'Good.' He pressed a kiss to her forehead. 'Take the spell off.'

'Sleepy,' she complained.

He stroked her hair. 'Please?'

She muttered, fumbled to get hold of the dampening spell and released it.

His wide chest moved in a deep sigh. 'That's better.'

'Shh,' she scolded. She turned on her side. He wrapped his body around her. Her check rested on one bulging biceps while he curled his other arm around her torso. He pinned her legs with one heavy thigh. She cast a sleep-blurred glance down at their entwined bodies. The pale glow of her form was caged in possessive, dark bronze male. It was a jealous, suffocating hold. She should want to break free of it. She sighed. Something deep inside settled into place and she closed her eyes, content.

This time when she fell asleep there were no more dreams.

A long, restful time later something brought her out of deep unconsciousness. She drifted for a while in a twilight state. A large hand played down the front of her torso. Gentle fingers trailed from her flat stomach up her rib cage to circle first one breast and then the other.

She sighed and stretched. She turned onto her back as she arced toward that roaming, pleasurable touch. Lips brushed against her bare shoulder, caressed up the graceful curve to her neck. Teeth scraped against sensitive skin and nipped at her earlobe.

Bare shoulder? She opened her eyes. It was shocking all over again to lie naked with him. She rubbed a foot on his leg, crisp hairs tickling her toes. Predawn bloomed outside and brought the room to a light gray. Dragos rested his weight on one arm as he leaned over her. His severe face was intent as he studied her with a heavy-lidded gaze. The etched line of his mouth was curved in a lazy, sensual smile.

He was so gorgeous her whole body throbbed. His fine-cut nostrils flared and she knew he had sensed it.

She licked her lips. His gaze dropped and he watched the movement. 'I'm quite sure I went to bed with clothes on,' she murmured.

'So you did,' he said, his tone languorous. He circled the areola of one breast. She watched him swallow as her nipple puckered. 'I found them in the way.'

'You undressed me while I was sleeping?' She shivered as he circled the areola of her other breast. 'I must have been pretty out of it.'

'I might have helped you along.' She arched a brow at him. He told her, 'It was just a little beguilement. You needed to rest.'

'Without my clothes.' There he went, messing with her head again. Making note to self: they've got to discuss how she was not his personal Barbie doll to dress and undress whenever he felt like it.

'I needed to rest too,' he said in a bland voice. 'And they were bothering me.'

She snorted out a laugh. Who knew this exotic, terrifying male would be so funny? She loved it, loved the surprise of him.

He traced her lips next. She got the feeling she was being stalked without ever having left the bed.

She took his finger in her mouth and sucked it, and set him on fire.

He pulled his finger out. Shadowed gold eyes flashed with ravenous heat. His head came down hard. He drove her into the pillow as he plunged into her mouth with a hard, hungry tongue. At the same time he cupped her between the legs, probed her damp sex and pushed two fingers deep inside her.

She groaned and clutched at his arm. His aggression pulled a helpless response out of her. She grew liquid and swollen, drenching his fingers. He growled and pushed his tongue and fingers into her in a simultaneous penetration. Her hips bucked against his hand.

She dragged her mouth away from his and gasped. 'Wait . . . I don't want . . .'

He hovered inches above her, the raptor waiting to plummet, while his thumb found and rubbed her clitoris. She moaned and pulled his hand harder against her. 'You don't want?' he murmured, giving her a ruthless smile.

She found his hard penis and grasped it. He hissed and pushed into her hand, pulsing against her palm. 'I want to explore you too before you wreck me again.' She looked into his eyes, uncertain. He was so dominant. She didn't have a clue what he might like. 'Would you enjoy that?'

He paused and she watched him struggle with contrasting impulses. Then he pulled her hand off him and pinned it over her head. 'I'd love it,' he whispered in her ear. 'After we get you to just a little climax first.'

He pushed in deep with those long clever fingers and rubbed the heel of his palm against her, finding just the right spot. She jerked and struggled against his hold, pushing against the pressure, straining to find release. 'Come inside me,' she coaxed.

'No,' he purred against her ear, drinking down every response. 'Not yet. You come just like this, lover.'

'Damn it!' He was diabolical. The pressure built, and his fingers felt so fine as they stroked inside – God! – but she wanted him thick and hard and buried inside of her. She turned and bit his shoulder.

He laughed, a sexy, husky sound. He bent down to suck one of her nipples into his mouth, drawing on it and flicking it with his tongue while he worked her.

There it was, a climax burgeoning inside like a match flaring alight. She arched and gave him her sounds of pleasure. He left her nipple to brush his mouth over hers as she moaned, her inner muscles contracting. 'That's it, there it is,' he whispered against her lips. He eased rubbing the heel of his palm against her, bringing her down again with care. 'Beautiful.'

They lay quiet a moment, breathing together.

Then she stirred and gave him a wicked smile. 'You wanted to know why I said I wasn't right in the head.'

One corner of his mouth lifted. 'Yes, I did, didn't I?'

She walked her fingers across his chest. 'I kept having sexual fantasies of you at very inappropriate times.'

'Like when?' he asked, stroking her hip and down her thigh. He ran his fingers through the tangle of white-gold curls between her thighs, his touch delicate and light. He looked very interested.

She sighed in pleasure. How did he get so wise in all the ways to arouse her? 'Like when you dropped out of the sky and sat on me. You looked like the wrath of God, and it scared me half to death. Then all I could think about was that blasted dream and how hot you were. It's just not right to be scared and turned on all at the same time.'

'That's all I could think about as well.' He lifted her hand and kissed the scab on her palm. 'I meant to lay a trap for you with that dream. I trapped myself instead.'

'And then,' she whispered, eyes sparkling, 'remember when you were chained up in the Goblin stronghold?'

'Not a memory that will soon fade,' he replied in a dry tone.

'It was terrible,' she said. 'I felt awful, the cell was filthy and I was scared again. And there you were chained and spread out like a gourmet feast. In spite of everything, for a moment there the sight of you made my mouth water.'

His interest sharpened, became electric. 'I've got to remember to add shackles to all the bedrooms.'

She chuckled and nestled closer. 'It was just a fantasy. The real thing was pretty disturbing.'

'So, we'll pretend.' He rolled onto his back and took hold of the bed rails above his head. The posture stretched the muscles of his arms and chest, accentuated his rib cage and hollowed his abdomen.

She stared at him heavy-lidded, her body tingling. Banked sensuality smoked in his gaze. His aroused body and his face were the sexiest things she had ever seen. It was even more arousing that he volunteered to lay supplicant before her, this big dangerous male.

She slid over him until they lay torso to torso, her breasts pressed against his chest. She bent her head and rubbed her open lips along his. She licked and kissed and nibbled. His breathing roughened. He nipped at her, trying to coax her down for a harder kiss, but she pulled away and slid down him.

She slid her open mouth along the bulges and hollows of his chest, kissing his breastbone and rubbing her nose in the sprinkle of dark crisp hair that arrowed down his long body to his groin. He shifted underneath her, stretching like a cat. She played with his dark, flat nipples, making them harden.

She was arousing herself as much as him. She reached down and took hold of his penis. He hissed and pushed his hips up. She looked down at her pale, glowing hand gripping him, her breathing erratic. He was beautifully contoured, his erection big and thick, the skin of the shaft and bulb of the head velvet soft. His testicles were drawn up tight underneath. She massaged them. They were heavy, voluptuous round globes.

He lifted his head to watch her fondle him, eyes glittering. He was all hard angles and edges. The muscles in his arms shook. She glanced at his hands fisted at the bed rails. They were white-knuckled.

'This is my game now. Don't let go,' she warned him. She held his fierce gaze as she slid down his body. Whatever major issues or questions that lay unresolved between them, when it came to this they generated combustible magic together.

She crouched over him, lifted his erection, took the head in her mouth and suckled at him. He gave a short, sharp shout, his head slamming back on the pillows. His hips left the bed as he pushed at her mouth.

She gripped his penis at the root with one hand, cupped his sac with the other and feasted. The taste and feel of him was intoxicating. She crooned as she worked to get him deeper, opening her throat muscles as wide as she could, pulling back slow and tight and then pushing to take him in deep again. Hunger spiraled out of control, wild and hot.

Their game forgotten, he gathered her hair in one fist and pumped in her mouth. He put the other hand between her legs and probed and fondled the wet, silken folds.

Then he pulled her hair, forcing her head away. She made a noise of complaint as his cock left her mouth. He yanked her up for a devouring, openmouthed kiss. He was shaking all over, and it made her crazy. He pulled her on top of him and she parted her legs to sit astride, curling over him and rubbing her sex on his erection as he continued to hold her by the hair, imprisoned for his assault.

Overcome with greed, she lifted up and positioned him so that his thick broad head breached her entrance. Then he took over, grabbed her by the hips and thrust all the way in to the root. His whole body clenched and he gave a shout.

She was making noise too, urgent animal sounds, shivering all over as her body adjusted to the heavy invading length. He found a rhythm, pistoning into her with escalating urgency, fingers digging into her soft white flesh.

She tried to brace herself any way that she could, elbows propped on his chest. His head was lifted so that he was nose to nose with her, face etched with sexual aggression, fierce lambent gaze fixed on hers. He bared his teeth at her.

His feral beauty sent her into a liquid meltdown. She stretched out her arms and pushed openhanded at the pillows, lips parted, reaching, reaching, and then she was overwhelmed with a shock of pleasure so intense as he impaled her, she writhed in orgasm.

He joined her with a harsh groan, pushing up and up as his climax spurted into her. They held tense for long moments. Her lungs worked as she tried to suck in some air. Her damn hair was all over the place. She pushed it out of her eyes in time to catch a glimpse of his face. He looked desperate, out of control.

He shook his head, muttering, 'Not enough.' Holding her low at the hips with one arm to keep them joined, he flipped them so that she landed on her back on the mattress with him on top. He was still hard. He began to move again, sliding in and out of her juicy, tight sheath.

'Oh God, you're going to kill me,' she groaned. He paused and searched her eyes. She wrapped her arms around his neck and whispered, 'You better not stop until you're done. Remember, I can take any pace you can set, big guy.'

His face lit with a savage smile. Then he lost the smile, lost the words, lost everything to uncontrollable passion that swept her right along with him. He didn't stop until he had spent all that he had.

Wrecked. He had wrecked her again. He took her so far and deep outside of herself, she came back changed in fundamental ways she didn't understand. She made noises with him and did things she never had before, things she had never conceived of doing. She had never realized how the act of sex could be a total loss of all civilized behavior. He brought her face-to-face with the animal that lived inside her. She had nothing left to cling to, either inside of herself or outside in the rapid changes that had overcome her life. There was only him, the destroyer of her world, and she hung on to him with everything she had.

They lay together in a tangle of limbs, his head on her shoulder, as the morning light advanced across the ceiling. She might have dozed. She had lost count of her orgasms, let alone his. He pressed a kiss to her breast. He said, 'I marked you up again.'

She yawned and tried to figure out how he sounded. Complex, that was the word, his voice filled with both regret and satisfaction. 'You've got a few bite and scratch marks you didn't have before too, big guy.'

He smiled against her skin. Regret fled and left pure male satisfaction the victor on the field. 'That I do.'

A knock sounded on the door, and it opened to a faerie pushing a food cart into the room. 'Good morning,' she piped.

Quicker than thought, Dragos yanked up the sheet and threw himself to cover her. He roared over his shoulder, 'What are you doing!'

She threw the dampening spell on herself as fast as she could. Dragos looked murderous. She put a hand against his cheek, kissed him and peered over his shoulder.

The poor faerie turned dead white and looked like she was about to faint. She stammered, 'I always – it never mattered—'

Pia said in a gentle voice, 'What he means to say is, "Thank you very much for breakfast." And you didn't do anything wrong. He's not really mad at you. He just got surprised.' Underneath the covers, she pinched him hard. He grabbed her

176

hand but didn't contradict her. 'Things are a little different right now, so maybe it's a good idea to knock and wait next time until someone says you can come in.'

The faerie bobbed several times in frantic curtsies. 'Of course! Of course! Thank you, my lady. I'll—' She pointed at the door and bolted.

The door settled back into place. Pia looked at Dragos in bemusement. There were so many things that had just happened. She didn't know what to make of it all or what to say. She stroked his face and waited until he calmed.

'She called me "my lady," ' she told him in a plaintive voice. 'I don't know who that is. I'm no lady.'

The last of his fury faded away to be replaced with a quick gleam. He peered under the sheet. 'I can attest to that.'

'Ooh!' She smacked his shoulder.

They looked at each other, then burst out laughing.

He piled the pillows up, settled back against them and pulled her against his side. She put her head on his shoulder and tried to reach for her earlier drifting sense of peace. It proved to be a fugitive feeling and began to slip away.

He stroked his fingers through her hair. 'You owe me a lock of hair,' he said.

She closed her eyes and tried to ignore the realities of the morning. She asked, 'How much do you want?'

'A lot,' he said, holding up a few strands so that they glinted in the light. Then he frowned. 'Not too much.'

She started to smile. 'Make up your mind. I can cut it short and you can have all of it, if you want.'

'Don't you dare. I want just enough.'

'Oh, like that makes any sense.' She raised her head to give him a quizzical glance. He was scowling. She sighed. 'Hold on.'

She padded naked into the dressing room, pulled her thigh-length pink robe from a hanger and belted it on. She dug through the dresser drawers that held her things, found her portable sewing kit and walked back into the bedroom. She sat cross-legged facing Dragos on the bed. He laced his hands behind his head, regarding her with interest.

She took the scissors from the kit, isolated some hair close to the scalp at the back of her head where the cut would be hidden and snipped it off. She held the lock up for his inspection.

It was a good-sized piece, the width of her little finger and the full length of her hair.

'Perfect,' he said, eyes gleaming in satisfaction.

'Debt paid?' she asked.

'Debt paid.' He rubbed the ends between his fingers.

'What are you going to do with it?' she asked.

He frowned again. 'I don't know.'

'Here, I'll braid it for you. Otherwise you'll have it all over the place.'

He watched in fascination as she cut two lengths of gold thread almost the exact same color as her hair. Almost but not quite. It was the closest she could find in her sewing kit and wouldn't be noticed at any distance, but the thread lacked the lustrous quality of her hair.

She put one piece of thread between her teeth. She wound the other thread several times around one end of the hair and tied it. She used a safety pin to pin that end to a pillow and with swift competence braided the lock. She said between her teeth, 'You're not going to do some kind of black magic hoo-doo on me with this, are you?'

'Oh no,' he said, gaze on her fingers. 'I just like the color.'

She smiled to herself, both warmed and weirded out by how they were acting with each other. It felt so natural, so right. There were so many reasons why it shouldn't. She took the second length of thread to tie off the end of the braid.

Some foolish impulse made her offer, 'I could tie it around your wrist if you like.'

She waited for him to tell her not to be stupid. Instead, to her surprise, he raised his eyebrows and said, 'I would like that.'

He held out his right wrist. She wound the braid around it. Despite how thick his wrist was, the braid was long enough to go around it almost twice. She took more thread and worked on sewing the braid together. After she was sure she had it on secure, she tied it off and snipped the ends of the thread.

He held up his wrist and admired the pale gold gleam. He ran a finger around his wrist, feeling the soft bumps of the braid. The dark bronze of his skin seemed to make her hair gleam brighter.

'Dragos, am I a prisoner?' she asked. After weighing on her since last night, the question slipped out easily enough after all.

His eyes narrowed as he looked up. She kept her attention on putting things back in her sewing kit and willed her fingers not to shake. 'No,' he said after a thoughtful moment. 'Why do you ask?'

'The guards last night.' Relief had her offering him an unsteady smile.

'The guards are for your safety. When I'm not with you, they will be.' As she opened her mouth, he said, 'That's nonn-egotiable.'

'But—'

His face hardened. 'No arguing, Pia,' he said. 'I am at war now. Until I bury Urien, he's going to continue to be a serious danger. Whether he knew about you before or not is a moot point. After what happened on the plain, you have just become a major target.'

'But guards even here?' She felt any hope of even an illusion of freedom slipping between her fingers.

'A couple thousand people work here every day. Several thousand more visit. Yes, there is security and there are restricted areas, but no place is a hundred percent secure, not when Power is involved. You remember how I got to you with the dream. What if some magical attack occurs? You will have guards until this is all over. End of discussion.'

Her lips tightened. His logic was irrefutable and his autocratic attitude all but intolerable. When she thought she had her temper under control, she gave him a short nod. She didn't necessarily disagree with him once he had explained things. She just expected to have a say in what happened in her life.

He settled back against the pillows and laced his hands behind his head again. He gave her a relaxed, ruthless smile. 'Now that it's come up and we can have that long-overdue conversation, why don't you tell me all about your mother and how you healed me?'

═ TWELVE ═

After a frozen moment, she threw herself off the bed. She grabbed her sewing kit and stomped into the dressing room. 'I can't believe you're asking me that.'

He followed and leaned a shoulder against the doorpost. He had slipped on a pair of black silk pants. His gold eyes gleamed. 'It's pretty evident you healed me with your blood. That's why you were so desperate to destroy it. Your blood tells something important about you. You couldn't leave any behind.'

She took in his dark lounging figure and looked away with determination. Yes, he was too sexy for words. He was also utterly insufferable and he didn't have an ounce of shame or embarrassment to his name. 'I guess when you promised not to ask me about it, you meant you wouldn't ask when you didn't want to,' she said in a grim voice. She shoved her sewing kit into a drawer and brushed past him.

'Of course.' He turned to track her. 'I learned that from someone I know. You know, the one who promised not to argue only when she doesn't want to,' he said, raising his eyebrows at her. 'Now who could that be?'

She stormed up to him and stuck her finger under his nose. 'That was different.'

'How do you figure?'

'We were in a bad situation. I reserve the right to sometimes know better than you do what should be done. So I'll argue with you whenever I feel like arguing, big guy.'

His mouth flattened. He folded his arms. It was obvious he was unimpressed with her finger or her posturing. 'Like you did when we were in the car with the Goblins watching?'

She scowled. 'That was a mistake. I already said that and apologized. I would also like to point out that if I had been a good little girl and followed every single thing you told me to do when you were throwing orders around, I might still be sitting in my cell. My initiative saved your ass.'

'I already said that too,' he said, eyes narrowed. He went nose to nose with her. 'You're deflecting. You really don't want to talk about this, do you?'

She backed away from him, rounding her eyes. 'What part of "don't ask me any questions about this" gave you that idea?'

He followed, on the prowl, his body moving with liquid grace. 'So, let's see, what do I know? No lock can hold you, you're an herbivore, you have to wear a dampening spell to appear human, and your mother was revered by the Elves.'

'Stop it,' she whispered. It felt like he was peeling her alive, exposing everything.

There was no mercy in that predator's gaze. 'You know, I felt the Power in your blood when I cleaned you off in the car. Then on the plain, when you put your hand on me, I thought you were going to knock me to the ground. But you weren't sure it was going to work. It's because you're a half-breed, isn't it? All those abilities are from your Wyrkind blood. You got them from your mother.'

She turned away and looked around the room. It seemed so much smaller than it did before. She went to the French doors, threw them open and rushed outside, desperate for fresh air.

That was just before she saw there was no railing or wall, just a straight, flat ledge to open air. Sharp whistling gusts of wind teased her hair. Everything whirled around her and started to tilt. Hard arms caught her and held her fast.

'Shit,' she said, shaking. She clutched his arm. 'There's no railing.'

'You did so well on the flight. I thought you weren't afraid of heights,' he said. He pulled her back inside and kept one arm around her waist as he shut and locked the doors. He frowned down at her. 'You're white as a sheet.'

'I don't have a problem with heights – when there's a rail! Or a wall, or some kind of barrier!' She pointed out the window. 'That's a straight eighty-floor drop. Not so small a deal to someone with no parachute or wings.'

'Pia, the edge is a good twenty feet away now.' His hand was gentle as he rubbed her arm.

'I know that. Did I say I was being rational?' she said. Embarrassment and fright made her even more irritable. She found her balance and straightened out of his hold. There was a sharp rap on the door. Rune and Graydon walked in. She threw up her hands and snapped, 'And does anybody in this place wait for an answer when they knock?'

The two men froze. They stared at Pia, with her disheveled blonde hair and furious face, pink thigh-length robe and delicate contoured legs down to the red-tipped polished toes. Then they looked at Dragos, in his black silk pajama pants, bare chest and blonde braid of hair on one dark wrist.

Dragos stalked after her as she stormed into the bathroom. She slammed the door. He put his hands on his hips and raised his voice as he told her through the panel, 'We're not through discussing this.'

The bathroom door yanked open. She snapped, 'And my mother is none of your business!' She slammed the door again.

Dragos turned to look at the two men. Graydon, the brawniest of the gryphons, had begun shaking his head and backing out of the room. Rune just stared.

Dragos said, 'What.'

'Who are you,' Rune said, 'and what have you done with Dragos?'

He gave them his machete smile. 'I had no idea this could be so much fun.'

Rune said, 'We just thought you'd be ready to get on with your day. There's a backlog of issues waiting for your attention.'

Graydon said, 'We'll go now and come back much, much later.'

'No, don't bother.' He strode over to the serving cart and started inspecting the contents under the silver covers. One hid oatmeal with walnuts and apples. He covered it back up. The other had a pound of fried bacon and a half-dozen scrambled eggs. He picked up the plate and a fork.

He told Graydon, 'Make us a pot of coffee.' He paused and looked thoughtful. 'Please.'

Graydon turned his head to the side and widened his eyes at Rune while he said, 'Yes, my lord.'

Dragos settled on one couch, grabbed the remote and turned on CNN. He ate breakfast in quick, efficient bites. Rune sprawled on another couch. Graydon brought three cups of coffee from the wet bar.

Eyes on the morning headlines, Dragos said, 'No more barging in.'

'Never again,' Graydon said. The gryphon had a fervent note in his voice. 'We'll pass the word.'

'The breakfast faerie has no doubt already done that,' Dragos remarked around a mouthful of bacon. 'You two clowns just missed the memo.'

'The breakfast faerie.' Rune pinched his nose and coughed. Amused gold eyes met his, then turned back to the running ticker tape on the plasma flat-screen.

'What things need to be addressed?'

He finished his meal as he listened. They ran down a list of things, a variety of domestic, administrative, business and military issues. He responded with his customary decisiveness. The two gryphons started relaying his orders telepathically to the appropriate people.

The bathroom door opened and the scent of Chanel wafted across the room. The men fell silent. Pia walked out wearing her short pink robe. She entered the dressing room and shut the door.

Dragos scowled. 'Get a personal shopper for Pia. Make sure a longer robe is on the list.'

'Right.' Graydon looked like he was being tortured.

'Are the contractors done repairing the other bedroom?'

'Almost,' Rune said. 'There was some structural damage when you, uh, punched the wall. They're working hard to be as quiet as possible. Since it's on the other side of the building, the noise shouldn't be too bad. They already know they may have to stop at times, and they're prepared to work around your schedule if necessary.'

He looked out the windows and rubbed his chin. 'When they're through, have them put up a balcony wall. Tell them to go halfway around the building and put gated fences on each end. That'll still leave plenty of open ledge.'

Pia emerged wearing low-rider jeans and a tight blue long-sleeved jersey shirt that bared her midriff. She carried a cloth zippered bag under one arm. She paused, looking from the three men to the food cart and the unmade bed, her expression uncertain. She looked much calmer.

Dragos unfolded from the couch and walked toward the cart. 'Come eat your breakfast with us,' he said. He put his empty plate on the cart and retrieved her bowl of oatmeal and a spoon. 'Would you like some coffee?'

She nodded, trailing behind him to the couches. Graydon started to his feet.

Dragos put her oatmeal and spoon on an end table by the couch where he was sitting. 'I'll get you a cup,' he told her. Graydon paused halfway out of his seat.

She gave Dragos a wary scowl. 'Are you sucking up?'

'Of course.' He bent to give her a swift kiss. Dusky color touched her cheeks. He touched one high, delicate cheekbone.

She glanced sidelong at the two other men. They were dressed in jeans and T-shirts. Leather jackets were thrown over the back of the couch, and each man wore a shoulder holster and gun. She suspected they both had several other hidden weapons.

Graydon looked like he was watching a train wreck. Rune sprawled, long legs stretched out, his expression unreadable. She curled up at one end of the couch, thanked Dragos for the coffee as he set it beside her and concentrated on keeping her head down and eating her breakfast while the men talked. She was so hungry again she almost inhaled the apple walnut oatmeal.

She pulled out of her bag a bottle of nail polish remover, cotton balls and a bottle of Dusky Rose nail polish. She cleaned the chipped red polish off, tucked cotton balls between her slender toes and began to paint her toenails.

From what Dragos had described, Cuelebre Tower was a small city. Just from listening to the men, she got the merest glimpse of how vast and complex Cuelebre Enterprises was. It was quite the global corporation.

There was a pause in the conversation. She looked up. Dragos had angled himself toward her, one long leg hooked up on the couch cushions, an arm draped across the back. His head was tilted as he watched her work. She glanced at the other two men. Still not a whole lot of friendly coming from that quarter. She looked down at her half-painted toes and her cheeks burned.

'I'll go into the bathroom,' she said.

'No,' Dragos said. 'You are to be comfortable here.'

She sighed and muttered, 'You just can't dictate things like that happening, big guy.'

'I can dictate anything I want,' he told her.

She rolled her eyes. She decided to try to ignore the other two men and went back to painting her nails. She finished one foot and started on the other.

'Anything else?' Dragos asked the gryphons.

'One last thing,' Rune said. 'The Elven High Lord is demanding a teleconference and proof of Pia's well-being. She's become somewhat of a problem.' The gryphon's tawny, expressionless gaze flicked to her; then he looked away.

Sudden anger burned. 'I am not a problem,' she announced. She finished painting her little toe. 'I am a "tactical consideration."'

Dragos dropped his hand to her shoulder. He squeezed her. She glanced sideways at him. He smiled at her. He said to Rune, 'The Elven High Lord can go fuck himself. You can quote me.'

'Ms. Giovanni,' Rune said. 'Forgive me. I did not mean to imply that *you* are a problem. I meant to imply that the Elves are turning the subject of you into a problem.'

Chin resting on upraised knee, she looked at the gryphon. The apology seemed too easily offered, his handsome face too smooth.

I don't think you meant that, slick. She looked at him hard and made sure he saw it.

But now was not the time to pick another confrontation. Instead, she said, 'If they're turning the subject of me into a problem, why don't we just make it go away?' She turned to Dragos. 'You could have the teleconference and let me be there.'

His white teeth showed a little too much as he enunciated, 'I have no intention of pandering to that son of a bitch's demands.'

She set aside the nail polish and put her hand over his. 'Is this important?' she said to him. He looked at her from under the dark slash of his brows, gold eyes obdurate. She rubbed her thumb over the back of his hand. 'Wouldn't it be better if the Elves would just shut up and go away? Hey, what if they stopped throwing a fit at you walking across their backyard. It's not like you ate their tulips or dug holes in their lawn. You didn't piss on any trees when I wasn't looking, did you?'

The thundercloud that had darkened his face broke apart. He laughed. 'I would have if I'd thought of it.'

Rune grinned. A snort exploded out of Graydon, who covered his smile with a hand as big as a dinner plate.

She ducked her head and wiggled the cotton balls from between her toes. It wasn't acceptance. But at least it was something.

While Dragos showered and dressed, Pia gave in to the urge that had been eating at her ever since Rune and Graydon entered the room, and she made the bed with quick efficiency. She felt better when it was done, less exposed, even though it was crystal clear that she and Dragos had shared that bed the night before. She kept her face averted from the gryphons' covert stares while CNN continued in the background.

Dragos strode out in boots, fatigues and a black shirt that molded to his muscled torso. The symbolism of his attire didn't escape her. He was still in a combative mood. She ducked past him to pick out a pair of sandals to wear. She chose black slip-ons with silver sequined straps and low heels. She mourned her tennis shoes. They had been a big splurge, custom-fitted, and she doubted the dried blood and filth could be cleaned from them enough so that she would feel comfortable wearing them again.

Dragos led the way to the floor below. Pia had to trot to keep up. Rune and Graydon fell in behind them. She looked around, taking in as much as she could while on the move. She felt adrift. She didn't know the layout of the penthouse, and she couldn't get a feel for this floor's layout in the route they took. They did pass a massive gym with aerobic equipment, weights and a weapons training area. She stared through the windows at four Wyr engaged in a sword-training exercise and almost ran into a wall. Dragos's hand shot out and corrected her course.

186

His presence was a battering ram that cleared their path. People gave way as they approached, greeting him with a variety of nods, bows and other gestures of respect. She avoided focusing on any one of the sea of unfamiliar faces and curious gazes.

They arrived at an executive conference room, as richly appointed and built on the same massive scale as everything else. A couple of people were already present. Cuelebre Enterprises' PR faerie, Thistle Periwinkle, stood in a formal pose, hands clasped at her waist. She was dressed in a pale blue silk pantsuit and gladiator-style sandals. Standing no more than five feet tall, she looked even more diminutive when she was surrounded by oversized Wyr. The faerie faced one wall and was speaking Elvish. The teleconference had already begun.

Dragos took Pia by the hand and strode forward. Looking curiously at Pia, the faerie backed out of the way. Dragos turned to face the large flat-screen on the opposite wall. Rune and Graydon assumed places behind them.

Three tall, slender Elves filled the screen. They stood in a sunlit office much like the conference room. Ferion stood to the right. A gracious Elven woman with long black hair and a starlit gaze was on the left. The Elf in the middle had the same ageless beauty as the others, but the Power in his eyes was palpable even through the distance of the teleconference.

They all wore cold expressions as they regarded Dragos. The Elven High Lord's gaze glittered. Dragos appeared unimpressed, his body stance aggressive. His face had turned dangerous, and his eyes flat and wicked.

Alrighty. Maybe this wasn't such a good idea.

The Elven High Lord looked at her, and spring came to his winter-cold elegant face. 'We see that Ferion did not exaggerate,' he said in a deep, musical voice. He inclined his head to her. 'My lady. It is our very great pleasure to meet you. I am Calondir and this is my consort, the lady Beluviel.'

A fine trembling took up residence under her skin. The sense of exposure was back, and this time it was all but unbearable. In a whole long string of bad ideas, doing this teleconference in front of witnesses came close to topping the cake. Dragos's fingers tightened on hers to the point of pain.

She took a deep breath. It was too late to back out now. Might as well see what she could make out of yet another screwup. 'I'm honored to meet you,' she said. 'Please forgive me. I don't have any formal Court training.'

The Elven woman smiled at her. 'Such things count as nothing compared to a good heart.'

Dragos said, 'You wanted to see if she was all right. She is. We're done.'

'Wait. We wish to hear that from her,' Calondir said icily. The Elven High Lord looked at Pia. 'Lady, are you well?'

She glanced at Dragos's stone-cold profile and then back at the Elves. She said on impulse, 'I am being treated with extraordinary graciousness, my lord. While I did not want to, I actually did commit a crime. Dragos has heard the circumstances of what happened and what compelled me. He's chosen to forgive me. I would respectfully ask that you consider doing the same for him. No harm has come to you from his actions. But a great deal of harm has come to him from mine, which I very much regret.'

Something stirred through the conference room, a sigh of movement. Dragos turned to look at her. The High Lord regarded her for a long, grave moment. 'We will think on your words,' he said at last. 'If the Great Beast is capable of grace, perhaps we can do no less.'

Feeling awkward, she bowed to the Elven High Lord. 'Thank you. I appreciate it.'

'In the meantime, we would ask that you come and visit us,' Beluviel said. Her smiling eyes were warm. 'Your presence would bring us much pleasure. We would speak with you of . . . well, of things from long ago.'

Pia translated that to mean Beluviel had known, and loved, her mother. Her eyes misted and she nodded.

Dragos stepped forward and pulled her behind him. The gesture was unmistakably possessive. Even from her limited view behind his shoulder, she could tell that the Elves had stiffened. 'Stop that. What's the matter with you!' she whispered to him. He was going to unravel all the good she tried to do for him. She shoved at his arm. It was like trying to move a boulder. He twisted to glare at her. She leaned sideways to look around him and she promised the Elves, 'I'll talk to him.'

The Elven High Lord raised his eyebrows. Ferion's face

was the picture of offense. Beluviel looked startled. The Elven woman had just begun to smile when the screen went blank.

Dragos rounded on her. He looked furious. 'You are not going to visit with the Elves!'

'Did I say I was going to visit the Elves?' she snapped. 'I was being polite! You might look that word up sometime in a dictionary!'

He glared around. 'Out.'

The room emptied. Thistle gave Pia a gleeful ear-to-ear grin, eyes sparkling. The faerie held her hand up to her cheek, thumb and pinkie out, mimicking a phone. 'We'll talk,' she mouthed as she bounced out the door.

Pia tugged hard. Dragos refused to let go of her arm. She sighed and put a hand over her eyes as her shoulders sagged. She muttered to herself, 'How did I get here and what the hell am I doing.'

Beside her, Dragos took several deep breaths. She could feel the air around him burning with Power. He was very angry with her, maybe for the first time since the beach. He dropped her arm and began to pace around her.

'The Elves know more about you than I do,' he snarled in her ear as he passed by. 'Unacceptable. They know who your mother was. Also unacceptable. They want you to come live with them. They're enemies of mine.'

The exposure, the constant stress, the uncertainties of her present situation, all became too much. 'All I wanted was to try to help you!' she burst out. She threw her arms over her head and burst into tears.

He started to swear, a steady stream of vitriol. His hands came onto her shoulders. She jerked away and turned her back to him. His arms came around her from behind. He pulled her against him, curving around her, and put his head down next to hers. 'Shh,' he said, still sounding angry. 'Stop now. Calm down.'

She sobbed harder and hunched her shoulders, resisting his hold.

His body clenched. He said, 'Pia, please don't pull away from me.' He sounded strained.

It caught her attention so that she let him turn her around. He leaned back against the conference table, pulled her arms down and held her tight. She leaned her body against him and rested her head on his shoulder.

'I wasn't supposed to tell anybody anything about me,' she said. The tears streamed down her face and soaked his T-shirt. 'I was supposed to live my life in secret. But I didn't want to be alone. All I told was one damn secret and it keeps snowballing on me. First Keith, then you, then the Elves, then Goblins, then the Fae King, then more Elves again, and all the people in this room watching, and you just keep digging and digging at me and you won't stop until I feel like I'm going to scream.'

He rested his cheek against her head and rubbed her back. 'I am cursed with a terminal case of curiosity,' he said. 'I am jealous, selfish, acquisitive, territorial and possessive. I have a terrible temper, and I know I can be a cruel son of a bitch.' He cocked his head. 'I used to eat people, you know.'

If he meant to shock her out of crying, he succeeded. A snort burst out of her. 'That's awful,' she said. Her nose was clogged. 'I mean it, that's awful. It's not funny. I'm not laughing.'

He sighed. 'It was a long time ago. Thousands of years. Once I really was the beast the Elves call me.'

She closed her eyes, took a deep, shuddering breath and rubbed her fingers along the seam of his T-shirt. 'What made you stop?'

'I had a conversation with somebody. It was an epiphany.' His voice was rueful. He rocked her. 'From that point on I swore I would never eat something that could talk.'

'Hey, that's kind of your version of turning vegetarian, isn't it?' she said.

He laughed. 'I guess maybe it is. All of that is a long, round-about way of saying I'm sorry. I don't always get the emotional nuances of a situation and I didn't mean to make you cry.'

'It's everything, it's not just you.' She turned her head and put her face in his neck.

He held her closer. 'I want you to trust me more than you trusted that dumbass boyfriend of yours.'

She sighed. 'When are you going to let go of that? Ex-boy-friend. Ex. And anyway, he's dead.'

'I want you to tell me what and who you are, not just because I want to know but because you want to tell me.'

'Why?' she whispered.

'Because you're mine,' he snapped.

'I'm not just a possession, like you'd own a lamp.' She pulled back and glared at him. He just looked back at her, face hard and eyes unapologetic. She sighed. 'I guess that's the possessive and territorial bit, isn't it? You know, I don't want to fight with you.'

Like any efficient predator, he scented weakness and acted on it. 'Then don't,' he said. He gave her a coaxing smile. 'Just give me everything I want.'

She groaned and let her head fall back. She stared at the ceiling. She had to grant him a lot of respect. At least he was all out there, nothing hidden. He was up front with who he was and what he wanted, and he wasn't ashamed of a single bit of it. Not like her.

'I guess I've got a lot to think about,' she said.

Even as he enjoyed looking at the pure, clean line of her throat, he frowned. That wasn't what he wanted to hear. He cupped the back of her head and pulled her upright so that he could look into her eyes. They were a drenched dark violet blue, bigger and more beautiful than ever. She gazed back at him, waiting to see what he would do next. That wasn't what he wanted either.

There she was, inside of her skin, and she was more of a mystery to him than ever. It was driving him crazy. Curiosity gripped him, and without realizing he was taking a momentous step, he asked, 'What do you want?'

Surprise lit her face. She tilted her head and smiled at him. Did she dare to have the kind of courage he had and just say what she wanted out loud? 'I guess I want what a lot of people want. I want to feel safe,' she said, lifting one shoulder. 'I want to have a say in my own life. I want to be loved. I don't want to live this half life of not being either human or Wyr. I wish I were one thing or the other. I want to belong somewhere.'

He had a strange, intent expression on his face as he listened to her. His eyes were open and accepting in a way she didn't think she had experienced from anyone else before.

'I don't know what love means,' he said. 'But you belong somewhere. You belong here with me. I will keep you safe. And I think you might be more Wyr than you realize.'

She frowned. 'What do you mean?'

'You're stronger since we were in the Other land. I can sense it in you.' His eyes narrowed. 'Haven't you noticed?'

'Well, yes, now that you mention it.' She gave a half laugh. 'I mean, I've been kind of too busy to process everything that's happened, but I do still feel like I did over there – I don't know, more alive. My hearing, eyesight, everything is . . . more.'

'You weren't sure that you could heal me,' he said, as he had earlier. 'And maybe you couldn't a couple of weeks ago. Remember, I said it can make some half-breeds that way when they get immersed in magic from the Other land. Sometimes the magic triggers a reaction and they're able to come fully into their Wyr nature.'

She gripped fistfuls of his T-shirt. Could what he was telling her be true?

He covered her hands with his, watching her. 'How long has it been since you last tried to shift?'

'Years ago,' she whispered. Her eyes went unfocused as she thought back. 'After puberty. It was before my mom died. I think I was sixteen. We tried every six months or so. Once I was an adult, medically speaking, we decided there wasn't any more point in putting either of us through it anymore. She was fine; she loved me no matter what. But I kept getting too disappointed when I couldn't change.'

He touched her nose. 'Sixteen is a very young age to give up. Most Wyr have life spans much longer than humans, even mortal Wyr, and they mature at a later age.'

She hardly dared to breathe. 'I don't know what to think.'

'I can't make you any promises,' he told her. 'But over time I've helped a lot of Wyrkind through a difficult first change. If you want to try again and you trust me, I'll do everything I can to help you.'

≋ THIRTEEN ≋

She threw her arms around him, hugging him hard. Then she pulled away and paced in a circle, her mind racing. She flung herself at him and hugged him again. He laughed and gripped her by the hips to hold her in one place.

'Did you hear me when I said I can't make any promises?' he demanded.

'Yes, of course I did,' she said, distracted. She focused on him, her face grave. If it worked, she would be hunted for the rest of her life. But the way her life was spiraling out of control, she was going to be hunted anyway.

'All right, then.' He paused. 'Think about it. Let me know what you decide.'

She nodded. He kissed her, stroking her cheek. Then he strode over to the door and opened it. Clusters of talking people in the hall sprang to attention.

'Who needs to be here?' he asked. Most scattered like buckshot. A few of his sentinels, including Rune and Graydon, remained. Pia wiped her face on her sleeves in a vain effort to make herself more presentable.

Cuelebre Enterprises' PR faerie slipped around Dragos and into the conference room while he talked to the others. Beaming, she bounced over to Pia. 'Hi! Oh wow, am I pleased to meet you.'

Taken aback, Pia took the little hand the faerie stuck under her nose. 'Hi, thank you. You're Thistle Periwinkle, right?'

'Oh please,' the faerie groaned. 'That's my stupid TV name. Don't call me that. Call me Tricks; everybody else does.'

'Okay . . . Tricks. I'm Pia.' She smiled. Much as she had never cared for the faerie in television appearances, it was hard not to smile at this compact package of ebullience.

'Listen, I know we don't have much time.' Tricks waved her hands. 'I'm busy, you're busy, everybody's busy. I've got a lot I want to say to you, though.'

'All right,' Pia told her. 'Hit me with it.'

'First, I'm so sorry about what my uncle Urien did to you guys. I hate him, he killed my family, and we're going to cut off his head, and then I have to be Queen, but before that happens let's do lunch, okay?'

Pia felt like the faerie had just jumped on her head and started tap-dancing on it. She said, 'Are you serious?'

'As a heart attack,' Tricks told her. 'And I wanted to say you did an awesome job with Mr. and Mrs. I-Keep-My-Dignity-Stuck-Up-My-Ass. Really awesome job.'

Pia burst out laughing. 'You're talking about the Elves.'

Tricks blinked and wrinkled her freckled nose. 'Of course. You want a job?'

'*What?*'

'I need to hire someone to take over my PR job, with the upcoming assassination and taking the throne and all, and I think you'd be great. Oh, never mind; we don't have time to talk about that right now. We'll talk about that over lunch.' The faerie looked over her shoulder. She made a V with the first and second fingers of both hands and waved them like President Nixon. 'Two more things real quick. One, just so you know, not everybody's happy about you being here. A lot of folks are great, I mean, you know, in a Wyr kind of way, but there are also some people that I think are nasty-dangerous characters. Not that I'm talking about anything specific, just . . . There are a lot of predators that work here. That means there are some pretty hot heads and sometimes things blow up without much warning, so you just want to watch out for yourself.'

'Predators, hot heads,' Pia said, watching the faerie in fascination. 'Right. I think I do want to have lunch with you.'

194

'Of course you do!' Tricks said. She lowered her voice in a whisper. 'And last but not least. Dragos? Oh my God, he's so gone on you!' She giggled. 'I've lived at the Wyr Court for two hundred years and I've never seen him this way. Everybody's freaked because *nobody's* seen him this way, not even folks who are way older than me. So, you know, he's a man and a dragon and all that, and I know that means he's got communication issues, but hoo, honey, he's so hot he smokes without ever having to light up, if you know what I mean, so . . . way to be, my mama!' The faerie giggled again and held her hand out for a fist bump. 'Okay, that's what I wanted to say.' She beamed at Pia. 'Lunch today, one o'clock, got it?'

'Got it,' Pia said in a dazed voice as she fist-bumped the little hand held out to her. Dragos, gone on her? Really gone on her? Not just having a sexual fling? Not just having a possessive fit?

Oh God, I hope so. Don't I? Do I? She chewed her lip.

'Gotta go.' Tricks winked at her and bounced out just as Dragos, Rune and Graydon stepped back in. The faerie tapped Rune on the arm. 'Be sure to have Pia at my office at one o'clock, hear?'

'Do I look like a social secretary?' Rune said.

Tricks's eyes narrowed and the happy good humor she had shown Pia vanished as if it had never existed. She pointed at her own face. 'Do I look like I care right now? I have a million and one things to do before I go, so don't give me any grief.'

Rune laughed and gave her a one-armed hug. 'I'm sorry, pipsqueak. I know you're having a challenging week.'

Tricks readjusted her finger aim and pointed at Rune. 'Yeah, well, don't make me come find you either.' She charged away, tiny heels clicking down the hall.

'Looking rather shell-shocked there, lover,' Dragos said to Pia with a lazy smile. He strolled across the room to kiss her. 'Tricks tends to have that effect on people.'

'I guess.' Pia's smile was uncertain.

'When she's in her manic phase, she's a little like trying crack for the first time,' Rune said. He blinked at them, his face bland. 'Not that I would know what that feels like.'

'Right,' Dragos said in a brisk voice. 'I have things to do, Tiago to talk to, a beheading to plan.' He looked at her. 'You good?'

She smiled at him again with more surety. 'Yes.'

'Good.' He paused. 'Thank you for what you did in the teleconference.'

'You're welcome.'

He looked at Rune and Graydon. 'She gets to do what she wants. Got it?'

Graydon looked at his feet with a long-suffering expression and rubbed the back of his neck. Rune pursed his lips and said, 'Dragos, that might call for . . . a lot of tactical consideration. Don't you think it would be wiser to restrict her movements?'

'Why are they talking about her in the third person while she's standing right here in the room?' she said in a resentful mutter. Hot gold eyes met hers. Was it her imagination or did his lips tighten with some kind of suppressed emotion? Then he turned to give Rune a machete smile.

'Fuck you,' Dragos told him. 'I'm not the boss of her.'

He strode out. The conference room seemed to darken and expand at the absence of his nuclear presence. Then Pia stood, looking up at her two huge, stony-faced guards. Oh boy.

'Ms. Giovanni,' Rune said in a smooth voice, as he stared at a point beyond her left shoulder. 'For your convenience and pleasure Dragos has sent for a personal shopper to attend to you today. The shopper should be arriving any minute now.'

Pia stared at the gryphon. She turned away, pulled out the chair at the end of the conference table and sank into it. She flattened her hands across the polished surface. Clothing rustled as someone shifted behind her.

Okay. She nodded. Okay.

'Would you both please have a seat?' she asked.

After a moment, Rune took the seat at her right and sprawled long limbs out. Graydon took the seat at her left. The two men exchanged a look. She bet they were wondering what she was going to do next. She was kind of wondering that herself.

Her fingernails had gotten ragged. She rubbed at the uneven edge of her right index finger. Never enough time in a day.

'So,' she said in a quiet voice as she looked at her hands, 'is this passive-aggressive smarmy attitude working for you, slick? Because I've got to tell you, it's not working for me. In the last week and a half or so, I've been blackmailed, chased, threatened, in a car wreck that would have turned me into hamburger

196

if it hadn't been for your boss, kidnapped, beaten up and chased again. I was in a showdown with a Goblin army and the Fae King and forty or fifty of his favorite guys, and what life I had has been destroyed.'

She heard Rune suck in a breath. She said, 'I'm not finished yet. I'm also stuffed to the eyeballs with autocratic macho behavior since Dragos is all over that one. Just so you understand when I say I'm running low on patience right now. I get you guys don't want to be babysitting me. You've made it loud and clear. I don't want it either, but it is what it is. So can we do this easy, or do we have to do it hard? I'm trying to be nice, but I don't have any problem at all with doing it hard if that's really what you want.'

She looked up at the two men. Graydon had put his elbows on the table. He was watching her. For the first time she noticed he had nice slate gray eyes. She didn't see acceptance in his craggy face but at least it was no longer outright rejection.

Rune had folded his arms across his chest and narrowed his gaze on her.

'Slick,' Graydon said. 'She got you with that one, my man.'

'Fuck you,' Rune said.

'Believe it or not,' Graydon told her, 'he's the diplomatic one of the bunch. Dragos sends him out to do all sorts of smarmy passive-aggressive shit.'

Rune leaned forward and planted his elbows on the table. 'Shut up, asshole.'

She bit her lip and refused to smile.

Rune looked at her. 'Okay, Ms. Giovanni, let's try a do-over. See how it goes.'

'Call me Pia.'

He nodded. 'Just so you know, though, you do anything to betray Dragos and I'll disembowel you myself.'

She rounded her eyes. 'Wow, slick, that makes us practically BFFs, huh?'

Graydon exploded. After a moment, Rune grinned too. 'All right, Pia,' he said. 'What would you like to do today?'

She considered him. 'We already know I'm meeting Tricks for lunch. What do you think I should do?'

That must have been the right thing to say, because both men relaxed.

'Well, now that you ask,' he said, 'safest thing would be for you to hang out in the penthouse.' She sighed. He went on, 'But I can see how that wouldn't appeal. Next best thing, stay in the Tower. We'll follow orders and take you out if you really want to go, but I don't think that's a good idea right now, and to be blunt, I don't think Dragos does either.'

She turned thoughtful. Dragos's brief struggle with something had not just been her imagination. He had reined in his own impulses and opinions to allow her at least some freedom of choice.

Rune continued, 'Also, sometime today I'd like to go to the gym and run through some safety pointers with you.'

She refocused on him and nodded. 'Okay. I've taken classes that should help with that.'

'I know about them classes. Cardio Kickboxing,' said Graydon. 'Turbo Dance. I watch the infomercials.'

'You're not helping, Gilligan,' Rune said.

She smiled. 'How about this? If you don't mind, I would like a tour of the Tower.' They both nodded. 'I would also kill for a Starbucks soy vanilla latte if that isn't too much trouble. There's got to be a coffee shop close by. And I have to have new tennis shoes. Mine got trashed. I've got about twelve hundred dollars in my savings account if I can just get at it. Then, maybe after Tricks and I have lunch, we can hit the gym.'

Rune dug in his pocket and pulled out a card. He put it on the table and pushed it to her without a word.

She stared. And stared.

An American Express Black Centurion card. With her name on it.

A half-dozen emotions shuttled through her at high speed, starting with offense. Was he trying to *pay* for her, like she was some kind of whore? Was this to keep her widdle self entertained while he was busy, until he got tired of her and decided to get rid of her? She gripped shaking hands together and took deep, measured breaths until she found some self-control.

As she calmed she remembered what Tricks had said. Dragos was a man and a dragon, which meant he had communication issues.

Amusement was the last emotion to shuttle in to the station.

It braked hard and stayed. Dragos wasn't treating her like a whore. He was trying to give her a treat.

The gryphons were watching her with their game faces on.

'That card is so wrong I don't even want to talk about it. It's kind of fun to look at, but it's wrong.' Moving as though the card might explode on her, she put one finger on a corner and pushed it back to Rune. 'Look, all I want is a couple hundred dollars of my own money, a latte and new shoes. Okay?'

Rune smiled a real smile this time as both he and Graydon relaxed further. 'How about I loan you some money until we can get you access to your bank account? There's a Starbucks on the ground floor, along with some other shops, a CVS and a decent restaurant.'

'Okay, thanks.'

Just then a slender dark-haired man burst chattering into the conference room. He was the personal shopper, a Wyr-mink named Stanford. 'Hi, girlfriend, it's nice to meetcha. Look at what I got for yoo-hoo. A black Dolce & Gabbana satin robe, ooh, it's going to look so stunning with your hair and coloring.' He put a Saks Fifth Avenue box in front of her, opened it and, with a dramatic flick of his wrist, shook out the robe. 'Go ahead and feel it, honey. It's divine.'

Pia listened to the Wyr's incessant chatter. She looked at the robe. From Saks. She pressed fingers to the skin over her right eyebrow, where a headache was beginning to throb. She asked, 'Hi there, nice to meet you too. Stanford, how much did that cost?'

The shopper stared at her as if she had sprouted horns. 'Cost?'

'And why did you get it for me? I have a fine robe already.'

Graydon cleared his throat. He tapped her arm. She leaned over and he whispered, 'I think the boss wants you to have something that's more than a tiny scrap of pink that barely covers your ass. Don't get me wrong. It's a lovely ass.'

She jerked back and stared at the gryphon. 'Excuse me?'

The huge man's cheeks darkened. He raised a finger. 'Not that I meant to say that or to notice or anything. Fuck. I mean, I get it about the card, but if I were you, I'd think about letting the boss give you a robe. You know, 'cause sometimes things happen and us guys are around without a whole lot of warning. And I don't think he's okay with us seeing you wrapped up in that cute little pink handkerchief.'

She ground her teeth. After a moment she said to Stanford, 'Thank you for getting me the robe. It's beautiful.'

The Wyr-mink beamed. 'Atta girl, now we're talking. Let's get down to some serious shopping. You and me, honey. I'll help you look like a queen!'

'Stanford,' she said, regarding the little man. 'Do you get paid on commission or on an hourly basis?'

His nostrils pinched and he shook his head. 'Oh, I don't do commission, honey. Unh-unh.'

She turned to Rune. 'Got any cash I can borrow right now?' He dug out his wallet and handed her a hundred-dollar bill. 'Can I have the card back too?' He raised a tawny eyebrow and handed her the Centurion card.

She turned to Stanford and gave him the cash and the card. 'I want two things, please. First, I want you to take the cash and buy me a pair of size seven New Balance running shoes, and bring them back here with the change. After you do that, I want you to take the card and stock up every food bank in New York.'

The little man paled. 'Every food bank? In the city or in the state?'

Her mouth dropped open. 'I didn't think of that. Let's do every one in the state. How soon can you be back with the shoes?'

'I'll have them to you this afternoon,' Stanford said. His face had turned glum.

'Thank you.' She looked at Rune, tongue between her teeth. 'He did say I get anything I want.'

The gryphon grinned. 'He sure did, didn't he?'

They stood as Stanford slunk away, and the two gryphons took her on a tour of the Tower as promised. They had relaxed enough to chat, which made everything more endurable. She got a feel for the general layout quickly enough.

The penthouse floor housed Dragos's private quarters. The painting that had snagged her attention the night before was indeed a Chagall, and it sat across the hall from a Kandinsky. Aside from the bedroom suite they occupied last night, there were two other bedroom suites, one of which was draped in heavy construction plastic, undergoing repairs that were being done under the close supervision of security guards. The penthouse kitchen looked like something out of a professional cooking magazine. It was next to a dining room that could seat twelve large Wyr in comfort. There was an extensive library with two skylights, battered, comfortable leather furniture and over twenty thousand volumes on a wide variety of subjects. The library also had a glass case that housed the older, more fragile books.

The living room area was like their bedroom suite, with one wall comprising floor-to-ceiling windows interspersed with French doors. It had two fifty-inch plasma televisions at either end of the room, several sitting areas with sofas and chairs and a bar that was comparable in size to the one at Elfie's. Only sentinels and selected kitchen, security and domestic staff had access to the penthouse floor.

The next floor down held the large communal areas for key personnel, like the executive dining room, the teleconference room, the gym and training area, Dragos's personal offices and a large meeting hall. Below that were quarters for the sentinels and certain executives and Court officials and guests from other Elder demesnes.

Then the rest of the Tower was taken up by business offices – international corporate affairs, domestic, Wyrkind and Elder Races. Two floors were devoted to law offices. An entire law firm worked for Cuelebre Enterprises on anything from international corporate law to Elder-human relations, and matters that arose between the Elder communities such as the imposed Elven trade sanctions on the Wyrkind demesne. The law firm litigated matters in front of an Elder tribunal, which was composed of representatives from the seven demesnes, rather like the human United Nations, that heard and settled legal disputes.

The richness, the extravagance of the Tower, with gold-veined Turkish marble flooring, gleaming frosted glass lights and polished brass fixtures, was a massive architectural proclamation of Cuelebre's money and power. She thought of the Forbidden City, Versailles, temples to Egyptian gods. Not quite as tall as the 102-story Empire State Building, this building was no less a palace in a city that worshipped the god of commerce.

In the center of the Tower's ground-floor lobby stood a third-century sculpture that rose over the heads of the pedestrians. An intact sister to the damaged *Winged Victory of Samothrace* housed at the Louvre, the sculpture depicted a beautiful, powerful goddess with a stern face. She was draped in flowing robes, with her great wings swept high into the air behind her. She held a sword in one hand, while the other cupped her mouth as she called a battle cry to unseen troops. The statue was from ancient Greece, but the inscription in the modern pedestal was Latin, and very simple.

REGNARE.

To reign.

She had reached overload by the time they reached the ground floor and was extra grateful to get her soy latte and that kick of caffeine. Graydon got a grande mocha, and Rune had a black iced coffee. The men ordered a dozen pastries and several sandwiches. Then they picked a corner table. While their manner was relaxed and casual, Rune and Graydon angled their chairs so that they could keep an eye on the rest of the Starbucks. They also could watch the general ground-floor traffic through the windows.

Pia kicked a foot as she drank her latte. She tried not to stare too much at how fast the mountain of food disappeared between the two men. She said, 'People use words like "empire" but it's impossible to understand unless you get a chance to see all this in person.'

'Dragos is the one that did it,' said Rune as he demolished a piece of carrot cake. 'About fifteen hundred years ago, he realized the Wyr had to come together and form our own society. It was the only way we could protect our own identity and interests as human societies and other Elder Races developed.'

'Yeah, that dragon's one nasty motherfucker,' Graydon chuckled. 'I don't think anybody else could have done it. He united the immortals with the mortals, shoved his laws down our throats and kicked predator ass hard and long enough until we all started to behave. We had to or die. Those were some bloody years in the beginning.'

'It seems awfully feudal,' she said. She rubbed her finger around the rim of her coffee lid.

'It doesn't just seem feudal,' Rune said. 'It *is* feudal. I don't think there's any other way to run things. A lot of Wyr are peaceful creatures, like Stanford, who have no problem blending in with human society. A lot more need to know they'll get the living shit kicked out of them if they don't follow the rules. The world's gotten too small for anything else.'

'That's what you guys do, isn't it? I mean, when you're not babysitting.'

'Each of the four gryphons command Wyr forces that patrol a quadrant of the Wyr demesne,' said Graydon. 'We're sort of like police chiefs. But we've been pulled in occasionally for babysitting detail before.' He bumped her with his shoulder. 'You're not that special, toots.'

She sat back with a grin. 'Thanks, I feel so much better now.'

Just then Rune's wristwatch beeped. He pushed a button to silence it. 'It's your turn for lunch. Time to head up to Tricks's office now,' he said as he stood up.

As they rode the elevator, the men chatted to each other with the ease of long friendship. Pia fell silent as she considered her upcoming lunch meeting with Tricks. She turned to face the mirrored back wall of the elevator car. Like her pink robe, her jeans were from Target and she had trimmed her own hair.

Tricks's silk pantsuit had the classic lines of a famous designer, like Ralph Lauren or Dior, and her chic gladiator-style sandals probably cost as much as a good used car. And how crazy was it to go talk to the faerie about such a relentlessly famous public job? Even if the position were offered to her, she couldn't take it. Funny, how she hadn't noticed things like that before when she had been talking to Tricks. Self-conscious, she tugged at the waist of her jeans and smoothed back her hair as she tried to think of graceful ways to back out of the upcoming conversation.

She turned to face the front again along with the two gryphons as they neared the seventy-ninth floor. The doors slid open to reveal Tricks sprinting toward them, her small fists clenched and sweet pixie face transformed with fury. The faerie leaped around a corner and pressed back against the wall, her attention clearly focused on the hall behind her.

Pia slid an uncertain glance from Rune to Graydon. The two

gryphons exchanged a look. In a casual-seeming movement Rune took hold of her arm, silently urging her into a corner while he pressed the door-open button to hold the elevator. Graydon laid a hand on his sidearm.

Hard on the faerie's heels stormed the gigantic American Indian male Pia had noticed in the group of sentinels greeting Dragos's return to New York. At six foot four and 250 pounds, with barbed-wire tattoos circling thick, muscled biceps and swirls shaven into short black hair, the Wyr male was no less a frightening sight in broad daylight than he had been at night. His face looked like it had been hewn with a hatchet.

Thunder rumbled in the distance. Graydon's eyebrows rose. Either not noticing or not caring about their presence, the male charged around the corner. Tricks stepped out behind him and smacked him flat-handed in the back of his head.

The American Indian spun on one heel with blinding speed. He grabbed Tricks by the shoulders and hauled her up so she was nose to nose with him.

Pia made an involuntary noise. Instinct took over and she tried to move forward, to do something to help the delicate faerie. Rune's hand tightened on her arm, anchoring her in place. He whispered, 'Not when there's thunder in the air.'

What the hell did *that* mean?

Tricks shouted point-blank into the Wyr male's angry face, 'I've had it up to here with your mulish bad-tempered crap, Tiago! I'll thank you to remember my name is not "Tricks god-dammit" or "God damn you, Tricks." Henceforth those phrases are against the law – when you yell at me again the next one out of your mouth better be "Goddammit, ma'am"!'

For one throbbing moment they stared at each other. Then the rage in Tiago's face splintered. '"Henceforth?"' he said. He started to chuckle. 'You're kidding, right?'

She kicked him in the shin. 'Don't you dare laugh at me!'

He laughed harder, and the ruthless hatchet-faced assassin transformed into a handsome man. 'But you're so damn cute when you're mad. Look at you. The tips of your ears turned pink.'

As the Wyr male's anger dissipated the faerie seemed to compress, even vibrate, with deeper fury. 'Wrong thing to say, moron,' she snapped. She drew back her fist and planted it in his eye.

204

Tiago's laughter hiccupped. 'Ow.' He put a hand over his eye and glared at her. 'Have all the hissy fit you like – you're still not leaving New York without a Wyr security detail.'

At some unspoken signal she didn't catch, Rune and Graydon relaxed. Graydon's hand fell from his sidearm as Rune let go of Pia's arm. She glared at him and rubbed the spot, even though he had been quite careful not to cause her discomfort. She followed the gryphons as they stepped out of the elevator.

'Tiago,' Tricks said, sounding severely tried. 'First of all, Urien isn't dead yet.'

'I give it a week,' said Tiago.

'Second,' the faerie continued, 'after he's dead, Dragos and I have already decided there will be no Wyr allowed when I leave. The Dark Fae would never accept the presence of a Wyr force, and if any of the other demesnes even suspect that the Wyr are trying to control the Dark Fae succession, shit would really hit the fan.'

'That's suicidal,' said Tiago flatly. He crossed his arms, thick muscles bunching. 'And it's not happening.'

'Third,' Tricks continued through clenched teeth, 'I'm going to be *Queen*. It's the scissors-paper-rock game. Queen trumps Wyr warlord asshole. I get that you're used to commanding your own army, running around and killing things and doing whatever the hell you want. That doesn't happen in New York, and it doesn't happen around me. Get over it or go home. If you have a home. If you even live in a house.'

Tiago scowled. 'I live in a house when I have time.'

Rune strode forward, demanding, 'When did you and Dragos decide you would leave New York without Wyr bodyguards?'

The faerie threw him a hassled look. 'We discussed it this morning.'

Graydon joined the triangle. 'Sugar, I think we should revisit that decision. It's gonna be a hell of a shock when you go public with your real identity. Most people think your whole family's dead. There's gonna be some Dark Fae who will feel mighty displaced when they find out you're the real heir to their throne.'

Tricks slapped her fists over her ears. 'We're not talking about this. I'm not talking.'

Still standing by the elevator, Pia watched the angry quartet in fascination. She didn't understand everything that had just

205

happened, but it was clear the four of them were tied together with much more than just inter-Elder politics. They were in the middle of a knockdown, drag-out family fight.

She looked around, feeling awkward and quite the outsider. She recognized where they were from the earlier tour. At the end of the hall were large double oak doors, at present propped open. They led to Dragos's offices.

Overcome with curiosity, she inched down the hall and peered into the inner sanctum to find yet more luxurious appointments and a rampant display of wealth. She sucked in a breath. She didn't recognize a lot of the artwork she had seen in the penthouse, but she was pretty sure she was staring at a painting by Jackson Pollock that hung directly opposite the open doors.

Dragos stood nearby. He was deep in conversation with a large shaggy young man who managed to look rumpled and somewhat shabby despite wearing an expensive suit. Dragos caught sight of her and he smiled. The warmth of his smile spread through her, and she smiled back.

A moment later his face darkened with rage, the swift trans-formation so inexplicable and unexpected, she recoiled. He strode toward her and yanked her against his side.

'She's not alone. We're here. We've got her,' said Graydon from around the corner, behind her. The gryphon had followed her. He stood not five feet away, relaxed but alert with his back against the wall.

She looked around as Dragos glared down the hall. Rune had planted himself several feet farther away. He was still arguing with Tiago and Tricks, but he had positioned himself between them and Graydon and Pia.

The rigidity left Dragos's body and his expression eased. That was when Pia caught up. She pinched her lower lip between thumb and forefinger. His look of rage hadn't been for her. It had been for her bodyguards. She said to him, 'If I ever make you that mad – again – you will give me a chance to apologize, right?'

He pulled her hand away from her mouth and kissed her swiftly. 'You won't make me that mad again.'

She was all too aware of the young shaggy male's fascinated

gaze. Dusky color painted her cheekbones. She patted Dragos's arm and murmured, 'As long as you believe that, big guy.'

He turned, pulling her with him. 'Pia, this is one of my assistants, Kristoff.'

She met the shaggy Wyr's gaze, which was lit with appreciation. He gave her a shy smile. 'Hi.'

Pia's day brightened. Not everybody disliked her at first sight. She said, 'It's nice to meet you.'

'Take ten,' Dragos said to Kristoff. He led Pia into his office.

Vertical blinds were pulled back from the two outer walls, and the large office was filled with bright, hot, early-afternoon sunlight. She blinked, dazzled. She gestured at the door and said, 'I didn't mean to interrupt. They were all busy talking outside and I thought I would just take a quick peek—'

'They were the ones interrupting. They're making enough noise to wake the dead,' Dragos said. He punched a button on the wall. With a near-soundless motor purr the vertical blinds closed over the windows, remaining half open but providing some shade from the blinding blaze of light. 'Your arrival was a welcome bonus.'

Her attention returned to the windows and the cloudless bright blue sky outside. 'We heard thunder?'

He sighed. 'Tiago's Wyr form is the thunderbird. Lightning and thunder come when he really loses it. It's something to see in battle. Normally his temper is much better controlled, but everybody's on edge right now.'

Pia caught sight of the two landscapes hanging on the inner walls. 'Oh, these are magnificent,' she breathed. She walked toward them. The aerial landscape effect had been created by a mix of media, with paint, cloth, glitter and beads. The day landscape had a river cutting across the canvas. The night landscape conveyed an impression of towns scattered over a patchwork land. They couldn't be more perfect for him. She could just see him sitting at his desk and looking at them as he imagined flying overhead, and he contemplated all the parts that comprised the whole. She turned to smile her delight at Dragos. 'More patterns.'

His expression lightened with surprise and pleasure. He said simply, 'Yes.'

A tapping made them both turn. Tricks stood with a sheepish smile in the open doorway. She said to Pia, 'I'm so sorry you had to witness what happened in the hall.'

Grinning, Dragos said to the faerie, 'Goddamn, ma'am.'

The faerie's cheeks darkened. She said, 'What, you've never said something stupid in a fit of temper?'

'Never,' said Dragos. He snagged Pia's wrist and pulled her with him as he leaned back against his desk. As she settled at his side, he drew light circles on her back.

Pia coughed. He looked at her. She muttered behind her hand, 'Big roar, last week?'

His fingers slid under the hem of her shirt, and he pinched her. Pia jerked upright and huffed at him.

Preoccupied with her own sense of grievance, Tricks didn't notice their byplay. She said, 'Dragos, you've got to do something. Tiago's giving me fits.'

'Clearly,' said Dragos.

Tricks scowled. She told Pia, 'I'm great friends with all the other sentinels, but I barely know this guy. He's always off somewhere fighting things. Over the last two hundred years we've had maybe a dozen conversations whenever he's been called back to New York. Suddenly he's seething and snarling around the place, thinking he can tell me what to do?' The faerie turned to Dragos. 'He's a junkyard dog. He shouldn't be allowed in the house. Would you please send him back to South America?'

'The South America contract is unimportant. I canceled it a half hour ago,' said Dragos. 'We're pulling the rest of the troops home.'

Tricks's slender shoulders sagged. She wore the expression of someone watching her life crash in pieces around her. Pia's mouth slid into a sympathetic pout. She knew just how the faerie felt.

Tricks gave her a grim smile. 'How about some alcohol with lunch?'

'Sounds good to me,' said Pia.

≈ FOURTEEN ≈

Pia and Tricks said good-bye to Dragos and left his offices. In the hall, Graydon and Rune were talking to Tiago. Tricks ignored the trio as she sailed past them. Tiago glared after her. The handsome laughing man Pia had glimpsed so briefly was once again supplanted by the hatchet-faced assassin. Pia matched the faerie's shorter stride and kept her expression scrupulously neutral.

Tricks took her down to Manhattan Cat, the restaurant on the ground floor. 'It's owned by a Wyr-fox, Lyssa Renard,' the faerie said as they walked across the crowded lobby. 'Lyssa's a bit of a snobby bitch but she does know her food.'

'I've heard of the restaurant,' Pia said. She caught a glimpse of Rune and Graydon keeping pace a few feet away, their eyes constantly roving over the crowd. 'It's gotten some decent reviews.'

'You're a vegetarian, right?' Tricks pushed the restaurant door open. 'Of course, there's a lot of dead animal and fish on the menu, but there are also some good salads and a few tofu dishes I like. Best of all, they stock this 2004 Piesporter that makes me crazy. You like white wine?'

'Absolutely.'

'A girl after my own heart.' Tricks turned as the hostess, a dark, slender young Wyr-cat with slanted eyes, approached with menus and a smile. 'Hi, Elise, I'm sorry we're late.'

'No problem, Tricks,' said the hostess.

The restaurant's decor was simple and sleek, featuring dark wood, white linen tablecloths and fresh flowers. Every table was filled, and while one or two people called out a greeting to Tricks, most of the occupants paid no attention to them. The sounds of conversation and cutlery accompanied them as the Wyr-cat led them to a small private room at the back that was, Tricks explained, on permanent reserve for Cuelebre executives.

There were three tables in the empty room. After letting Pia precede them, Tricks stopped in the doorway. She said to Elise, 'We'll have two orders of the tofu stir-fry, a bottle of the Piesporter and no men allowed.' This was thrown at the two gryphons who were hard on their heels. Elise nodded with a smile and slipped away.

'Aw, Tricks, come on,' said Graydon.

'No,' said the faerie. 'You know this room. You know there's only one way in or out. And you know she's with me. Deal with it.'

Tricks slammed the door in their faces. Pia started to laugh. 'There's nowhere for them to sit out there,' she said.

'I know. I'm still mad at them. Besides, these walls are soundproofed. You know, supersensitive Wyr hearing, corporate secrets, confidential business lunches and all that.' Tricks grinned. 'That means you and I get to have some girl talk.'

Pia wasn't under any illusions about what she had witnessed. The faerie's utterly fearless confidence around the Wyr sentinels was based on two hundred years of residence with them. They were dangerous, powerful men and Pia was going to have to carve out her own way with them. Still, it was heartening to see they had a soft side.

Lunch came quickly. The waiter propped the door open as he served them. Just outside Rune leaned against a partition opposite the door. He sucked a tooth and regarded them with narrowed eyes until the waiter left and shut the door behind them.

Some impulse had Pia say, 'They're worried about you. It's clear they're going to miss you when you leave.'

Tricks's grin slipped. 'I'm going to miss them too.'

Was that a wet glitter in those pretty, overlarge, gray Fae eyes?

Pia looked away as she took a seat. 'I'm sorry,' she said. 'That was pretty personal. I didn't have any right to say anything.'

Tricks slipped into a chair beside her. 'It's okay. You're right.' Pia's gaze slid sideways. She watched as the faerie flexed delicate hands and looked at them. 'They're such good guys, Pia. Even that crabby mountain Tiago. Every last one of them would take a rain of bullets for you.'

'Well,' Pia said in a gentle voice, 'they might take a rain of bullets for *you*.'

'Oh no.' Tricks looked at her, eyes wide. 'I mean, yes, they would take them for me. Without question. But they would take them for you too, just because Dragos wants you safe.'

Damn, the faerie's sadness was making her own eyes prickle with tears. 'I think I know some of what you're going through right now,' Pia said. 'Not the impending Queen stuff. That's way out of my stratosphere. But the other stuff.'

'You mean the end of life as you know it?'

'Yeah, that.'

Tricks gave a sudden giggle. 'How'd we get so downtrodden? We haven't even finished our first glasses of wine.' She picked up her glass and clicked it against Pia's. '*Salut*, new friend.'

Pia picked up her glass. '*Salut*.'

Tricks knocked back her wine. 'Now for the good stuff. Gossip! You need to know who is lying, cheating, backstabbing, revenge-seeking, who-done-who-wrong and who is just plain hard to get along with in this place. I'm here to give you the road map every girl should have before she starts working in this loony bin.'

Hungry, Pia forked some stir-fry into her mouth. She remarked, 'It sounds like I need a flowchart.'

The faerie gasped. 'Beauteous. I need a pen.'

Pia watched her pat the pockets of her silk suit, then trot to the door to flag down a passing waitress. Tricks returned triumphant. She started to scribble on the white tablecloth, drawing circles and arrows between names as she chattered. They finished their lunch. The waiter came and left with their plates. More wine flowed.

Sometime later Pia rubbed her nose. She looked at her empty wineglass, then at the empty bottles on the neighboring table. She squinted at her new best friend, who listed to one side in her chair. 'What is your name again?'

The faerie snickered. 'It's gotta be on this chart. I'm sure I wrote it down somewhere.'

Pia looked over the dense black scribbles that covered the tablecloth. 'We were going to talk about something. Weren't we?'

'Sure we were. You're going to take over my PR job.'

'Okay.' She nodded. It was the perfect solution. Of course it was.

But wait. There was something she needed to remember about that. Doubts, other considerations, deadly good reasons why she shouldn't accept. There was something. . . .

Something that twinkled in the air, a feminine Power so light and delicate and effervescent she only just noticed it, after hours of sitting saturated in its presence.

Her best friend was writing something down. T-r-i-c-k-s. The faerie drew hearts and flowers around the word as she hummed to herself.

'Tricks,' said Pia.

Tricks looked up from the doodling, tongue between her teeth.

Pia put one elbow on the table, her chin in her hand, and smiled at the other woman. 'Is your Power by any chance related to charm or charisma?'

Tricks scratched the tip of one ear. 'So what if it is?'

'I don't think I should say yes to anything you ask me while we're in the same room together and I'm drunk, that's all,' Pia said.

One of Tricks's eyelids lowered to half-mast, a crafty, unrepentant look. Then the faerie grinned, and sunshine and happiness burst into the room. 'Oh, pfft!' she said.

The afternoon descended into early evening. Dragos, Kristoff and Tiago watched the evening news in Dragos's office. Kristoff stood with an arm wrapped around his middle, one hand covering the back of his neck. Tiago stood with his feet planted apart, arms crossed. Barbed-wire tattoos flexed as his biceps clenched.

Dragos sat at his desk. He tapped his steepled fingers against his mouth as he watched Cuelebre Enterprises get bitch-slapped on national television.

Two beautiful people were on the screen. One was a human female reporter. The other was the Dark Fae King.

For the first time in many decades, Dragos looked on the face of his enemy. Urien had typical Dark Fae coloring and features, with overlarge gray eyes, high cheekbones, white skin and black hair that fell to his shoulders. His hair was pulled back, revealing elegant, long pointed ears.

'. . . of course, scrapping the project is quite a financial blow to the people of this community and to the state of Illinois,' said Urien, with a charming, regretful smile. 'And not only for potential jobs that have been lost. We lost a valuable source of clean and economical power that would have been produced by a new electric-generating nuclear power plant, and we have Cuelebre Enterprises to thank for that. As you know, the nation faces the challenge of reducing our carbon emissions. The only way we can achieve lower emissions is by developing energy efficiencies and clean technologies, such as wind and solar power. Nuclear energy has got to be part of that mix. . . .'

Dragos punched the mute. He looked at Tiago and his miserable assistant.

Tiago said, 'Urien looks good for a dead man.'

'Too good,' Dragos growled.

'I can't believe what a fucking hypocrite he is,' Kristoff said bitterly. 'He's talking about clean energy and lower emissions when he's still blowing up mountaintops and he has one of the most polluting companies on the planet. You know our DOE contact, Peter Hines, rejected the RYVN grant application like we asked. He got fired today. And Urien's media blitz hit earlier this afternoon. Stocks are down in six of our companies.'

'The ones headquartered in Illinois,' said Dragos.

'Yup.'

'Oh, buck up, Kris,' Tiago said, impatient. 'Did you think Urien would take losing his pet project lying down? Of course he was going to strike back. At least you've got the satisfaction of knowing you really pissed him off. Usually he has nothing to do with human media.'

Kris chewed a nail. 'I know what's going to happen next.

RYVN is going to reapply for that grant with Hines's replacement. After this, public sentiment will be on their side.'

'They'll get that grant over my dead body,' Dragos snapped. 'I said do what it takes to tear the RYVN partnership apart and I meant it.' He surged to his feet and slapped his hands on the desk. Tiago was silent and Kris looked at his feet while Dragos battled his rage. After a moment he continued, with a semblance of calm, 'Get ahold of Hines, offer him a job. He's a bureaucrat – he must be able to do something we like.'

Kris said, 'Maybe he can join our Washington lobbyist team.'

'Go.' Kris fled. Dragos turned his hot gaze onto Tiago. 'And for God's sake, will you go find that slippery motherfucker so I can tear him to shreds?'

'Working on it,' said Tiago. 'He can run from me but he cannot hide forever. We'll get him, Dragos.'

He glared as his sentinel strode out. Locating Urien wasn't happening fast enough. He snarled down at his desk and made himself lift up his hands and get a grip on his temper. I've got to stop tearing the furniture up. There's too goddamn much to do. No time for another repair and remodel.

His thoughts shifted to Pia. He glanced out the window and frowned at the early-evening light. He left the office and jogged the stairs up to a silent penthouse. He strode through the rooms. They echoed with emptiness.

He didn't like it. His frown turned into a scowl. But what else had he expected? Did he think Pia would be here waiting for him whenever he decided to look this way – like an employee or a servant? Fuck.

Rune, he said telepathically.

Rune replied, *They're still at lunch.*

Still at lunch? Dragos reversed direction and headed toward the elevator. Minutes later he entered Manhattan Cat and made his way across the restaurant to the executive room.

Rune and Graydon stood on either side of the closed door. Graydon bounced on his feet. Rune leaned against the wall with arms and ankles crossed. Dragos put his hands on his hips and looked at them.

Rune said, 'Tofu stir-fry lunch at one thirty. Four bottles of wine. Waiter took in a tray of chocolate desserts and a bottle of cognac about forty-five minutes ago. Last time the door opened, they were singing "I Will Survive."'

'What's that?' Dragos said.

Graydon grinned. 'It's a seventies hit by Gloria Gaynor. I think they were singing it as a kind of "female bonding over bad ex-boyfriends" type of thing.'

His head jerked up. He had one of the most startling and unwelcome thoughts of the last century.

Am I a *boyfriend*?

He growled and jerked the door open.

Pia and Tricks were on their hands and knees on the floor, snickering in fits and snorts. The tables and chairs were shoved against the wall. Pia was folding a white table cloth that was covered with black writing.

'Give me a minute,' Pia was saying. 'I swear I just saw it. If you fold the flowchart just right – look, the names match up. All of those people slept together too.'

Tricks giggled. 'How did you notice? That's like something out of *National Treasure* or *The Da Vinci Code*. We need to get some weird antique glasses with special lenses and maybe we'll see something else. Wait. Here we go.' She let out a long, loud burp.

Pia counted through the burp. '. . . two ten thousand, three ten thousand, four – oop, you win.' She stared at the little faerie in awe. 'Where did you put all that air?'

'It's a gift,' Tricks said.

Dragos's bad mood burst like a soap bubble, and he grinned. Pia's blonde ponytail had loosened and slid over one ear. Tricks had kicked off her sandals and rolled her designer silk pants to the knees. She looked like a refugee from Pucci's on Fifth Avenue. He leaned against the door and waited to see which one would notice him first.

Pia did. She sat back on her heels as surprise and delight lit up her face. 'Hi.'

Surprise and delight, a gift-wrapped present all for him. He smiled at her. 'You're drunk on your ass.'

In inebriated slow motion, Tricks noticed him and the two gryphons at his back. She shrieked and spread her arms over the tablecloth. 'Nobody can see this!'

Rune slid around Dragos, his head angled in curiosity. 'Why, what is it, state secrets?'

'Pretty much!' Tricks started to wad up the cloth. Rune grabbed a corner and tugged. She threw herself on top of it. *'Nooo.'*

Dragos ignored them. He squatted in front of Pia and tucked a strand of hair behind her ear with a gentle hand. Her pale skin was flushed, and her sparkling eyes couldn't quite focus. 'You're going to be sick as a dog in the morning.'

'We just thought . . .' she said. The sentence trailed off. She stared at him in astonishment. 'You are the handsomest man I've ever seen. I would tell you that if I were sober too.' Then she gave him a sloppy grin as she shook her head. Her ponytail slid farther. 'No, I wouldn't. I'd be too self-conscious.'

His fury and frustration from earlier slid into the past as if it had never existed, an alchemical transmutation brought on by this tipsy enchantress. Laughing out loud, he slid his hands under her elbows and lifted her with care to her feet. 'What else are you drunk enough to tell me?'

She leaned forward and staggered, as she confided in a whisper, 'You're the sexiest guy I've ever seen too. You know, your long, scaly, reptilian tail really is bigger than anybody else's. Not that I've been with very many guys. Or was comparison shopping or anything.' She hiccuped and watched him worriedly as he guffawed. 'Have I just gone over a conversational cliff?'

'Pretty much,' he said. He put an arm around her and guided her around Rune and Tricks as they wrestled over the tablecloth. 'That's okay, lover. I'm here to catch you. So, how many guys have you been with?'

She held up two fingers and looked at them with one eye closed. 'One of them doesn't count anymore, 'cause he's dead.' She poked herself in the cheek with both fingers. 'I can't feel my face. How was your day?'

'Fine,' he said. He captured her hand, folded down one finger and pressed a kiss against her remaining index finger as he led her out of the restaurant. 'It was good.'

The next afternoon Pia changed into workout clothes along with her new shoes. She wound her hair up and bound it in a tight queue at the nape of her neck.

Her memory of the night before was fuzzy. She remembered talking and flirting, feeling brilliant and beautiful and witty, while Dragos teased her, his dark face creased with laughter. She remembered falling into bed, shrieking and kicking at him as he tickled her unmercifully. She remembered falling asleep, wrapped around him, his hands fisted in the waterfall of her hair.

She had been alone in the bed when a hangover had finally hammered her into consciousnesses late the next morning. She had rolled away from the windows with a moan to discover a vial resting on his pillow. It tinkled with magic. A note was tied to the neck. It said, *Drink me*.

That potion had saved her life. She hoped someone had been kind enough to get one for Tricks as well. Even with the potion's help, it had been some time before she could face putting anything else into her stomach. Now after a light lunch, which she had eaten with caution, she, Rune and Graydon were finally going to the gym as originally planned.

She opened the door. The two gryphons in the hall broke off their conversation. Their expressions were entirely too bland. She frowned. 'Did I do or say something yesterday that I should apologize for?'

'Not you, cupcake,' said Graydon. 'But apparently a lot of other people in the Tower have. Rune thinks we should rename it Melrose Place. I think Peyton Place has a more classic feel to it, don't you?'

'Oh no,' she said. 'You got the tablecloth away from Tricks.'

Rune grinned. 'Not before the little shit bit me.'

They took the stairs. Perhaps twenty people were in the gym. Some worked on equipment and others sparred with each other in the two large workout areas. One area had hard-used but well-kept hardwood floors and the other area was covered with tumbling mats.

Rune commandeered the space covered with tumbling mats while Graydon went into the locker room and changed. Then Rune went to change too. As he came back out he beckoned her and Graydon to the center of the mat. Both men wore tight tanks and black cotton pants. They seemed bigger than ever as she stood between them, totaling five hundred pounds of solid Wyr muscle.

Those that Rune had displaced loitered at the edge of the area, watching. Pia took deep breaths, trying to dispel the jitters that had taken over her stomach, all too aware of the curious, not entirely friendly stares directed their way. She balanced on the balls of her feet, shook out her arms and legs and stretched her neck.

Rune said, 'Okay, we're going to run through a few basic self-defense techniques. Pia, the main takeaway is we're the bodyguards and we know best. You've got to do what we tell you, when we tell you to do it. If I tell you to duck, you damn well better duck. If Gray tells you to drop to the ground, you plant your face. The toughest thing is that an attack will most likely happen without warning so following orders without hesitation or argument is absolutely essential.'

'In other words,' Graydon said, 'if we tell you to duck, don't stick your head up and look around and say, "Huh?" That's what your instinct may tell you to do, but if you're saying "huh," it probably means you're getting your head shot off.'

'Right,' she said, looking from one to the other. 'No "huhs."'

Rune said, 'Gray, get behind Pia. You're going to be her attacker. Pia, Gray is going to come up behind you and grab you like he's going to drag you off. I want you to pay attention to how he gets hold of you and the position of your bodies. We're going to work on ways you can break out of his hold, okay?'

'Okay,' she said.

Graydon moved behind her. For such a big man he was silent on his feet. She focused on the floor in front of her and continued to breathe deep as she sank into her training.

Stay firm but flexible, rooted but yielding.

She reached behind with her awareness and – there he was. She got a lock on him, stronger than she ever had on anyone before. She could hear him breathe, feel his weight shift with his intent. Her hearing, eyesight, her sense of everything in her surroundings was . . . more than it had ever been before.

He came up on her, inhumanly fast.

Flow like water.

She slid sideways, bending at the waist, and felt his hand graze along her arm. A twist, and she balanced on one foot, felt him extend, and that was her leverage.

Graydon landed on his back in an impact that shook the

floor. Silence filled the gym as exercise machines slowed and stopped. Both gryphons stared at her.

Graydon swore, letting his head drop to the mat. 'The hell'd you do? That weren't no Turbo Dance move.'

Rune put his hands on his hips and started to laugh. 'She smacked you down, is what she did.'

'I'm sorry, did I do that wrong?' she said, growing anxious as they continued to stare at her. 'I didn't follow orders, did I? Was I supposed to let him grab me?'

'No. No, I think you did that just fine,' said Rune. He offered a hand to Graydon and hoisted the other gryphon to his feet.

Graydon glared at her. 'Okay. I was sleepwalking through that. My bad. You said you had classes, and we should have listened. But we're gonna do that again, cupcake, and you're not gonna get me by surprise this time.'

She nodded. 'Okay.'

They assumed their former positions, and she balanced on the balls of her feet again, head tilted as she focused on the floor. This time, intrigued with her heightened senses, she locked on both Graydon and Rune. Their Power and physical energy made their positions easy to hold in her mind.

Graydon moved to the attack, his lethal body honed by countless centuries of combat. She flowed and slid away from him. This time he shifted with her, snaking one powerful arm out to wrap around her waist.

But she wasn't there. She moved, counter to his point, sensing the force of energy he put into his arm and how he threw his body forward, and that was her leverage. The floor thundered as he hit the mat.

He pounded the mat with his fist. 'Fuck me!'

Rune shouted in laughter.

Graydon flipped to his feet. It was a startling show of strength, agility and speed for such a large man, and she flinched back. He snarled at Rune, 'Laugh it up, asshole. It's your turn to try.'

'Quit being such a crybaby,' said Rune. He shifted around to Pia, the predator in him roused and full of smiling menace. 'You good to go?'

Mainlining adrenaline, she lifted her shoulder in a quick, jerky shrug. 'Give me what you got, slick.'

He lunged, using both cunning and speed, and she could tell he was really giving it to her, no holding back. She fell back in a graceful curve as he reached her, and the power in his momentum was her leverage. She hit the mat, and as she went backward she used her feet and one hand to propel him over her head. For one brief moment he was airborne. Then he slammed into the mat even as she completed her somersault and came up light on her feet.

Rune coughed hard, his expression frozen. Somebody whistled and shouted. Distracted, she looked toward the noise. Their audience was clapping.

'That was goddamn balletic!' Graydon roared. He pounded her on the shoulder and knocked her sideways. She grunted and stumbled, and he grabbed her. 'Oh shit, cupcake, I'm sorry. I didn't mean that. Did I hurt you?'

He looked so concerned as he steadied her she didn't have the heart to complain. She rubbed the spot where he had hit her, and he pushed her hand away to rotate her arm and probe her shoulder muscles with careful fingers.

'I'm fine,' she told him. 'It's good.'

Rune rolled to his feet. 'Go get Bayne and Con,' he told one of their watchers, who took off running. He walked over to her, eyes narrowed. 'What all have you studied?'

'Wing Chun, jujitsu, some weaponry,' she said. 'Basic stuff, sword and knife work. I can load and shoot a gun or crossbow. I'm not so good with a longbow.'

He studied her like she was a Rubik's Cube he hadn't quite figured out. 'Dragos said you weren't a fighter.'

'I'm not.' Graydon refused to be shooed away. She gave up trying to push him away and let him massage her shoulder muscles. 'Not like you guys are. I wouldn't choose a fight if I can avoid it, I don't have a killer instinct and I don't like the weaponry stuff.'

'Could you kill if you had to?'

'If I had no other choice,' she answered without hesitation. 'I think I could do it to survive. But otherwise, all of my focus and training is on getting away.'

'Excellent. We can work with that. Which of the disciplines you've worked with do you like the best?'

She considered. 'I'd have to say the Wing Chun. I like the principles of efficiency, practicality and economy of movement, and sensing the energy in your opponent's movements. It's elegant. I had a teacher once who told me the best kind of fighter was like haiku, very spare and simple, and the fight very short. Wing Chun seems to have something of that philosophy.'

He nodded. 'What would you say is your strength?'

'That's got to be speed. Let's face it, if you guys were really out for blood and got your hands on me, I'd be toast.'

'Very good. And your weakness?'

She bent her head, rubbed at the back of her neck and confessed, 'Following orders. I haven't done any of this before. I'll try my best, but if one of you yells duck, I could end up being that idiot that sticks up her head and says, "Huh?"'

'Well, that might not matter if you were slow enough to pin down,' said Graydon. 'We've got to yell duck 'cause you might get all startled and hop out from underneath us if we try to tackle you, even if it's for your own good.'

She winced at him.

The other two gryphons, Bayne and Constantine, had joined them while they talked, until Pia was surrounded by an enormous wall of solid muscle and close male attention. Rune said to them, 'You guys have got to see this. Pia, you up for more?'

'What do you mean, am I up for more?' She snorted and tossed her head. 'I haven't yet broken a sweat, slick.'

'Them's fightin' words, cupcake,' said Graydon with glee. He cracked his knuckles.

Bayne and Constantine took turns at trying to tackle her. Each gryphon hit the mat. They had better luck when they went after her in pairs. Pia's tank top grew damp with sweat. Not only were they formidable warriors with centuries of experience, they were motivated, fast learners. Very soon she had to ratchet up her effort.

She shifted into high gear, knowing she needed to learn even more from them than they did from her. All her focus was on the four Wyr who were intent on bringing her down. While they laughed and did a lot of joking, she knew now that what they were all working on was no mere exercise class but could be a matter of life or death.

. . .

Dragos had enjoyed a completely captivating evening with Pia. This morning he had held her soft sleeping form and watched the sun rise, and he had discovered another strange new experience, a feeling of absolute contentment and peace in the quiet, a certain knowledge that all was right with his world.

That was all in the past. His mood since had turned foul.

The Goblin stronghold had been abandoned. There had been no one to question. The enchanted shackles had vanished without a trace. Urien's media blitz had been pretaped. He had been long gone by the time they got someone to investigate the interview site, and nobody could pinpoint the whereabouts of the bastard. Those investigating the trail from Pia's ex-boyfriend and his bookie had come up against a dead end. And the stock value from the companies in Illinois continued to tumble.

There was also the not-so-small consideration that if the Fae King had been able to conjure a spell that had found his hoard, then the location was compromised. Didn't matter if the charm had only worked once and Pia was the only one who knew of the hoard's present location. Urien could make another charm, couldn't he? And maybe Pia was the only one right now who could navigate through Dragos's locks and wards, but once something had been breached it was just a matter of time until someone else found a way to do it again.

There was also no telling what else a finding charm of that strength would work on. He thought about warning his Elder allies about what had happened, but if he did that he would have to admit to his own vulnerability. He wasn't willing to go that far just yet.

On top of all that, the Chinese water torture had started as soon as he strode into his office.

The New York mayor was demanding to talk to him. No one else would do. His constituents were insisting they come to an agreement on noise control so that last week never happened again. Drip.

The governor of Illinois called personally to talk about his persecution of the RYVN partnership. Drip.

The Elder tribunal had issued a summons to him to discuss his 'act of aggression' in Elven demesne, and allegations of an

Other land Fae mass murder. Apparently they had decided to ignore the fact that he didn't answer summons from anyone, ever. Drip.

A personal courier had already arrived from the Elven High Lord, with a written invitation for Pia to visit with them at the summer solstice. Just Pia, nobody else. Certainly not him. The High Lord would be pleased to lift the trade embargo with the Wyrkind as soon as he received her acceptance. In writing. Drip fucking drip.

Then there were the endless business decisions on everything else. His administrative assistants and management teams were excellent. Everything that reached his office really did need his direct attention. As a norm, he enjoyed working with all the international ventures pursued by Cuelebre Enterprises. It was like playing several games of chess at once. But today it felt like wearing tight clothes over abraded skin. He wanted to tear it all off of him and claw at the walls.

He paced. He couldn't stop thinking about Pia. There she was, front and center, no matter what else he tried to turn his mind to. He didn't want to be working on all this shit. Business was boring. Who gave a flying fuck if stocks in the six Illinois companies tanked for a while? It's not like he needed the money. All of the entities clamoring for attention were like a pack of yapping Chihuahuas nipping at his heels. The thought of finding another secret location and moving all his treasure was a serious pain in his ass.

And why couldn't someone just FedEx him Urien's head?

He planted his hands on the window and leaned on them as he stared out over his city. When he had asked her last night if she was interested in Tricks's PR job, caution had stolen the sparkle from her beautiful gaze like a thief.

She had said, *I'll have to think about it.* Again. Just like she had yesterday when she'd told him, *I guess I've got a lot to think about.*

What the fuck did she have so much to think about?

She looked at him with desire in those gorgeous midnight-colored eyes. He would swear when she hugged him it was with sincere affection. She was generous and giving and held nothing back physically. He could make himself crazy at just the thought of how tight she felt when he was inside her, how gorgeous she was when she climaxed. He hardened as he remembered the sounds she made when they made love.

He was astonished at how easy she was to talk to, how much he *wanted* to talk to her, and fighting with her was the best fun he'd ever had. He had seen her just hours ago, goddammit, and he couldn't wait to fight with her again, to talk with her and hear what ridiculous thing she said next, to cuddle and laugh with her, to pin her down and drive into her again until there was nothing left inside of him, nothing left inside of her except his name.

She was *his*. Why couldn't she admit it?

Whenever they got to that point, whenever he thought he had a good grip on her, it felt like the beguilement dream when she had turned into smoke and melted through his fingers.

Those protection spells in her mind. That's where she disappeared to. She pulled back into that elegant citadel. He couldn't get at her unless he smashed through the barrier and broke her mind.

He scowled. Somehow he would figure out a way to get inside that citadel. He would have her. So help him, if it took the rest of his considerable life, he would have all of her.

Anything else was unacceptable.

Determined to try to shake it off and focus on something useful, he opened his door and strode out of his office to see if Kris had an update for him.

Nobody was in the outer offices. That was when he noticed the uproar. His pace increased as he stalked down the hall. He rounded a corner.

People had collected in the hall outside the gym. They were staring in the windows. As he approached a shout went up, and people inside cheered and clapped.

He brushed people out of the way as he entered the gym, caught sight of Graydon and Bayne at the edge of the tumbling mats. The gryphons stood with their arms crossed. They were watching something on the floor and laughing.

As Dragos approached, Graydon caught sight of him over the onlookers' heads and grinned. 'Hey, boss. Thanks for the new toy.'

Dragos demanded, 'What are you talking about?'

Graydon told him, 'We're playing pin the herbivore. None of

us can figure what the hell she is, but damn, she's fast. So far Team Gryphon is two for ten. Get her greased up and I bet we couldn't pin her at all.'

He reached the edge of the mat and looked down.

Constantine was crouched, arms out, intent on the struggle that played out in front of him. 'Get her – get her—'

Rune and Pia were in a tangle of limbs on the mat. Rune's powerful body strained as he fought to cover hers. Pia's smaller form twisted and flowed underneath him, her face fierce and reddened. They were both panting and slick with sweat. Pale, slender muscles flexed as she avoided his grasp. The gryphon swore as he shifted with her, into a position that was reminiscent of the very one Dragos had used yesterday morning when he had taken her from behind.

The dragon detonated.

⇒ FIFTEEN ⇐

The attack happened without warning, just as Rune said it might.

One minute she was immersed in the move/countermove of her match against Rune, mind racing to strategize against his flow of intent. He'd gotten her down on the mat. Not good. It meant he was more likely to pin her. She had to get out from underneath him fast, or between him and Constantine she was done.

Then his weight vanished.

Thrown off balance, she tumbled onto her back. She gasped to catch her breath and tried to make sense of what was happening.

Constantine lay sprawled against a wall. He spat blood, rolled over and got a knee underneath him.

Bayne shoved people toward the door. 'Out. Everybody out.'

Graydon knelt, slipped an arm around her and lifted her to a sitting position. He had gone pale. 'You okay, cupcake?'

She said, 'What happened?'

He wasn't paying attention. She followed the direction of his gaze.

Dragos had Rune pinned to the wall, one hand at his throat. Rune held still in the larger male's grip, arms lax and hands held open. His alert gaze was fixed on Dragos while his face darkened.

Constantine got to his hands and knees and coughed. 'He's killing him.'

Pia found her feet, avoided Graydon, who tried to grab her, and leaped forward.

There was nothing rational in Dragos. The dragon looked out of his eyes. He had partially shifted. The lines of his body and face were monstrous, all wrong. Talons dug into Rune's neck. Blood trickled from the punctures.

She didn't pause, didn't think. She eased up to Dragos and touched him on the shoulder to signal her presence. She stroked his arm as she slid under it, insinuating her body between the two men. She put her hands to that alien, deadly face and stroked his cheeks.

His Power was an inferno. She tried something she'd never done before and brushed her own cooler, gentler energy against his.

'Hey there,' she said. Gentle, soothing. She took a deep, slow, controlled breath. 'Dragos, I want you to look at me now, please. I forgot to tell you about the earlier part of my day yesterday. I sent my personal shopper to feed New York. The state, you know, not the city. So you're going to get a really big grocery bill soon. Sorry about that except, well, I guess I'm not.'

The dragon blinked. He looked at her. She had never seen anything so magnificent.

She smiled up at him and smoothed his inky hair as she kept up the soft patter. 'Come to think of it, I bet you're going to get lots of grocery bills. I can't imagine Stanford will be able to get so much food from just one supplier. Stanford is the shopper. He's a Wyr-mink. And my new robe is beautiful. It's black satin, very soft and elegant. I wore it this morning and thought of you when I took a shower.' She put a hand on the rigid muscles of his arm as she leaned against his chest. 'Come down off the ledge now. Let go of your friend. You like him. You're going to remember that soon and then you'll be upset if you've damaged him. Besides, I want you to give me a kiss, so I can thank you properly for the robe – and for the potion you left on your pillow this morning. They were very thoughtful of you.'

The dragon's eyes narrowed. His Power shifted to wrap an invisible cloak of warmth around her.

'I'm still not right in the head,' she whispered to him. Sexuality flared in those gold raptor's eyes. She slipped the tip of her finger between his lips and rubbed the inside of one thigh along his leg. 'Come on, big guy, you know you want to.'

He slid an arm around her, took hold of her chin with those long bloody talons and tilted her head up with exquisite care. She rose up on her toes, closed her eyes and lifted her face to him in total trust. His hard mouth brushed against hers.

She could feel the quick movement at her back as Graydon pulled Rune from them. The gryphon gagged and coughed. Then the rest of the world fell away as Dragos deepened their kiss. She slid her arms around his neck. She felt his body shift and flow back into more familiar contours.

He slid his mouth along the curve of her cheek, down to her collarbone, and he buried his face into her neck.

Her gaze slid sideways. The sober gryphons had arranged themselves around the area. Bayne leaned back against a wall near Constantine, who sat on the floor with a bottle of water. Rune was farther away, near the free weights, as he blotted his neck with a towel. The puncture wounds were already healing.

Graydon stood not three feet from them, arms crossed, watching her with an anxious expression. Okay, so that was maybe a little too close when she was busy getting lost in Dragos's kiss. She shooed him with her fingers.

He shook his head. Then he mouthed, 'What the fuck?'

She rounded her eyes, mouthing back, 'I dunno.' She shooed him again.

The gryphon was stubborn as a mule. He cleared his throat and said aloud, 'Boss, you gotta know we would never hurt her. We were just going through some self-defense maneuvers. She turned out to be so damn good we started to have some fun, that's all.'

Dragos lifted his head. He cupped the back of her head and pulled her closer as he turned away from the gryphons, putting his body between her and them.

Realization dawned. He wasn't being protective. He had almost killed his First because he was jealous.

She planted her hands on his chest and shoved. He let his hold loosen. She glared up at him, but when she saw the strain on his dark face her quick flare of anger died. Maybe she didn't understand what was going on. Maybe she would never understand.

She drooped. 'Is there anything more I can do?'

'I need to talk to my men,' he said.

She bent her head and nodded. She looked around the empty gym. 'Okay. I'd like to take a shower.'

He let her go. 'We'll all go upstairs.'

As he spoke to his men, she turned toward the doors.

A tall powerful woman stood in the hall, looking in on them. Armed and dressed in leather, she had a strange beauty, with lean muscles, tangled black hair and stormy gray eyes. It took Pia a moment to recognize her. She was one of the sentinels from the Tower rooftop. Aryal, the harpy.

The woman turned away as she watched, but not before Pia looked upon the merciless gaze and cold white face of judgment.

Pia, Dragos and the four gryphons went up to the penthouse. Pia took the Saks box from the bed and disappeared into the bathroom without a word. A few moments later the shower started.

The gryphons raided the wet bar for bottles of Heineken. Dragos opened up the French doors. He stood in the doorway as a sharp breeze gusted in. The fresh air was brisk and calming.

Rune joined him and stood casual and relaxed, hands on his hips as he too looked out over the city.

He said to his First in a quiet voice, 'I owe you an apology.'

The gryphon searched his face. 'It's all right, my lord. I can imagine how things must have looked. You'd already warned us to take care with her.'

'No,' he said. 'It is not all right. It's clear I am not in control. I am well aware that I am not acting or thinking normally or even rationally.'

Rune's gaze was keen, perhaps more keen than he was comfortable with. 'Dragos,' he said, 'we've all seen Wyr acting this way before, you know. We've just never seen *you* acting this way.'

He tilted his head. 'What do you mean?'

'Come on, think about it,' said the gryphon, a smile creasing his tanned face. 'When have you seen Wyr acting too jealous, possessive and obsessed? When have their tempers become too volatile? Too irrational?'

His mouth twisted. 'I've always been bad-tempered.'

'Well, yeah, you can be one crabby son of a bitch, especially when things don't go your way. But you know, when you lose your temper you have a reason. There is a reason for all this too.'

His thoughts twisted and turned. He considered the drama that played out when Wyr passions ran hot. 'You think I'm mating.'

His First shrugged. 'The possibility occurred to me. There's also a lot going on right now. You've been under considerable strain. It's rare when you've been in real danger of being killed.'

He took a deep breath and nodded.

Mating. Hmm.

He was a solitary creature by nature. He might interact with others, but inside he had always been alone. He counteracted the stresses of constant socialization in modern life by escaping for regular long flights where he could lose himself in wind and sunlight.

That was the juxtaposition that perplexed him. Instead of feeling relief at escaping Pia's presence earlier today when he had left her sleeping in his bed, he had felt her absence as a loss.

He had . . . missed her.

'I guess I've got a lot to think about,' he said. The irony of that statement occurred to him, coming so soon as it did after his annoyance at it being Pia's favorite refrain. He rubbed his chin and started to pace around the large room. 'Just – don't any of you touch her right now. Not until I figure this out.'

Rune strolled to join the others on the couches around the fireplace and accepted the bottle of lager that Bayne offered. He said, 'Understood. Unless, of course, her life depends on it.'

He explored the strange landscape inside himself for a moment and nodded in agreement. He changed the subject. 'Still no lock on Urien's location,' he told them. 'Whatever Goblins that might have survived have scattered. The mayor's whining, the governor of Illinois is trying to tunnel up my ass, the Elves are being manipulative, and . . .' He stopped and shook his head. 'She didn't say she's feeding the state, did she?'

Graydon rubbed his face, covered his mouth with a hand and said, muffled, 'Ayup.'

Rune and the others weren't so circumspect. They shouted in laughter at his expression. Rune explained, 'She asked the shopper to stock up all the food banks in the state. To be honest, I think the credit card freaked her out a bit. Maybe she's more of a flowers-and-candy kind of female.'

As he scowled, Graydon added, 'She liked the robe, though. Said it was real nice.'

'Whatever,' he said, dismissing the subject with a wave of his hand. 'I think it's pretty clear to everyone I can't be around too many people right now or I really might tear somebody's throat out.'

Bayne grunted. 'It is pretty tough to apologize after the conversation degenerates to that point.'

He gave them a grim smile. He finished one circuit of the room and started another. 'Another day like today isn't going to happen. We're going to start selling off some of the businesses and get life more simplified.'

'Maybe it would be a good idea to go upstate to Carthage for a few weeks instead,' said Constantine in a cautious voice. He referred to Dragos's 250-acre country estate in northern New York. 'You know, take some afternoons and fly out over the Adirondacks, figure out what you really want to do, let stuff settle in your head?'

'Going upstate for a while isn't a bad idea, he said. 'But I'm settled on a few things right now. Aside from the fact that Urien's got to die, I want to downsize my life and get rid of some of the white noise. And while we're at it, I want you guys to help me figure out what to do with all the crap I've got crammed underneath the subway.'

Under the cover of the shower, Pia sat on the bench with her head in her hands. A backlash from fear and adrenaline hit, and she cried until her throat hurt and her nose was clogged and she couldn't cry anymore.

The last couple of days had been so full of extremes, she felt like she was suffering from some kind of psychic whiplash. Everything was strange, full of hidden currents and nuances, with bouts of intense joy and sudden sharp spikes in anxiety and isolation. Reality had become a kaleidoscope that kept breaking up and re-forming.

For a while when the shit had hit the fan, Dragos had been her center, her one stable point. Odd, but she had been okay with all the danger and uncertainty that surrounded them. Here Dragos was part of everything else – unpredictable and unknown.

She had moments of clarity when she felt she was connected to him in a way that went deeper than either of them comprehended. She felt like she understood him better than he understood himself.

Then all the certainty slid away and she was left clutching at air. When that happened, she felt fractured inside. Maybe she was the kaleidoscope, breaking and re-forming. Maybe she was part of everything else that was unpredictable and unknown.

He was beyond splendid. He made her breath catch and her heart race, her temper flare and her sense of humor sharpen. He had her sexuality dancing for joy.

He wanted her to trust him, but how could she trust someone she didn't understand?

How could she love someone who admitted he didn't even know what love was, who claimed her as his possession, and who was capable of almost killing his oldest, most trusted ally and friend?

Wait a minute. She didn't just think that, did she?

Well, it wasn't true. She was suffering from a supersized value meal of Stockholm syndrome. She would admit to having a mouthwatering crazy going-on for him. Heh, not like she could deny that at this late stage. But she would not admit to the *L* word.

Oh God.

She wanted to go home, but she didn't have a home. Her apartment wasn't hers anymore. It might be let to someone else already. Even if it wasn't, she was afraid that if she were able to step back inside that space, she would find it was cramped and too small and just as alien as everything else had become in her life.

The shower stall opened. She started and shrank back, covering her breasts in a reflexive gesture, as Dragos stepped in fully clothed.

He knelt in front of her, gripping the bench on either side of her thighs. The severe lines of his face and muscled body were drenched in moments, the gold of his eyes shadowed. She plucked at the collar of his soaked T-shirt and sighed. 'What are you doing?'

'You've been crying again,' he said. 'Why?'

She chuckled, a small, hollow sound. 'Hard day, I guess.'

'Don't deflect,' he said. 'Tell me why.'

'What if I don't want to,' she snapped.

'Tough,' he told her. He took hold of her shoulders and drew her into his arms. 'You have to tell me so I can learn not to do whatever it is I did.'

Damn him. How could he end up saying the exact right thing just when she needed it most?

'Who said it was you? I already told you, everything's getting to me.' She tucked her face into his neck and nuzzled, reveling in his warm, wet skin.

'Still deflecting,' he said. He reached for a bottle of herbal scented body wash, squirted some into a palm and began to massage her neck and shoulders. 'You were having a good time with the gryphons. It was me.'

'We weren't always having a good time,' she grumbled. She bit back a moan at how good his hands felt as he dug into tired muscles. 'I've had to exert a great deal of my considerable charm on them these past few days.'

His chest moved in a silent chuckle. His fingers roamed the pale violin shape of her back, trailing suds. He paused and said in a dark tone, 'You have a hell of a bruise on your shoulder.'

'Don't even start that with me,' she said. She rubbed his back. 'After all my hard work we did end up getting along pretty well today. I'll have you know I was having a perfectly splendid time mopping the floor with them when you broke the party up.'

He pulled back and stood to strip off his sodden clothes and fling them into one corner. She stared at the sleek strong lines of his nude body and her heart started to pound. She couldn't deal with the strength of her reaction to him right now. She averted her gaze.

He sat on the bench and picked her up. She tried to pull away. 'Dragos, don't. I can't.'

'Hush. Trust me.'

He put her on his lap and tugged her around so that she was facing him. Then he leaned back against the wall, wrapped his arms around her, laid his head on her shoulder and just held her. She laid her head on his shoulder too, and he rocked her.

He said, 'Take it off.'

'You're such a pain in the ass.' She sighed, removing the dampening spell.

'I know.' He pressed a kiss to her clavicle.

His erection pressed between them, but he made no sexual moves. She sniffled as warmth and comfort stole through her limbs. 'And I'm such a wuss.'

'So speaks the young lady who Rune said tossed four of my toughest fighters around like throw pillows,' he said. He squirted shampoo on top of her head and lathered her hair. 'I frightened you again, didn't I?'

'No. Yes. Oh, I don't know.' She straightened and looked at him. Water trickled down the hard planes of his face and spiked his black eyelashes. 'How could you do that to him? He's your second-in-command. You've known each other for . . . for far longer than I can comprehend. If you could do that to him, who else could you do it to?'

'Right now, I could do it to anyone but you.' He eased her off his lap, stood and lathered. He washed his groin and genitals. He handled his erect penis with brisk practicality, but she still had to glance away from how mouthwatering he looked. She finished rinsing her hair as he sluiced off. He turned off the shower.

She wrapped her hair in a towel and dried off with another, while Dragos rubbed a towel over his head and body. The domesticity of the scene was both bizarre and seductive. She fought against giving in to a sense of belonging. It was an illusion. She slipped on the black Dolce & Gabbana robe and saw his eyes light with approval.

'Why anybody but me?' she asked. 'Why am I the only one who's safe?'

Why can I trust you? she wanted to ask. But the strain had

eased from his features and she didn't want to disturb the peace that had crept in to take its place. She took the towel from her hair and started working a brush through the wet length.

He stood behind her, a towel slung around his hips, and took the brush from her. He smoothed out her hair as she watched him in the mirror. The wet braid at his wrist was the same darkened shade of honey.

After several moments of looking thoughtful, he said, 'You don't know much about living in Wyr society, do you?'

She shook her head.

'I forget how secluded you've been.' He kissed the nape of her neck. 'It will all come clear in time. I promise. Just believe me when I say that not only will I never hurt you, I will protect you from anyone else who would hurt you.'

She did believe him. It fit with how he responded to her when she worked to calm him, with everything that he had said to her and with all his actions. Things settled back in their rightful places. 'All right,' she said. 'But how do we make sure that you don't hurt the others then? They're so loyal to you, Dragos.'

'I know they are. They're good men. You'll have to take my word that they understand what happened earlier, maybe even better than I do. We were all a bit too careless today. It won't happen again.'

'Can you be a bit more enigmatic?' she asked. Irritation brought out the sarcasm in her like nothing else. 'A few of those sentences made sense, you know. What won't happen again?'

He smiled. 'Are you hungry? Let's have supper. It should be set up in the dining room by now.'

Once he mentioned eating, she noticed how famished she was. All of a sudden she felt hollow and shaky. 'I'm starving. All I had for lunch was a salad.'

He frowned as he strode into the dressing room. 'You should eat more than that. It must take a lot of lettuce and carrots to keep up any kind of normal body weight.'

'Very funny.'

He cocked his head at her. 'I wasn't aware I was making a joke.'

She followed him and picked out a sleeveless red tank top and a matching white skirt splashed with large red poinsettias. She slipped on lace panties but didn't bother with a bra or shoes. Dragos's eyes gleamed with approval when he saw her.

He had dressed simply as well, in another white Armani silk shirt, rolled at the sleeves, and black slacks.

They walked to the dining room. Her stomach growled at the appetizing smell of roasted meat, fresh bread and garlic.

Appetizing smell . . . roasted meat . . .

A dizzying wave of nausea hit her. What the hell? She came to an abrupt stop, braced one hand on the wall and pressed the other to her stomach as saliva flooded her mouth.

Dragos whipped around. He snaked an arm around her waist. 'What's wrong?'

She held up a hand as she concentrated on deep breathing. The dizzy nausea passed after a moment. She straightened. 'I'm all right.'

'You're going back to the bedroom,' he said. His face set into harsh lines. 'I'll send for our Wyr doctor.'

'No I'm not, and no you won't,' she told him. She tugged against his hold. He refused to let go of her. 'Dragos, please. Cut it out. I'm all right. I didn't eat much earlier today and I'm just – a whole lot hungrier than I realized. All the good smells are down that way and you want to go in the other direction? Don't be so mean.'

He acquiesced and let go of her with obvious reluctance. She raised her hands and shrugged at him. He continued to watch her as they went to the dining room.

Two places were set at one end of the large polished mahogany table near the window, surrounded by several covered dishes. White candles were lit, and there was a bouquet of large white roses in a fluted crystal vase. The city skyline was the backdrop for the setting.

Pleasure flooded her. 'How beautiful. I adore roses.'

He smiled. 'Good. I hoped you would.' He held her chair for her and then sat too.

A platter of some kind of sliced roast meat was near Dragos's elbow, along with roasted potatoes and gravy. Revolted by the sight and confused, she averted her gaze. Near her was a dish of bow-tie pasta with red peppers and broccoli in a garlic sauce topped with vegan grated 'cheese' and a spinach salad topped with mango slices and pecans. Between them was a basket of white and whole grain rolls. An opened bottle of Pinot Noir sat nearby.

Her stomach gave another unsettled lurch, but she was so hungry in spite of it that she forced herself to take a bite of the pasta. The nausea disappeared like it had never been. She said, 'This is delicious.'

'If you have a sweet tooth, you might want to save room for dessert,' he said. 'There are strawberries dipped in dark chocolate.'

She sighed. 'I've died and gone to heaven.'

Silence fell as they concentrated on their food. She felt again that sense of the bizarre, sharing such a simple domestic scene as eating supper with him. Caught in the grip of compulsive hunger, she ate like there was no tomorrow. Then it eased so she was able to think again.

Feeling tentative she asked him about his day, and she was surprised and flattered when he responded with every appearance of prompt frankness. He told her of Urien's disappearance, their corporate conflict, the mayor, and the Elves. She bit her lip as disquiet intruded. 'This isn't going to have a quick or easy resolution, is it?'

He regarded her from under lowered brows as he took a drink of wine. 'It doesn't appear that way. It might be a good idea for us to spend some time at my country estate. Not only is it quieter and more private, it's well defensible.'

Us. We. Her clothes in his bedroom. Sleeping in his bed. She thought of their confrontation with the Fae King on the plain and how Dragos had denied his instinct to pursue so that he could protect her.

'Dragos, what's going on here?'

'What do you mean?'

She put down her fork. He watched her, thoughts shifting in his gold shadowed gaze. After a few moments she said, 'I would like to ask you a series of questions, if I may.'

He put his fork and knife down as well and rested his elbows on the table, hands clasped loosely, steepled index fingers pressed against his mouth. 'Go on.'

She began to pleat the edge of her linen napkin. 'Would you be hunting Urien yourself if I weren't here?'

'Yes,' he replied without hesitation.

For a moment she lost her breath. Implications tried to

crowd her mind. She shied away from them and focused on another question. 'What happened to my apartment?'

'I presume it's where you left it,' he said. 'Why? Do you want something from it?'

She clenched her hands. 'What if I wanted to leave? What if I wanted to go back there?'

'You promised you wouldn't.' His voice was steady, ruthless.

Fair enough. She started pleating the napkin again. 'What if I want my own room?'

Silence.

She forced herself to continue. 'What if I want to go see my friends? What if I want to start working at my job again?'

Silence. She looked up and met the dragon's gaze. He hadn't changed position, but his hands had clenched. His fingers were longer and tipped with razor-sharp talons.

She wasn't sure what emotion moved in her at the sight. He was far too dangerous a creature for pity. She did feel concern. She reached across the table, holding her hand out to him, and said in a gentle voice, 'They're just questions, big guy.'

He regarded her hand as it lay on the table, her fingers curled over an empty palm. For a moment that became more terrible than she could have imagined, she thought he was going to ignore her reaching out to him. Then those long taloned fingers wrapped with the utmost delicacy around hers.

He said without expression, 'What do you want?'

Something was on the line in this undefined place they were in. She chose her words with a great deal of care. 'I'm not sure, other than I would like to know my wishes matter. I don't want to be talked about in the third person while I'm standing right there or for my life to be arranged without my consent. I would like to make sense of what we're doing.'

'That would help both of us,' he said. Lines bracketed his mouth.

She studied him. 'Five days ago, more or less – at least for us – I was in danger of my life and on the run from you. Now my clothes are in your bedroom, we're sharing a bed and I'm worried about how I can fit in here. That's aside from all the rest like Urien and Goblins and Elven relations. My past feels like it's gone. I have no friends here. Tricks doesn't count since she isn't staying. The future has no definition, and it feels like whatever we're doing hasn't got any context or foundation to it.'

'You're right, your past is gone,' he said. 'You will make friends here if you want to. As far as the future is concerned or any possible context or foundation we may have, you've got to make some decisions. I think you'd better make them pretty fast.'

He spoke with the same direct incisiveness as he had when he told her how to negotiate the dangers of their capture by the Goblins. Instead of being put off by his attitude, a deep quiet settled into place inside. She squeezed his hand, and his fingers returned the pressure.

'All right, what kind of decisions do you think I have to make?'

'Rune thinks I may be mating with you,' he said, the dragon still looking out of his eyes. 'I think he may be right.'

Mating with her. All the air left the room, and her earlier dizziness came back in full force.

She may not know much about the intricacies of living in full Wyr society, but she knew that Wyr didn't always mate. When they did it was for life. It happened to her mother, who had bonded with a mortal man. After he had died, she had held on to life for the sake of her daughter, but when Pia was no longer quite so dependent on her she lost the will to live and faded from this world.

'Oh God.' Her face felt bloodless. 'You can't mate with me. I'm a mortal half-breed. It'll kill you.'

'That does not appear to be a relevant factor.' He sounded composed as ever but he gripped her hand so tight she couldn't feel her fingers. 'Besides, what you are seems to be in some question. Was your mother mortal?'

'Not until she mated with my father and he died.' She rubbed her forehead. 'She held on for a long time. He died before I was old enough to remember him. When I was little I didn't know any better. But when I got old enough to take care of myself, I could feel her slipping away. She wasn't interested in life anymore. It was a terrible thing to watch.'

'If you are able to come fully into your Wyr abilities, you will be whatever your mother was.'

'But what if I can't?' she whispered, staring at him with horror darkening her eyes.

'It is what it is, Pia.' He looked as unafraid as ever. 'Everything has an end. Even I will end one way or another. At the moment it's beside the point. If you want to leave my bedroom or my life, you'd better decide now. I'll do my best to try to let you go. If that is really what you need. I can't guarantee anything. It goes against all my instincts, *because you're mine.*'

His growl shook the floor.

It shook her too. She tugged at her hand and after a moment he let her go. She wrapped her arms around her middle and stared at the olive oil and bits of garlic congealing on her plate. The silence between them became weighted, sulfurous.

The quick rhythm of booted heels sounded in the hall. Graydon rounded the corner to the dining room in jeans and a Harley Davidson jacket. 'Hey, boss, I got what you wanted.' He stopped and stared from Pia's distressed face to Dragos's darkening expression. 'I'll just come back—'

'No.' Dragos stood in a swift movement. 'Give it to her and stay with her. I'm going for a flight.'

A flight, at a time like this? She looked up and said, 'Dragos, no.'

His reaction was immediate. He jerked to a halt and looked at her.

'The Fae King,' she said. 'He can still trace you. It's not safe.'

She could tell it was not what he wanted to hear from her. The darkness came back to his face. He said with deliberate brutality, 'I'm a lot safer on my own.'

She flinched and looked away.

Dragos looked at Graydon. 'I'll be in telepathic range.' He strode out.

'What does that even mean?' she said. 'Telepathic range. Anybody I know with the ability can only speak if they're within a few feet of each other.'

'Dragos has a range that's more like a hundred miles,' Gray told her.

She pushed her plate setting away and put her head in her hands.

Graydon sighed and came to sit beside her.

'I'm sorry,' she said into her hands. 'I know you don't want to be here.'

'You shut that up,' he told her. 'I'm fine with being here. I just think it would be better if Dragos were here instead.'

She looked at the gryphon over her fingers. He had picked up the bottle of wine and was eyeing the liquid left inside, his weathered features contemplative. The bottle was about a third full. He tilted back his head and drank it all down.

She said, 'Feel better?'

'No,' he said. 'That would take a bottle of scotch. Or two. Been one of those days, know what I mean?'

She nodded. Yeah, buddy, she did.

He reached into his jacket and pulled out a gold-wrapped package. Giving her a grimace, he put it in front of her. 'I'm pretty sure it wasn't supposed to go like this, but okay. This is from the boss.'

She stared at the slim package. 'Is it going to blow up in my face, like everything else has today?'

'I dunno. It might, judging from what I just walked in on.' Graydon flattened his hands on the table and stood. 'Be right back.'

She picked up the package and tore off the paper. The black case was inscribed with TIFFANY & COMPANY. The sense of the bizarre came back stronger than ever as she opened the lid.

A necklace nestled on ivory velvet, a ring of opal cabochons set in gold. The opals were bigger than the size of her thumbnails and had a multihued brilliance unlike any other opals she had ever seen. Tears prickling at the back of her nose, she set the case down and lifted out the necklace. It spilled over her fingers, the stones flashing with intense colors in the candlelight.

Graydon appeared with a bottle of scotch under one arm. He carried another opened bottle in his hand. He nodded when he saw the expression on her face and took a drink. Then he came around the corner of the table and sat by her side again. He slid the opened bottle over to her.

Johnnie Walker Blue. Alrighty. She took a healthy swig and looked at the bottle. Damn, that stuff was smooth. Cutting it with ice would just be wrong.

'A dragon just gave me a piece of jewelry,' she said. She took another swig and handed the bottle back to Graydon. 'Have I been added to his hoard?'

He shook his head and drank too. 'No, cupcake,' he said. 'I'm pretty sure you've replaced it.'

═ SIXTEEN ═

She stared at the gryphon. 'What do you mean?'
'He's downsizing. He's decided to sell some businesses, and he's making plans to either vastly reduce the size of his hoard and move it, or shit, I don't know, maybe he'll ditch it altogether. Says he wants to get rid of the "white noise."' Graydon rubbed his forehead. 'I guess maybe hell really does have a cold day now and then. Doesn't sound like he's quite right in the head, does it?'

Her eyes glittered wet. Looking alarmed, he reached out to pat her hand, then seemed to rethink the gesture.

He said, 'I know he's not a romantic guy. I mean having me just hand you your present and all. Even I know that was lame, but I think he's tryin'. There's even nice flowers on the table and shit . . .'

His voice trailed off as she just looked at him. He offered her the bottle. Her stomach gave another inexplicable lurch. She shook her head. She folded her napkin and whispered, 'I need a friend to talk to.'

The gruff gryphon's voice turned gentle. 'What am I, chopped liver? You beat the crap out of me this afternoon. That pretty much makes us pals in my book.'

She picked up the necklace again, turning it so that it caught fire in the light. 'I did not beat the crap out of you.'

'If you had one mean bone in your body, you could have,' Graydon told her. 'Now Rune's scouring the city for a Wing Ding expert for us to train with. We're all gonna learn to go with the flow or whatever the fuck it is you said you did. Think we'll look as pretty as you did doing it?'

'Not a chance,' she said, smiling as she looked at him sidelong.

His steady gray eyes smiled back. 'That's what I said too. Con, though. He thinks he'll look like hot shit, but then, he always does. Guy spends an hour every morning getting his hair just so. I'm tellin' you. Hair styling products for men? That's just not right.'

She chuckled. A companionable silence fell between them. She played with the necklace while he sprawled in his chair and drank scotch.

'So,' the gryphon said at last, 'tell Uncle Gray all about it. Dragos hurt your feelings or something?'

'Wow, that would be simple,' she said. 'Been there, done that, going to do it again sometime soon, I imagine. He said he might be mating with me.'

'Oh,' said Graydon. 'That.'

'Yes, that.' The words started tumbling out of her. 'We've known each other a matter of days, and he's taken over my life. He demands I trust him, claims that I'm his, like I'm some piece of property. He doesn't even know what I am and it's driving him crazy.'

'Well, none of us know that, cupcake. We can't figure you out and you're not inclined to talk about it.' Graydon drank some more.

'I have my reasons.' She shivered. 'And I'm a half-breed. It'll kill him if I can't make a full change.'

'So you two talk about this and he walks out,' said Graydon. 'Doesn't sound quite right.'

'Well, no. He said I had to make up my mind about what I wanted fast, so he could try to let me go. Then he said he wasn't sure he could. Then he left. Meanwhile there's the Fae King to deal with, and this is all so strange.' She waved a hand in a gesture meant to include everything. 'I barely know anybody here, and it seems like I've already stirred up hard feelings.

Everything my mom taught me was to run and hide. This isn't running and hiding. This is insanity.'

'Hey, don't go all 90210 on me,' said Graydon. 'Let's pull back from the curlicues for a minute and untangle things. Urien has to be dealt with, and he's a dangerous fact of life at the moment, but he's not part of the real issue, is he?'

After a moment she shook her head.

'Okay. Now, who hates you? None of us do. You're sure as hell a game changer, and I'll admit it took us by surprise. We didn't take kindly to the idea at first and some of the sentinels are still grumpy about it. But we'll adjust. Changes happen. That's not to say there won't be others who'll have issues if you mate with Dragos. He's very powerful, financially, politically and magically, and I won't lie to you. Court politics can get pretty spiky. You gotta know that's part of the package.'

She narrowed her eyes on him, remembering the woman outside the gym. She described the woman to him. 'That's one of the sentinels, isn't it? It looked like she's got a real hate-on going for me.'

He tapped the tips of his blunt fingers against the bottle, frowning. 'That's Aryal, and yeah, she's one of us. She doesn't exactly hate you. Harpies just aren't known for being real forgiving types. Give her time. She'll come around.'

She nodded. 'Tricks mentioned some hotheaded predators.'

He grinned. 'Yeah, there's a lean and hungry pride of Wyrlions in the corporate law division. They bring a comprehensive new meaning to the word "bitchy," but they have their place. If anybody gives you any trouble, all you gotta do is let me know and I'll take care of it.'

'Thanks.' She gave him a wry look. She didn't say it, but if she was going to make a go of living here, she would have to fight her own battles and carve out her own niche.

He said, 'This might be hard, but it's all simple at the same time. You know what it boils down to. Do you want Dragos or not? Do you want him bad enough to overcome what your mom taught you and let your guard down, to put up with all his shit, the Wyr Court, and deal whatever the future holds? Or do you want to run away and leave all this behind? That's all you gotta figure out. The rest will work itself out over time.'

She tried to imagine running away and starting over. She could go south. She would be alone. She knew without ever discussing it that if she said good-bye to Dragos, there would be no second chance. She said, 'It's all happening so fast.'

'Often the Wyr mating bond does. I've known times when it has happened the moment two Wyr laid eyes on each other. Now, there were some bumpy roads.'

'Have you ever known of the mating bond to happen to one person and not the other?'

He blew out a breath. 'That's a tough one. It's a lot trickier if a Wyr bonds with a non-Wyr like a human, since non-Wyrs don't go through the same experience we do. As for Wyr mating, I remember once a couple hundred years ago it didn't take right. At least I think. Were they going through the bonding process or were they just fucked-up? She killed herself when he wouldn't have her.'

Her forehead wrinkled. 'That's awful.'

'Tell me about it.'

'What if I remain mortal?'

He shrugged. 'Dragos doesn't appear to be running away because of that. Will you deny yourself a mate and the chance of happiness just because you're gonna die someday?'

'That's different. I'm going to die one way or another if I can't change. It just seems terrible to think that Dragos would die because of me.'

He hunched his shoulders and watched his hands as he turned the scotch bottle in circles. 'There aren't any guarantees in life. Just because some of us are exceptionally long-lived and call ourselves "immortal" doesn't mean we can't be killed. I would jump at the chance to have a mate, mortal or otherwise. Most of us would, you know. We never expected it to happen to Dragos, but I bet you every last one of us is thinking what a lucky son of a bitch he is.'

They fell silent again. Then she slid her hand over to touch the back of his. 'Thank you, Gray. You're a good listener and a wise man.'

He took her hand and pressed a kiss against her fingers. 'Shh,' he whispered over her hand, eyes crinkling. 'Don't tell anybody.'

She smiled at him. 'Your secret's safe with me.'

She was tempted to change into gym clothes and spend an hour on a treadmill, but then tiredness swept over her. It had been another long day and the gryphons had already given her quite a workout before Dragos stopped them.

Over Graydon's protests, she put the necklace back in the box, cleaned off the dining table, put the leftovers in the large stainless steel refrigerator and rinsed the dishes and stacked them in the dishwasher. Then she decided to wait for Dragos's return in the library. Rune came to join them as she browsed through the volumes.

She greeted him, picked an early history of the Wyr and curled up to read in a large leather armchair. The chair was the most battered piece of furniture in the room, the dark brown leather buttery-soft and bearing a faint but unmistakable familiar masculine scent. She could just imagine Dragos relaxing in this seat as he read his scientific journals. Rune and Graydon respected her unspoken desire for privacy and settled across the room to play chess.

After a while she let the book rest on her chest as she closed her eyes.

A gentle touch on her shoulder woke her. Rune squatted by her armchair, his eyes kind. She sagged back in the chair and yawned. 'Time's it?'

'After two,' he said. 'You look beat. Why don't you go to bed? Better yet, Dragos said he'd stay in telepathic range. You could call him back if you wanted.'

She shook her head. 'I don't want to do that. He needed some space. He's had a tough day. And I don't want to go to bed without him.' Her eyes started to drift closed and she forced them open. 'Unless you guys need to go to bed?'

He smiled. 'We're up until he gets back. Don't worry about us; we're fine.'

She nodded and felt soft warmth as he tucked a cashmere throw blanket around her. 'Thank you.'

'Thank *you*, Pia.'

He walked back to the chess table and Graydon. She closed her eyes again. Soon she was walking in a very old forest, breathing in its fresh loam scent. A small, pearly, luminescent dragon lay draped around her shoulders like a stole. She stroked a graceful sinuous leg, and the dragon lifted up his head to look at her with beautiful, dark violet blue eyes. She was full of emotion as she looked into his wide-open innocent gaze.

I love you, said the little dragon.

She kissed his delicate snout. *I love you too, peanut.*

She came full awake with a start and sat up, looking around. For a moment she felt disoriented and abandoned as she put her hand to her empty throat and shoulders.

Graydon and Rune watched her from across the room. Both men were wide-awake and alert. Graydon said, 'What is it?'

She shook her head. 'Just a dream.'

They stood. 'What kind of dream?' Rune asked, eyes sharp.

She frowned at them, not wanting to share it. 'Nothing happened. It was just a dream.'

They both looked toward the ceiling. 'Dragos is back,' Graydon told her. 'He'll be right here.'

'Okay,' she said, hurt that Dragos hadn't reached out to her telepathically and determined not to let it matter. Now was not the time to develop a thin skin. In fact, as long as she remained in the Tower she ought to jettison any delicate sensibilities she might have altogether.

Dragos entered and the atmosphere in the room turned electric. He looked invigorated. He glanced at the gryphons and jerked his chin toward the door, and they slipped out as he strode over and squatted in front of the armchair. She gave him a tentative smile as he leaned his forearms on the chair's arms and regarded her. His gaze was moody, his mouth tight.

'It's almost four A.M.,' he said. 'If you wanted to avoid my bed that much, you should have crashed in one of the other rooms.'

Her smile vanished. She struggled to sit upright and pull the jewelry box out from under the open book. She threw the box at him. Impossible to miss at point-blank range. It smacked him in the chest.

'I was waiting up to thank you for the gift,' she snapped. 'That you, oh, by the way, didn't give me yourself. Move.'

He stayed crouched in front of her, eyes narrowed.

She stuck her face up to his, giving him a full-on glare. She bared her teeth. 'I said move out of my way.'

He snatched her against his chest and drove his mouth down on hers. She struggled, managed to get one arm free and smacked him on the shoulder. He grabbed her by the back of the head to hold her still as he devoured her. She mmphed against his mouth and gave him another, weaker smack. He wedged her lips open and drove his tongue in deep.

Damn him! She wound her free arm around his neck and kissed him back furiously. All the electricity in the room shot into her body in one thunderous strike.

After a moment he eased up, turned gentler. She sucked his lower lip between her teeth and bit him hard.

He jerked back, gold eyes flaring. He touched his lip, looked at the smear of blood on his fingers, and his face creased with laughter. He said, 'You liked me kissing you.'

She didn't try to deny it. 'Well, there's a whole lot happening over here besides that. I've got quite a bit of angry still going on. Not that you asked. Did you come in here looking to pick a fight? How do you expect me to trust you when you act like such a pig?'

He didn't like that and glared at her. Struck by the strength and ferocity of the expression, she stared at him. If she were meeting him for the first time and he looked at her like that, she would be spinning on her heel and on the run before you could say Kentucky Derby. How things had changed.

His hold loosened on her. He eased back on his heels. She straightened and inspected the open book that had gotten crushed between them. Some of the pages had gotten creased. She smoothed them out and then set the book on a nearby table. All the while she was focused on him crouching too close in front of her.

'I'm sorry,' he said.

Her anger wasn't so quick to die away just because he knew how to say the word 'sorry.' But she didn't want to start escalating things again, so she just nodded. Maybe waiting up to talk to him had been a mistake. She avoided his gaze as she folded the throw blanket and draped it over the arm of the chair.

'Pia.' She looked at him. He held the jewelry box out to her. 'I have a present for you.'

The starch keeping her spine ramrod straight melted. Damn him again. 'Do you?'

He opened the box and lifted out the necklace. Gold and rainbow fire glittered in his dark fingers and was reflected in the gleam of his eyes. 'I wanted to see how the opals would look against your skin.'

'It's a beautiful present,' she told him. 'Thank you.'

'I'd like to put it on you.'

'All right,' she said.

She pulled her hair into a hand and held it aside as she twisted in the chair. His fingers worked at her nape, securing the clasp. Then the weight of the necklace settled into place around her neck, much heavier than the slim chains she was used to. It was longer than a choker and fell to the top of her breasts. She looked down at it and touched one of the stones.

His fingers stroked the hollow at the base of her neck and trailed along her skin. 'Lovely,' he whispered. He bent and angled his head to press a kiss against her throat. She stroked his black hair, her eyes half closed.

He drew back. The lines of strain were bracketing his mouth again. 'Do you want to stay or not?'

'I'll be honest with you,' she told him. 'It's hard to want to stay when you're being impossible. But I don't want to go.'

His gaze flared with something, triumph or relief, or maybe both. He started to pull her back into his arms.

'Wait.' She braced both hands on his chest. 'I'm not done. I don't see how we can finish this conversation until something else is concluded.'

'And what is that?' His eyes narrowed.

'I need to know for sure who and what I am. We both need to know. That's got to come before anything else. You think you want me to stay, but what if you change your mind?' She put fingers over his mouth when he started to speak and said, 'It doesn't matter what you say right now, since this is actually about me. I won't be able to trust things between us until I believe you know who I am. Hell, until *I* know who I am. I want you to help me try to change, please.'

He took hold of her hand and removed her fingers from his mouth. 'Can I speak now?' he demanded.

He sounded mad again. She wondered if anyone had ever told him before that it didn't matter what he said or thought. She licked dry lips and said, 'Yes.'

'All right. You want to do this, we'll do it right now.' He stood and pulled her to her feet.

'Now?' She looked at a nearby wall clock. 'It's four thirty in the morning.'

'The hell difference does that make? I'm not going to give you time to overanalyze things and chicken out. You napped, didn't you?' He took her by the wrist and strode out the door.

'Well, yes.' She trotted to keep up with him. 'Damn it, that's another thing. You've got to stop dragging me around like a sack of potatoes.' It was always some kind of he-man issue with him.

He shifted his hold to lace his fingers through hers. 'Better?'

'Maybe,' she grumbled.

He led her to the bedroom and into the dressing room. 'You're going to want to put on jeans and some shoes, maybe grab a sweater or jacket. There's a pocket of Other land about fifteen minutes' flight west of the city. I've used it before for this kind of thing. It's not very big, but the magic is strong and steady.'

'Okay.' She walked into her closet and stopped. Nerves started to tie her insides up in knots.

Was she going to let him railroad her into doing this now?

Yes. Because he was right, she would overanalyze and she was already tempted to chicken out. It was hard enough to try on her own and fail to change. So much seemed to be on the line with this one.

Not giving herself a chance to think, she tore out of her skirt and hopped into a pair of jeans. She sat on the floor to tug on socks and her new running shoes, then grabbed a black zippered sweatshirt. Then she removed the opal necklace with care and laid it out on her dresser beside her small jewelry chest. She went into the bathroom to run her brush through her hair a couple of times, and she yanked the length back into a scrunchie.

Dragos appeared in the bathroom doorway. He had kept the jeans on and changed out of the Armani shirt, into another black T-shirt that molded to his muscled torso. He wore black boots and had a gun holstered at his waist and a sword strapped to his back.

She drew up short at the sight. 'Oh-kay.'

'It's just a precaution, Pia. We're leaving the city,' he said. 'We're not going far, the gryphons are going with us, and we'll

251

still be well inside my demesne, but you've got to get used to this. Going out armed is a fact of life now.'

'Of course. It's just another thing to get used to.' She looked at the holster. 'A gun?'

'It's for any trouble we might run into on this side of the passage. They're safe enough to pack if you don't fire them on the other side.'

She grimaced. 'I guess I'll adjust.'

'You're doing more than fine with all this,' he told her. 'I'm proud of you.'

She smiled at him as pleasure welled. She figured it was a measure of how far gone she was that his praise could affect her so. But she also suspected he didn't offer praise lightly or often.

'All set?' he asked.

'Yes.' This time when he reached for her she was ready for him and took hold of his hand.

Bayne, Constantine, Graydon and Rune were armed and waiting for them when they went up to the roof. She looked from one to another. They were relaxed and alert and gave no hint that being called out before dawn was anything unusual. Graydon winked at her and she gave him an uncertain smile.

She hadn't envisioned having quite such an audience when she tried to shift again. She struggled to not let it matter but the terrible sense of exposure from earlier that day came back, turning her nervousness to fear.

Dragos walked with her to the center of the roof. Some signal passed between the men that she didn't catch. The four sentinels shifted into gryphons. She lost all sense of fear as wonder overcame her and she stared. They had the body of a lion and the head and wings of an eagle. No drawing of a gryphon she had ever seen had quite managed to capture their strange majesty or fierce dignity. They were smaller than Dragos in his dragon form but still huge to her eyes, each one's sleek muscled body the size of an SUV.

Dragos's Power shimmered at her back. She turned and looked up at the bronze and black dragon and forgot all about the gryphons. He bent his immense, horned, triangular head down to her. She spread her hands over his snout, eyes shining.

He gave her a very careful nudge and whuffled. She pressed a kiss to the warm hide between her fingers. He picked her up, gathered himself on powerful haunches and launched from the Tower.

Just as Dragos had promised, the flight was short, which was good since it was so unpleasant. She kept her eyes closed so she didn't have to look at the cityscape scrolling by underneath. She breathed through her mouth in an effort to control the nausea that welled as they took to the air.

After five minutes or so the violent nausea subsided and she felt herself acclimate to the flight. They had already passed over the Hudson and crossed into New Jersey, the gryphons winging in a protective formation around them. It was not long until they banked and began to glide downward.

She tried to make sense of what she was seeing. The spray of electric lights that blanketed the land broke up ahead of them, and a darker mass rose up ahead of them against the night sky. She asked, *What is that?*

First Watchung Mountain, said Dragos. *This is a short, tight passageway along a deep ravine. Hold on.*

The sense of land magic came on fast. The gryphons fell back as he went into a steep descent and glided very low. They passed between trees that topped the edges of a ravine. She could have sworn Dragos's wingtips brushed the rocky edges on either side.

The lights in the distance behind them wavered and disappeared, and she could tell they had crossed over to the Other land. Dragos climbed in altitude but just for a few more minutes. Soon they dropped into a large clearing.

She found her land legs as Dragos put her on her feet. She stared around, reveling in the wind and the quiet. The night sky on this side of the passage was strewn with filmy clouds. The shimmer of land magic was stronger than she had ever felt before. It called to her on a silver moon tide, rousing the caged creature that lived in her so that it wailed and threw itself against the inside of her skin, beating to get out. She stared at the etched silhouette of trees that rippled and swayed in the wind, wondering what this little jewel of a place would look like in the daytime.

Dragos shifted, but the gryphons didn't. They took watch in four points around the clearing. Dragos walked up behind her. He put his arms around her, pulling her back against him. She breathed deep, crossed her arms over his and leaned her head back against his chest. Her blood ratcheted too fast through her veins. She said, 'I feel like I'm at home and in exile at the same time. I wish I could settle down.'

'We have time. We're not going to rush this. And this is not an all-or-nothing situation. If it doesn't work the first time, we'll learn from it and try again.' His voice was calm and quiet. He pressed a kiss to her temple. 'I'm going to tell you some things now. Some of it is stuff I know, and some is just my opinion. I want you to listen to me: I am not asking you to do anything. If you want to turn around right now and go back to New York without trying, we'll do that. All right?'

I love you, she almost said. She caught the words back just in time and instead gave him a jerky nod.

'You stand a greater chance of shifting if you give me your true Name.' His arms tightened, although she hadn't moved. 'I'm not asking you to give me your Name. We can try this without it. I'm just telling you that I can help you better if I know it. Sometimes half-breeds get caught in midtransition and they're unable to complete the change. If that happens I can pull you over with your Name.'

'All right,' she said, her breathing choppy. 'What else?'

'I've been giving this some thought. I know your mother has put protection spells on you. I could feel them right away when I first tried to beguile you. How long have you had them?'

'Ever since I can remember,' she replied. She tilted her head back to look up at him. His head was dark against the night sky, but she could see the faint lines of his face and the dark glitter of his eyes. 'Mom was always worried that something might happen to her before I grew up. She was also worried about me being a half-breed, since I wasn't as strong as she was and I couldn't do half the things she could. I think she felt guilty for having me.'

His hand circled her throat underneath her chin. He kissed her mouth. 'It's clear she loved you very much and all she meant to do was keep you safe. She never meant to hurt you in any way.'

'She did,' Pia said.

Dragos continued, 'I don't know this for sure, but I'm guessing those protection spells are hampering your change. They're very tightly woven around your core. So the way I see it, you have a couple of choices. You can try to shift just the way you are, and for all I know you'll be able to. But if you want to give this your strongest shot, I think you should at least remove the protection spells while you try to shift. Sharing your Name is another issue altogether. It's a pretty radical step. But I wanted you to know it's on the table too.'

Panic tried to take her over. She fought an overwhelming urge to bolt. What the hell was she doing? This was going in the exact opposite direction of everything she had ever been taught. She gritted, 'Give me a minute.'

'Take your time,' he said, his voice quiet and calm. He rubbed her arms.

Could her mother have trapped her with the very spells that were meant to keep her safe? How could she trust Dragos so much?

They were standing in the open, but she still felt the cage inside. She had always felt she was never strong or good enough. Next to her mother's shining, radiant beauty, she felt dull as dirt and inadequate.

She knew her mother had loved her and would have hated to find out she had made her feel this way. But her mother had always been so afraid for her. Had her father's death made her mother that fearful?

'I don't want to live this way any longer,' she whispered. Dragos's hands clenched on her, but he remained silent. She turned to face him. 'I can't take off the protection spells. I don't know how. Can you remove them?'

'Not without hurting you.' He cupped her face in his hands. 'And I will not do that.'

What if I tell you my Name? she asked, unable to say the words out loud.

Then yes, I could.

She looked up at the sky and told him her Name.

The breath left his body. He shuddered and held her tight, bowing his head and shoulders, wrapping himself around her. 'You'll never regret it,' he murmured. 'Never. I swear that on my life.'

She laid a hand against his cheek as she rested against his chest.

He nuzzled her hand and began to whisper.

The whispers curled around her body, stroking her, urging her to relax, to open up to him. She looked up into his dark face and shadowed, hypnotic gaze. He stole into her like a thief in the night.

The dragon filled her to the deepest part of her being, coiling his bronze, serpentine body around her, whispering, whispering. The intricate citadel of spells inside her fell away. Great gold eyes filled her vision, as fathomless as the world. There was not a single part of her he did not hold.

Then with consummate skill, he began to withdraw. She looked at what he showed her, how to tap deep into herself for her Power when she willed the shift. Then she was alone inside her head. He cradled her and whispered, 'Are you all right?'

'Yes,' she whispered back. 'But I feel so strange.' She felt stripped, all her senses wide-open. The tiny hairs on her skin raised as the wind blew through the clearing, and the world breathed magic.

He smiled. 'Are you ready?'

'Ready as I'll ever get, I think.'

He let go of her and stepped back. She could feel his Power as he maintained a light connection with her. She looked around the open space. The gryphons were shadowed, motionless sentinels.

She reached deep inside for her Power. It came readily to her, welling up more plentiful and richer than it ever had. It filled her with a roaring gush of light. She stretched and extended everything she had toward the trapped wild creature that lay inside, the elusive part of her she had never before been quite able to reach . . .

And the world shifted.

≈ SEVENTEEN ≈

She looked intensely startled for a moment before her human form shimmered and disappeared. An exquisite creature glowing with a pearl luminescence took her place. She was the size of a small Shetland pony, but she was as far different from a pony as a greyhound was from a Saint Bernard. Her small body had willowy, racy lines. Long slender legs were tipped with dainty hooves. She had a graceful arched neck and a delicate equine head tipped with a sharp, sleek horn.

'Holy shit,' Dragos whispered. The possibility had crossed his mind from the various clues he'd been given but not with any real seriousness. In the whole of his life he had never laid eyes on a unicorn. He had heard for many centuries that the rare creatures had been hunted to extinction, but he had always been inclined to consider them just a myth.

A unicorn's horn could dispel any poison. She could heal with her blood. She could only be captured by unfair means. No cage could hold her. Her life sacrificed could bestow immortality.

No wonder all her mother taught her was how to run and hide.

Her large, dark violet blue eyes were Pia's. They were wide with alarm.

Predators. She was surrounded by predators. She reared and wheeled, looking for a way to escape.

The tall dark man started crooning to her. She stamped a foot and lowered her horn at him. 'Shh, my darling, you're safe. Be calm. You're safe.'

He took a step toward her. She scrambled back, tripped over herself and looked down in confusion. She had so many legs. She looked behind her. And a tail.

The large predators at the edge of the clearing were creeping closer, their eyes wide. The man snarled at them and they froze, then changed into men too. She galloped in a circle and made a sound of distress.

Then the dark man whispered her Name. She skidded to a stop and stared at him. 'Remember who you are.' He spoke the words softly but with Power.

Pia shook her head and snorted. She lifted up a foot and looked at a hoof.

Hey.

She had changed. She was Wyr.

Dragos went to his knees. Everything in him was in a suspended state of apprehension. After all they'd been through, after she had taken such a radical step and trusted him with her Name, she looked close to panic again at just being near him. It was her Wyr side. It had to be. The animal had taken too much control.

'Come on, darling,' he coaxed. He held his empty hands out from his sides. 'There's no reason for panic. You remember all of us. You like us. God, you're the most beautiful thing I've ever seen.'

She arched her neck and looked at him sidelong. Was that awareness in her eyes? Did she understand what he was saying?

'Give me a sign, sugar.' Gentle, gentle. Now he had the barest hint of what she experienced when she talked him back to himself. 'Let me know you're in there.'

She looked across the moonlit open field and then back at him. A run sounded pretty nice. But there he was with his face all lit up. He looked like it was his birthday, Christmas and New Year's, all rolled into one.

She took a couple of steps toward him. They were eye to eye when he was on his knees. The breath shook out of him. She walked the rest of the way to him and laid her shining head against his shoulder.

258

He stroked her velvet nose. She lipped at his fingers. His eyes glittered with a damp sheen. He sat cross-legged and pulled her onto his lap. She curled her legs underneath her like a cat. He put his arms around her and rested his cheek on the top of her head. They listened to the sound of the wind in the distant trees.

'Thank you,' he whispered. 'Thank you.'

She had trouble changing back and came close to panicking again. He had to guide her through the transition. He held her the whole time and talked to her until she was back in her human form again and kneeling on the ground in front of him.

'Why was it so hard to change back?' She gasped, clinging to his hands.

'It won't always be,' he told her. 'I'm told it's like learning to walk or ride a bicycle. Once you've mastered the shift it will soon become second nature. You could shift and change back to yourself now that you've gone through it once, but I don't recommend it right away. The first time, especially for a half-breed, can leave you wrung out.'

'Tell me about it.' Her tone was grumbling but her eyes were bright.

He helped her to her feet as the gryphons drew closer. All four men were staring at her in wonder. She looked at Graydon, who smiled at her.

'If you ain't a sight for sore eyes,' he said. 'I thought you were just going to end up being something small, fast and weird, like a marmoset or something.'

On impulse she went over to him and flung her arms around his neck. 'Thank you for being such a good friend.'

The big man held very still and looked at Dragos over her shoulder. Dragos's expression turned dark, but after a moment he gave the gryphon a short nod. Graydon patted her back, his gray eyes smiling. 'My pleasure, cupcake.'

Dragos put a hand on her arm and drew her away. He told her, 'We should head back now.'

He and the gryphons changed. She paid close attention to the ease and skill with which they shifted form. She wanted to try it again on her own, but that was going to have to wait until she had some rest. She felt like every nerve was exposed and hyperaware. At the same time, her eyelids expressed their own opinions by closing on her whether she liked it or not.

She fell asleep on the flight back. She didn't even wake up when Dragos changed, which he did with extreme control and dexterity. He held both front feet underneath her as the shift began. As he compacted, his forelegs shifted to human arms underneath her knees and shoulders, until he was standing as a man on the roof of the Tower, holding her sleeping form close to his chest.

The gryphons had already changed. They gathered around, staring at her along with Dragos. She was still shining.

Rune stood hipshot, his thumbs hooked into the belt holes of his jeans. He said in a quiet voice, 'You realize, don't you, that if this gets out she's going to be hunted for the rest of her life.'

'She's already aware of that, and so am I.' Dragos's face was grim. 'So it doesn't get out. Nobody hears about it. Understand?'

'What about Aryal, Grym and Tiago?'

'Not even the other sentinels, not right now. This stays between us.' He looked down at her sleeping face resting against his shoulder. 'She's had a hell of a week for a lot of reasons. I want to give her a break and let her just be for a while. Then she can decide who gets to know and who doesn't.'

She came half awake as Dragos eased her clothes off and tucked her into bed, only to roll over and bury her face in a pillow, one leg bent. He stripped, slid under the covers beside her and molded his body to hers, hooking his leg under hers, one arm tucked around her. She laced her fingers with his. He buried his face in her hair.

She slept hard and then dreamed of running. She woke with a start when she realized she was running on four legs, and the memory of what had happened sent a glow of happiness through her. The morning sun had brightened the room.

She looked at Dragos, who lay on his side facing her, one heavy arm draped around her. The hard lines of his face were quiet in sleep. The bedcovers had slipped to their waists, and the muscles of his chest and arms were relaxed. His eyelashes were twin curls of black against his bronze, lean cheeks, his inky hair tousled. His morning erection pressed against her hip.

He would never be a soft man. The capacity for violence

lived and breathed under his skin. But he had shown her moments of extraordinary gentleness, and she suspected seeing him so relaxed in unguarded sleep was a rare gift of trust.

I love you, she almost said. But he had already confessed he didn't know what love was. Her hands fisted.

Maybe he never would. Maybe this was as close as she could ever get if she accepted him as a mate. If she had to choose between being alone with him and being alone without him, she would far rather have what she could of him. She would have to learn to adapt to whatever relationship he was capable of having. It would have to be enough.

She curled her fingers around his thick penis and pressed her lips to his. He made a sound deep in his chest and kissed her back as he pushed his hips at her caressing hand. Then he nudged her legs apart, rolled on top of her and eased his erection inside. They both sighed when he was full in.

'That's it,' he murmured. He nuzzled her ear. 'That's right.'

'Right where you belong,' she whispered. She hooked a leg around him and rubbed his broad back.

He rocked in her, flexing his big body over her, in her. It was so good, so good. He brought her slow and easy to a climax that was so rich it brought tears to her eyes. He was kissing her, hands framing her face, when he came.

She felt him begin to pulse inside as he leaned on his elbows and hunched over her, gasping, and his face was so transformed, so beautiful, she had to whisper it. 'You're mine.'

He opened his eyes and looked deep into hers, still shuddering.

'I'm yours,' he said.

They both fell asleep again with him inside her, basking in the morning sun. Sometime later she stirred and murmured a protest as he withdrew and lifted his weight off of her.

'I have things I need to do,' he said in a soft voice. 'You stay in bed and rest.'

She gave him a sleepy pout. He kissed her forehead. She curled into his warm spot, hugged his pillow and dozed.

Such a funny little white dragon. His head was too big for his body. He focused on her, pure, determined love in his beautiful

261

eyes as he wobbled toward her. He couldn't get his hind legs coordinated with his front. He tumbled to the floor.

She couldn't laugh. It would hurt his feelings. She clasped her hands tight together to avoid helping him. She said, *Hey sweet baby.*

Mommy, he said, crawling fast toward her. *Mommy.*

She lunged up in bed, heart knocking like a crazy thing. What the –

The bed spun. Nausea surged, this time uncontrollable. She jumped out of bed. She couldn't get to the toilet in time but at least made it to the bathroom sink before she vomited until she couldn't vomit anymore. Several times when she thought she was done, her stomach would lurch again until tears ran down her face and she was dry heaving in painful spasms.

Oh no. Oh no, no. This couldn't be happening, not on top of everything else.

One of the advantages to being Wyr, for either male or female, was the ability for natural contraception. She had never been quite sure how it worked. It had something to do with fixing in one's mind a barrier to pregnancy, and somehow that was connected to the ability for shape shifting. It was all part of control over one's body.

Being half human, she had never had the ability, so she had to rely on human contraceptive techniques. She'd had a copper IUD implant for over a year now. It should be good for up to twelve years.

Except now Dragos was in her life, pouring everything into her, flooding her with his Power and semen over and over again.

Claiming her any way he could.

Reeling from shock, she barely remembered to check if the transparent strings from the IUD were still in place. They were. But – she stretched her newly expanded senses down into her body. There. A tiny new life spark nestled deep inside.

Betrayal filleted her. That bastard.

She showered and dressed. T-shirt, knee-length khaki cargo shorts, running shoes. Thirty-five dollars borrowed from Rune, left over from buying the shoes. She walked out of the room.

This time it was Bayne and Aryal who lounged in the hall. Pia drew up short at the sight of the tall, powerful, leather-clad

262

woman with tangled black hair, a strange gaunt beauty and stormy gray, judgment-filled eyes.

Bayne greeted her with a wide smile. Aryal did not. The harpy gave her a level look, her angular face cold.

'Where's Con?' Pia asked.

'He had other business to take care of,' Bayne told her. 'Aryal's filling in for the afternoon.'

'Got a problem with that?' Aryal asked, one eyebrow angling up insolently.

Pia's mouth pinched. What the fuck ever. She was just grateful she didn't have to look Graydon in the face. She ignored the harpy's question and jerked her thumb at the open doorway. 'Go on in and see what's on TV. Could you make some coffee, please? Better make it a pot if you want some. I'm going to grab some breakfast. Be right back.'

'You got it,' Bayne said with a cheerful smile.

Act casual. Go down the hall. Past the kitchen and dining room.

She glanced over her shoulder as she rounded the corner. Bayne and Aryal had disappeared into the suite. She ran for the elevator and the stairwell that opened into the huge living room area. The elevator was key-operated at the penthouse level, a problem she couldn't solve since she couldn't pry the doors open. The stairwell door was locked.

No problem there. It would be the work of a moment to push open that door and ease through.

She flattened her shaking hands on the door panel and leaned on it, breathing hard as the feeling of being trapped in a cage came back stronger than ever. The urge to run was overwhelming. She fought to get past panic, pain and betrayal to think things through with some semblance of rationality.

Even if she tried she might not make it out of the Tower. There were a hell of a lot of stairs down to the street level. She might have five minutes to get out of the building, ten at most if she locked the bathroom door and the sentinels thought she was taking her own sweet time doing female things in the bathroom.

And what would she face if she did manage to get out? The danger from Urien and his forces hadn't gone away just because she was having a bad day and needed to get the hell out of here.

Be smart for once. Don't add another thing to your stupid list.

Nausea surged again. She closed her eyes, clenched her fists and fought her body for control.

Behind her, Bayne said, 'Pia? Is everything all right?'

She took a deep breath, braced her shoulders and turned. She said, 'Dragos said I could go anywhere. I need to go out.'

God knew what the expression on her face revealed. It could not have been good, for the gryphon regarded her with a sober face and concerned eyes, quite unlike his earlier cheer. 'Can you tell me what you need?' he asked. 'I would be more than happy to get you anything you want—'

Her self-control slipped its leash. She went into a meltdown. She whirled and kicked the door, which resonated with a hollow, metallic boom. The sound was kinda like a bomb going off in your face. It was kinda like finding out you're pregnant when you shouldn't be. Yeah, kinda like that.

'I need to go out,' she shouted. She pushed against the closed door with her fists. 'I am not all right.' Kick. 'I need to *not talk about it*. I need for Dragos to leave me the hell alone.' *Kick*. 'I need for you to stop asking me questions and just take me where I need to go. Will you fucking do that for me or not?'

Suddenly Aryal was there. Both sentinels moved to stand on either side of her, their faces turning still and watchful. They moved like soldiers, athletic bodies light on their feet. Bayne's easygoing demeanor had vaporized. He blanketed her in protective male energy and put a gentle hand on her back. 'Of course we will,' he said. 'We will take you anywhere you need to go.'

'Bayne,' Aryal said.

'Standing orders,' he said to her. The harpy's lip curled but she said nothing.

Pia's breath shook out of her. She turned blindly to the elevator. Bayne guided her inside. He kept a steadying hand on her shoulder while Aryal shifted to stand between her and the elevator doors. She wrapped her arms around her middle, staring blindly at a point between Aryal's shoulders as the penthouse elevator plummeted eighty stories to the ground floor.

The doors opened and they strode out. Aryal remained on point while Bayne moved so close beside her his shoulder brushed hers while his sharp gaze roamed over the large, crowded ground floor. Then they pushed out the revolving doors into sunshine and a busy New York street.

She paused, one hand pressed to her abdomen. She could hardly believe it. They had actually kept to their word and taken her outside the Tower.

Silently Bayne urged her forward, toward a black Porsche SUV that had appeared as if by magic and idled at the curb. Aryal glanced around with a sharp gaze, tangled hair blowing across her angular face as she slid into the driver's seat. Bayne opened the rear door for Pia. She climbed in, twisted around and barred him from sliding into the seat along with her. For a brief moment his gaze met hers, and the kindness and concern in his eyes pierced through her internal upheaval. Then he stepped back, closed her door and moved to the front passenger's seat.

'Okay, Pia,' said Bayne. Aryal's frigid gaze met hers in the rearview mirror. 'Where to?'

'Brooklyn.' As Bayne's hand went out to hover over the car's GPS system, she said, 'I'll give you directions as you need them.'

The two sentinels exchanged a glance. 'All right,' Aryal said.

The Porsche pulled into traffic.

Pia huddled in her seat and stared out the window as they passed the Fifty-ninth Street subway station. Dragos said in her head, *Pia, what are you doing?*

She closed her eyes. It had been too much to hope that the sentinels would keep quiet about their outing. What she wouldn't give for a little privacy right now.

Don't talk to me, she said to Dragos.

You left the Tower. His mental voice was so quiet and controlled it sent a chill down her spine. *You promised you wouldn't.*

She snarled, *I said don't talk to me, you son of a bitch.*

A heartbeat, and then, his calm quite stripped away, he demanded, *What's happened?*

Shut up. Get out of my head.

Pia, goddammit. When she didn't answer he roared, WHAT THE FUCK DID I DO NOW?

His telepathic shout reverberated in her skull. She clapped

a hand to her forehead. *Don't yell at me like that. I can't think! Give me a minute.*

Her body felt numb, her seat belt the only thing anchoring her in place as Aryal suddenly cut across traffic. How could Dragos even ask her that? How could he not realize that she would know, now that she had made the full change to Wyr?

I'm sorry for shouting at you. He turned coaxing. *Bayne and Aryal won't say anything, just that you're upset and they're taking you where you need to go. Gray's worried about you. We can talk about anything that's wrong, can't we? Pia, please. You're killing me here.*

Whatever else anyone might say about him, he had a wily wisdom that could slip inside a person like a stiletto. She wiped her eyes and tried to process. *You don't know . . . anything . . . about what's going on?*

I swear I don't. His response was strong and immediate. *Whatever has happened, we can fix it.*

Could they? How?

Tell me where you're going, he said. *We'll do it together.*

Dragos, just give me the afternoon. She held on to a door handle as the Porsche hit an open stretch and gathered speed. *I need to calm down and think, and I need to find out some things before I can talk to you.*

Silence pulsed. Then, quiet and silken, he said, *I could use your Name to call you back.*

She sniffled as she stared out the window. She said, *Threats aren't a good idea right now, big guy.*

Seconds trickled by. Then he told her, *You have the afternoon. After that I'm coming to get you.*

You're giving me a whole afternoon of my own time? Gee, thanks. Big of you, said the part of her that was sarcastic with hurt. She managed to bite it back and stay silent.

Then he was silent too and she was alone.

Without him.

Rune and Graydon stood in Dragos's office, their hands on their hips as they wore identical scowls.

'At least she's protected,' Graydon said. 'She's got Aryal and Bayne with her.' He did not look reassured by his own words.

Rune asked, 'Did she say where she needed to go or what was wrong?'

'No.' Dragos prowled the perimeters of the room. It was too small, closed in. 'She just said she needed time. I told her I'd give her the afternoon.'

Rune said, 'You're really going to give her the whole afternoon?'

'Fuck, no. I lied.'

He threw open the French doors with such violence the glass shattered. The sharp May wind whipped through the room. The fresh air lessened his sense of confinement, but he still vibrated with the need for action.

'The witch isn't answering her phone,' he said. 'Find someone to put a tracking spell on this and do it fast.' He held up a fist. It was the one with her pale braided hair on his wrist.

'On it,' Gray said. He dove out the window and changed in midair.

Dragos and Rune regarded each other. Bayne and the harpy were excellent warriors. They were a couple of his finest.

But an afternoon could be a very long time in New York with the Fae King at large and intent on mischief.

An afternoon like that could be a very long time indeed.

Pia gave Aryal directions when necessary, but other than that the trip to Brooklyn remained mercifully silent. Soon they arrived at the large Brooklyn Wyr health clinic she had used for the last couple years. The clinic was housed in an unadorned square, concrete-block building in a neighborhood filled with pawn and barber shops, liquor and rent-to-own stores and businesses offering paycheck loans. A fugitive dereliction hovered around the edges of the streets, a sense of something sharp and desperate that huddled in shadowed places waiting to show its teeth after nightfall, but the clinic itself was open during the daytime, and it had a professional, caring staff and a high number of half-breed patients, so it was perennially busy.

Aryal pulled the Porsche to the curb and switched off the engine. Both she and Bayne snapped open their seat belts as they scanned the street.

Pia's stomach clenched again. 'Stay here,' she said.

'Sorry, Pia,' Bayne said. The gryphon moved fast. He was out of the car and standing guard before she could get her car door open. Aryal slid around the front of the Porsche and joined him.

She strangled the impulse to yell at them as she climbed out. She looked from one sentinel to the other. Aryal's expression was stony, Bayne's eyes carefully blank. She wondered what they thought of their destination, what kind of telepathic conversation might be going on behind those killer faces.

'Here's the thing,' she said. She pointed at the building. 'Nobody in there knew we were coming. You guys are not going to go in and scare the shit out of anybody who happens to be inside, so just guard the entrances and stay the hell outside.'

Bayne pursed his lips as he considered her. She narrowed her eyes and said, 'I could have left without you. I really wanted to, Bayne. Don't make me regret trying to play by your rules.'

Aryal said suddenly to him, 'Take the back exit.'

Bayne scowled. 'Fine,' he said. He spun on one booted heel and stalked away.

Pia didn't wait to hear more. She took off for the front doors. She had almost reached them when Aryal grabbed her by the shirt and shoved her against the side of the building.

'What the hell!' she sputtered. Shock ignited into outrage. Her fists came up to knock the sentinel's hands away.

With almost contemptuous effortlessness, Aryal held her pinned in place with a forearm across her throat.

'Shut up,' snapped Aryal. 'I'm not hurting you. You and I are going to have a talk.'

'Let go!' Pia dug in her heels and tried to yank the harpy's arm away from her throat. Aryal caught her wrist. Slender steel fingers bit into her flesh.

Aryal gave the street a quick scan with blade-sharp eyes. 'You have caused more trouble in the last couple of weeks than a street gang of Wyr-rats running amuck,' the harpy said. 'I want to know what the fuck you're up to now.'

'That's none of your business.'

'It is my business if it puts Dragos in danger again.'

Pia tried to shove the knuckles of her free hand into the harpy's midsection, but Aryal avoided her with a neat twist of her hips. 'I'm not hurting anybody. All you need to know is Dragos promised me the afternoon.'

'And you believed him.' Aryal barked a short laugh. 'Good one, genius girl.'

Had he lied? That hurt. She turned a look of dismay onto the harpy and felt like a fool. Her eyes burned. She gritted, 'Take your hands off me.'

Aryal released her so quickly she almost stumbled, standing too close between her and the street, crowding her. The harpy wore a leather jacket that gaped open as she put her hands on her hips. Pia caught a glimpse of the sentinel's shoulder holster.

'You know, I could get over that cheerleader ponytail of yours,' Aryal said, giving her a smile that could cut glass. 'It would take me a while, but I could. I could get over the gryphons losing their goddamn minds for whatever reason and fawning all over you. What I can't get over is this: you broke the law. You endangered the life of the Wyr lord, and by doing *that*, you endangered all of us, and you haven't been punished for it. So I've got to admit, that one pisses me off.'

'You have no idea what you're talking about,' Pia snapped, even as her gut clenched. She rubbed at her burning eyes. She had felt trapped at the time, but could she have done anything differently to avoid what had happened? She felt off balance and stupid and completely at sea.

'What have I got no idea about – that you may or may not be Dragos's mate?' said Aryal. 'Well, cupcake, that's the intractable problem and why I can't just kill you.'

Pia's hands fisted. She said between her teeth, 'No, you can't, can you?' She shot her fist out with such speed she got past the harpy's guard. She slammed it into Aryal's shoulder so hard that the sentinel staggered back. 'You don't have to like or approve of me. You don't have to agree with Dragos's decisions. You have to do what you're told. Did he tell you to bring me back to the Tower?'

Aryal glared at her and remained silent.

'No, I thought not. So you have to back the fuck off. You don't get to question or intimidate me and demand answers like I'm some kind of grunt under your command because I'm not and I never will be.' She strode forward until she was toe to toe with the sentinel, her body combat tense. 'And Graydon's the one who gets to call me cupcake – you don't. You haven't earned it. Now I'm going to do what I came here to do. You're going to do your job or Dragos is going to want to know why you did n't.'

Surprise flared in Aryal's stormy gaze, followed by a thoughtful expression.

Pia didn't wait to see any more. She turned away and pushed through the front doors of the clinic.

Half a dozen people sat around the waiting room. A few were watching *All My Children* on a TV set high on a wall. She went to the receptionist window. A nurse she recognized gave her a perfunctory smile. 'Afternoon. What can I do for you?'

'My name is Pia Giovanni. I need to see a doctor or a nurse practitioner,' Pia said, keeping her voice quiet so other people couldn't hear. Her face and neck muscles ached with tension. She twisted her hands together. 'Dr. Medina knows me. I'm sorry. I don't have an appointment. I—' Her eyes glittered. 'I'm afraid it might be an emergency.'

'Oh, honey,' said the nurse with quick compassion. She handed Pia a Kleenex and motioned her through the doors and into an alcove with a sink, a chair and a weighing scale. 'All right, what's going on? Are you sure you should be here and not in the ER?'

'I don't know. There's been so much happening.' She swallowed. 'I'm a half-breed Wyr so I have an IUD. You know, the one with copper, not the one with hormones, because of not being quite human. And I'm in this new relationship with a full Wyr, and I managed to change last night—'

'Congratulations!' offered the nurse with a wide smile. RACHEL, her name tag said.

'Thanks.' She tried to smile as she remembered how happy she had been. 'But all of a sudden I've gotten sick the last couple days. It was really bad this morning, and I'm pretty sure that somehow I got pregnant. I can feel it now that I've changed. And the IUD's still in place.' She focused on the nurse, her expression intense. 'I'm in shock. I can't think straight, but I do already know one thing. I do not want to lose this baby.'

The nurse put her hand on Pia's abdomen, her gaze going inward. Pia stood still. She felt the tingle of magic as the nurse scanned her. 'Oh wow, you're right, you are pregnant,' said the nurse, her eyes lighting up. 'What a sweet little strong spark.'

'Did changing last night hurt it?' she asked.

'No! Oh no, shifting is the most natural thing in the world. Your nausea does sound a little different, though. And with the IUD, you did the right thing by coming in. We'll get you in to see a nurse practitioner or doctor. Just go ahead and take a seat right there, and I'll pull your records. In fact, I'm going to see if I can catch . . .'

Muttering to herself, the nurse rushed off. Pia slumped in the chair and put her head in her hands. Thank God Dragos had stopped roaring in her head, because otherwise she thought she might spin into the air and fly into pieces. She thought his silence was ominous, but she didn't care as long as she could hear herself think for just a little damn while.

She felt shaky and on the edge of nausea again. She put her hand on her abdomen. Stay in there, peanut.

Luck continued to flow her way, as Dr. Medina was getting ready to go on vacation and had just seen the last of the patients she'd had scheduled for the day. Pia was acquainted with Dr. Medina and comforted by the familiarity. She was a brisk, gray-haired canine Wyr with a no-nonsense attitude and a sense of humor Pia found calming.

After a quick examination and a pulse of Power, the doctor removed the IUD and grinned at her. 'Good news. You, my dear, are in excellent shape and it isn't ectopic, which is one of the major risks when pregnancy occurs with an IUD. That baby is exactly where he's supposed to be, all snuggled in right and tight in your uterus and not in a fallopian tube or anywhere else. I'm glad you came in so soon though. Women who put this off for too long run a high risk of miscarriage or other serious complications. Now tell me about this nausea you've been experiencing.'

Pia sagged with relief. She described the last few days. 'I've not ever been tempted to put meat in my mouth,' she said with a shudder. 'But it's smelled so good. And that's so wrong.'

The doctor regarded her over half-glasses. 'Are you by any chance with a predator?'

'Yes?' She didn't mean that as a question. Did she?

'Well, that's your problem.' The doctor sat back and smiled

271

at her. 'Predator/herbivore mixes are much more unusual than homogenous matches, although they do happen, of course, since we Wyr are much more than just our animal natures. I'm not going to lie to you. You're in for a bumpy ride for the duration, and it may seem at times like your instincts have gone haywire.'

'Will it be a high-risk pregnancy?' Her hand went to her abdomen again.

'I wouldn't say that. There's no reason to go there right now. Think protein and calcium. If you can't force yourself to be omnivorous for the duration of the pregnancy, you'll need to stock up on protein drinks. Soy is fine. Whey is better. Along with the prenatal vitamins, I'll prescribe an anti-nausea charm that should help. It won't block pain, mind you. Pain is too important a messenger. But it should help you keep your food down. Keep it with you everywhere but in the shower. It loses its efficacy if it gets wet too often.'

'Thank you so much, especially for seeing me before you left on vacation,' she replied with heartfelt feeling. The doctor scribbled on a prescription pad and handed her a slip. She said, 'One last question, if you don't mind.'

'Sure, go ahead, as long as it won't take too long. I've got a flight to Cancún this evening and a mate who won't be happy with me if I miss it.'

She hesitated, not sure how to word things, and plucked at the edge of her examination gown. 'The pregnancy is a real shock. I mean, I had the IUD, so I thought it should have prevented things, right? It hasn't even come up as a topic of conversation with my . . . partner. I was starting to feel nauseated before I changed this morning, so I must have already been pregnant. So it had to have been the father who . . . changed things?'

The doctor's eyes were shrewd and kind. 'No single birth control is a hundred percent foolproof, for either Wyr or human. Yes, all things being equal, the IUD is a very effective method of birth control, for the most part. And yes, Wyr can control their reproduction cycle. For the most part. But I've also known Wyr to lose control during the first days of the mating frenzy. Only the two of you can say whether or not he's just your lover or your mate. If I were you, though, I'd think about going easy on your partner on this one, if he's your mate. Does that help?'

272

Her throat worked. She had to swallow hard before she could reply. 'Yes. It helps a lot. Dr Medina, thank you so much.'

'My pleasure. I love the babies. Should have been an obstetrician.' The doctor closed her file and stood but paused before stepping out. She regarded Pia curiously. 'By the way, you never did tell me what you shifted into?'

Caught off guard, she stammered, 'Oh, a . . . a marmoset.'

'Odd,' the doctor murmured, giving her a quizzical look. 'I wouldn't have classified marmosets as herbivores. And your mate?'

'He's . . . not one.'

The doctor narrowed her eyes on Pia. 'You will tell me, won't you, if it becomes medically relevant?'

'Yes, of course,' she said with a sheepish smile. 'I promise.'

The doctor pointed at her. 'Take your vitamins. See you next month.'

She changed into her clothes, giddy with both relief and hunger. She could eat a horse if it weren't somehow cannibalistic. She bent and tied her shoelaces.

Pregnant. Mate. I'm going to have a dragon baby.

Nope, that didn't get all the way inside. Let's say it again.

I'm going to have a dragon baby.

She straightened as black stars danced in front of her eyes. Maybe she really was going to spin into the air and fly into pieces anyway, with or without Dragos's help. She had so many things going on inside, random thoughts and feelings were popping like fireworks at the Fourth of July.

Panic at possibly losing the pregnancy had receded, to be replaced by panic at being pregnant. She was relieved not only that the pregnancy was viable but, even more, that all the evidence said Dragos hadn't intentionally trapped her with it. It looked like she owed him a big apology.

But of all times for it to happen! She had only just, literally hours ago, decided to stay with Dragos. Then there was the war with Urien, which had only just begun. And who knew how Dragos was going to react when he heard the news. He might spin into the air and fly into pieces too.

She pressed her hand over her abdomen. Oh, peanut, I always had the sneaky hope I might have a child someday, but I have to tell you, this timing sucks.

She ran into an unexpected snag as she started to leave. The nurse checking her out asked, 'Still the same insurance and co-pay?'

Same insurance. From Elfie's. And her with thirty-three dollars in her pocket and no checkbook. She pinched the bridge of her nose. Offering a mental apology to all concerned with a promise to pay the bill for real, she lied, 'Yes, thanks.'

She forked over the twenty-five-dollar co-pay, waved away the offer of a receipt and tried to not look shifty about any of it while she continued her internal dialogue with the peanut. *What if he hates the idea of the pregnancy? What if he doesn't want you? He has to want you, that's all there is to it. Anyway, I want you. I just don't know what I'm going to do with you. Just one more thing I'll have to figure out, along with how to live with the rest of the crazy-ass changes going on in my life.*

Business concluded, she made her way through the lobby toward the clinic door where she paused. She didn't think she had the Power to reach Dragos telepathically, but she decided to give it a try anyway. *Dragos?*

His response was immediate and, thank God, calm. *Yes.*

I'm done. I'm headed home, she told him. *I've got some news and I owe you a big apology.*

We can talk about whatever it is later, he said. *Where are you? I'll come get you.*

You don't know? She thought for sure Bayne or Aryal would have told him by now. She pushed through the glass door, squinting in the bright sunlight. Where was the harpy? She shaded her eyes as she looked around. *See, I went to my doctor's –*

She stepped on something and shifted her foot as she looked down. She had stepped on – was that a dart?

Sudden pain pricked her neck. She brushed at the pain and saw another dart fall to the sidewalk. Numbness spread through her body at unbelievable speed. The world went sideways and the sidewalk slammed into her.

Bayne. Aryal. She tried to call for them, but her mouth wasn't working.

Somebody was shouting in another part of her head, but she couldn't connect with it or understand what they were saying.

Three people walked into view and stared down at her. Two

were Dark Fae males with long tilted eyes, high cheekbones, pointed ears and dark hair.

One was a Hispanic woman, with a queenlike beauty and eyes that connected to hers with a snap of Power. The witch Adela, from the Cauldron.

'Oh, it's you. Again.' Adela's mouth pursed and she sighed. 'I was afraid of that.'

You stupid bitch, she tried to say. I'm so going to kick your ass.

If Dragos doesn't get to you first . . .

Everything floated away.

⟅ EIGHTEEN ⟆

A Mephistophelian voice thundered in her head. It called her Name.

Use your Power, damn it. I can feel you're there. Try hard, the imperious voice demanded. *WAKE THE FUCK UP.*

Everything whirled around her. It stank like oil and exhaust. She lay on something hard that vibrated, her cheek pressed against a rough carpet. She felt dizzy, sick. She breathed in shallow pants.

Someone was making a thin whining sound. Oh, it was her. Shut up, stupid.

She fought to do as the voice demanded and reached deep inside. Her training instructor would have said she reached for her chi, her energy flow, the seat of her breath.

For a terrible moment she was disoriented and rudderless in the dark. Then she connected. Power flowed up from the base of her spine and flooded her body. It didn't dissipate all the effects of the drug, but it helped to clear her head some.

She was bound with her arms behind her, gagged and in the trunk of a car traveling at high speed. She drooped. Apparently it really did never rain but poured.

Answer me now, Dragos commanded.

Having a hell of a week, she managed to articulate.

Her mental voice was thready and lacked control, but he heard her.

There's my girl. The thunder was gone, replaced by desperate relief. *Talk to me. Are you hurt?*

No, some kind of drug. She struggled to find words that made sense. *Tied up. In the trunk of a car. We're traveling fast.*

All right. Stay calm, said Dragos.

Bayne and Aryal. She tried to figure out how to articulate their names into a question.

We found them outside the clinic. They were drugged too. They're okay; they're shaking it off. Dragos sounded composed again. *We finally got ahold of someone who can cast a tracking spell. I'll be able to follow you in just a moment. How are you tied? Can you get loose?*

Nausea lurked. She clenched down on it hard. She couldn't afford to vomit with the gag in her mouth. She bent back in a bow so she could feel along her lower legs with hands that were prickling and starting to go numb.

They're those plastic restraints. No locks. I can't get them off.

All right, he said again. *Don't worry about it.*

She had important things to tell him. What were they again? For how long would he be able to talk to her? Graydon had said something about his telepathic range being over a hundred miles. She had no idea how long she had been unconscious or how far away they were from each other.

She said. *I have to tell you things in case we lose contact.*

We're not going to lose contact, he snapped. *That's it. I've got a tracking spell on your braid. I'm on my way.*

She kept her breathing deep and regular. It seemed to help keep her stomach settled, although the exhaust fumes made her want to gag. She tried to think. Was that land magic she felt in the distance?

Will the tracking spell still work if we cross over to an Other land?

He said, *I'm not going to let you get that far away.*

He didn't tell her the spell would work. She had a feeling that meant it wouldn't.

She said, *It's two Dark Fae. They're working with a witch from the Magic District.*

His voice turned ominous. *Describe her.*

She's dark-haired, a human, first name is Adela. She owns the shop Divinus. I can't remember her last name. She struggled to think.

Don't worry about it. It doesn't matter, he said. *Can you describe the Dark Fae to me?*

She tried her best, but she had gotten just that brief look at them before falling unconscious. *I'm sorry.*

He turned gentle. *None of that matters right now. Let's just focus on getting you back.*

Her sense of land magic grew stronger. Uh-oh. *But I have to tell you. I'm pregnant.*

His roar filled her head. *WHAT!*

She talked faster. *I never had control over that so I had an IUD implant. When I realized what was going on this morning, I was so scared I was going to miscarry, all I could think was I had to get to the doctor fast and get the IUD removed. And I was so damn mad at you. I thought you'd done it on purpose.*

Pia. My God.

I dreamed about him this morning. I think it was real. He was a white dragon, the most beautiful little boy you've ever seen. They went into a wide turn, picked up speed for a brief while, then slowed into another turn. She told him with enforced calm, *We're leaving a highway and slowing down. I can feel land magic close by.*

Quickly, he said. He sounded more shaken than he ever had before. *The car trunk has a lock. Try to push it up, and tell me what you see.*

If her hands were free or bound in front of her she could just spring the catch of the trunk lock from the inside. She struggled to get her knees underneath her and push up on the trunk with her shoulder. The catch gave just as they rolled to a stop.

Why the hell not. She pushed the trunk open wider so that she could wriggle through and spilled onto pavement with a painful thud. She stared up at the front end of a Dodge Ram pickup coming straight for her. The truck slammed to a halt inches away from her face. The car she had been in pulled away from the stop and turned left.

'Hey!' a man yelled from the truck.

Shut up, you stupid man, shut up.

A truck door slammed.

She sat as a middle-aged man appeared. He knelt beside her, his face filled with shock and outrage.

'What the hell?' he said. 'Oh sweet Jesus, lady, you've been kidnapped?'

Ya think?

Yards away, car brake lights showed. She yelled against her gag at the man.

'Just hold on, honey. You're gonna be all right now.' The man worked to get her gag loose.

I slipped out at a stop, she said to Dragos. *They noticed. They're in a gray Lexus and they're turning around. I'm seeing signs for . . . Highway 17 and . . . Averill Avenue or State Road 32. There's a state park sign. I can't see the name. It's the same two guys, no witch.*

I know where you are, he said in satisfaction. *Well-done.*

The man got the gag loose and pulled it over her head just as the Lexus pulled up. She screamed at the man, 'Run!'

The two Fae stepped out, looking pissed. They had guns.

No, it's not well-done. I made a bad mistake. Oh God, oh God, oh God.

Dragos was trying to talk to her, but she couldn't shut up, couldn't run, couldn't do anything but stare in horror as the man stood and turned around. One Fae lifted his gun and shot him.

She sobbed, *I think I just got somebody killed.*

Then the other Fae lifted his gun and shot her. She looked down at the pain in her chest. Another dart stuck in her T-shirt.

Fade to black.

The dragon roared in anguish as he hurtled north with every ounce of his strength and speed. He was followed by all his sentinels but one who had been left behind to deal with the witch.

He was too far, too far, and now she was gone again.

His enemies had taken his mate. *His child.*

She had to be alive.

Anything else was unacceptable.

279

. . .

A burning cold Power yanked her awake. She coughed and rolled to her side. Her gag was gone and so were her ankle and wrist restraints. Her arms and legs crawled with prickling pain as her circulation returned.

She was lying on a floor. She touched the polished hardwood. Inside then.

'There's our thief,' said a cultured male voice overhead. 'Time to rise and shine.'

Inhuman. Fae. Didn't she just know who that was. Too bad his head was still attached to his body. She had been hoping she would meet him the other way.

'I'm asleep, then I'm awake. Then I'm asleep and now I'm awake again,' she croaked. 'Make up your mind already.'

The male laughed. 'Well, you have not been boring, I'll give you that, but haven't you been one slippery bitch to get ahold of. And apparently for Cuelebre to hold on to.'

Yes, well, let's not talk about that. She looked at the sleek black boots near her head. They belonged to legs that went up farther than she could focus just yet. 'Can I have some water?'

'Sure, why not.'

He threw cold water in her face. She was too depleted to react much other than gasp. 'Alrighty,' she said after a moment. 'Can I have some water to drink now, please, Your Highness?'

He laughed again. 'Not boring and not dumb. That's so much better than your boyfriend, who both bored me *and* was dumb. To be honest, I don't know what you saw in him.'

'Ex. Ex-boyfriend,' she said. 'I swear to God, I'm never going to live that down.'

Finally it felt like her limbs would function. She pushed herself to a sitting position. She was in a very large room that had a medieval feel. There was a large stone fireplace and a nearby cluster of chairs, a long wooden table with benches, lit sconces that gave the scene a flickering illumination she found eerie, and a high-raftered ceiling.

There were also Fae guards at long metal-hatched windows. The two who had snatched her were stationed at large double doors.

Again she had no idea how long she had been unconscious,

or where she was. She hoped the drugs hadn't hurt the peanut. Her hand slipped to her abdomen. She gave herself a surreptitious scan. She sighed in relief as she located the tiny bright life inside her. There you are. Looks like it's just you and me, peanut. For now, anyway.

The Fae King squatted beside her. He handed her a goblet. She took a cautious sip. Cold, crisp, clear water. She sucked the contents down.

Then she looked up at Keith's murderer. A few weeks ago she had not known there were so many people in the world to hate. Urien. The witch Adela. The two Dark Fae males at the door who had shot an innocent human without so much as a blink of an eye. Her revenge to-do list kept getting longer and longer.

The few Fae she had met had looks that ran from those who had a puckish quality, like Tricks, to those who had a strange stern beauty, like Urien. It was too bad he was such a monster. With his lean supple build, high cheekbones, white skin and raven black hair, he should have been one of nature's miracles.

'This is one of my country retreats,' he told her, having noticed her curiosity. 'No full Court in attendance, just me and my men. And now you, of course.' He gestured to the goblet. 'More?'

'Yes, thank you.' She handed it to him and pushed to her feet as he refilled it from a silver pitcher sitting on the table. She drank that goblet down as well.

'Have as much as you like. The sedative can leave one with quite a thirst, or so I'm told,' said Urien. 'I suspected you'd wake up thirsty since you had two doses back-to-back. Which rather surprised my men, since one dose should have been sufficient for the trip.'

'I've always had a high metabolism,' she said. She filled the goblet one last time and drained it. The hydration made all the difference in the world. Things stopped spinning at the edge of her vision and she felt stronger. 'Local anesthesia at the dentist? Forget about it. It doesn't take until they pump enough in me to numb an elephant.'

'I see.' The Fae King strolled to one of the high-backed chairs near the fireplace and sat. He gestured to the chair opposite him with a smile. 'Please join me. We have a lot to talk about, you and I.'

The worst thing you could do with a predator was show your fear and run. She suspected dealing with the Fae King would be a similar experience. She took the chair he indicated, leaned back and crossed her legs.

Urien regarded her across steepled fingers; then he reached for the glass of wine on the table by his chair and took a sip. 'What a surprise and a mystery you've been, Ms. Giovanni.'

'It wasn't intentional,' she said. 'Well, maybe the mystery part was, but that was supposed to go unsolved.'

He gave her a grin that didn't reach his cold black eyes. 'I knew I liked you the moment I got that penny. Now that made me chuckle.' His eyes sharpened. 'There is something about you. . . .'

All these stupid old people. Had every last one of them met, heard of, gossiped about, or smelled her mom in the distance? Way to be inconspicuous. Thanks a lot, Mom.

She pinched her nose and sighed, 'Yeah, I look like Greta Garbo. I get that a lot.'

'Really, and this Greta Garbo is who?'

She looked at him over her hand. 'An old movie star.'

'I do not follow such newfangled human pastimes.' He dismissed the subject with a flick of his fingers. 'This pissant nobody kept annoying my men, so when I heard about his preposterous claims about his girlfriend, I thought, Let's throw a kind of finding charm out there and see what happens. You know, just to try out a prototype of a little something I've been cooking up in my spare time. Imagine my surprise when everything he claimed came true. Then imagine my surprise when he wouldn't say a word about you.' He leaned forward. 'Not after he was gelded, not after he was eviscerated, not after he was blinded. I didn't think the boy had that kind of loyalty in him. I thought he would give you up in the first ten minutes.'

She covered her mouth, fighting hard to show no emotion. After a moment, she had enough control to say, 'He couldn't tell you anything. I made him take a binding oath.'

Urien snapped his fingers. 'That explains it. One mystery solved. So tell me what the dragon's hoard looked like. Was it as magnificent as legend says?' His expression had turned avaricious.

'To be honest, I was too scared to look around.' She closed

her eyes, remembering the terror. How long ago that seemed. 'For all I knew he was going to show up at any minute. I got in, found a coin jar by the entrance, took the penny and ran. I could have grabbed something else, but I was so damn mad at Keith I wasn't going to give him the satisfaction of handing over something of real value. And I hoped that if I took only the penny, just maybe Cuelebre might not kill me if he ever caught up with me.'

'Which is a great segue into our next mystery,' said Urien. He cocked his head, studying her like she was a bug under a microscope. 'Why hasn't Cuelebre killed you yet?'

She laced her hands in front of her stomach. Hold on, peanut. If anyone has truthsense, he does. Here comes some tricky tap dancing.

'You'd have to ask him,' she said. She widened her eyes. 'Because I've got to tell you, it has surprised the heck out of me.'

His eyes were narrowed, unblinking. She felt his cold Power drift across her skin and struggled not to shudder. 'How did you escape the Goblins?'

She shook her head. 'Again, you'd have to ask him. I was locked in my cell when he came for me. Taking the penny didn't help a bit. He was in a hell of a rage when he caught me, and you have to know he's not the forgiving type. He was determined to be the one to pass judgment on me, nobody else.' Then something occurred to her. 'You know, I never thought of this before, but he also wouldn't have wanted me to get away alive because I know where his lair is.'

The Fae King's eyebrows lifted. 'Very true.'

'Not that it matters anymore,' she added.

'What do you mean?'

She shrugged. 'One of my guards said Cuelebre decided to move his hoard. I suppose now that the location has been compromised . . . ?' She let her voice trail away.

He shrugged as well. 'I guess that's to be expected. Too bad. He's kept so much from me. I would have liked to have stolen more from him. Maybe I'll have you take something from the new location.' He waved a long white hand. 'But that's a conversation for another time. What I want to know is how you did it.'

His Power enfolded her and squeezed tighter, an invisible boa constrictor coiling around her body. Goose bumps rose along her skin. She bit her lip to keep her teeth from chattering. Her mind raced, working to find and eradicate any loopholes in her story before she said them.

'You know how marmosets are little, weird and quick?' she asked.

'Marmosets,' he said.

'Didn't Keith or someone tell you by now that I'm a half-breed Wyr?'

'Someone did mention it, yes,' he replied slowly.

'Well, I'm weird and quick. And I have a gift for getting through locks.' She raised her fingers and wiggled them. Infer, imply, don't state. Careful now. 'That's how I was planning on getting away . . . today? Earlier, anyway. My guards don't know I can do that. I was going to trick them into looking the other way, then slip out of the locked area where they've been keeping me.'

He gave her a charming smile and the chilling compression eased somewhat. 'Impressive. So, my dear, you have not only humiliated Cuelebre by stealing from his hoard, but you have the ability to escape from his Tower too. I knew you would be worth tracking down.'

How lucky for us, peanut.

'This leads me to our last little mystery,' Urien said. 'What happened between you and Cuelebre on that plain? You two seemed quite the team. Something happened, some kind of Power surge, and he was able to shift. We had been assured he wouldn't be able to quite so soon.'

A chill trickle of sweat slid between her breasts. He had in so many words just confirmed an Elven accomplice. She closed her eyes and rubbed at her temples. She was beginning to feel depleted and her hands trembled.

'Did you know that the Goblins beat me quite badly?' Her voice shook too. 'They were trying to get a rise out of Cuelebre, which didn't fucking happen, of course, because he watched the whole thing with this stone-cold look on his face.'

Huh, didn't know she was still upset about that, which was mighty irrational of her, wasn't it? It wasn't as if Dragos had had any choice. That game face of his might have saved her life.

The Fae King sipped wine and watched her.

'Well, we faced a whole damn plain of those stinking

Goblins. I would have done anything to get away. In New York I at least had some hope of survival if I could find a chance to escape. There was this white place on his shoulder where the Elves had shot him with their magic crap.' She gestured on herself. 'It was right about here. So I made a last-ditch gamble. I convinced him to let me lance the wound. And apparently you were there – you must have been on the bluff? As you said, you felt his Power surge.' She let the horror of the memory show in her eyes. 'He killed everything on the plain except me.'

Silence filled the room. She searched Urien's face, which was smooth and expressionless. You think he bought it, peanut? Can't tell. Maybe, maybe not. Don't ever play poker with this creep.

But wasn't what happened even more outlandish? It had all happened to her and even she had trouble believing it.

She felt the same disorientation she always did after she and Dragos had separated for a while. She told herself fiercely, he *is* coming after me. He said he was. We're mates, maybe. Probably. Or now, according to Graydon, I'm his hoard. Which makes no sense. Anyway I'm pregnant with his son. He may not love us, but that's got to matter to him. Right?

'I see,' said the Fae King at last. He finished his wine and set the glass aside. 'Well, you have been through quite an adventure these last several days, haven't you?'

'Look,' she said. She felt so hollow it hurt, and the edges of the room were too far away. 'Am I a guest or a prisoner? Are you going to torture me for some strange reason I don't understand – because just in case you're not, I want you to know I haven't eaten since yesterday and I'm not doing so well right now.'

The Fae King made a moue and tsked. 'Cuelebre didn't take care of you at all, did he? My dear, why in the world would I have any reason to torture you?'

'I don't know.' She threw up her hands and let them fall into her lap. 'It's been a hell of a day for a couple of weeks now,' she said. There was no reason to hide the exasperated exhaustion in her voice so she didn't try. 'And I don't understand half the things that have happened to me, not least of all why you would have your goons drug me instead of walking up to me in the street and introducing themselves.'

'That,' said the Fae King, 'is a very good point. Let's just say we were unsure how you would react and we were unwilling to let you slip away again. Since, from all reports, you were surprisingly protective of the Wyrm when talking with the Elves in South Carolina.'

She froze. She hadn't seen that one coming. What could he have been told? How should she respond?

She said through numb lips, 'If that confrontation had escalated any further, two Elder demesnes could be at war right now. If that happened, a lot of people would have gotten killed. Sure, I stole from him, but I'm not a murderer. If you had a report of that confrontation, then you know I was going to see him to the Elven border and take off, but then we had some Goblins in trucks smash into us. And somehow that event leads back to you, doesn't it.'

He gave her a heavy-lidded smile. 'Well, you see, one of these days I'm going to finally succeed in killing Cuelebre. You just got in the way. Unfortunate, but all of that is in the past now.' He waved a hand. 'I think we should consider you more as a conscripted employee, rather than a guest or prisoner. I can see a lot of uses for you. So many people have so many things I want.'

'I didn't know this was a job interview, or I would have put on a suit,' she said, fury making her reckless. Whoa, throttle back there, filly. He's not torturing. Remember, that's a good thing.

He threw back his head and laughed. 'I do like you, Pia. This is very simple: you will do as you're told. If you do you will have, comparatively speaking, a very comfortable life. If you don't? Oh, I don't recommend that one. I really don't.' He stood. 'Conversation's over. Piran, Elulas, see her to her room and make sure she stays put. Remember to pat her down for anything she could use to pick a lock. Oh, and find her something to eat. Poor thing has purple circles under her eyes. She looks like she's ready to pass out.'

Her kidnappers approached. Her own personal Thing One and Thing Two. She stood and went with them. What else was there to do?

They let her use the bathroom on the ground floor. She was relieved to find that the house wasn't too medieval. At least it had running water and a flushing toilet. Then they took her up a flight of stairs and down a long hallway to a bare room with nothing in it but a narrow bed and two folded blankets and a barred window.

Then Thing One gave her an infuriatingly thorough search while Thing Two watched. The Fae felt along the seams of her clothes, ran his hands up the insides of her legs and squeezed her crotch, probed between and underneath her breasts and made her take off her shoes so he could inspect them.

She gritted her teeth and suffered through it. She was able to hold on to her rage only because it was obvious from the Fae's flat, bored expression that the search had no sexual undertones. There was no way she could have sneaked a thin, flat lock pick in with her if she'd tried.

They locked her in the room. She shook out a blanket on the bare mattress and fell on it, listening as the two Fae spoke to each other in their Celtic-sounding language. One set of footsteps walked away, hopefully to bring her some kind of sustenance. She was going to have to choke down whatever they brought her so that she could stabilize and get ready for the next steps, whatever those were. She hoped it wasn't meat.

It looked to be evening outside, gray and leaden with the promise of rain, which left the room shadowy. Her gaze tracked across the bare walls as she rested. *Dragos?* she tried. *Are you there?*

Nothing but a deadened silence. What did that mean? Cautiously she expanded her awareness. She couldn't feel anything, no land magic, no other Fae, nothing but the chill heavy blanket of Urien's Power. Was he able to suppress magic in his vicinity? If so, that was a pretty handy self-defense mechanism.

Her eyebrows rose as she looked down at herself. She wasn't glowing. He must be able to suppress magic but not undo those spells already in place. Whatever the specifics, she was guessing he could sense any nearby upsurge in Power.

She went over her story again. Hey, peanut, get me under pressure and I rock.

But the story wouldn't hold up for long. For one thing, she didn't know the extent of Adela's knowledge about her or how deeply the witch was involved with the Dark Fae. If she knew anything of the truth, sooner or later Pia had to assume she would tell Urien.

287

And about that Elven connection. Ferion knew of her real heritage, had spoken to the Elven High Lord and Lady and had been present at the teleconference. Did she dare hope that Urien's Elven contact was not Ferion? He had treated her with such warmth. Did that mean he would not have spoken of her to the Fae King?

She tried to remember what Ferion had said aloud at Folly Beach and what he had said during their private telepathic conversation. She couldn't. That was worrisome. But at least it looked logical that Ferion was not Urien's Elven connection.

There were too many unknown variables, and not least among them was the fact that *she* didn't have truthsense. Urien could well have been playing her or lying for his own reasons. So the only thing she dared hope for was that she had bought herself a little time.

Footsteps approached. She sat up as a key grated in the lock. Thing Two took a step inside. He set a tray down on the floor. He stepped out and locked the door again. She checked the contents of the tray.

Half a loaf of plain dark bread, apples and more water. Score.

She fell on the food. The bread was maybe a day old as it was just beginning to go stale, but it was still chewy and grainy and delicious. The apples were wonderful. They had a quality that made her think they were from an Other land, perhaps even this place. She ate everything, drank half the water and felt an immediate energy surge. Way better.

Now what? There were two ways out of this room. She pushed the tray against the wall so she wouldn't knock over the last of her water. She went to inspect her window.

She stared, hardly daring to believe her luck. The bars on the window were on the outside of the glass pane. They were two simple vertical metal grills with supporting crossbars at top and bottom. They were hinged on either side of the window and secured with a padlock and metal chain wound around the end bars. What they looked like were replacements for old-fashioned window shutters. Someone had prepared this room for her arrival.

She eased the window open as quietly as she could and

then paused to listen. Her two Fae guards continued to talk, undisturbed.

Urien might be able to suppress magic, but her mother had always said that magic versus intrinsic natural ability was a tricky thing to define, and in her demonstration Dragos hadn't been able to feel her do anything. She took hold of the padlock and pulled. It fell open.

She slipped the lock off and unwound the chain. She hefted it, considering. It was nice and solid, more than a good yard in length. She doubled it, wound one end around her hand and swung it to get the feel for its weight.

It wasn't a bad weapon for someone low on options. She dropped the padlock on the bed, drank the rest of her water and eased the metal grill open a couple of inches as she tried to peer down at the ground surrounding the house.

Either Urien or whoever was in charge of his security was clever enough to keep the area around the house free of shrubbery. The landscaping wasn't very attractive, but it also didn't give anyone a place to hide. She pulled back as a guard came around the corner and walked by underneath. Her luck only went so far, it seemed.

She watched for a while, counted to estimate the passage of time and kept track of the guards. The fifth guard was the original one, so there were four outside guards, one to a side, as they patrolled in a circle. Four plus Thing One and Thing Two, the inside guards at the windows in the meeting hall and no doubt some she hadn't seen. Maybe Urien had a total of twenty men with him, a reasonable number if he wanted to move fast and quiet.

The way she looked at it, she had two choices: She could lock herself back in and bide her time, which was dicey. Or she could jump out the window, take out a guard fast and run like hell was after her. Extremely dicey.

She had no defenses or options if she stayed. She would be at the Fae King's mercy and the story she had spun had its own built-in time bombs. And she didn't dare come under any closer scrutiny. She couldn't bear to think what would happen if he discovered she was pregnant with Dragos's child.

So, in reality, she had no choice at all.

She watched the guards rotate again. Which one looked the sleepiest, the slowest, the most incompetent? Damn, they all looked good.

Well, dying just wasn't an option. She was fighting for two now. 'Hang on, peanut,' she whispered, bracing her foot on the windowsill.

As the next guard walked by, she pushed open the metal grill and leaped out. The thud as she hit the ground had the guard raising his crossbow even as he turned around.

He was fast.

She was faster.

She spun and used every ounce of centrifugal force she could muster as she lashed at him with the chain. She could tell by how it struck him in the temple that he was dead as he hit the ground.

She felt nothing, no mercy, no remorse, as she watched his body crumple. Huh. So this is what a killer instinct feels like.

Alrighty.

She snatched up his crossbow and assessed it at a glance. It was already loaded, a modern compound bow, light and sleek, with a telescopic sight and a quiver mounted to the main arm that held half a dozen bolts. She knew this weapon.

Hey.

Heart pounding, she sprinted for the corner of the house where the next guard would appear in just a few seconds. She pressed her back against the wall, took a deep breath and waited with the crossbow up.

She came face-to-face with the next Fae guard as he rounded the corner. His eyes went wide. She shot him point-blank and peeked fast around the corner.

From the glimpse she had of that section of the house it was longer, and there was part of another building visible nearby. Perhaps that was a stable? Where would they keep those dragonfly thingies, inside a building or outside?

She pulled back, reloaded the crossbow and counted.

Four ten thousand, three ten thousand, two ten thousand . . .

She couldn't hear him but the guard had to be there. She rolled around the corner, shot him and yanked his body around, piling it on top of the other guard. She reloaded and counted.

She couldn't believe it when the last guard dropped. She

stared at his body, grateful that she was still numb. She had just killed four people in as many minutes, all so she could get more than just a few seconds' head start.

Better make their lives count for something.

She dropped her bow, snatched up the last dead guard's crossbow with a full load of ammunition and ran.

≡ NINETEEN ≡

A half hour had passed since Dragos had lost the connection with Pia through the tracking spell. Then he and his sentinels arrived at the junction of Highway 17 and Averill Avenue. They found police cars, an ambulance and a fire truck surrounding a black Dodge Ram pickup. He sent Tiago, Rune and Grym winging southeast into the Harriman State Park to look for a gray Lexus.

At almost forty seven thousand acres in size, the park was the second largest in New York and had over thirty lakes and a couple hundred miles of hiking trails. It also had a passageway to a large area of Other land.

Still shielding their presence from human sight, Dragos arrowed to the ground, followed by Graydon, Bayne and Constantine. After shifting, he raced toward the emergency response vehicles, flanked by the gryphons.

Graydon walked up to a policewoman and introduced himself. 'What happened?'

'There was a shooting,' said the woman, glancing from Dragos to the gryphons with wide eyes. 'The victim's a middle-aged guy who was gunned down in the street. Couple kids found him—'

Dragos ignored the rest. He strode past the truck. There

was one pool of blood. Bayne stopped to inspect the spot. The ambulance doors were open. He looked inside. Two EMTs were working over a man.

'He conscious?' he asked one of the EMTs.

'You can't be here right now,' said the man, without looking up.

He reached inside, grabbed the man and threw him out of the ambulance. He said to the other EMT, 'This man conscious?'

He nodded, eyes wide. 'We're working to stabilize him. We've got to get him to the hospital.'

Dragos climbed in and crouched by the stretcher. The victim's eyes were glazed with shock. Dragos pulled the oxygen mask down. He demanded, 'Was she alive when they took her?'

The man's mouth worked. He was panting in short, shallow breaths and his color wasn't good. 'What . . .'

Dragos leaned closer. 'The woman who was kidnapped. *Was she alive when they took her?*'

'Y-yes, I think so . . .' managed the man between gasps. 'Shot her . . . shot her—'

The EMT's hand came over his to take hold of the oxygen mask and ease it back into place. 'Please,' he said to Dragos. 'He's already arrested once. You've got to go.'

Constantine released the EMT he had evicted as he climbed out of the ambulance. He stood, face white and hands clenched, as Graydon and Bayne jogged over. He said through white lips, 'He thinks she was alive. He said they shot her.'

'Ah shit,' said Graydon as he blanched.

Constantine gripped Dragos's arm hard. 'Don't go making her all dead in your head,' he said. 'Remember, they drugged and kidnapped her the first time – they didn't kill her. They want her alive.'

'You're right,' he said. He looked at them, his eyes bloodshot. For the first time he managed to articulate what she had told him earlier. 'She's pregnant. Urien has my pregnant mate.'

The gryphons stared at him in equal measures of horror and dismay.

Then Tiago said, *We found the Lexus. They crossed over in here.*

Galvanized, the four raced away from the human scene and

took to the air to join the others. Good news: the Lexus didn't have any traces of blood. The constriction in his chest eased. He started to breathe again.

They located the passageway and crossed over to the Other land. Dragos had hoped against hope, but the tracking spell laid on her braid didn't survive the disconnect and crossover. They would have to track her and her kidnappers by land.

Good thing they had one of the best trackers of any species on their side. Tiago loped across the ground in wide arcs, studying the ground, until he took off running in one direction. Rune and Graydon scouted farther afield while the others kept to the ground with Tiago.

Dragos kept to the air, shielding his presence as he scouted in circles, projecting ahead of Tiago's trajectory.

Death was another good friend of his and flew in his shadow.

Pia had no idea where she was or where she was going. Story of her life, apparently. She had one goal: to run as far away from Urien as fast as she could get. She hoped he didn't have any of those dragonfly thingies with him. If it came down to a ground race, she had a good fighting chance.

The rolling countryside was carpeted with thick clusters of forest and open areas carpeted with riotous profusions of wildflowers. She paused at the edge of a wood and ran her gaze quickly over the scene behind her. No sight or sound of pursuit.

Gold and purple and scarlet dusted the emerald green field she had just traversed. Her gaze landed on a brilliant purple flower with fluted petals like a lily as it spat out a long, feathery, stamenlike stalk, whip fast, and it caught a buzzing insect on the sticky end, which then retracted into the flower with its prey.

She recoiled. Let's not consider that a metaphor for anything.

She slung the crossbow on her back and plunged into a forested area for ground cover. She avoided anything that looked like a path. If she managed to get far enough away, she would start thinking about how to hide her trail better, but right now she didn't have time to consider finesse.

A light rain started to patter in the treetops, the occasional drop making it far enough to land on her. Maybe she'd get lucky and it would start to pour. A heavy rain would help to dissipate her scent.

The newly released Wyr in her was eager to stretch out her legs and dig into a hard run, but Pia's human mind couldn't help but be frustrated. Six months from now she would have had a chance to practice many of the tricks her mother had tried to teach her about how to obscure her path from pursuers. As it was, she didn't dare try to tap into her Power in case she made a mistake and gave away her position.

She got maybe fifteen minutes of peace and quiet. Then Urien hissed in her head, *You have just made a very bad mistake, Pia Giovanni. What I did to your boyfriend is nothing compared to what I will do to you when I catch you.*

Snot, snot. Threat, threat.

The lunatic inhabiting her body said to the Fae King, *I can beat any pace you set, asshole. Catch me if you can.*

Okay, let's face it. It wasn't the smartest thing she'd ever done. But she had so had it up to here with mean people today.

The rain started to come down harder. She ran faster.

Her awareness narrowed to what was around her, watching for obstacles, plotting her course ahead through the trees, and working to keep her footing on ground that became increasingly slippery. Soon she was soaked to the skin. The forest grew more shadowy and treacherous.

Then she saw a break in the trees ahead. She managed to skid to a stop before she went tumbling head over heels down a rocky incline.

Oh, that's not so good. Ahead of her stretched a very large expanse of rolling meadow. It wasn't the size of the plain where she and Dragos had been trapped, but it was still far too large and exposed for her liking.

She bit her lip and tried to think. Couldn't go back. Shouldn't go to either side. Urien would spread his men out as they pursued her. Damn. Nothing to do but go forward. Maybe she could get to the other side before she was seen.

She bounded down the incline, hit the bottom and sprinted with everything she had.

Pia, Dragos said.

She stepped into some kind of animal hole and went down.

Pain lanced up her leg. She clutched it and rocked. *Dragos!*
Damn it.

She thought she heard him say, *Thank you, gods.* Then he
demanded more loudly, *Where are you?*

Well, I don't know that, do I? she snapped. *I got drugged
again and carted off to one of Urien's vacation homes. Then I
escaped, and now he's chasing me, and I just stepped into some
damn gopher or rabbit hole. Damn,* DAMN, *damnedy damn it –*

Did you break anything?

I don't know. She bit her lip and with a gigantic effort flexed
her ankle. The pain was a railroad spike shooting up her leg.

Can you run?

I don't know! She pushed to her feet and tried to put her
weight on the ankle.

Describe where you are, he demanded.

She pushed her hair out of her eyes, looked around and told
him what she saw. The ankle protested but bore her weight.
Barely. She lurched into a limping run, but her former speed
was gone.

Hey, big guy, she said, gritting her teeth against the pain. *I
can't tell you how glad I am that you came or how good it is to
hear your voice.*

How glad you are that I came, he said in a flat voice. *What
the hell does that mean?*

What do you think it means! she snapped. *Forget it. I can't
talk right now. This is too hard.*

She tried to push harder, to eke out a little more speed, but
there wasn't any more to be had. Jagged splinters of pain shot
up her leg with every step. If she were a horse, she would have
herself put down.

She wasn't going to make it.

She put her hands on her hips, caught her breath and walked.
The rain felt good, nice and cool on her overwarm body. She
was about halfway across the meadow when a sense of malevo-
lence made her turn around. She looked back to the tree line
from which she had just come.

Urien and his men, mounted on horses, stood staring down
at her.

She had passed the in-for-a-penny-in-for-a-pound road sign

a long time ago. Hell, she was cruising the neighborhood streets of tonnage by now. Limping backward, she raised her middle finger to the Fae King.

Their horses plunged down the incline. With a casualness that spoke of contempt, he and his men trotted toward her.

She pulled the crossbow from her back. As soon as they were in range for her, she would be in range for them. She must stand out against the twilight like a lighthouse. She tore off her white T-shirt and tossed it aside, then turned her body to present less of a target.

I'm so sorry, peanut.

She located Urien in the crossbow telescope. The bastard had started a nasty smile. He kicked to a canter. She shot just as a blow slammed into her.

It knocked her down.

She lay sprawled on her back and blinked up at the rain that felt so good, so maybe she was the only one on the ground who saw the dragon plummet, screaming, out of the sky.

Forelegs extended, talons spread, wicked teeth bared, Dragos snatched Urien from the back of his horse. He pumped his wings to rise in the air above the trees; then he threw back his head and roared as he ripped the Fae King apart.

'There's my bad boy,' she whispered. God, he was breathtaking.

A strange melee played out in the meadow. It was like something out of a nightmare. Gryphons attacked Fae while horses screamed and plunged in terror. She thought she saw a winged, demonic-looking creature rip out the throat of a Fae. There was a huge dark bird that caused thunder with the beat of its massive wings. Lightning flashed out of its eyes, but maybe by that point she was beginning to hallucinate.

Graydon bent over her. 'Oh fuck, no,' he whispered. He grabbed for her crumbled shirt and pressed it around the crossbow bolt sticking from her chest. 'Hold on, honey.'

She touched his hand. 'I'm okay,' she tried to tell him. 'Everything's going to be all right now.'

She didn't think she managed to get the words out because he wiped his cheek on his shoulder and shouted, 'Dragos!'

Then Dragos fell to his knees beside her, and her world

turned right again. His face was ashen, his eyes stark. He added pressure to the wound at her chest and laid a hand against her cheek.

'Pia.' He spoke like the words were ripped out of him. 'Don't you dare leave me. I swear to God, I will follow you into hell if I have to and drag you back by the hair.'

One corner of her mouth lifted. She put her hand over his on her cheek. She said, 'You say the most god-awful things.'

She was tired so she rested her eyes for a minute.

Afterward she remembered a series of images, like pearls on a string.

She opened her eyes to find that Graydon held her back against his chest, one arm across her shoulders, the other arm clamped low around her waist. They sat in a cage made of talons formed by Dragos's two front feet. Rune stood over them, looking through the talons. 'Hold her just like that,' he said with his face grim. 'Don't let her get jostled.'

'I got her,' Graydon said. 'Let's go.'

They were acting so dramatic, like it was life or death or something. So much for being big tough warriors. They were worse than a bunch of high school girls.

She faded out as Dragos launched.

The next thing she knew Dragos was the one holding her. She could have carried a brimming wineglass and not spilled a drop as he raced up a flight of stairs. 'I don't care!' he roared. 'Get any goddamn doctor fast as you can. Steal one from Monroe if you have to. One of you fly to New York and get our Wyr healer!'

She tried to focus her blurry gaze. Is this Urien's house again? I'm awake, I'm asleep, I'm awake, I'm asleep. I'm in the house, I'm out. Now I'm in again. This is getting ridiculous.

And she faded out.

Then things got really strange.

She was immersed in the dragon's Power. He had consumed her. With every breath, he worked her lungs. Her heartbeat faltered. The great engine of his heart took over the rhythm. Her Power started to fade, but he had her Name. He demanded she stay in her flesh. She drifted inside him, inextricably woven with his life force.

She thought she heard her mother say, *He cannot hold you forever. You may come to me if you wish.*

But there was somebody else with them, a bright, tiny, stubborn spark. He was just a new creation, but he already had his own opinions. Dragos held her life to her body, but her son's Power pulsed inside her.

He was trying to heal her. She roused.

Oh no, sweet baby, she crooned. *You're too small for that.*

The peanut begged to differ.

A warm glow of energy suffused her body, so like her mother's healing Power, so like her own. For one moment everything was shining and well and right. Then, with infinite gentleness, the dragon laid his Power on that tiny spark of life that glowed too bright, too strong, and eased it back until it nestled into place.

Precious baby boy.

Her fingers crept an inch across a sheet. They were grasped by a much larger, more powerful hand that held on to her hard as she fell asleep.

≈ TWENTY ≈

When she woke up again for real she was in their bed at Cuelebre Tower. She gazed at the ceiling for an unmeasured time as the light changed. It was quiet. She was warm, clean and dry and pain free.

Dragos lay beside her, his arm around her. She looked at his sleeping face and saw something she had never seen before. He looked exhausted and worn, as if something inside of him had stretched too thin. She frowned. Had he gotten hurt in the battle?

She tried to raise her right arm to stroke his face but she couldn't. She tugged at her arm, and all of a sudden Dragos rose up on his elbow. He put his hand on her arm to hold her down. 'Sweetheart, don't do that.'

'My hand's caught on something,' she mumbled. She looked up at him with sleepy anxiety. 'What's wrong? You look so sad. Are you hurt?'

He smiled down at her, gold eyes alight, and the careworn look vanished. 'I did not get hurt, other than in my heart.'

'Somebody shot you in the heart!' She tried to jerk her hand up.

'Pia love, stop. Look at your arm.' She turned and followed the direction of his pointing finger. 'You have an IV drip. You keep trying to pull it out in your sleep, so we had your hand tied down. We didn't want you to hurt yourself.'

'Oh.' Feeling foolish, she subsided. She turned back to him. 'Somebody shot you in the heart!'

'Yes.' He kissed her nose. 'You did, metaphorically speaking.' He kissed her mouth, his caressing lips infinitely gentle. 'You were dying, you little shit. Your heart shut down and your lungs stopped working. I had to take over for a while. Then our son decided to help and almost burned himself out healing you. It scared centuries off my life.'

He nuzzled at her, his eyelids closed. She breathed him in, rubbed her cheek against his and let his presence soothe the jagged edges inside.

'I'm sorry,' she whispered. A tear slid out of a corner of her eye and soaked her hair, followed by another. 'I'm so sorry for everything.'

'Stop that.' He cupped her face and wiped the tears away. 'It's not your fault. I flew your doctor back from Cancún and had quite a talk with her. First I found out what an IUD was and how it could have endangered both you and the pregnancy. I understand why you panicked and why you were afraid I had forced the pregnancy on you.'

'I should have known better.'

'How could you? We've been together for less than a week and under far less than ideal circumstances. But of course I didn't mean to make you pregnant. You've ruined me.' His voice and face were rueful. He stroked her hair. 'I had no idea my control had slipped to that extent.'

Her gaze clung to him as her free hand slid to cover her abdomen in a protective gesture that was fast becoming habitual. Something tentative and fragile in her expression seemed to catch his attention. The dark slash of his eyebrows contracted. He covered her hand with his, lacing his fingers with hers.

'The pregnancy is a total shock,' he told her. 'Connecting with our son when he healed you – he's one of the most beautiful things I've ever seen. I can't begin to describe my reaction to him. I've never felt these feelings before.'

'That's actually a pretty good way to describe it,' she whispered. 'Me either. I'm terrified.'

He kissed her, his lips moving slow and easy as he savored her. 'I have no idea how to act around small new creatures. But I'm *glad*.'

'I am too,' she whispered. Her eyes glittered with easy moisture as she smiled at him. Then her gaze turned inward and grew haunted. 'I killed five people.'

His eyes narrowed. 'How do you figure?'

'It's my fault the man in the truck got shot—'

He tapped her lips. 'That one's easy. He's not dead. It was touch and go at first, but they say he's going to pull through just fine.'

'Thank God,' she said, sighing.

'There were, however, four dead guards around Urien's house that we've been mighty curious about. Was that you?' He searched her face. His fingers couldn't seem to stop stroking her cheekbones, her jaw, her throat.

She grimaced and nodded.

He showed her his teeth. 'I am so damn proud of you. You stepped it up when you had to. You did what needed to be done and got yourself away.'

'Yeah, well, you're a bloodthirsty monster. Who cares what you think,' she muttered. She drifted for a few minutes and he let her be, stroking her hair. She roused enough to say, 'To be honest, I was feeling bad about not feeling bad. Except for the guy in the truck. Him I just felt bad about.'

'That's stupid and convoluted. You are going to stop it right now,' he ordered.

She gave a ghost of a giggle. 'There you go again, giving orders. His Majesty is starting to feel better. Oh, speaking of majesties.' Her eyes opened very wide. 'Urien actually thought he was going to be the boss of me.'

'Which was one of the things that finally got him killed.' His eyes crinkled. 'Imagine that.'

She slept for a while with the easy exhaustion of a convalescent. She woke up once to say with sudden urgency, 'Don't go anywhere.'

He was dressed in cutoffs and stretched out on top of the covers, reading files, pillows piled at his back. He set them aside and gave her a steady look. 'I'm not going anywhere, Pia. Not anywhere. And neither are you.'

His much-loved face was as immovable as a mountain. She nodded and relaxed. He did not pick up his reading again until she was sound asleep.

Almost dying can sure take it out of a body. The brief healing flare of Power from the peanut had taken care of essentials, but she had to do the rest on her own.

She had been unconscious for two days. Dragos had a present for her, an anti-nausea charm set in a two-carat diamond pendant necklace. The day after she woke up, when they were sure she could keep liquids and solid food down, the doctor had the IV drip removed.

She couldn't concentrate on anything more substantive than magazines and TV shows, and she napped often. When she was awake, Dragos coaxed out of her every detail of what happened.

Then he shared the story of their pursuit, down to the final part when all the sentinels had taken to the air to search for the meadow she had described. With his keen raptor's gaze, Bayne had caught the movement as Urien and his men had plunged down the incline toward her. They had still been a couple miles away and had hurtled forward with every ounce of speed they possessed.

Every ounce of Dragos's formidable energy had been focused on taking Urien out before the Fae King had a chance to draw on his considerable Power and fight back. He hadn't seen Pia get shot, but he had seen her bolt hit Urien high in the shoulder. It hadn't been a killing shot, but it was enough to distract the Fae King for those few final seconds as Dragos and the sentinels dove down to the attack.

They had all seen her give Urien the finger. The sentinels made much of it as they sprawled on the couches with their feet up on the furniture, ate pizza, drank beer after beer and watched SOAPnet.

'I like that evil twin,' said Graydon, pointing his bottle at the flat-screen. 'The other one's too sickly sweet. Nobody's that nice.'

'Fuck, no,' said Constantine comfortably. 'But you gotta admit, that actress is smoking hot. You think they're real?'

'Doubt it,' said Graydon. 'They're too globular.'

Constantine nodded. 'I can handle globular.'

'Pun,' said Graydon. 'Groan.'

Pia looked at them over the top of the *Cosmopolitan* she was thumbing through but refrained from comment. She supposed it could have been worse. At least they were more or less housebroken.

She was curled on one end of the couch, tucked under a light silk throw. After she had started to feel steadier, she had been able to convince Dragos to go take care of a backlog of things, but that only meant she had a steady, rotating stream of sentinels as visitors. She hadn't had a moment to herself since the kidnapping.

When she complained to Graydon, he told her, 'It's just a precaution, cupcake. A few of Urien's Fae are still being hunted down, and that Elven connection we were hunting for has disappeared. Damnedy damn it.' He snickered.

'I can't believe he told you guys that,' she said. 'I'd just twisted my ankle and was having a bad day. I wasn't responsible for what came out of my mouth – or head.'

'You handled yourself like a pro,' he soothed.

'Yes, I did. I kicked ass,' she grumbled. 'And anyway, I'm in the Tower penthouse. This place is locked up tighter than Fort Knox. Nobody's hunting me anymore. I'm sure not going anywhere right now.'

'Yeah, but you gotta remember,' said the gryphon as he tapped her nose. 'You scared the shit out of the boss. He's not used to fear. If you don't let him fuss, I think he might blow up. You scared the shit out of us too, by the way. Besides, you're family now and we're having fun. It's like a vacation.' He winked.

Family. Wow.

'Okay,' she muttered. She tried not to wiggle for joy and pretended to still be grumpy, but she gave him an affectionate smile.

A depressed Tricks came to thank her for her part in killing Urien and to say good-bye. The faerie was leaving to be crowned Queen at the Dark Fae Court. She had had the lavender dye stripped from her hair and no longer wore it with a perky flip on the ends. It was its natural raven black. Pia was surprised to see how much it changed the faerie's appearance and made her look more serious.

'Please God, come visit soon,' said Tricks. 'Don't abandon me to the Dark Fae Court. We'll do lunch again.'

She groaned. 'Okay, but next time let's do without the Piesporter and cognac.'

Tricks gave her a sly one-sided smile. 'We'll see.'

Pia told her, 'I'm going to miss you.'

The faerie threw her arms around her. 'I'll miss you too.'

Lunch sometime with the Dark Fae Queen. Invitations to visit with the Elven High Lord and Lady. How strange her life had become.

On impulse she asked, 'Did you find somebody to take over your PR job?'

'No,' said Tricks. 'There hasn't been time. Why, do you want it?'

She lifted a shoulder, feeling self-conscious. 'Maybe I'll talk to Dragos about it. You know, when I'm up for it.'

'Whatever you decide, you keep that dragon twisted around your little finger,' the faerie advised with a giggle. 'It's his karma after so many centuries of being the center of everybody's universe around here. It'll do him a world of good.'

Another visitor came one afternoon. Pia looked up as Aryal threw her six-foot body onto a couch beside her. The harpy's black hair was tangled again, which seemed to be its usual state. She wore low-rider jeans, a sleeveless leather vest and the requisite sentinel weapons.

Pia studied her as Aryal fidgeted. The harpy's odd gaunt beauty had nothing to do with dieting, and while lanky, her body was sure cut. Pia looked at her arm muscles and rippling stomach, thinking of all the hard work it took to look like that. Not in this lifetime.

Aryal glared at *General Hospital* playing on the flat-screen and jiggled a foot. She picked up a *Harper's Bazaar*, thumbed through a few pages and tossed it aside. Pia thought she heard the harpy mutter, 'I'm no good at any of this girlfriend shit.'

She raised her eyebrows and wondered if she was supposed to say something.

Aryal looked at the TV. She said, 'Can you believe it – first, the witch Adela sold you a binding oath, the next day she put a tracking spell on you for Dragos and this week she contracted with the Dark Fae to find you. You turned out to be quite the cash cow for her.'

She shook her head. 'That's pretty wrong. I never did feel quite right about her.'

The harpy continued, 'We found her body in the Hudson River. Her throat had been slit. Apparently she contracted her services out one too many times. The forensic report is inconclusive, but we're guessing the Dark Fae killed her. The estimated time of death is shortly after you were kidnapped. It looks like the Dark Fae were trying to cover their tracks after taking you.'

'I see,' she said, her tone neutral. Maybe she should care that the witch had been murdered. Whatever Adela had done, Pia wasn't sure that she had deserved to die for it. At the moment she couldn't seem to muster much of a reaction.

Silence fell between them. Then Aryal's strange stormy gray eyes met hers. 'Bayne and I feel like shit about the kidnapping. But I'm not sorry about the rest of it.'

'I didn't ask you to be. You're entitled to your own opinion, and you were trying to protect Dragos in your own way. I respect that and there's nothing more to be said.' Pia took the end of her cheerleader ponytail and flicked it at the harpy.

A feral grin spread across Aryal's face. 'Uh, listen, sometime when you're feeling up to it, I'd like to have a round or two with you on the mat. For a while the gryphons couldn't talk about anything else.'

'Sure, why not,' she told the sentinel. 'The way things have been going, I had better keep up on my training.'

'Okay.' Aryal put her hands on her knees and started to push to her feet.

'Just one thing,' Pia said. The harpy paused and looked at her. Pia regarded her with a cold, steady gaze. 'Try shoving me into a wall again and I'll smack you down.'

Aryal's grin turned into a scowl. She looked like she had just swallowed something sour, but after a moment she nodded.

Pia returned the nod and looked down at her magazine. It was a dismissal. The harpy took it as such, launched off the couch and disappeared.

Pia also had time to give Quentin a call. She went out onto the balcony on a sunny afternoon and closed the door for some privacy. Then she leaned against the new wall and looked out over the city as they talked.

It was quite an exchange. She had to fill Quentin in on all that had happened since her brief stay at his beach house. It was a lot to tell, including that she was now apparently Dragos's mate and carrying his child.

306

When she finished, there was a long, long silence on the other end. She toed one of the flagstones and watched traffic below as she waited. 'That's going to take me a while to process,' Quentin said in a scrupulously neutral tone of voice.

'Tell me about it.'

'How . . . is he?'

'You know Rex Harrison in *My Fair Lady*?'

'The professory, growly son of a bitch?'

'Yeah, well' – she closed one eye, squinted at the skyline and grinned – 'Dragos is a lot worse.'

That caused another rant that went pretty much along the lines of he'd-better-treat-you-right-or-I-don't-care-who-the-bastard-is-I'll-kill-him-myself kind of thing. She bent over, put her forehead on the wall railing and endured it with as much patience as she could muster, making noises every once in a while to pretend she was actually listening.

Finally he said, 'I want to see you in person. I want to make sure that bastard hasn't addled you with some kind of beguilement.'

'He hasn't,' she said. 'But I'll come to Elfie's soon for a real visit.'

'You'd better.' Quentin sounded grim. 'Or as allergic to the Tower as I am, I'll come break you out.'

'Tell everybody I miss them.'

'I will. See you soon.' He stressed the last.

'Yes, you will, I promise.' At last she was able to extricate herself from the conversation and hang up.

She was wrung out. This starting a new life was a hell of a lot of hard work.

She and Dragos didn't talk much after they had shared stories, and she didn't see much of him after she had convinced him to go back to work. He was soon immersed in stabilizing some businesses in Illinois before he sold them, and he mentioned something about initiating a hostile takeover of an investor-owned utility company.

She wondered if the distance between them would be the definition of her life now. He slipped into bed with her every night and wrapped her up in his arms, and she derived a lot of comfort from his nearness. But they didn't make love, or have sex, or . . . mate.

Changing and becoming full Wyr enhanced her healing capability. After three days of convalescence, she was climbing the walls. Finally Dr. Medina, who had been making daily house calls, cleared her for treadmill walking and other light exercise.

'Yes!' She'd been hoping for the go-ahead.

'No running until I say so, no matter how good you feel. And I'm not going to say so till at least next week,' the doctor warned. 'That crossbow wound gave your respiratory system quite a knock.'

'No running. Gotcha.' She grabbed her clothes, black Lycra exercise tights and sports tank top, and put them on. 'Thank you!'

'You're welcome.' The doctor smiled. 'I'll let myself out.'

She sat on the edge of the bed to put on her running shoes – another new pair – as the doctor left the suite. After her last shoes were ruined in her flight through the rain-drenched forest, Dragos had bought her six new pairs.

The door opened. She looked up, ready to tell the guys they could hit the gym. Dragos strode in. As usual, he took total command of the air space in the room.

He gave her a long look, then shut the door. He had dressed that day in black jeans and a black silk shirt that emphasized the strong athletic lines of his massive body and the bronze of his skin – and did nothing to lighten the severity of his face.

Even in his human form he looked capable of ripping the Fae King apart with his bare hands. Should she find that as sexy as she did? She scratched her head. She wondered about herself, she really did.

'Hi,' she said. 'I wasn't expecting you.'

'Apparently you don't expect much from me,' he said.

'Excuse me?' she said, taken aback.

He began a slow stroll around the large suite. It was his prowling stroll, his long muscular limbs moving like liquid under the silk and denim. She twisted to watch him with equal parts pleasure and uncertainty.

'The doctor has cleared you for exercise,' he said. 'So I

figure that means you're strong enough to face other things now as well.'

'Oh-kay.'

'Go ahead and call me obsessive, but I have a bone to pick with you,' he said. He was frowning.

It made her forehead crinkle in response. 'What's wrong? What else did I do?' Hadn't she done more than enough for a week? At this rate she was going to have to turn catatonic to make sure nothing else happened.

He turned to face her, hands on his hips. 'Do you remember when you stepped in the rabbit hole?'

She snorted. 'I'm not likely to forget.'

His narrowed eyes glittered like gold coins. 'You remember what you said?'

She shrugged, her face and mind a blank.

He stalked over, put his hands on her shoulders and shoved her back. She fell back on the mattress. 'Hey!'

Then he crawled on the bed until he was on his hands and knees over her. He glared down at her, every inch the dominant angry Wyr male. 'You said and I quote, "I can't tell you how glad I am that you came or how good it is to hear your voice."'

'So what?' She smacked his shoulders with the flat of her hands. Didn't quite work out the same way when she did it. Of course he didn't move an inch. 'Quit with the primitive crap already.'

'You might have noticed I'm a primitive kind of guy.' He showed his teeth and got into her face. 'All those centuries of civilization? Just a veneer.'

'Oh, for God's sake.' She went lax and just stared at him, helpless as usual against the flood of arousal that swept over her. 'Have you been sulking about what I said this whole time?'

He tilted his head, his eyes lava-hot. 'You said it like I was some kind of visitor. Or like you weren't sure I would come when *you had been kidnapped*. When you had just told me you were *pregnant* with *my child*. I don't know what the hell you think of me other than I am a bloodthirsty monster.'

'Dragos!' Her eyes went wide. She touched his face. 'I was kidding when I said that.'

'So? I am a bloodthirsty monster, and you are my mate.' There was not a hint of softness in that aggressive face. He

309

growled, 'And I am yours. What will it take for you to accept that?'

'I do. I promise I do,' she said. Incredibly, she had hurt him in more ways than one. She stroked his cheek. 'I just don't know how to be your mate. Somewhere between that horrible Goblin stronghold and when you flicked your tail at me on the plain, I fell head over heels in love with you. But I come from a strong human background. Love, being in love, making love – those things make sense to me. They're part of who I am. And you already admitted you don't know what love is. So I still don't have that frame of reference I was looking for. Even though we're together, I don't know how to behave or what it means.'

His expression had eased as she talked. He kissed the palm of her hand. 'It means, you stupid woman, that I am learning too. Now you listen to me. I never stop thinking about you. You're with me everywhere I go but I miss you when we're apart. I've already shown that I will kill for you. I would also die for you. You make me laugh. You make me happy. You're my miracle and my home. If you as much as twitch, I get a hard-on. I will always come for you, always want you, and always need you. We clear?'

She had begun to glow. 'Sounds a lot like love to me.'

'I thought so too,' said the dragon. In a move too fast for her to track, he snatched her hands and pinned them over her head. She startled but made herself relax in his hold. His fierce raptor's gaze flared in the light. He descended until he was nose to nose with her. He hissed, 'So say it.'

She gave him a gentle, radiant smile and whispered, 'I'm yours.'

'It's about goddamn time,' he growled. He straightened off the bed and yanked her up with him. Then he took hold of her tank top in both hands and shredded it. 'Say it again.'

She started to laugh. Even to her own ears, she sounded drunk. She reached for his shirt and tried to undo the buttons with clumsy fingers as she told him again, 'I'm yours.'

He spun her until she faced away from him. The controlled violence in his movements jettisoned her laughter. Her knees started to shake. He tore the rest of her clothes away and pushed her onto the bed until she was on her hands and knees, facing away from him. He widened her legs until she was fully exposed to him. The sense of vulnerability was almost too much to take. She shivered spasmodically.

She heard the tiniest of sounds from behind, the catch of his breath and a rustle of cloth. She tried to look over her shoulder to see what he was doing.

Then he put his hot lips on her from behind and licked along the delicate folds of her most private, hypersensitive flesh. He tickled her clitoris with his tongue and mouthed against her, 'Say it again.'

Arousal roared over and through her. It knocked her off her hands. She collapsed forward, turned her damp cheek into the bedspread and gasped it.

Her collapse exposed her even more to him. He licked, nibbled and suckled, coaxing pleasure from her with a soft and dexterous touch, then turning demanding and rough, gripping her by the hips and holding her in place as he feasted on her with a ruthless carnality that sent her squealing into a climax that peaked and peaked until she writhed, utterly helpless in his grip as she fought for enough breath to scream.

All the while he insisted she admit that she was his. She gave it to him every time he demanded. She moaned it, sobbed it, until finally she lay boneless on her back, a mass of quivering, exposed nerves.

There was no part of her he had not pleasured or taken when he finally moved over her body, positioned his cock at her drenched, inviting entrance and pushed his way inside. She stroked the strong curve of his back with trembling hands as he filled her and she whimpered, drugged with pleasure. Tears spilled out of the corners of her eyes.

He framed her face with his big hands as he came all the way inside, seated to the root. At last he had burned even his own ferocity away, until all that was left on his severe dark face was tenderness.

'I have learned so many things over the long years,' he whispered as he moved inside of her. 'I've taken tribute from sovereigns and witnessed the end of empires. But you are my best teacher.'

She stroked his lean cheek. 'I love you.'

A smile filled with simple wonder lightened those fierce gold eyes. 'I know.'

Laughter threatened to take her over, but then he lost his smile and grew intent as he drove harder, deeper inside her. She arched up to him as he hit just the right pleasure spot, and his powerful body shook as he spilled inside her. She cradled him close as he gasped and hid his face in her neck. Afterward she stroked his hair as they drifted.

Then he roused just enough to shift his weight off her. He lay on his back and pulled her against his side.

'Good to have that settled,' he said with satisfaction. He ran his fingers through her hair and with a gentle pulse of Power smoothed the tangles out.

'What, that we're mates?' She stroked his hard, beautiful mouth.

'Yes.' He kissed her fingers. 'Because we're getting married.'

'We're—' She bit her lip. 'That's your proposal. Just like that, we're getting married.'

'Oh.' He reached over the side of the bed, dug into his shirt pocket and then dropped a massive diamond ring on her chest. 'There.'

She rolled her eyes and flopped onto her back. This was too good to pass up. 'Well, Dragos, it's one thing to agree that we're mates, but I don't know about marriage,' she said. 'I read *Cosmo*. You eat people. I think divorce court might call that the definition of irreconcilable.'

He rolled onto his side. The sheet slid from his muscled chest as he propped himself up on one elbow and regarded her from under lowered brows. It was his moody, stubborn look. God, she loved that expression. She could just about see the wheels turning in his head.

After a moment, he said, 'Please.'

'That's better, big guy.' She nodded and put the ring on.

Turn the page for a special preview of
the next Novel of the Elder Races
by Thea Harrison

STORM'S HEART

coming soon from Piatkus!

Motel 6 wasn't so bad. In fact, it was kind of cute in a polyester sort of way.

Sure, it wasn't the Regent, or the Renaissance, or the Ritz-Carlton. But the desk attendant had been cheerfully disinterested when she had checked in, the prices were affordable and, most important, they had smoking rooms. Score.

On the one hand, there wasn't any room service or those darling little liquor bottles in a small refrigerator. On the other hand, there weren't any assassination attempts or a pending coronation. Hm. Tricks wondered if they offered a twelve-month lease.

She limped into the room. She pulled her new sunglasses down her nose and took a long careful look over the rim at the surrounding scene. The bright, warm afternoon sun toasted the asphalt of the motel parking lot, and a fitful wind swirled dirt and exhaust fumes into a toxic soup. The motel was located near some interstate exit, along with several fast-food restaurants, gas stations and a Walgreens. The sound of traffic was a constant in the background, but it shouldn't be too disruptive once she had the door closed.

She couldn't see or hear anything unusual in the motel's immediate vicinity, and her sight and hearing, along with her sensitivity to magic, were inhumanly acute. She wasn't up to a more strenuous inspection. A visual scan from the doorway would have to be good enough.

After she shut the door and put on the security chain, the first thing she did was kick off her stylish four-inch heels. Ah, thank you, god of feet. She set her sunglasses on the TV. The double room was either painted or wallpapered beige. It had bright bedspreads patterned with an insistent orange, a window covered with short, heavy curtains that hung over a long, thin, wall air-conditioner unit, and a plain table and chair that were pushed against the wall. She dropped her shopping bags on the nearest bed, limped to the air conditioner and turned it on full blast.

Life had sure gone to hell since Dragos had killed her uncle. Oh, Urien had to die, without a doubt. She was *glad* he was dead. She just wished it could have happened in a couple of decades or so. This business about her becoming the Dark Fae Queen? She was so not in the mood.

She dumped out the contents of the shopping bags. The items chronicled a long, busy day.

She'd had a lot to do once she had killed her second cousin Geril and his two cohorts. First item on her agenda was to run away. The second item was to get stuff and keep running. She had walked into a twenty-four-hour pharmacy, bought bandages, a pair of sweatpants, sunglasses and a T-shirt, changed in their bathroom and walked out.

Sunglasses at midnight. Huh. Idiot.

Those had gone into her first shopping bag until daybreak. Then she stole a car and drove in aimless circles while she tried to think past the frozen tundra in her head. She stopped at a superstore and bought more stuff, left the stolen car in the parking lot and got a cab, took the cab to the airport where she got another cab, and here she was.

Her path had been so random, so erratic, made up as it was by stress-induced on-the-spot decisions, that she defied anybody's ability to figure out where here was. Hell, even she didn't know where here was, just that she was still somewhere in the greater Chicago area. Neither ride had been long enough to get her anywhere else, more's the pity. She hadn't wanted to imprint herself too deeply in the memory of either cabdriver so she had tried to keep both trips as normal as possible. She could always steal a car again and drive away from the area, but first she needed a few hours to recuperate while she considered what her next moves should be. At the moment she was too awash with conflicting impulses, pain and exhaustion to be sure of anything.

One shopping bag held her crumpled red halter dress and the matching evening bag that carried a compact powder, a lipstick, and her two small stiletto knives. She kept the tips touched with poison and had a variety of places she could wear or carry them, in the side pocket of a purse, strapped to her arms, or underneath her dress and strapped to her thighs.

Good thing the red color of the dress hid the bloodstains or she might have occasioned more attention at the pharmacy. She set that bag aside. Another bag held an unopened bottle of vodka, a bag of Cheetos, three packs of Marlboro reds and a lighter.

Say hello to tonight's hot date. She set it all on the bedside table near the head of the second bed.

The third bag held a first aid kit, extra bandages, toiletries and underwear. The last bag had jeans, flip-flop sandals, a pair of shorts, a couple of tops, and a dozen wallets.

She sat on the edge of the bed and inspected the blisters on her heels. Should have changed into the flip-flops as soon as she bought them. Should have bought the flip-flops at the first store and the sunglasses later but all she could think after the attack was, oh gods, I can't be recognized.

Shoulda, woulda, coulda. They were the Three Stooges of regret. All they were good for was saying *whoop-whoop-whoop* and smacking one another over the head.

She gritted her teeth. She had slapped a temporary bandage on herself when she had changed in the pharmacy bathroom, but she needed to clean and bandage her knife wound properly. Instead she picked up the wallets. They weren't new wallets. They were other people's wallets. They were from all the people she had bumped into today, when she had wrinkled her cute widdle nose at them and said sowwy. She bet every last one of them was very unhappy with her right about now.

Why did she pick pockets and start smoking and drinking when she was under stress? Can we say maladaptive coping mechanisms, class? If she wasn't careful, she was going to go to prison where people would call her Light-Fingered Stinky.

She pinched her nose and sighed. She was good at a dog-and-pony show. She could clean up well and pretend to be respectable enough, often for hours, even days at a time. She had, after all, been excellent at her job as head of PR for Cuelebre Enterprises. It was all an act. She had known for a long time now that she was really nothing more than a Sackville-Baggins kind of hobbit.

She showered first. It was harder and more exhausting than she had counted on. Afterward she sat on the toilet and hissed as she blotted the knife wound with fresh cotton pads. She poked it to see if there were any cloth fibers from her dress or any other kind of dirt still in the wound. Gray stars bloomed in front of her eyes. Damn, that hurt. A deep puncture, it kept seeping a slow, steady stream of crimson.

She put antibacterial goop on it, doubled up on the padding and taped it in place as best she could. She smeared more goop on the blisters on her heels and put Hello Kitty Band-Aids on them. Then she put on her new underwear. Teeny-tiny little camo boxer shorty-shorts that rode low on the hips. Weren't they cute?

The next bit wasn't so easy. She grunted as she worked her way as carefully as she could into a sports bra. Structurally she may not be very big, but her perky pair of puppies made her a C-cup. Shoulda bought a bra with a front clasp, but today hadn't been a shining example of her best thinking. Whoop-whoop-whoop, smack. After she managed to get the bra on, she eased on a matching camo spaghetti-strap T-shirt that stopped above her pierced navel.

Then she put her hair in pigtails. Because it was layered to fall in an outward-flipping bob, the pigtails stood up on her head like twin black starbursts. She pouted at herself in the mirror and said, 'Sowwy.'

Yep. This look is good for several more wallets. NOT that I'm going to steal anymore, because I'm stopping right now. I'm just sayin'.

And now it was past time for that hot date. She limped to the bed and eased her sore, bruised body onto it, lit a cigarette and flipped on the TV. She started to look through the contents of the stolen wallets. Hey, some of these had good family pics. She pulled out the photos and started to lay them across the bed.

Then what was playing on the television registered in her tired brain.

She stared. Put the cigarette in the ashtray. Put down the wallets and photos. Picked up the vodka bottle, opened it and took a stiff drink.

That was the first time she saw the cell phone video footage of the attack in the alleyway, where she had kicked the crap out of her second cousin Geril's dead body.

It wasn't going to be the last time. Not by a long shot.

Tiago believed in giving credit where credit was due. The little shit had tried like hell to avoid being tracked down.

By the time he had reached Chicago, the SUV Rune had requisitioned was waiting for him, along with a detailed list of assorted supplies, including cash, a couple changes of clothes, a laptop and an assortment of his preferred type of weapons. Tiago picked up the vehicle in Lakeview from their Wyr contact, Tucker, who had already stashed the supplies in a large duffel bag in the backseat.

Tucker was, like his Wyr-badger nature, a short, powerful, stocky and antisocial male. He did well living in relative isolation outside the social structure of the Wyrkind demesne. The badger was content with a job that had sporadic, often strange duties and irregular hours, as long as he could live within walking distance of his beloved Wrigley Field.

Although Tiago hadn't thought to ask for one, there was also a cell phone tucked into a side pocket of the large, heavy canvas duffel bag. He discovered it when it rang as he climbed into the driver's seat.

He clicked it on. 'What.'

Dragos said, 'Preliminary autopsy report is in on the three dead Dark Fae males.'

His eyebrows rose. 'That was fast.'

'With the next ruler of the Dark Fae demesne missing, the authorities put a rush on the job,' Dragos said. 'All the Dark Fae males died of the same kind of poison Tricks favors on her stilettos.'

Tiago adjusted the seat and pulled into traffic. He grunted.

'At least she kept her weapons poisoned when she left New York. Good for her.'

'The fucker who filmed the footage is cooperating with police,' Dragos said. 'He's claiming he didn't see anybody else in the vicinity when she took off down the street.'

'I want to know where he lives,' said Tiago. He drove fast and aggressively as he glared at the other vehicles on the road.

'Later. Check out the airport. Security footage shows someone that looks like it could have been her climbing out of a cab.'

Dragos hung up without saying good-bye. Tiago turned off the phone and tossed it into the passenger's seat.

When Urien had assumed control of the Dark Fae government, Tricks had taken sanctuary with Dragos in 1809. While young, she had already reached her adult size. She was small and delicate, even for one of the Fae. She had a mere fraction of the strength the Wyrs had. She also had her uncle Urien, one of the nastiest and most Powerful men in the world, who had been determined to see her dead.

The Wyr sentinels had proceeded to teach her every dirty trick they could think of in order to help keep her alive, which was where she got her nickname. Nothing was off-limits, or so Tiago had heard. He had been busy elsewhere, helping to keep the peace in Missouri when the Osage signed the Treaty of Fort Clark and ceded their land to the U.S. government.

Everything added up. She had left the hotel with three males, and three males were dead. She had either been taken from the site of the attack, or she was on the run. Logic said she had gotten away and was on the run.

But if so, why hadn't she called New York for backup? Tricks was family. Any of them would gladly have rushed to help her, but she still hadn't tried to call anybody and she hadn't replied to any of the phone messages left on her cell.

Tiago planned on asking her that very question when he caught up with her. She might be hell to track down, but he was old and steeped in Power, and most of his talents were concentrated on the hunt. There wasn't anything on this Earth he couldn't track once he put his mind to the task. He recovered lost scent trails, made intuitive leaps no one else would think of, and shit, more often than not, luck just fell his way. It might take him a while, but in the end he always brought down his prey.

His prey, in the end, appeared to be holed up in a motel room off the I-294 Tri-State Tollway.

He paused for a moment outside the door and listened. Tricks's scent was all around on the surrounding sidewalk, but it was close to midnight and he didn't want to knock on the wrong door by mistake.

He heard her inside. She was singing in a clear, sweet, pure voice. His eyebrows rose.

'*"Down in the valley, the valley so low, hang your head over, and hear the wind blow . . ."*' The singing stopped. He heard her mumble, 'Can't remember what comes next, something, something . . .'

He grinned as he relaxed and leaned against the doorpost. If she was singing and talking to herself, she was't dead in a ditch. It was all good.

She said, 'Oh, that's right . . . No, wait, that's another song. Crap, I'm too drunk.'

That sounded like his cue. He knocked.

Silence. He imagined there was a startled quality to it.

He knocked again. 'Tricks, it's Tiago. Open up.'

She said with the slow incredulity of the inebriated, 'Is that you, Dr. Death?'

'Come on, open the door.'

'No, thank you for stopping by. I'm okay. Everything's okay. It's all taken care of now. Just don't watch any TV for a while, okay? You can go back to New York, or wherever it is you lair when you're not killing things.'

He scowled. Dr. Death? No, thank you and don't watch any TV? What the hell did she mean by that? He muttered, 'I do not live in a lair.'

He settled his shoulder against the heavy metal door that was constructed to meet fire safety codes and to keep thieves out. After pushing with a steady increase of pressure, the lock and chain broke.

Cigarette smoke billowed as the door opened. He coughed, waved a hand in front of his face and stared at the scene inside.

The motel room was a pigsty. Shopping bags were piled on the bed nearest the door. Tricks lay on her back on the other bed, which was littered with photos, credit cards, and driver's licenses. She was dressed in some kind of porno version of camouflage, in very short shorts and a tiny, stretchy T-shirt that left her narrow waist bare. Her head was hanging off the end of the bed. She held a bottle of vodka in one small hand. It was significantly low in liquid. She clutched a remote control in the other hand. A cigarette smoldered in a half-full ashtray and an open bag of Cheetos was on the floor.

Her compact, curvaceous body was laid out like some kind of offering to a pagan god. As someone who had once been a pagan god, he knew what he was talking about, and he definitely appreciated the view. As her head hung over the end of the bed, it accentuated the thrust of round, luscious breasts that curved over a contrasting narrow waist. A gold ring glinted at her navel, just begging to be licked. Her graceful hip bones and the arc of her pelvis were outlined by shorts that Congress ought to make illegal. Slender, shapely bare legs tipped with toes painted a saucy pink completed the package, and his appreciative cock swelled to salute every visible, succulent inch of her.

He glowered, thrown off balance by his own intense, unwelcome reaction. Rein it in, stud. Under the reek of smoke he could smell feminine perfume and – was that the scent of blood?

'Oh, you shouldn'ta done that,' Tricks said. Large upside-down Fae eyes tried to focus on him. 'Breaking and entering. That's against the law.' She snickered.

Tiago took refuge from his strange feelings in the much more familiar emotion of aggression. 'What are you doing?' he demanded. 'What do you mean "go back to New York"? Do I smell blood?'

'I can only answer one question at a time, you know,' she said. With remarkable dignity, considering. 'I am hanging my head over to hear the wind blow. I never did get that bit in the lyrics. Who hears the wind blow when they hang their head over? Hang their head over what? What does that even mean? Do you know?'

He had no idea what she was babbling about. Something about the stupid song she had been trying to sing. He pushed the door shut with a foot and strode over to stub out the smoldering cigarette. 'This is disgusting,' he snapped. 'Why haven't you called? We've been worried sick about you.'

'Whoa,' she said. She looked up – or down, as it were – at Tiago's crotch, which had stopped right in front of her. He was one scary, mean-looking, oversized barbarian, in black jeans, black boots and black leather vest. He bristled with weapons and anger, and muscles bulged everywhere. His crotch sported a significant bulge too. A very significant bulge. She licked her lips. She might be drunk but she wasn't dead. She wouldn't be forgetting this sight in a hurry.

He squatted and suddenly his upside-down face was in front of hers. Obsidian eyes glittered. 'Tricks, what the hell? Seriously.'

She tried to track where that mouthwatering bulge in his crotch had gone, couldn't, and focused instead on his face. Brown skin, strong hawkish features, and a sensually shaped mouth that more often than not looked like it could cut through concrete. She had always thought he was a proud, aloof man with the longest legs and the sexiest moves she had ever seen. He walked everywhere with a quick, ground-eating, lean-hipped stride.

'Has anybody ever told you, you look a lot like Dwayne Johnson?' she asked.

He scowled. 'Who the hell is Dwayne Johnson?'

He tried to take the vodka bottle away from her. She clung to it.

'You know, the Rock? Hot, sexy football player–wrestling guy turned movie actor? Only . . . you're a whole lot meaner.' She concentrated very hard, tongue between her teeth, and touched the tip of her forefinger to his scowl. The vodka bottle bumped his nose. He jerked his head out of the way.

His eyes narrowed on her. Was that male interest in his dark, glittering gaze? She didn't trust her powers of observation at the moment.

'Hot, s—' He stopped dead. When he spoke again, his normal growl had dropped to a husky murmur. 'You're comparing me to a movie actor? Fuck yeah, of course I'm a whole lot meaner.'

Huh. Wasn't he the cock of the walk?

'Whatever, don't let it go to your head,' she said with scorn. 'You're not as sexy as I think you are.' She squinted. Wait. That hadn't come out right. She tried to sort it all out in her vodka-befuddled head. It didn't help that he gave her a swift white grin that scrambled her brain even further.

All too soon that grin disappeared. Then Dr. Death was back and scowling again.

Ooh. Sexy. No, scary. No, sexy. Oh phooey.

He grabbed her hand. He could feel how delicately formed the bones were. He could crush her so easily. Any one of those Dark Fae males could have snapped her neck effortlessly if they had gotten her in the right hold. He took care to keep his touch gentle, even as he said, 'Goddammit, faerie, you'd better start answering some questions.'

'Or what?' She pointed the remote at him and pushed the mute button. 'Pleh. I'm gonna get someone to make me a magical mute that really works.'

A kind of desperation came over his harsh features. He snatched the vodka bottle from her and took a swig. She watched with acute interest as shock shot across his face. He gagged and spat the mouthful out on the carpet. He glared at the bottle. 'Bubble-gum-flavored vodka? *Bubble gum*?'

'What? It's good.' She reached for the bottle.

He held it out of her reach. 'No way.'

She scowled. 'That's my dinner. You give it back.'

'Oh no, young lady. You've had more than enough.'

Only a gazillion-thousand-year-old Wyr could get away with calling a two-hundred-year-old faerie 'young lady.' Holy cow, he was one devastatingly good-looking barbarian, upside down or not. But so preachy! She remembered the vodka. She reached for it again.

He stood, grabbed the ashtray and strode for the bathroom. She could just barely see what happened in the corner of the bathroom mirror as he turned the bottle upside down in the sink. There went the rest of her hot date.

'Screw you,' she called after him. There was a thought. She scoped out his lean, tight ass with interest.

Tiago ignored her and dumped the ashtray in the bathroom trash. He paused, looking down in the trash can. If anything, he looked even angrier than he had before. He looked fit to murder somebody. The strong, proud bones of his face clenched like a fist.

Her eyelids closed in a slow blink as she tried to process. If he was that mad at her, she should give some serious thought to running. And she would too, just as soon as she found her feet again.

A shiver rippled down her spine. She rolled onto her side, tucked her knees against her chest and wrapped her arms around them. She didn't want him that mad at her. She didn't want anybody that mad at her.

Tiago walked back to the bed. She could have sworn she heard a rumble of thunder in the distance. He squatted by the bed and rubbed her shoulder with a giant callused hand. 'Where are you hurt, faerie?'

His gentleness was so unexpected, coming as it did from such a wrathful, clenched-fist face, that it almost did her in. Her eyes filled with tears. She gestured to her side.

Icy shock ran over his skin, followed by a blast of heat. Tiago didn't know where to put his rage. That bastard Fae hadn't punched her in the alley. He had *knifed* her.

'Let me have a look.' He tried to raise her T-shirt.

She resisted. 'I already cleaned and bandaged it.'

He exploded. 'Goddammit, woman! I said let me have a fucking look!'

Her eyes went wide and she froze. The force of his anger was palpable. It beat against her skin. Thunder rolled, this time closer. It was almost overhead.

She had heard the stories about Tiago. The thunder and lightning came when he really lost it. Cautiously she uncurled, her eyes wide. She made herself lie passive as she stared up at him. Sometimes with dominant Wyr warriors the best thing you could do was stay quiet and get out of their way – or in this case, acquiesce. Sooner or later their rampaging always ground to a halt and then they could listen to reason again.

He put one knee on the bed and leaned his weight on it as he lifted up her T-shirt. The bandage covered her ribs under her left breast. She winced as he peeled back the bandage to look at what was underneath.

'Do you know how irritating you are?' she said. 'Because if you don't, I've got time.'

'This looks deep,' he said in a quiet voice. Lightning flashed outside. Thunder exploded with a boom. She jumped and shivered. He put his hand briefly against her narrow waist. 'Ssh now, be easy. The dressing is soaked. I'll change the bandage.'

325

She knuckled her eyes. Damn it. She hadn't slept in two days. She was starting to come down from the singing part of the drunk. He was acting far too serious and concerned, a storm was brewing outside, and all the fun was packing its bags and ditching the party. She tried to hold on to it.

'You know, technology in the twenty-first century is pretty cool,' she told him. 'I'm going to DVR my own meltdown and e-mail it to my therapist.'

He didn't so much as crack a smile.

She drooped. She uncurled as he urged her to lie flat. He removed the soiled bandage and with a careful, velvet-light touch he cleaned the wound and covered it with cotton padding again. At one point he bent down close to her skin and sniffed the wound. Okay, so that looked a little weird but she knew what he was doing; he was checking with his Wyr sense of smell to see if he could detect poison. He caught her eye afterward and gave her a tight, quick smile that was probably meant to be reassuring, but he didn't speak. He seemed busy with his own internal issues. Lightning struck the parking lot. Her shivering deepened. That was just downright sexy. No, spooky. No, sexy. Damn it!

'All right, I'm all done for now,' he said. His soft, even voice was somehow so much worse than his yelling voice. He taped the bandage in place. Then he looked at her, and the fury in his dark eyes stabbed her. 'We know everything that matters.'

She rubbed the pointed tip of one ear, which was burning in embarrassment. 'Apparently the whole world does,' she muttered. 'I never even saw the guy with the cell phone.'

'That asshole is going to be lucky to live out the week if I have anything to say about it. I can't fucking believe he didn't call 911 as soon as he realized someone was being attacked.' He took her hand and held it. 'Now I want you to tell me, why didn't you call, and why do you want me to go home?'

She pulled her hand away and tucked it against her chest. 'Don't be nice to me.'

'I'll be whatever the hell I want to be,' he snapped. 'Why didn't you call?'

She muttered, 'I'm supposed to do this on my own. No Wyr allowed.'

'That's old news,' Tiago said. 'Plans have changed.'

Just like that? Plans have changed? She scowled at him. 'Hey, cowboy, I'm gonna be Queen. I don't think you get to boss me around like that.'

He rubbed the back of his head and raised his eyebrows at her. 'How are you going to stop me?'

'Screw you,' she said.

'You've said that already,' he pointed out. 'I'm getting bored now.'

'Yeah, well, it's the only thing I can think of at the moment,' she muttered. With a Herculean effort she managed to keep from looking at his crotch again.

'The game's changed. Deal with it.'

Her gaze bounced around his dark, saturnine features. The force of his presence was such that the tiny hairs on her arms rose. It cremated the numb state she had managed to achieve with the alcohol. He had the extreme physicality of a Wyr who was an apex predator, his body tempered by years of fighting, the thick muscles corded with sinew and veins. His Power was a heavy sulfurous force that pressed her into the mattress.

She struggled to sit up. Suddenly he was bending over her. He eased one huge arm underneath her shoulders to help her upright. Damn it, don't be nice to me! She sniveled. 'Look, you can't stay, and that's all there is to it. I'm all right. I handled everything.'

He snapped, 'You have a knife wound between your ribs!'

'You should have a look at the other guys,' she told him.

Her words hit a stone wall. 'We're done discussing this,' he said. He walked over to the other bed. 'What do you want to take with you?'

'All of it.' She spoke in an absent tone of voice as she stared at his ass again. Really, it was the sexiest ass she had ever seen. First she got a close-up of his front, and now she got treated to the back view. Tight, taut, and clothed in black like it had been gift-wrapped just for her. She patted him on the butt and told him, 'Nice buns.'

As he started gathering up her packages, she opened up his wallet.

A plain white card was just inside. Strong masculine writing slashed across it. It said, 'Put me back.'

She drooped. Rats. He must have talked about her with the

other sentinels who were much better versed in her character flaws. She tucked the wallet into his back pocket. He reached back and patted her hand. 'I'm taking the bags out to the car,' he told her. 'Be right back.'

He walked out. Just like that she lost what little control she'd had over her life. She tobogganed right out of the fun bit of the drunk and plunged into the snowdrift labeled the sorry stage.

He came back and scooped her into his arms. He was such a mean barbarian and he was being so careful with her, so gentle and nice. And she couldn't let herself rely on him. She couldn't let herself totally rely on anyone ever again.

Her head fell against his arm as he carried her out of the motel.

She sang, '*Sad, sad, sad, sad.*'